Please Stand By!

EMILY RENNIE

PLEASE STAND BY!

Printed in the United Kingdom.

For more information, or to book an event, contact :
emilyjrennie@gmail.com
@EmilyRennie3 on X

Cover design by Natcha Chirapiwat

ISBN - Paperback : 978-1-7384179-0-2
ISBN – Ebook : 978-1-7384179-1-9

First Edition: October 2023

This book is dedicated to Grandma, Aileen Rennie.

I did it – I wrote and finished a proper book! Thank you for letting me scribble all over your printing paper back in the day to make my stories.

I have a feeling you would've loved this book, though I know you wouldn't approve of the swearing in it.
Sorry.

Love you always.

.

Chapter 1

When I was eight-years-old, I was confronted with the horrible realisation that I could no longer ride my tricycle.

It seemed that only yesterday I'd been able to pedal around the neighbourhood with my sister, ringing the tinny bell with pride. Now it lay discarded on the grass, dejected and pathetic. Suddenly my legs were too gangly, the seat uncomfortable. The pink paint – once so pristine – was stripping away from years of use. I found myself sitting down next to it on the grass and I wailed.

"Eva!" my mother attempted to enthuse me. "This is exciting! You can now get a proper, grown-up bike!"

Weeping, I told her I didn't care. No one could understand why I was so upset. Even I didn't know why, not really. All I knew was that one day I'd been able to ride it and then, just like that, I would never be able to again.

I don't like thinking about the tricycle. Sometimes it'll creep back into my brain, prodding right at the sides like a persistent puppy wanting attention.

Anxiety sets in, the kind where your entire body gets taught and heat pulses in your forehead. Push it down. Lock it away. I don't need to think about the tricycle. I only need to think about Lila.

Chapter 2

When I think about Lila, everything is exactly as it should be. I feel like I've always had Lila in my life, and I suppose everybody must feel the same way.

The Lifetime Lila Show is on every day; from the moment I wake up to the moment it's time for bed. My mum would call it an obsession, but that's the joys of being an adult who lives alone. I don't need to be told what to do anymore. Besides, my mum is wrong about a lot of things.

Just before bed, I stare at the black-and-white television screen, and Lila gazes right back at me with colourless eyes. "Goodnight," she trills, her smile so wide. I wonder what colour her lipstick is, because of course she *must* be wearing lipstick. I imagine a deep crimson, or sometimes it's a soft pink. I don't think I've ever worn makeup in my life; even if I did, I'd never look as perfect as Lila.

"And remember!" Lila says. I mouth along the next words. "I do this because I love you!"

Chapter 3

You can have a house anywhere, but it takes a special kind of love to make it a home, my mum is fond of saying. So that's what I've tried to do.

My day begins at 7 AM sharp. The sound of the TV is already coming in from the living room by the time I crawl my way out of bed. Time for my usual morning routine.

First, I send a text through sleep-blurred eyes to my twin sister, Ali. She'll typically get back to me by 1PM.

I change into my favourite loose dress. It's a different shade from the hot-pink of my nightie. This dress is light and pastel, like the cherry blossoms of spring. The sleeves are ever-so-slightly puffy, which makes it look elegant rather than over the top. Last, but certainly not least, I pin part of my hair back with the pink butterfly clasp my mum got me when I was eight. The colour has slightly worn off – tiny slithers of rust poke through the pink, but the actual butterfly itself is as vibrant as ever.

The house is small, I'll admit, and the entire

connected kitchen and living area could use a lick of paint. I used up the only paint pot I had on my bedroom, and it's *adorable*. Pink walls, pink desk, pink wardrobe. No doubt about it, the rest of the place is decidedly bland in comparison. The only thing that really matters in the living room is the TV, isn't it? So, who cares what the rest of the place looks like?

I make my way into the kitchen, tiles cold against my bare feet. I don't like socks. If I don't wear socks, I can sometimes recollect the feeling of bare toes digging into the grass. If I close my eyes and pretend *really* hard, I can almost smell the summer flowers.

Push it down. Lock it away.

Breakfast consists of a cup of coffee, a tiny splash of milk. No sugar. You know when you take your first sip in the morning, and it seems all your worries (not that I have any!) are washed away in a scalding second? Lila always swears that coffee is the best way to start your day, and she's of course right. It'll get me through until lunch, where I'll ransack the cupboards and see what I can make.

Years ago, Mum would make Ali and I the most delicious tteokbokki, with chillies we had grown ourselves in the garden. Nowadays, I don't really see the point in those kinds of excursions, though I'm sure the two of them are still making an effort.

There's not much to say about the bathroom – the shower is a cramped cubicle that takes up most of the space, and no matter how hard I scrub, there's still a thick layer of grime that lingers on the tiles. The mirror above the sink is slightly cracked, which I hope doesn't mean I'll have seven years of bad luck. When I lean over the small basin to wash my face, my long, black hair floods over my shoulders. Definitely dry at the ends, and straggly rather than sleek. Sometimes I'm tempted to chop it off right to my chin, because trying to take care of it all the time is such a pain, but Mum loves my long hair. She always took such pride in brushing it for me. Seems like I'm still eager to always please her, even if I *am* an adult.

I stretch. I yawn. I sit down by the TV for a moment, just to wake myself up by looking at Lila. I don't bother sitting on the sofa – it stopped being comfy years ago, and besides, it's better to be closer to the tiny screen. This morning Lila looks as immaculate as ever, dark hair pin-curled and her eyes wide and welcoming. I wonder what colour her eyes are. Usually I'll switch them up in my mind, and today I hope they're brown like mine. I like to think one day I'll be able to know for definite; for now, I'm confined to guessing.

"It's going to be a beautiful day," Lila says as she shuffles the papers on her desk. "Did you know it's officially the first day of spring? It's true! That time of year again already!"

I rest my chin in my hand, staring at her in adoration. The seasons come and go so fast, but with her by my side, it's not so bad.

The intro music to the show plays, an upbeat little jingle that I've memorised by heart.

We're keeping you safe,
so you don't wander and roam,
because after all – there's no place like home!
She's your loveable host,
when there's no place to go.
It's the Lifetime Lila Show!

Lila beams her dazzling smile. "That's right! And I have a feeling that this spring is going to be a hot one!"

As unpredictable as British seasons can be, spring for the past few years *has* been lovely and warm without fail, so this is welcoming news indeed.

"So, what're you waiting for?" Lila asks cheerfully. "Remember, you've got your portable fans that we sent to you last year! Keep them on throughout the day so you can stay cool and fresh!"

Certainly shall. I give her a little salute, even though she can't see me. She'd probably think I was cute though.

"And just to get us all in the spirit, here's one of my favourites!"

The sound of Elvis Presley's *Burning Love* fills the living room, which is fast becoming one of my favourite songs too, and not *just* because Lila likes it. She's definitely taught me a lot about the old crooners; Bobby Darin is another one of her cherished singers. I down the rest of my coffee and begin to dance.

I dance until I'm all out of breath, my black hair sticking to my sweaty forehead. Collapsing on the sofa, I'm laughing through my short gasps.

Somewhere, sometime in the future, maybe Lila will be dancing with me.

Chapter 4

Lila's tips for you to have a perfect day:

1. *Wake up bright and early! Don't waste a single second.*
2. *Coffee is ALWAYS a must!*
3. *Put on some lipstick. If you don't have any, make sure you're still smiling nice and wide.*
4. *Don't bother yourself by thinking too hard. If there's nothing to feel, then there's nothing to fear, and vice versa!*
5. *Above all else, remember I do this because I love you!*

Chapter 5

The next morning, I'm up at 7AM, my usual time. The early bird catches the worm, which is of course unfortunate if you're a worm, but that's hardly *my* fault.

I slept well. At least, I think I slept well. There's a nagging thought somewhere in the back of my brain, and the more I try to chase it, the further it retreats. If it's the remnants of a nightmare, I can't remember anything about it.

Push it down. Lock it away.

My coffee doesn't taste as good as it did yesterday. Maybe the milk is off.

The Lifetime Lila Show instrumental music is playing when I shuffle into the living room. No matter what's going on, Lila is going to cheer me up. She'll turn my silly frown upside down.

Except Lila is sitting at her desk in silence. The intro music to the show continues to play, but she's not doing anything. Just sitting and staring right at us, eyes wide and unresponsive.

Before I can decipher what *exactly* is going on, the

TV monitor blurs, and the picture distorts for a split second. I gasp, scrambling forwards as if I'll be able to fix it with sheer willpower, but then it's back to normal. Lila's still there. Still silent.

And then suddenly, like a light being flicked on, she smiles. A big wide grin as she looks right at me.

The corners of my mouth tug up too, by pure instinct. Her smile is just so contagious. With a roll of my shoulders to loosen the tight muscles in my upper-back, I sit down by the TV.

"Good morning!" Lila exclaims, a hint of tetchiness in her voice that she tries to disguise. "We seem to have had a few technical issues getting started this morning. Not to worry! Never happened before, and I'm *sure* it never will again, or I'll be *very* upset!"

My brief period of panic has subsided, and I'm glad. While Lila continues to chat away in the background, my eyes drift up to focus on the wall behind her. I'm going to need to dust some of those picture frames – I can't remember the last time I did a proper clean of the house. The joys of adulthood.

In hindsight, I don't have many pictures up on the walls. There's the one of me, Mum, and Ali, on a family holiday in Tokyo, standing underneath the pale blossom trees. Ali and I are probably around five-years-old, wearing matching blue sundresses, eating ice-creams the size of our faces. All of us are smiling at whoever the photographer was – probably another tourist who decided to indulge us.

"Oh well," Lila continues. "Nothing to fear, so nothing to feel, isn't that right?"

Nodding in silent agreement, my eyes linger on the family picture for a moment longer. My mum and my sister are very close. Dad left before both Ali and I were born, and I don't have any pictures of him. I don't feel sad about it. It's just always been that way – and you can't be sad about what's always been that way.

Then there's a framed photograph of Lila that I had delivered from the television company. It's signed and everything!

Dear Miss Eva Jeong, love from The Lifetime Lila Show.

It's just a picture of Lila sitting at her desk, in the usual black-and-white colours. It was probably taken during one of the broadcasts. Imagine working on the television show, being so close to her every day! I don't know how they do it.

As far as photographs go, that's all I seem to have. There were more, once upon a time, but I can't seem to ever find them. These are the only two I need. I smile fondly, my eyes darting back to the TV to see Lila shuffle her papers again. And then something happens.

Her eyes momentarily dart away from me. From *us*. I know she's talking to the whole community, but sometimes it's nice to pretend she's talking to *just* me.

It's disconcerting. Lila never looks away from us. A deep, uncomfortable feeling stirs in my stomach. There's something in her eyes that I can't read. It's only a flicker, and if I'd blinked I probably would've missed it.

But I didn't miss it. I saw the look in her eye. It was fear.

Lila is afraid.

What could Lila possibly be afraid of? There's nothing to fear, there's nothing to feel. And if there's nothing to feel, then there's nothing to fear. Right, Lila?

I wish I could call the show, just to do *something,* just to check everything with her is alright, but I don't have any data or Wi-Fi. Nobody here does anymore. All we need is *The Lifetime Lila Show*, but something is clearly, extremely wrong, and I don't know what to –

Lila is smiling.

My heart is beating ridiculously fast in my chest as I scan her face. There's no tell-tale sign that anything strange ever happened. That she ever glanced away with that *look* in her eyes.

"Anyway!" she says brightly. "Don't you just love the smell of lavender before bed? Remember your little jar of lavender pills are always at the back of your cupboard, for whenever you need them! For the best nap of your life, from our sponsors, Lavender Slumber."

For a moment, my mind screams at me to keep the focus. I trip over my own feet as I get up, collapsing with a thud on the carpet before scrambling to stand again. Where do I keep my pen? I find a biro lying on the kitchen table, and rip off a piece of paper from the kitchen calendar that I made myself. It's mostly blank, so I don't feel too bad.

This pen is awful. I stab at the flimsy paper uselessly, trying to get it to work. My head is throbbing and I'm struggling to focus on what I'm doing, but I know this is important. *Lila looked a –*

"Shall we take a moment to think back to last spring?" Lila's voice bleeds through into the kitchen.

My grip on the pen loosens, as I let her words wash back over me. Closing my eyes, I nod, even though no one can see me.

"It was a lot colder at first, wasn't it! I know we had to send out a few extra blankets to some lucky viewers. Don't you feel good knowing that it's so nice and warm outside now?"

I fold the note up, keeping it close to my chest as I slowly make my way back into the living room. My breathing is no longer ragged by the time I sit back down in front of the television, looking at Lila's lovely face.

The paper falls from my hand. I let it flutter to the ground, and allow Lila's gentle voice to soothe my soul.

And then there's nothing to worry about. Nothing at all.

Chapter 6

Years ago, there used to be a café round the corner of our home that sold the most amazing milkshakes. Literally, they could make you any kind of milkshake you could imagine. Ali and I would always drink ours so fast that we'd simultaneously get brain-freeze. We were never too fancy with our choices – she'd always choose strawberry, I'd choose vanilla.

This morning, the niggling feeling at the back of my brain is back, so I'm trying to redirect myself into a more positive train of thought. It's almost working. I just picture those milkshakes as I stir my instant coffee. Officially no milk left. I make up for it with a spoonful of sugar, even though I'm sweet enough, as Lila would probably tell me.

I wonder if Ali remembers the milkshake café. The text from her yesterday was a bit bland, just a simple *Everything's fine* kind of thing. I guess she's not up to much. Still, a love heart emoji wouldn't have gone amiss.

I can't help but feel I'm forgetting something, no

matter what I do. If I'm not careful, I'm going to get cross at myself.

Just as I'm walking over to the television, ready to let Lila's voice relax my agitated mind, I spot a scrap of paper lying on the carpet. From where I'm standing, it looks like a handwritten note. Was it pushed through the letterbox? I wrack my brains, trying to think of the special occasion. It's not my birthday, surely. My twenty-third wasn't *that* long ago, and I quite like being twenty-three, so I'm not ready to give that up.

Sipping my coffee, I walk over to take a proper look. The joints in my leg protest as I bend down to pick the paper up. Maybe I should start incorporating some exercise into my daily routine.

Lila looked a –

I frown, turning the paper over, but no. That's all the note says.

Lila looked...what? Looked amazing? She always looks amazing.

That nagging feeling in the back of my brain picks up speed. The writing seems to swim on the page the harder I attempt to focus. For some reason, the image of my pink tricycle circles around my mind, but I quickly push that aside in an attempt to focus.

This is ridiculous. I'm tempted to scrunch the paper up, but I can't stop scanning it over and over, hoping to find the crucial clue I need to piece this all together. It's *my* handwriting, I'm sure of it now. Why would I write a note to myself?

I sit myself down in front of the TV, paper still in

hand. Lila is chatting about the best kind of lipstick to wear to compliment your complexion, which sounds like important content for me to pay attention to. Her blazer is stripy today. Her dark hair is, as always, neat and immaculate. I wonder what shampoo she uses.

"And now for some *really* important news," Lila says. She rests her arms on her desk, leaning in as if sharing a secret. I find myself inching closer to the screen, completely enraptured by her eyes. Today, I can't shake the feeling that they're blue. I bet they're so blue that you could almost swim in them – the deepest, glittering sapphire of the ocean, captured in her gaze. "Aren't you all excited for the upcoming Giveaway?"

The giveaway competition! I slump back, groaning. I'd almost completely forgotten about it.

The show hosts an annual competition, where viewers have the opportunity to win some kind of reward 'beneficial to the home'. It has to be something practical – you can't ask for a fancy Bentley or anything like that. You write into *The Lifetime Lila Show* and tell them what you would be particularly grateful for this year, and whichever answer Lila likes the most is the winner. I've never won. Just thinking about it makes my stomach churn in anger. My face is probably molten red.

My fingers itch to text Ali, before I remember I've text her already this morning, as per my routine. I'll just have to wait until she gets back to me. Still, I wonder if her and Mum have been planning anything for the competition. Maybe I can steal some of their ideas.

I glance down at the note again, my brow furrowed. Nope. Still not making any sense.

"I'm really looking forward to reading your entries," Lila continues. "We're humble and modest in our noble country, and I love to see it. It's important to live a simple life, don't you think?"

"Yes," I mumble. I still feel a little annoyed, but I'm beginning to relax now that I can see Lila is genuinely happy about the competition. I keep getting drawn to the note in my hand, and force myself to rip my eyes from it, so I can focus on the only person that matters. Lila would never be as rude as I'm being, she'd never –

Then it hits me, like a punch to the throat. Her eyes. Lila. Lila looked *away*.

I'm stuck in time. Frozen. Lila continues to talk, but her words are lost in the ringing of my ears. She looked away from us. She looked away, and there was something wrong. How could I have just *forgotten* that? If my mum was here, she'd tell me I'd lose my head if it wasn't screwed on. Annoyingly, she'd be right.

Focus. I should see if I can contact the show. Maybe with the upcoming competition – I can send in a note alongside my entry. Something to show Lila that I care about her.

A cold sweat is prickled all over my skin. My long hair sticks to the back of my neck, so I gather it and pull it back into a scruffy ponytail. It takes a few attempts, seeing as my hands won't stop trembling. What do I do? Should I ask Mum or Ali if they noticed anything? No. No, I don't want to alarm anyone. It could have been my own mind playing tricks on me.

But I need to know for sure. I need to focus entirely on *The Lifetime Lila Show* until I go to bed. I roll back my shoulders, and stare at the screen until my eyes ache and that's ok because if Lila does this because she loves me, I do this because I love *her*.

Chapter 7

Lila isn't saying much this morning.

The uneasy feeling in my stomach is back, and I don't have any desire to finish my coffee. The smell of it seems too sharp, too acidic. I force myself to relax my jaw. Breathe in through my nose, out through my mouth.

I've had the image of her looking away, playing on a constant loop in my head. By the time Lila said good-night, I was absolutely exhausted and had no problem drifting off to sleep. This morning, the anxiety is back in full-force, fizzing through my bloodstream.

I sit closer to the screen, my eyes burning as I scan Lila's face. I didn't see her look away again all through-out yesterday. Maybe I *did* imagine it.

I hope you and Mum are doing ok, is the text I sent Ali at 7:30AM. *I'm feeling a bit weird.*

I ache for her response. Suddenly I'm hit with a wave of longing for my family. Ali would be able to calm me down, to stop my head from aching. But no-body knows Lila as well as I do – so I'm in this alone.

A sharp *bang* from behind me. Breath stutters and hitches in my throat. Oh no no no.

The loud hammering continues, over and over. The sound of my front door being kicked wide open. My head snaps round, and I scramble backwards, before realising there's nowhere for me to go. There's a high-pitched noise that reminds me of a dog whining in fear, and I realise it's coming from me.

Two women stand in the doorway. Harsh sunlight streams in, hot and foreboding. The way it shines behind them suddenly gives me the overwhelming notion that they're some kind of angels, here to take me away, into the next life. Angels, or *devils.*

Get out, I try to say, but my voice won't work. *You can't come in.* I scramble to my feet, any defences completely forgotten. Instead, I throw my hands up in surrender. *Don't hurt me,* I also try to say. *Who are you? What do you want?* All that comes out is a useless whimper.

"Calm down," the taller woman says. She speaks with an accent that I can't place. Spanish? Possibly Spanish. Her dark eyes then fall on the television, where Lila is talking about the best tips for a good night's sleep. The woman's mouth curls in disgust. There's a long pink scar above her top lip, bright against her brown skin. "Turn that bitch off," she tells her companion.

Now I've found my voice. "Turn – you can't turn *Lila* off!" I manage, horrified. The words tumble and trip over my tongue.

The smaller woman walks towards me like she's coaxing a wild stray. Through blurry eyes I scan her up and down, waiting to see what her next move is. Her afro hair is pulled up in two buns. Her dungarees have a lot of holes in them. Dusty glasses sit on the bridge of her nose, and her skin is smooth and dark. No weapon on her, as far as I can see.

I stand in front of the TV, my arms spread out, teeth bared in a snarl. Whatever these strangers want, they will *not* turn off *The Lifetime Lila Show*.

"Who – who are you?" I demand, and that's when I spot the small revolver holstered at the tall woman's hip. Bandits? I have nothing worth stealing. "Take – whatever you want. Then leave! Get out of here!"

"I'm Val," the tall woman says simply. She points at her friend in the dungarees. "That's Tabby. What's your name?"

"*You're* the ones who've broken into my house!" my voice pitches into a scream. I allow myself a few seconds to breathe, to listen to Lila. I have to keep calm. I can't antagonise *criminals*. "Please – just get out. Get out now!"

"Miss Eva Jeong," the smaller woman, *Tabby*, reads from the photograph on the wall. "That you?"

My silence says it all. For a moment the three of us stand looking at each other. The only audible sound is my harsh breathing, and Lila chatting away in the background.

"It's you who needs to get out of here," Val eventually says. She's walking around my small open-plan house, and I can't quite make out the expression on her face. My eyes follow her as she approaches the door to my bedroom.

"What do you want?" I whisper. I'm ignored. She's already walking on in, as if she's lived here all her life.

"It's like Barbie's fucking dream house in here," Val's voice is heard from my room. "I guess pink is your favourite colour, huh?"

Flinching at her choice of language – swearing is completely unladylike – I self-consciously wrap my arms around myself, trying to feel comforted by the soft fabric of my pastel dress. I'm rooted to the spot in front of the television, my gaze darting back to Tabby. She's tapping away on her phone as she roams around the room, biting fervently at her lip as she concentrates.

"No data signals anywhere," Tabby calls. "The only thing I'm picking up is the TV."

Val emerges from my room. "No one else lives here." It's not a question, but I nod anyway. She walks over to Tabby, the two of them muttering to each other. This is my chance. Slowly, carefully, I start edging towards the kitchen. Val's head snaps up to look directly at me. I freeze in my tracks.

"You're alone?" she asks, as if she needs my actual confirmation.

"Of course I'm not alone," I say through gritted teeth. "I have Lila. We *all* have Lila."

Val snorts in clear contempt, while Tabby continues to tap away at her screen. There's still no clear idea of what these two actually want from me. They can't be robbers, otherwise they'd just start looting. They're certainly not friendly neighbours. Whatever they are – they're outsiders, and that makes them dangerous. I don't have time to be scared. I need to survive.

"Remember your next grocery orders are being processed next week!" chirps Lila. I can barely concentrate. "Get them in quickly, so you can have everything you truly need!"

Val storms over and switches the television off before I can leap over and stop her. Silence fills the house. Horrible, horrible silence, ruptured only by the ringing in my ears. I'm collapsing to my knees, clutching at my head as if to stop my thoughts cracking from my brain, spilling over my fingertips.

The pink tricycle. Walking along the street as I pushed it by my side, the sun beaming down on my face. Worn-out sandals on my tiny feet. My Mum and Ali waving at me as I approached them.

Push it down. Lock it away.

"Get out!" I'm screaming like a wounded animal, staggering to my feet. "Out, out, get out of here!"

"You can't stay here!" Val is shouting back, our voices clashing against each other like knives. "Don't you get it? None of this is – none of your little pink bubble-wrapped life is –"

Stumbling to the kitchen. Weapon. *Anything* to ward these people off. My sweaty hand grasps at the nearest cooking knife, and I swing around, brandishing it in front of me. My voice drops to a growl. "Out."

Tabby immediately throws her hands up, attempting to placate me. Val stands firm, clearly the leader of the two. She's smirking. I'm threatening her, and she's *smirking*.

"That's the spirit," Val says. "I like you already, Eva."

"You don't know me." My voice grates against my throat. "You don't know me, or Lila, or anything. You're –"

Some deep, foreign feeling is gripping at my chest. A wave of dizziness hits me, and I close my eyes. The knife almost falls from my hand, but I grip onto it like it's my last lifeline. "You need – you need to leave," is all I can say. "If you don't leave, I'm going to have to kill you, and I don't want to kill you."

Killing people is, of course, a terrible thing to do. Lila says it should only be used as a last resort, and these people are really pushing all those buttons.

"Let's not be drastic," Tabby says immediately. I tentatively open my eyes. Her voice is calming. Not as calming as Lila's, of course, but it's gentle and warm and it draws me in. "We can't force you to come with us. I mean, you know, you really *should*. We could use your help. There's really not that many of us, but we're grouping together –"

Val shushes her. Not in an authoritative way – more like a friend warning her to be careful. "You know something's not right here, Eva. Don't you? You know none of this is normal. When's the last time you stepped outside this horrible little house?"

"My house isn't horrible!" I find myself snapping,

even though that's really not the main problem at hand here.

"You can't stay here forever, rotting away," Val continues as if I haven't even spoken. "You could be useful. You could be *helpful.* We need all the help we can get if we're going to bring down Lila."

To – bring down Lila? Why would anybody want to bring down *Lila*? "You're dangerous," I whisper. "You want to ruin it all."

"*She's* the one who's dangerous," Val retorts. "Worms her way into your brain. Controls you. Manipulates you."

I'm throwing the knife before I can even register my hand moving. Val dodges adeptly, and the knife plunges into the back of the armchair rather than through her heart.

"We're going to stop her, whether you like it or not," she says calmly, as if she didn't just narrowly escape death's cold clutches. "We're in your neighbourhood for two days. After that, we're gone."

She gestures to Tabby and the two of them turn to leave. Tabby locks eyes with me, practically pleading, but I can barely focus. I'm already crawling over to the television.

The door closes behind them and the sound of Lila's sugary sweet voice fills the house. My breathing is still coming out in short, frantic gasps as I collapse in front of the screen, reaching my hands out to her.

Help me, I want to say. I wheeze and splutter,

hunched over like I'm praying. *Make me stop feeling like this.*

Eventually, Lila's calming presence begins to sink into my very soul. My breathing slows, and I can push those two women to the very back of my brain. All is as it should be. Nothing to feel, nothing to fear. If I stay right here, I'm safe. I'll always be safe with Lila.

Later, the camera closes up on Lila's face for her goodnight message. I've barely noticed the day ebb away.

"That's all for tonight!" Lila says. "And remember –"

For the first time in recent memory, I can't mouth along to the next part with her. A persistent ache swells in my chest. Tears are streaming down my face.

"I do this because I love you!"

Chapter 8

When I dream, I'm sitting on a knitted picnic blanket underneath a blossom tree, the spring sun beating down on my face. Ali sits next to me, in a checked blue dress, butterfly clips in her long black hair. I already know my outfit is matching, except it's pink. Of course it's pink.

An old-fashioned stereo crackles by our feet. Bobby Darin croons to us as we recline. Spread out in front of us are decadent bowls of fruit - my eyes are immediately drawn to a plate of strawberries, ripe and red and vibrant. My mouth waters.

"I'm having a lovely time," I feel the need to tell to Ali. I really want her to know.

Ali turns her head to look at me. There's a deep gash on her forehead drip, drip, dripping blood onto the white and red checked blanket. She doesn't mention it, so I feel it's rude to bring it up. She only hums in agreement.

"I had such a horrible day," I continue, reaching for her hand. Our fingers interlock in a firm squeeze.

"Oh?" Ali asks mildly, reaching for a crisp apple slice. She chews slowly, content. "What happened, Evie?"

I smile at the nickname. Nobody's called me Evie in a very long time. "Two women came to the house." I shiver as I remember the raw fear they'd caused me. "Burst right through the door."

"But nobody comes to the house," Ali says. The blood continues to trickle down her forehead, past her brown eyes, past her lips, until it splashes onto the blanket once more. "Nobody ever comes for us."

"I know." I stretch my arms above my head, frowning. "They said such strange things. I can't remember, exactly, but – Ali, they said so many horrible things about Lila."

Ali wears a matching frown. She bites down into one of the strawberries. Juice bursts, running down her chin, and she carelessly wipes it away. "I don't understand."

"You know Lila, *Ali," I say scornfully. "Everybody knows Lila. Everybody watches Lila! She's on TV, like, all the time."*

"How long has she been on TV for?" Ali asks innocently.

The sun doesn't feel so nice anymore. Now the heat is oppressive, caging us both in. My pink dress sticks to my sweaty legs, and I grumpily adjust my sitting position. "Don't be stupid."

Ali shakes her head sadly. Clearly we're not going to agree on this. "I'm sorry, Evie."

I wish she'd sort out that cut on her forehead. "You're getting blood on my strawberries," I say mournfully.

Quiet consumes us for a moment, apart from Bobby Darin continuing to sing Mack the Knife. *I reach for her hand again, already feeling bad. I've missed Ali. The last thing I want to do is fall out with her, even if she is being ridiculous.*

"Will the women come back?" Ali eventually asks. "What will you do if they come back?"

"I..." An all too familiar headache begins to pulse in my temples. "They said...they said they're staying in the neighbourhood for two days."

"Are they dangerous?"

There's no hesitation. "Yes."

"But maybe Lila is too."

I recoil away from her as if she's struck me. "No, Ali," I protest. "You don't – you can't say that."

"How long has Lila been on the TV?" Ali asks again, her voice frustratingly calm. Blood seeps on her pretty blue dress from an unknown wound. Around us, blossom flowers fall from the tree, gently twirling in the breeze.

I look at her helplessly. I don't know the right answer. I don't know what to tell her.

"Maybe the women are dangerous," Ali says. "But maybe – maybe you should think who's the bigger danger? Them, or..." She lets her sentence hang.

The music from the stereo crackles one final time before it fades out. We're left in total silence. "Ali," my voice cracks. "Why are you...why are you bleeding like that?"

Ali picks up another strawberry, holding it lightly

between her fingers. A thought seems to come to her, and she smiles when she looks back at me. "Eva," she says. "Do you still have your pink tricycle?"

Chapter 9

I jolt awake in a cold sweat, panting harshly as I try to catch my breath. For a moment I'm paralysed, staring at the shadowy outlines of my sparse bedroom, trying to process everything before it scampers away to the back of my brain. It's stifling hot, but I'm trembling hard enough to pull a muscle.

Ali is hurt somewhere. Maybe. Almost definitely. That's why her recent texts have been so curt. But what about Mum? They're supposed to be looking after each other.

Just a dream, just a dream, nothing to fear.

But I've had nightmares before, nightmares I can never quite remember, only the sour taste they leave in my mouth the next day. This was more than that. This felt – important.

Back to sleep. I need to be up nice and early tomorrow for a new day. Everything's better at the start of a new day.

There's no way I can lull myself back to sleep now, especially without Lila calming me down. It hits me, suddenly, the awful *silence* without her. I'm not supposed to be awake at this time. Everything about this is wrong.

Throwing the duvet away from me, I stagger around my room, hoping some movement will calm me down. I can't bring myself to turn a light on. In the dark, I can at least try to hide from my desperate thoughts. Sometimes things are just easier in the dark.

Wherever Ali is, something is clearly wrong. She's not been watching *The Lifetime Lila Show.* She's confused, lost. It's up to me to find her, and fix this, and then everything will be fine.

The silence is terrifying. I'm drowning in it, but nobody's coming to pull me out and stop my lungs from suffocating. I need Lila. In a fit of desperation, I push open the door of my room. Groggy and disorientated, I'm nowhere near as fast as I'd like to be. The entire house is shrouded in darkness, but I can just about make out the outline of the TV. I stumble towards it as if it's my only lifeboat.

The TV always seems to switch itself on and off like clockwork, perfectly in tune with my schedule. I've never attempted to turn it on myself, because there's never been any need. By the time I wake every morning, *The Lifetime Lila Show* is already playing.

I kneel in front of the screen, my throat unbearably dry. My body still shakes, to the point where it takes multiple attempts to switch the old-fashioned dial of the television on. I need her voice; I need her comfort. Please, Lila, I need you.

PLEASE STAND BY!

The bold words fill up the screen. No music. No Lila. Nothing. The low, persistent feeling of dread in my stomach bubbles up throughout my entire body, and then I'm howling in anguish, thumping my fist against the screen. The impact jars my knuckles horribly; I draw my hand back to do it again, stopping myself just in time. Lila isn't going to come back by my own brute force, and I *can't* break the television. Then I'll really be in trouble.

She'll just be sleeping. Even Lila needs to sleep. Because sleep is important, and good for you, and that's why we should be kind to ourselves and get as many hours of it as we can. I'm ruining it for myself, acting this way. It's not right. None of this is right.

Do you still have your pink tricycle?

Of course I don't have my stupid tricycle. Ali *knows* that. Ali knows that because –

Because we're not children anymore, neither of us are children, and I outgrew it. I outgrew it and it broke my heart because time selfishly moved forward when I was desperately trying to cling onto it and then I had to give my tricycle to that silly annoying girl down the street and I –

I grip fiercely at my head. No more of this. Push it down, lock it away. Push it down, lock it away, push it down, lock it away, *now*.

Lavender! Lila says that lavender is what you need for a good night's sleep. Everybody in the community has a little jar of Lavender Slumber, usually for a midday nap. I've never needed to take one – Lila is the only soothing I need – so the jar has been gathering dust for however long it's been since it showed up in the post one day.

The bathroom tiles are freezing against my feet as I burst through the door with newfound determination. Throwing open the cabinet, various useless items – expired creams, worn-out toothbrushes, rusted tweezers – are chucked over my shoulder as I search for that special little jar. It's nestled at the very back of the shelf, unopened and perfect, and I feverishly wrestle with the lid.

I dry swallow two of the little purple pills, and then grip onto the sink, breathing out shakily. With time, my furious heartbeat seems to calm down. I'm no longer trembling. As long as I don't think, I'm ok. Everything is going to be ok. I just need to go back to sleep, and wait for Lila.

That seems like an actual possibility now. My eyelids feel heavy, clouded by the familiar, welcome fogginess of exhaustion. Before I really know what's happening, I find myself back in bed, wrapped up in my duvet, perfectly content.

What do I have to worry about, anyway? I'm a safe, dedicated young woman, a crucial member of my neighbourhood, an avid Lila supporter. That's all that matters. That's all that's ever mattered.

And once I remind myself of my purpose, I know everything is going to be exactly as it should be. Right as I drift off to sleep, I thank Lila out loud for everything she's done for me. I like to imagine she hears me, and is thanking me right back.

Chapter 10

For the first time in what feels like forever, I can't bring myself to get up at 7AM sharp. Even though I'm sure I slept well, weariness clings to my bones, and my bed is *so* comfy. When I push myself up into a sitting position, stretching my arms above my head, I'm hit with a wave of dizziness that takes a while to dissipate.

What's going on with me? I need some coffee, pronto.

The familiar voice of Lila fills my ears over the boiling kettle. My mouth is frustratingly dry. I swallow a few times, but it doesn't seem to shift the invisible lump in my throat. It's only when I take my first sip of delicious coffee (with three added sugars to wake me up) that I realise I've neglected the first part of my usual morning routine – texting Ali.

How could I have forgotten to do that? My head really *is* all over the place. I scoff good-naturedly, the way Lila does when she's annoyed with herself while also showing us she's not self-deprecating. There's nothing worse than a self-deprecating complainer.

The Lifetime Lila Show is playing Elvis again – Return to Sender. I'm humming along as I make my way to my bedroom, opening up my bedside drawer where I keep my phone. Where I always keep my phone.

The drawer is completely empty.

My humming abruptly trails off. No phone. My eyes widen in horror as I fumble uselessly inside the drawer, on the odd chance my mobile's suddenly turned invisible.

Ok. Breathe. Maybe I just misplaced it somewhere. I pace around the whole house, gnawing at my lip until I taste the metallic tang of blood. Elvis continues to croon away as I ransack the kitchen cupboards. *Please, please, be somewhere.*

After what seems like hours, though it can only have been a few minutes, I slump on the sofa, defeated. My phone definitely isn't here. I let the annoyance cool down to a gentle simmer, swiftly making way for undiluted terror instead.

My phone isn't here, which means somebody must have taken it. Who could've possibly taken my phone, when I never have any guests?

I mentally retrace my steps. Yesterday I woke up at my usual time. I texted Ali, then I put my phone away, and then...Then I watched Lila, and I was worried about her, because...And then –

I leap from the sofa, my mouth open, my thoughts jumbling and tripping over each other. The two women! The two *thieves* who broke into the house, telling me all kinds of horrible things about Lila. No wonder I'd mentally shut them out. One of them must have stolen my phone, but *why?*

"We'll be in your neighbourhood for two days," the tall one had said. I'll bet all my non-existent money this was her idea. She was the one rummaging through my room, getting me all confused, spreading lies.

Focus, Eva. If these strangers have my phone, they have my only method of contacting my family. The image of Ali flashes into my head, and I feel a sharp pang in my heart. I can't quite remember the *exact* reason, but I know I need to be worried for her, and that's enough to spring me into action.

I need to find these women. I have to go outside.

"Another reminder about your groceries!" Lila says brightly. I can't help but be drawn back in. "Items are going out of stock fast, so make sure you write in everything you truly need!"

Oh no. The shopping order. In all the madness of the past few days, I've completely forgotten. Though, if I'm going to find these women, I suppose that doesn't necessarily matter right now.

Am I really going to do this? I can't do this. It's madness. What would Lila think of me?

But what will Ali think, if I don't text her? Her and Mum will be so worried, and I have to know they're alright. I can't abandon my family. Lila would support me in this.

I'm still standing helplessly in the middle of the living room, as if I'm frozen in time. Gritting my teeth,

I step forwards towards the front door. One foot in front of the other.

My head slowly turns to look at the television, Lila's soothing presence almost drawing me back in. It feels like a goodbye, which is of course silly. It's not a goodbye, it could never be. Not with her.

My cheeks are damp with tears. With a shaky hand, I blow a kiss towards the television screen, take a deep breath, and open up the front door.

I gasp as the heat of the sun thwacks me in the face, immediately bringing my hand up to shield my eyes. Paralysed in the doorway, unable to bring myself to take that tiny step. My home is safe; my home is where Lila is. The very thought of leaving that behind is unbearable.

But then, this persistent, nagging feeling that I *still* can't quite name is unbearable too. If I stay, I will be consumed by this thing gnawing away at my insides, rotting my soul. I can't be the good citizen Lila needs me to be if I don't fix this.

No more debating. Squaring my shoulders, lifting my chin high, I cross over the threshold.

I'm not quite sure what I was expecting. A life-shattering earthquake? A bolt of lightning to strike me down? The world doesn't crumble into pieces around me, despite the monumental thing I've just done. The air is calm, the sun continues to shine, and I slowly find myself smiling.

It's a beautiful spring day, and I'm standing outside. I take another tentative step forward, the gravelly pathway digging into my bare feet. It's a new kind of pain that I've not felt in a long time, so I find I don't mind it. Still shielding my eyes with my hand, I hobble onwards. The two women who stole my phone are somewhere in the neighbourhood, and I'm going to find them. But that doesn't mean I can't bask in the sun on my skin for a moment or two.

The sweet smell of blossoms fill the air, and straight ahead I can just make out the outline of a tree at the end of the road. Finally, finally, I'll be able to see the pink flowers in real life, and not just captured in a photograph in my living room. I move with newfound vigour, my feet tingling against the hot road with each step.

The silence creeps up on me slowly. I wish I had Lila's voice guiding me, so I opt for muttering a few of my favourite sayings of hers under my breath. *When in doubt, keep smiling,* stuff like that. It does the trick.

My eyes hurt from the sun, so unused to it directly. Little black spots dance in front of my face, but I fiercely blink them away. By the time I reach the tree I'm panting, and my feet are almost definitely bleeding, but what does that matter when I'm surrounded by all this beauty?

Blossoms fall in gently around me, and I twirl with them, my dress swaying as I do so. I'm laughing, and then I look back towards my home, and the laugh abruptly dies in my throat.

At first, I'm not quite sure what I'm seeing. I know this is wrong. I know this is horrifying. Still, it takes my brain a delayed moment to put the pieces together, and then I stagger back, the blossom tree holding my weight as I collapse against it.

My house stands alone against a midst of rubble and debris. A lone survivor.

There is nothing. Nothing is left but ruin.

How long have I been alone? Where is everything? When did everybody leave?

The spots in front my eyes multiply. The world spins and tilts and I go with it, colliding brutally with the road. The last thing I see before everything goes black is a flock of birds, circling over the rubble, before they fly away to pastures new.

Chapter 11

"I know how this goes," I say forlornly.

Ali and I stand outside our home, looking down at my broken tricyle. It seems so small, lying there on the grass, one of its wheels creaking as it rolls round and round. I can't believe I ever used to be able to ride it.

My sister inclines her head, her long black hair blowing gently in the spring breeze. "We should go," is all she says, nodding ahead. My eyes follow her gaze, to where our mother stands at the end of the street, waving at us. The spots in front my eyes multiply.

We both remain rooted in the same spot. "It's hard," I say. I'm attempting to fight the whine out of my boice, though I'm not sure how successful I am. I don't want Mum to scold me for being childish.

"I know," Ali agrees mildly. "Won't get any easier if we stay, either."

"Let's at least walk together," I say, practically bleeding. Mum's waving becomes more frantic. I'm too far away to see any expression on her face, but I can imagine all too well. Worry lines etched on her forehead.

Brown eyes filled with panic. We're not supposed to be playing out on the street alone. Not right now.

"Can't just yet," Ali murmurs. "That's something you have to do by yourself."

The two of us look at each other. I can't quite read her face. She continues to stay frustratingly calm despite everything around us.

"I'm dreaming," I say stupidly. "Right?"

"Of course you're dreaming," Ali says. "None of us live here anymore, silly."

My head turns to look at our old home, with its neat garden and its blue-painted door. Duck-egg blue. Ali's favourite. There's a pang in my chest at its familiarity, and I can't bring myself to say any more.

When I turn my head back, Ali's gone, and so has Mum. We should've walked over to her. We should've walked over to her, we should've walked over to her, we should've –

Chapter 12

My vision swims in and out of focus as I groggily blink back into consciousness. The first thing I register is that wherever I am, it's cold and dark, a far cry away from the spring sunshine I was just standing in. When I attempt to sit up, I lurch forwards.

"Easy," I hear a voice say soothingly. I think I recognise it. Warm hands gently hold onto my shoulders, keeping me still. For a moment I feel like my entire body is vibrating, continuing to move against its will, and then I realise that's because we *are* moving. I'm in some kind of vehicle.

"Eva, right?" the voice continues.

I force myself to properly open my eyes, blinking fiercely to clear them. Bright brown eyes framed in round glasses stare back at me. "You're..." I croak.

"Tabby!" She beams, pointing to herself uselessly. "I'm Tabby, from the other day? We found you passed out on the street. Congratulations on taking your first step into a new world!"

I groan pathetically. Leaving the house was a

horrible, *horrible* mistake, and this woman is clearly delighted about it.

"Have I been kidnapped?" I feel the need to ask.

Tabby frowns. "I prefer the term *rescued*," she says. "Kidnapped doesn't really fit this situation. At least, I don't think, but maybe – I can completely understand how you might think it's like that..."

I let her ramble on while I struggle to get my bearings. Whatever vehicle we're in, it's large. Larger than an average car or van. A small sun roof lets in slithers of light that rhythmically bounce along Tabby's eager face, but all the windows are painted black.

Swallowing a few times to help my voice, I push on. "Where am I? And where are you taking me?"

Tabby quickly nods her head in an apology. "Completely get the questions, yep. Should've started off by saying 'Welcome Aboard!' or something, but it didn't seem right. So, this is our mobile base. We call her Bessie." She pauses, as if waiting for me to ask why. I remain silent. "We call her Bessie because that was the name of Darryl's dog. Lovely little cocker spaniel, big floppy ears. I mean, I never met her, but the stories Darryl tells us are always *so* cute –"

"Ok, that's great, thank you," I grind out. "But why am I *here*?" I'm unused to hearing myself so angry. It's a sensation I despise. We're not supposed to be angry.

"You're lucky it was us who found you, and not anybody else," another voice says.

All of a sudden, I remember *her*. Val comes into view as she stands over the two of us, frustratingly smug. Her long dark hair is braided back, and I can see a cigarette tucked behind her ear. "*Hola*, Eva," she says. Her tone is sugary sweet, though her eyes remain guarded, like she's prepared to chokehold me in an instant, if she has to.

I've played right into their hands. Stupid, stupid, stupid.

"You stole my phone," I snarl. "You stole from me, so I'd leave my house."

Val digs into the pocket of her black combat trousers, and holds out my phone with a small smirk. "Guilty," she says. "Just had to cross-reference a few things with our tech genius over there. No hard feelings, right?"

I'm assuming Tabby is the tech genius by the way she proudly puffs her chest. What kind of tech do they need? All we truly need is a good, sturdy television, but so far I can't see a single one.

"*Lots* of hard feelings," I snap. As far as witty retorts go, it's not that great, but I'm so overwhelmed with anger and frustration that I can barely string a sentence together.

"Temper," Val says mildly as she leans against the wall of the mobile home – *Bessie* – perfectly balanced despite the speed we're going at. "What would your darling Lila say? That raising your voice isn't ladylike, I imagine. Let's follow her example, shall we?"

"Stop *antagonising* her, Valentina," Tabby says, her tone stern, before turning back to me. "We're really sorry about the phone, Eva, but we had no choice. You made it pretty clear you weren't going to come with us, and we didn't want to leave you by –"

"I want it back."

Tabby immediately takes my phone from Val's hand, holding it out to me. "Of course," she says. "We were never going to keep it. We were just...borrowing it."

I snatch the phone from her, holding it to my chest, suddenly overcome with a wave of relief. Within seconds I'm tapping away at the screen, but it's completely dead. The relief is quickly swamped by a now all-too familiar panic.

"What've you done? Turn it back on!" I thrust it towards Tabby, needing her to understand the urgency. "I need this phone! It's the only way to contact my sister!"

There's a silence. The phone is limp in Tabby's hand as she avoids looking at me. Val inspects her chipped black nail polish.

"What's the deal with your sister? You message each other a lot?" she asks.

"Every day. I *need* to. She'll be – she'll be worried about me." My voice cracks on the last word, and before I know what's happening, sobs are heaving in my chest. It's as if a chasm has been opened, deep inside of me, and all I can do is cry.

They both watch me for a moment, and then Tabby carefully reaches out to pat my knee, scuffed and bleeding from my earlier fall.

"It's ok," she attempts. "I can fix your phone, alright? I'm sure I can."

I try to get control of myself, but the more I attempt it, the more overwhelmed I feel. I hiccup a small thank you. I still can't trust these people – but I currently can't outrun them, either. I think of my home, and long to be sat on my floor with a cup of coffee, watching Lila.

And then I remember the devastation of my street, the birds circling the rubble, the charred husks of cars.

"Was it you?" I eventually manage to choke out. "All the houses – they were all gone. Everything was gone. Did you do that?"

The two women glance at each other. Tabby slowly stands, dusting down her dungarees, seemingly unable to look at me.

"You *really* don't know shit," is all Val says, sounding somewhat amazed. "They really did a number on you, huh?"

Tabby glowers at her, hissing something under her breath that I can't make out. Bessie lurches forward and she staggers back, while Val remains infuriatingly still.

"There's a bed if you want to sleep for a bit," Tabby says once she's found her footing again. "You know, for a few hours, if you're tired. We won't get to the safe spot until the sun sets."

I can barely concentrate on her words. "Do you have a TV?" I blurt out. "I should probably be watching Lila."

The look Val throws at me is the equivalent of

a punch to the stomach. "No TVs," she eventually growls. "Forget about that fucking show."

"*You* might be a liar and a – a *traitor*," I snap, "but I'm not. Never to Lila. We should all be watching –"

She's already walking away from me. My mouth remains open uselessly, and Tabby gives me a little shrug in solidarity. I scramble to follow Val towards the front of the motor-home, tripping over my own feet as we seem to pick up speed.

She sits in the seat next to the driver, untucking the cigarette from behind her ear and lighting it up. Most of the windshield is also painted black, save for a thin strip that allows a peak of the road. Probably explains why the driving has been so erratic.

I'm surprised when I finally see the driver. For some reason, I suppose I was expecting another woman. Instead, a young man accepts the cigarette from Val's outstretched hand, taking a long drag while his other hand lazily rests on the steering wheel. This must be the Darryl that Tabby mentioned, the one who's named this vehicle after a *dog*.

He's clean-shaven, with green eyes, and I can't decide if his hair's light brown or dark blond. He wears a blue three-piece suit, and similar to his companions, the clothes are tattered and worn-out. I've not seen a man for a very long time.

"Alright?" he asks me without even inclining his head to look at me. He's a Londoner. I've not been to London in years, but I'm certain that's where his accent is from. "Mind if you sit back down? Pretty distracting, you breathing down my neck like that."

"Darryl?" I guess. He grunts in response, so I suppose I'm correct. "Stop the van," I continue loudly. "I need to go home."

"What home?" Val asks flatly. "You said it yourself. Your street is a literal bomb-site."

I don't know what to possibly say. I can still feel the tracks of my tears on my face as I lunge for the steering wheel.

Darryl yelps, swerving erratically. "Val! A little help here, please!"

Val sighs, like we're not even worthy of her annoyance, and takes her feet off the dashboard. "Play nice," she tells me. "We'll explain everything once we're off the road. So sit down, and chill out for one second, I beg you."

There's no feasible way I'll ever be able to relax, but I can have some solace that eventually we'll be arriving *somewhere*. The moment they stop driving, I'll be out of here. No matter how long it takes, I'm getting home. My bloody knees and blistered feet seem to sting in protest at the idea. I'll have to ignore them.

"Maybe get her some brandy," Darryl suggests.

Val wrinkles her nose. "Brandy?"

"For the shock," he says. "I mean, she's obviously in shock. We were all like that, once upon a time."

Val looks me up and down. "She barely looks old enough to have a quinceanera," she says. "How old *are* you, Eva?"

"Twenty-three," I say, seeing no point in lying.

Val gives a surprised huff, but then shrugs in acceptance. "Alright. D'you want some brandy, Barbie?"

I've never had brandy before in my life, but if it'll make all of this horrible, endless sensation in my stomach and head stop, then I'll do whatever it takes. "Do you have any Lavender Slumber?" I ask meekly. "That really helped me the last time."

Darryl huffs a laugh, and then stops when he notices my eyes are full of tears again. "Sorry," he says. "We're in short supply of completely mind-numbing drugs."

"They're not drugs," I retort. "They're supplements."

The two of them look at each other before bursting into laughter, as if it's the funniest joke that's ever been told in the history of comedy. I feel my face flush, furiously blinking my tears away. Why am I wasting my energy on these uncultured mobsters?

I stumble away from them, and that's when I can properly appreciate the ingenuity of Bessie. The layout is undoubtedly impressive; to the left is a small sofa and armchair, made of similar black leather to the front seats. Further down is a tiny kitchenette, with a door leading to what I assume is the bed Tabby mentioned earlier.

Speaking of Tabby, she's sitting at a desk to the right of the motor-home, in front of several computer screens, typing away. I would like to assume she's working on how to fix my phone – out of all of them, she's the only one who seems to properly care. Either that, or she's just a really good actress.

She must feel my eyes on her, because she glances up and throws me a smile that makes her dark eyes shine. My stomach does a weird flip in response. Her hair is still up in two buns, but a few stray curls frame her face. My loyalty and love is, of course, always with Lila. But there's absolutely no denying that Tabby is beautiful.

Gesturing me over, Tabby swings her body round on the chair to properly face me. Talking to her will undoubtedly be a more pleasant experience than what I'm currently having, so I cautiously make my way to her, arms out to keep my balance.

"You get used to it," she says. "At first I thought Darryl's driving would make me literally sick, but it's not so bad after a while."

I don't plan on getting used to it, I almost say, but stop myself just in time. There's no harm in playing along. I can be polite and demure. If I can win their trust that's great; their compliance, even better. Maybe they'll actually listen to what I have to say. It's not necessarily *their* fault that they've lost their way.

"And don't worry about Val," Tabby continues. "She talks tough, but she always means well by it. She was the one insisting we go back and find you, and then when we saw you passed out on the road like that..."

"I was trying to find my phone," I say pointedly. "I need to know my mum and sister are alright."

"Sure," Tabby says softly, "sure, I know."

"You should never have taken it from me, and you should never have come in the first place." I feel my fists clench against my will. "Everything was fine! Everything was *fine* before you..." My words trail off, and my legs buckle uselessly. Tabby is there, helping me sit down.

"I'm sorry about the phone," she says gently. "But Eva, you know that everything wasn't fine, don't you? You know that."

"I don't understand anything," I whisper hoarsely. "What have you done? Who *are* you people?"

"Friends," Tabby says, "if you'll let us be. We're not your enemy, Eva."

The blood from my cut knees has stained my pink dress. I should clean the marks soon, or they may never wash out. And I didn't exactly pack a spare outfit. Tabby follows my gaze, and gives a small nod. "We have supplies. Shall we get you cleaned up?"

When she takes my hand, I don't recoil away. The strength has left my body, the continuous sick feeling in my stomach swirling round and round. If she's going to help me, I won't push her away.

Not just yet.

Chapter 13

The rumbling of the engine sputters and stops, and my eyes fly open. I'm tucked up in a small bunk-bed, where I'd only been intending to sit down for a minute or two. I must've fallen asleep.

I berate myself out loud, groggily pushing myself up, then remember being self-deprecating isn't an attractive quality.

It takes me a while to reorganise my scrambled thoughts. There's a pad of paper and a pen lying on the blanket that Tabby must have left for me, which I gratefully grab. She's drawn a little smiley face on it, nothing else. Maybe she left it specifically to help me get my brain in order. The thought makes me smile, and then I shake my head to stop myself immediately. Boy, is she *clever,* trying to get on my good side like that.

What I Know, I scribble, and underline it twice.

1) My street is destroyed.

2) My phone is broken.

3) Darryl is the driver. Tabby does the tech (for

what? Why do they need it??). Val scowls a lot. DO NOT TRUST THEM.

4) Bad feeling about Ali. Nightmares? Her and Mum in trouble??

I hesitate, and then add a *To-do: Find them,* before my final point:

5) Life without Lila is horrible.

A tear stain smudges the pencil as I write the last note. I hastily wipe at my eyes. I'll be back watching Lila soon enough, once these people realise how important she is to all of us. She would hate to see me cry for her, so I'll be brave. I just need to stick it out until we're outside.

These are important reminders that I can't let myself forget. Carefully, I fold up the paper and tuck it into the pocket of my dress so I can keep it safe, and then I'm aware of people talking on the other side of the door.

"...going to start to remember at some point," I hear Tabby say. "We can't just spring it all on her. We need to do it slowly."

"We may not have the time for that," Val says. "We're so close to finding the specific window."

I swing my legs out of the bed slowly, carefully, trying to be as quiet as possible. When my feet touch the ground I notice they're adorned in red fuzzy socks, which help me slide right along to the door. Now that the engine isn't running, I feel like they'll be able to hear my pounding heart. I'm sure that's not scientifically accurate, but I angle my body slightly from the door anyway.

"We don't know that for a fact," Tabby argues back. "I've been wrong before, or we've been too late, or they've caught onto what we were doing and had to retreat."

"I'm aware of our failures, thank you," Val says pointedly.

A silence. I fidget, trying to decide the best move to make. By the sounds of it they're right outside, so sneaking away isn't exactly an option. I could potentially barrel through them and make a run for it, but I don't think I stand a chance against a person like Val if it came to a physical fight.

Patience. Biding my time. That's all I can do for the moment.

With that in mind, I push open the door, feigning a yawn. All three of them are seated at the little kitchenette table, and all their heads turn quickly to look at me like a group of eager meerkats.

"Eva!" Tabby says, in a cheery tone that's obviously forced. "How're you doing? Did you sleep?"

"Head hurts," is all I say, which is the truth. The constant pounding in my temples refuses to let up, but I force myself to remember my manners. "I mean yes, I did sleep. Thank you. Have you fixed my phone yet?"

"Working on it," she says, far too quickly. "We have water for you, and this place will hopefully have some decent food. You must be starving."

Until she mentioned it, I hadn't even noticed. The nausea overpowered any kind of hunger, but I haven't eaten a thing since this morning, and I can now glimpse the crescent moon through the sunroof.

I accept the glass of water that's handed to me. It's slightly lukewarm, but I chug it down so fast that I practically choke. They all watch me in mild fascination. "Thanks," I eventually croak, wiping my mouth. "For your hospitality. I'm very grateful."

Val snorts as she stands up, tossing her braid over her shoulder. "You're very welcome," she says condescendingly, before gesturing to the others. "Let's go. I'll go on ahead and let them know we're here."

Tabby and Darryl are up and leaving the motorhome, ready for action, before I can even put down my empty glass. Val and I lock eyes for a moment, and I refuse to be the first to look away.

After what seems like a solid five minutes, the corner of her mouth quirks up. I *think* she's smiling.

"Got to toughen up sometimes, Eva," she says. "That pain in your head, that feeling you can't name? It's going to get worse. You're going to have to re-learn a lot of things. But you're not alone anymore. We all go through it. Nobody is immune."

Immune to what? I almost ask, but pure stubbornness keeps me quiet. Instead, I take a step closer to her, my eyes narrowed. "How did you get that scar?" It's rude of me, but she's been nothing but horrible, so I don't feel guilty. I want to know.

Val's hand goes to her top lip, lightly brushing the

pink scar, before it falls indifferently at her side. Her gaze is equally challenging. "They tried to shut me up," she says. And with that, she smiles, and turns, and leaves. I watch after her, feeling like a silly lost child in her presence.

*

For whatever reason, Tabby and Darryl are dismantling the motor-home's tyres.

I stand awkwardly on the side-lines holding a torch, watching them work, unsure if I should be offering any words of encouragement. It looks extremely laborious, and Val has gone off *somewhere,* so it's just the two of them.

There's no real telling where we are. Angling the torch slightly, I do my best to take in the surroundings. We've driven on a dirt track, and there's not a single house or building in sight. I move the light further on, and can't make out anything but rolling grass from every direction. Is this the countryside?

"In *this* direction, please," Darryl yells over. I jump, fumbling to swing the light back towards them. They're currently in the process of rolling one of the large tyres away.

"Are you...are you getting rid of your motor-home?" I feel the need to ask.

Darryl and Tabby stop wrestling with the tyre. "Get rid of Bessie?" Darryl asks in mock-horror. "Not bloody likely."

"It's just a precaution," Tabby explains through her staggered breathing. "We hide the tyres somewhere nearby. So that – if they drive past – they'll just think it's another demolished old van."

"*They?*" I echo dubiously, but they're already carrying on with their task. I glance back behind me. From the outside, Bessie looks like a load of junk with its blackened windows and rusted silver paint. A *deliberate* load of junk. These people are hiding from someone. By the sounds of it, they're hiding from a whole group.

The persistent knot of dread in my stomach tightens. Now that the sun has set, there's a chill in the air that creeps its way into my bones. I catch a flicker of my reflection in the large wing-mirror as I rub my arms to keep them warm. Even though I move away quickly, I've seen enough to know I look a complete mess. Long hair in disarray, face streaked with tears and dirt, murky blood stains on my dress. I barely recognise myself.

Finally, they seem satisfied with the state of their beloved Bessie. The tyres have been stashed somewhere that they assure me is safe, and then I'm being led along in the opposite direction.

It's too dark to get my bearings, and I've no idea what could be out here at this hour, which is the only reason why I don't start running. I'm not naïve enough to believe that I would survive a night here by myself.

Besides, wherever they're taking me might have a television. Lila should be doing her evening message soon. After that, she'll lull me off to sleep, and then I'll be ready for a bright and early positive morning.

Patience, patience, patience.

Chapter 14

"Is it four long knocks, then three quick ones?" Darryl hisses to Tabby. "Or is it *three* long knocks, and then four quick ones?"

"The first one," Tabby says, rapping her fist against the metal skip.

We've been walking for what must be at least half an hour, the only light source our torch and the glittering moon. It's been such a long time since I've properly seen the night sky. I tilt my head back. Stars twinkle above me. I suddenly have the overwhelming wish to just join them, to just *float* out of this sickness weighing down my body, to not have to feel so much.

"If there's nothing to feel, then there's nothing to fear," I mumble out loud.

Darryl turns to look at me in confusion. "You say something?"

I quickly shake my head. He's been complaining about a migraine for most of the walk; as we wait, he takes two small pills from a packet in his pocket. "No painkillers for you," he tells me before I can even open my mouth. He swallows the medicine dry. "Not 'til you've eaten."

I don't want painkillers; I want Lavender Slumber. In the glow of the moonlight, they reminded me of those perfect little pills. I grit my teeth, attempting to push the craving down.

Wherever we've walked to looks like a scrap heap. Large metal skips block us out, but I can glimpse towering piles of demolished cars, and the occasional plume of smoke makes my eyes water. Why have they brought me here? Maybe I should have ran when I had the chance.

A shuddering, grinding noise snaps me back into focus, as a portion of the skip in front of us creaks backwards, revealing a cut-out doorway. A woman stands in the opening, her greying hair pulled back in a bun. At first glance she seems like she *could* be kind and nurturing, but her steely gaze adds that she's not somebody to be messed with.

"Mrs. McIver," Tabby says in relief. "I hoped you'd be here."

The older woman's eyes crinkle as she smiles. "Lovely to see you, too," she says with an accent that lilts like a song as she gestures us in. Darryl goes first, bending down slightly to avoid whacking his head. Tabby quickly follows. I stand alone on the other side. A simple step feels like a giant leap off a cliff.

"Valentina filled us in on the new girl," she continues. "Eva, is it? Hungry?"

Her voice is quick and blunt, as if she doesn't have

time to even hear my answers. I simply nod to both. She stares at me impatiently until I force my legs to move. I'm through to the other side, but don't have long to weigh up whether it was a good idea or not; Mrs. McIver is already straining with the doorway. As it closes with a clang, I feel as though I'm encased in a tomb. The terror of it makes my eyes sting, but there's no time to cry. I'm already being led on, weaving in and out of piles of discarded junk.

Out of the corner of my eye I see a rusted bike, its frame all mangled. Somebody must've loved it, once, but it's ended up being abandoned just like every-thing else here. The same way all these people have abandoned Lila.

We pass others on the way – men, women, even some children, in simple patch-worked clothes that have been carefully stitched. I can't help but stare at them in bewilderment, though most of them refuse to even meet my gaze, hurrying along in the opposite di-rection as if I'm contagious. What are all these people *doing* here?

Tabby and Mrs. McIver are chatting away, their voices low. I hurry to walk by their side. "Where's your television?" I demand. "One of you must have a – a fucking *television*!" The swear word slips out of my mouth before I can stop it, and I wrench my mouth closed, horrified. Darryl looks amused, as if he can see my inner turmoil. "I – I'm so sorry," I say meekly. "I shouldn't have used that kind of language."

Mrs. McIver waves her hand. "That's quite alright,"

she says, "you're frustrated. It happens. But there's no television here, Eva. You won't be watching Lila tonight."

For a brief moment, I imagine wrapping my hands around her neck. She's bigger than me, but if I took her by surprise, I reckon I could choke the life out of her in a few minutes or so.

And then the overwhelming rage is gone, my legs buckling. Tabby quickly helps me up, but I can't even thank her. I'm utterly defeated. "Don't worry," she's saying to me. "Mrs. McIver makes the best soup. A bowl of that, and you'll be feeling much better, I promise."

Suddenly, I remember just how hungry I actually am. My stomach growls in agreement, and I allow myself to be led on without any more fuss.

*

After my second bowl of rich vegetable soup – as warming and delicious as promised – any fear I was previously feeling has long gone. It's hard to be scared when people are giving you a good meal.

Mrs. McIver likes to keep herself busy, apparently. Soup is her speciality, but I'm told she's a wonderful cook for everything else too, and I can believe it. The trio seem to know her very well, judging by their affection towards her. Even Val is smiling in her presence.

We're sitting in the centre of the junkyard around a

makeshift campfire; the source of the smoke I'd seen before. It's easing the chill that wormed its way into my bones. There had been others here, but they've all disappeared to bed. That's good. I don't have it in me for any small-talk, and all these new people are already making my head swim.

"Tell me about who you're hiding from," I say, clinking my spoon against the empty wooden bowl. Mrs. McIver takes it from me, filling it up again from the iron pot that's held above the campfire.

"Who says we're hiding?" Darryl asks.

There's a silence, and I observe him with narrowed eyes. His own shine back in amusement. "You're making a joke," I say flatly. It's a shame that I'm not in the mood to be laughing.

"Guilty," he agrees. "We make a habit out of hiding."

The others look at each other, and then Mrs. McIver gives Val a small nod, clearly deciding to give me some proper information.

"We call them the Creatives," Val says as she lights up another cigarette. "The men who help Lila run the show."

"The Creatives?" I echo dubiously.

"We called them the Producers for a while, but it never caught on," Tabby says. "Too..." she wiggles her fingers in little jazz-hands, and then looks at me expectantly. "Know what I mean?"

I don't know. I have no idea what she's talking about. The others around the campfire are chuckling, though, so I assume it's a witty joke. I force myself to smile.

"Why do you hide from them?" I ask, keeping my voice light. "Don't you think it would be so exciting to know more about the show?"

Val takes a deep drag of her cigarette. "You are so right, Eva," she says. "We think it would be very exciting indeed. That's why we need to find out exactly where they film it."

Darryl takes the cigarette from her outstretched hand. "They're sneaky," he says. "We can never seem to narrow them down to one specific spot, but this time we're sure we're close."

"Which is why we're jumping from one safe spot to another," Tabby adds. "If they know we're nearby – we just can't risk it. There's no telling what Lila would do to us."

I'm barely listening anymore. All I can think about is these Creatives, and if I'll actually be able to meet Lila face-to-face. My stomach somersaults. "What are they like?" I try to keep the excitement in my voice toned all the way down. I think I'm just about pulling it off. "The Creatives, I mean. What are they like?"

Val's expression sours. "Good question," she says. "We don't get close enough to find out."

"But – your scar," I prompt. "If the Creatives did that –"

"My scar wasn't the Creatives," Val says. "Men have always wanted to shut me up, Eva."

That's put me in my place. I'm not exactly sure

what expression my face is making right now, but I hope it somewhat resembles sympathy. A cacophony of information swirls in my brain, and I don't know which part to focus on the most.

"Thing is, Eva, there's a lot of people out there stuck inside just like you were," Darryl is saying. I force myself to focus. "But I bet none of them are as big a fan as you are."

A smug nod as I accept my bowl of soup. "I have an official signed photo," I say proudly.

He whistles in awe, and takes a deep drag of his cigarette. Smoke blows as he speaks. "Fancy that! That's why we need you. You're going to be a huge help to us. If anybody knows about Lila, it's going to be you. You've been watching for years, haven't you?"

"Since forever," I say, almost by default, but then I frown.

How long has Lila been on TV for? Ali's voice pipes up in my head. I push her away. Not now.

"So, what exactly has she been saying recently?" Tabby presses. "Has anything new been happening on the show? Anything that caught your attention?"

"If you'd been watching it like you *should've* been, you'd know it was time for our shopping orders." I don't bother to hide the contempt in my voice. "And the big competition is happening soon. Does anybody have any ideas about what I should be thankful for? I want to win this time."

Val rubs at her temples, irritation practically crackling through her. If I touched her arm I wouldn't be surprised if I got an electric shock. Maybe this isn't the kind of information they were looking for. *Has* anything caught my attention from the show lately?

"Oh!" I suddenly gasp. Everybody turns to look at me. "No, no, there *was* something! Lila looked away from us."

"Fantastic," Val begins to say in a voice dripping with sarcasm, but then Darryl holds up a hand.

"That is pretty weird actually, Val," he says. "Lila doesn't typically look away from the camera."

She throws him a withering look, but he only shrugs. "It's my turn." Val gestures to the cigarette, and takes it back from him, rolling it between her thumb and second finger as she mulls over my words. "Maybe she knows we're coming," she eventually says. "Maybe she's onto us. Maybe she's *nervous.*"

"I don't think Lila's the type to get nervous," Tabby says quietly.

I blow on my soup before taking a grateful spoonful. I barely make it halfway through my third bowl before my eyelids get droopy, the exhaustion of the day catching up with me yet again. I've not done this much exercise and socialising since...however long.

Mrs. McIver carefully takes the bowl from me, and helps me lie down by the fire. There are blankets, and various folded clothes that she fashions a pillow out of, and before I know it I allow sleep to pull me under.

Later on, I'm roused by two hushed voices that dip in and out of focus. My eyelids flutter the tiniest bit to see Tabby and Mrs. McIver alone by the fire. I force myself to keep still.

"And what makes you so sure she won't blow the whole thing?" I hear Mrs. McIver say.

I focus on my breathing, making sure it mimics the slow and steady state of sleep. For a while, the only other sound I hear is the crackling of the fire, but then Tabby begins to whisper.

"Eva won't be a liability. You heard her, she's a Lila fanatic. I bet there's loads she knows; she just doesn't trust us enough yet, and we can't blame her for that. Once she starts to remember properly..."

"There's no telling what she'll do," the older woman warns. "Absolutely no telling at all."

"But we'll be there to guide her through it," Tabby says. "Wouldn't that be better, than having her all alone again?"

Mrs. McIver scoffs in annoyance. "I'm not saying to leave her in the middle of the road! Leave her here, with us. We shouldn't jeopardise everything we've been working so hard on, just because you've got a silly crush."

I feel my entire body stiffen. There a sharp inhale of disbelief, and then the sound of Tabby stomping away. I realise that I'm forgetting to breathe, so quickly try to rectify it. It's too late. Footsteps approach, and Mrs. McIver gently nudges my shoulder with her foot.

"You can get up now," she says with a sigh. "I helped raise six nephews. I know a fake sleeper when I see one."

I squeeze my eyes tighter, even attempting to imitate a snore.

"Suit yourself," she says. I can practically hear her indifferent shrug. "I guess I'll have the rest of this soup all to myself."

My traitorous stomach growls, and she laughs. She's got me hook, line, and sinker with that, and she knows it. Sheepishly, I open my eyes and prop myself up, still unable to properly meet her gaze out of embarrassment. "I'll have some," I mumble. "If there's any left."

"There's always soup," Mrs. McIver says. "And always time to talk. So, Eva. Shall we talk?"

Chapter 15

"I don't understand a lot of things."

The fire has reduced down to a few glowing embers, so that Mrs. McIver's face is cast in shadow from where she's sitting opposite of me. I don't mind that. It makes talking easier if I can't see anybody.

As a way to keep my brain focused, I continuously tug at the hem of my filthy dress, staring at a loose thread until my eyes burn. "I thought I understood," I continue, "but things out here aren't the way they're supposed to be."

"And how *are* they supposed to be?" Mrs. McIver asks.

I don't answer. I can't answer.

"Valentina says they found you passed out on the street," she prompts.

"They stole from me. Tricked me into leaving. I never would've...I mean, only to...My mum and sister are together, you see," I suddenly blurt. "I'm in contact with them and everything, but I started getting worried. Ali – that's my twin – Ali was being a bit off with me, and now I can't shake the feeling she's in trouble."

I fumble for the scrap of paper that I'd tucked into my dress pocket, and wave it to emphasise my point. "*Nightmares*, that's what I wrote. I had nightmares about Ali. I think – I think she's in danger."

"We're all in danger," Mrs. McIver says cryptically, which does absolutely nothing to help me.

I fold my arms tightly across my chest. "I'm sick of all of you being so weird," I say with spite.

She only chuckles, as if I'm a baby acting up for attention. "Don't sulk on me, now," she says. "I understand. Your family is important to you, that's only natural. You want to find them?"

Slowly, I unfold my arms, turning my head to her. "I do," I whisper. "I think – I think that *is* what I want. For us to all be together again. Watching Lila at home."

"What about your father?" she asks. "Is he not in the picture?"

"I never met him."

She exhales slowly in sympathy. "I'm sorry to hear that."

"Oh, it's ok," I say quickly. "There's no point in being sad about it. I'm sure he was nice. Mum doesn't talk about him much, but he must've been nice, you know? Otherwise they wouldn't have been married."

"I'm sure," she agrees kindly, reaching over to pat my knee. I flinch away, unused to a stranger's touch.

There's a gold band around her fourth finger that glitters as she moves her hand.

"*You're* married," I say obviously. "Where's Mr. McIver, then? Does he stay here too?"

A sharp intake of breath that she tries to hide. "I'm afraid not," she eventually says. Her voice seems to catch in her throat. She coughs, hands now clasped together.

"Ok." I wait, but she doesn't elaborate. I need to fill this silence somehow. "Is he somewhere...else?"

Mrs. McIver straightens up. She clears her throat a few times. Perhaps she has a cold. "He died in the War," she says. "Ten years ago now. It was quick, but...That doesn't necessarily make it any better."

Died is such an ugly word. It hits me in the stomach with its bluntness. Why do we have to say such words out loud?

"I just like to keep the ring on," she's saying, but her voice seems dimmed. "I can't imagine not wearing it. Childhood sweethearts, we were. He'd buy me white roses every Friday, right up until the War began. It hit Edinburgh hard, you know. A lot of folk suffered."

"I'm sorry for asking about him," I force myself to whisper, if only so she can stop talking.

She dabs at her eyes for a moment, huffing a small laugh. "Never mind me! I'm glad you did. You should always remember your loved ones, Eva. Don't ever feel bad for that."

"I'm very sorry for all of you," I say truthfully.

These people must have lived such hard lives without Lila to guide them.

Mrs. McIver looks at me with gentle eyes. When she pats my knee again I don't pull myself away. She clearly needs to be comforted. "You're a sweet girl, Eva," she says. "I don't suppose you remember the War just yet, do you?"

Ba-dum. Ba-dum. Ba-dum.

My heart feels like it's going to beat itself out of my chest. A cold sweat tickles my forehead. "The War?" I ask. *Put on a big smile, nice and wide!* "Oh, no, Mrs. McIver," I say. My mouth stretches into a garish grin, even as a single tear trickles down from my eye. "I've never been bothered by any war."

Chapter 16

Over the next few days, it's easier to just sleep.

My schedule is all over the place without Lila to encourage me; I'm sluggish and grumpy and want to go home. These strangers are still being so kind to me, which almost makes it worse, because it's much harder to hate them. Mrs. McIver refers to themselves as a makeshift family, but I need my *own* family, and I need things to go back to normal. None of these people are *normal*.

So, the only comfort I've really had is sleep. If I can close my eyes and drift off, I don't need to worry so much. Lila is always talking about the importance of rest, after all. I was initially worried I wouldn't be able to, but if anything it's been far more effort to be awake than it has been to make myself drift off.

The sunrays piercing from the clouds are too bright to ignore now, though. I've been sleeping in a make-shift bed inside a hollowed out bus, a far cry away from my lovely pink room. Mrs McIver was able to wash my dress while I spent a day in a dressing gown – there's a river nearby, apparently – but some of the bloodstains proved themselves to be persistent. Still, at least I don't smell.

Mrs. McIver brings me a steaming coffee in a cup carved from metal. At least I'm following along with *some* of my morning routine. "Has my phone been fixed yet?" is the first thing I say.

"Not yet, hen," she says. I don't know why she keeps referring to me as a chicken. Maybe it's a subtle way of calling me a coward. "Try not to worry about that just now, I know it's hard. Drink your coffee."

So I do, and it does make me feel better. She lays a small rucksack on top of my blanket. "Spare clothes," she says. "You know, if you ever did want to change into something new. Try something different."

"Everything's different right now," I retort. There's no way I'm changing my dress. It's the only piece of home I currently have. The only piece of *me* I currently have.

She waves her hand. "Suit yourself! But keep them anyway. They're some of Valentina's old things, and I've certainly no use for them."

After she leaves, curiosity gets the better of me and I sneak a little look. Of course the clothes are all black and dismal. I toss the bag aside, but then can't resist looking again. I pull out a long leather coat, rubbing my fingers against the material. It's not exactly a *bad* coat. Maybe it could even be cute.

But Val used to wear it. So I'm certainly not putting it on.

It's another gloriously warm day when I step out

of the bus, and if I don't let myself think about my problems too much I could almost be in a good mood. That is, until I spot Darryl and Val walking together in the distance, looking decidedly shifty.

Time to start making some proper plans. Loathe as I am to do it, I creep back into the bus and snatch up the leather coat. It's comfortable and light on, and travels just past my knees, so my pink dress is covered. It's just a coat, but I feel different somehow. Different, and hopefully able to blend better in the background as I set off after them, making sure to keep a good few metres behind.

Their voices are low. I inch forwards, straining to make out anything they're saying. If they're plotting something insidious against me, I'll be ready. I've been ready all along, ever since they tried to drip their poison into my ears.

They come to a stop, and I hastily dive behind a rusted car.

"I'm just saying, you can relax for a moment," Darryl is saying. "The sun's out, we've got coffee, and nobody's tried to kill us for at *least* three months." He gives her a thumbs up, and takes a sip of his aforementioned coffee. "That, to me, is what we call a win."

Val only huffs in irritation. Her long, thick hair is loose today, cascading down her back. It's much prettier than mine, I note with envy, even though it's the exact same length and colour. Another reason to dislike her.

"You're so sulky," Darryl says, his tone teasing.

"Always so ready to act like you don't care about anything or anyone."

She opens her mouth – probably to say something scathing – but then closes it.

"But I know for a fact that's not true," he says, leaning in slightly. She doesn't move away, which surprises me. I didn't think Val would like anybody in her personal space like that. "'Cause of *Eva*."

I inhale sharply, and then duck further behind the car in case they heard me. After a few tense seconds of silence, I deem myself safe, and slowly peek my head back up. Val is glowering at him.

"What *about* Eva?" she says, her tone clipped.

"You rescued her," he says smugly. "Couldn't leave her all alone, could you? Heart of gold."

"Nu-uh," she shakes her head vigorously. "She was blocking the road. It was either move her, or let the raccoons eat her." She cuts him off before he can even open his mouth. "I *know* raccoons aren't in this country, you smug fuck. Something similar to raccoons."

"We have badgers," Darryl suggests. "They could probably be quite vicious if we gave them the chance."

"It doesn't mean I'm going soft," Val says. "I was being practical. I thought she could be helpful. I'm sure she *will* be once that brainwashing has been scrubbed out of her."

"No one could ever accuse you of being soft, Val," Darryl says. "Trust me."

Val suddenly turns to leave, but Darryl reaches out to hold onto her arm. From where I'm standing, I can see his touch is light, as if she's a wild animal that he's trying to coax back.

"C'mon, darling," I hear him say quietly.

"I am *not* your darling," she snaps. "You need to get a grip."

Darryl holds up his free hand in surrender, a now all-too familiar cocky smile on his face. "There must be *some* reason why you keep me around," he says.

"Sure," Val retorts, "you're our designated driver."

He laughs quietly. I shouldn't be listening in on this – it's not my place. Still, part of me can't bring myself to look away.

"Alright, then," he says, voice smooth as velvet before he slowly leans in. Her head tilts to meet him, seemingly against her better judgement, but then he pulls back.

"You owe me a cigarette," is all he says.

She whacks him in the chest, hard, but all he does is laugh. "You know you love me," he says teasingly.

"I don't," she says, her voice laced with acid. "I tolerate you."

I watch them both walk away in opposite directions, feeling lost and awkward. Maybe...Maybe they're not plotting against me after all. Maybe this all actually has very little to do with me.

I wrestle my way out of the coat as if it's laced with poison, scrunching it up in my arms. Why did they even bother bringing me all the way out here, sur-rounded by betrayers and liars and miscreants and –

"I like your dress," a little voice pipes up.

Through watery eyes, I spot a small girl standing by my feet. Her blonde hair is in two plaits, and her blue eyes blink up at me expectantly. She wears a grey patchwork dress that's too big for her. She can't be any older than six.

"Thanks," I say. And then: "Your dress is nice, too," because that seems like the right thing to do, even if it's a lie.

"My mum made it. She can never find pink fabric," the girl continues, "otherwise I'd match you. Are you Eva?"

Clearly people are talking about me, just as I suspected. "I'm Eva," I say. There's no point in pretending otherwise.

"I'm Lucy," she says with a gap-toothed smile.

I find myself kneeling down to meet her eye level, attempting a smile of my own. After so much stress, it's nice to be able to chat like this. "Is your mum here with you?" I ask.

She nods vigorously. "Mum, Dad, my two brothers," she says the last part with a scowl. "But they were annoying me. I wanted to walk by myself."

"Sure," I say in agreement. "Siblings can be annoying."

There's a mutual silence of understanding between us. I smooth out the coat that I still have in my arms, and lay it down by my feet. "Have you always lived here?" I ask. "Don't you have a proper house, with a good TV?"

Lucy doesn't respond right away. Instead, she chews at her lip, glancing over her shoulder.

"What?" I press. "What's wrong?"

"I'm not really supposed to talk to you," she says, having the decency to look ashamed. "Mum and Dad said not to."

"Oh," I say, sadness creeping into my voice. "That doesn't seem fair. Why can't you talk to me?"

"'Cause you only just escaped," Lucy says. "And you could be dangerous."

It's so absurd that I find myself laughing. I laugh for quite a long time.

"I didn't escape my *house*, silly," I manage through fits of giggles. "I didn't need to escape from anything! I'm just trying to find *my* family right now, that's all. I have a sister. A twin! We're identical. You know what that means?"

Lucy is edging away from me, but I reach out to grab her little arm. She turns milky-pale, her eyes wide like a startled bunny. "Eva?" she attempts. I don't let go.

"It's not me who you need to avoid," I tell her, desperate for her to understand. After all, this isn't her fault. She's so young. "It's all of *you* who need the help! You should all be watching *The Lifetime Lila Show*. I'm the only one here who knows how important it is."

"Lila's *bad* for us," Lucy whines. "Eva, please. You're hurting me!"

My grip tightens. "Don't ever say such horrible

things like that again," I hiss. "You have no right to spread such nasty lies."

She's crying. Big, shuddering sobs as she wrenches her arm away. I've left red marks against her soft skin. I allow myself a moment to feel bad about it. "I'm sorry, Lucy," I try. "I never meant to – I just want to *help* you."

For a moment, she just wails. I raise my voice to be heard. "You're going to be in huge trouble if you say untrue things like that. Lila does everything for us, and you're all being so *selfish!"*

Somebody grabs onto my shoulder, wrenching me to my feet. I yelp at the sudden impact as I'm swung round, coming face to face with a furious looking Val. I'm in trouble. Very big trouble.

"I'd ask if you've lost your mind, but clearly we're well beyond that," Val snaps, her eyes darting to Lucy. "Go to your mama, kid. *Now.* Beat it!"

Lucy sniffles, but does as she's told, running as far as her little legs can carry her.

"Jesus Christ, Eva," Val says, giving me a little shake. "Do you make a habit out of terrorising children?"

"I'm trying to help," I protest, fighting to keep the whine out of my voice. "I'm trying to help all of you!"

Her fingers dig into my shoulders. I can't look her in the eyes. "No," she grinds out, "you're not helping anybody. All you're doing is getting in my way, and – is that my coat?"

Both our gazes land on the discarded leather coat

by my feet. I swallow back the sudden lump in my throat. "Yes," I say.

"And why is *my* coat covered in dirt?"

"Mrs. McIver said you didn't want it anymore! I'm not a *thief*." I spit the last word, hoping to hit her where it hurts. "I don't want it! I only took it from her to be nice."

Val lets go of me with a disgruntled scoff. "Take it if you want," she says as she turns away. "None of this is my problem anymore."

I gawp at her departing back. "*You* brought me out here," I feel the need to shout after her. "*You* stole my phone and took me away from everything I knew. So stop being such a – a –"

Val abruptly stops in her tracks, tension radiating from her as she looks over her shoulder. "Gonna cuss me out, Barbie?"

"You're just a nasty piece of work," I say with an upwards tilt of my head. "I don't need to swear at you. I'm *better* than that."

"If you knew what we had all been through, just to get to this point," Val explodes, "you'd sit down, shut up, and be grateful I'm not *nastier*. You are not going to ruin this for us, do I make myself clear? Your precious Lila doesn't care about you. She doesn't care about any of us. She only cares about herself and keeping control."

I shake my head as I whisper, "She looks after us."

Val gestures wildly. I have a feeling it's taking all her self-control to not start firing bullets from the revolver strapped to her hip. "She's never looked after us! Don't you think it's fucking weird that you could never go out to do your own shopping? That they sent you pills in the mail to stop you from even daring to *think?*"

"For the last time," I growl, "Lavender Slumber is a useful supplement to help you –"

"Eva!" she yells in frustration.

I flinch wildly, my eyes screwed up, expecting the sharp crack of her fist against my jaw. It never comes. There's only the sound of ragged breaths. When I eventually deem it safe to peek my eyes open, I see her head is lowered, long hair masking her face. Defeated.

"It's not your fault," she says eventually, her tone tired and resigned. "But it's...It's so fucking *annoying.*"

"Sorry," I say, because I can't think of any other appropriate response. There's a silence that grows more and more uncomfortable. I bend down to pick up her coat, shaking the dust from it, if only so I can make myself look busy until she calms down.

Eventually, she pushes her hair away from her face, straightening her spine. Back in control. "Just try not to beat up anybody, alright?" she says, and there's a hint of a smirk on her face. I deem it safe to smile back. "Leave that to me."

Chapter 17

We're leaving the junkyard today, I'm told. The mismatched trio and I.

Mrs. McIver walks back with us all the way to the abandoned Bessie, despite Val's protests. The sun is hot, so her movements are slow. She stops several times, but always waves her hand away whenever any of us ask if we can help her, muttering something about not being an invalid.

When we arrive at the motor-home, Mrs. McIver hands me back the rucksack full of old clothes while the others sweat over mantling the tyres back on. I feel I'd just get in the way if I even tried to help. Not that I *want* to.

"I don't need these," I tell her, but she's so insistent that I decide it's not worth arguing. Besides, maybe it's not such a terrible idea to have at least *some* clothes that aren't splattered with blood.

"I hope to see you again," she says to me. "Be brave. Keep fighting."

She looks at me with such sincerity that I can't help but feel awkward.

"Sure," I say. "Whatever."

Mrs. McIver takes her time saying more heartfelt goodbyes to the others. Tabby has to take off her glasses, dabbing at her eyes as she nods at whatever is being said to her. They love her, I realise. The kind of love that breaks your heart, the kind of love you want to bubble-wrap and hold close to you forever. I think I understand all about that.

And yet, they keep brave faces as they watch her leave, determination plastered on in a heartbeat. I clutch at the straps of the rucksack until there are deep grooves in my fingers. Where do I belong now?

"We're heading to Dover," Darryl says, and I hope my relief isn't too obvious. "A boat should be waiting for us, to take us right up to Leith. You ever been to Scotland, Eva?"

"No," I say, fairly certain. "Is...Is that where the television show is filmed? In Scotland?"

"Currently in Edinburgh," Tabby says. "The base moves around, but we've finally managed to narrow it down. Right now, that's where Lila is. I'm 99% certain."

"And we're jumping on that 99%, so that's where we're going," Darryl says.

"You're going to Scotland to find Lila?" I ask just to make sure, trying to keep my voice light.

"Yes," he says with a smirk. "To find Lila."

I nod for far longer than necessary. "That's good," I insist. "Time to bring her down, right? We should go now." The sooner we go, the sooner Lila and her

Creatives can stamp them out. I'll be hailed a hero. Maybe I'll even get my own segment on the show. All I need to do is –

"Eva," Tabby says with a wince, "you said all of that out loud."

I swear I can *feel* my heart sinking rapidly in my chest. My mouth opens and closes like a useless goldfish as the trio look at me. "Did I?" I croak.

"Sorry, mate," Darryl says. "But you've got all the grace and subtlety of a pantomime villain."

Val taps at the revolver holstered at her hip. "If you want to stab us in the back, you are more than welcome to try," she tells me. "It'll probably be amusing. But don't think I won't hesitate to put a bullet neatly between your eyes, *querida*."

I don't need to bother asking her if she's serious. The stony expression on her face tells me everything I need to know. "I don't want to stab you in the back," I say meekly. "Honestly, I don't. You're...nice people."

Darryl taps his chest, right by his heart. "That's profound," he says.

"You're just wrong, that's all," I blurt. "You're wrong about literally everything, but that's not your fault. When we get to Lila, she'll be able to tell you better than I can."

"Maybe this is a bad idea," Tabby mutters. "I'd really hoped the impact would be wearing off by now, but..."

"I won't do anything." I say quickly. "I need to stay with you all. You're the only ones who can fix my phone, and I'll need transport to find Mum and Ali."

Darryl raises his eyebrows. "I'm not a bloody taxi service, Eva. We have one mission, and we're not diverting from it for a long lost family reunion."

"No, no," I agree, "we'll see Lila first. And then...then maybe you'll help me? Just a little help. I can't drive, and I don't have shoes to walk that far, and –" Once Lila sorts them out, her and the Creatives will help me, but I can't say *that,* because then they'll never –

"Eva," Tabby says kindly, "it's probably best if you just stop talking."

I realise I've said the last part out loud again. My face burns in humiliation.

"Ah, don't worry about it," Darryl says as he swings open the motor-home door. "Your optimism is to be admired. Now either hop aboard Bessie, or stay here and scheme. Your choice."

I mumble something about hopping aboard.

"Lovely," he says. "Maybe you can help pick a CD. You a fan of Chas and Dave?"

"Nobody is a fan of Chas and Dave," Val says darkly as she steps inside. Tabby hurries after her; I try to meet her gaze but she makes no effort to look my way. I hope I've not scared her.

"I've never listened to them," I admit.

"Ah, you'll love them. They're the pride and joy of my city," Darryl says as he ushers me in. "Great stuff. It's important to broaden your culture. There's more to life than Bobby Darin."

*

In the next few hours, Tabby attempts to explain to me what all her gadgets do. We've been listening to the constant sound of two Cockney men for the past hour, until Val finally changed the CD, though I don't exactly rate all these loud guitar solos and crashing drums. I sit on the floor, gazing up at Tabby as she works in her chair. For the most part, Darryl's driving is steady, though on occasion I need to cling onto the legs of Tabby's desk. Her enthusiasm is borderline infectious, even if I don't understand any of it.

"This is the built-in GPS," she points to one of the screens. "It's helping me map out where the Creatives are. This one helps me scan for any remaining data signals. I've been able to hack into theirs and changed the encryption so they can't trace it back to us. This –"

"Where did you learn all this?" I ask, before she goes into any more confusing detail.

"My auntie," she says immediately. I notice the way her eyes light up when she mentions her. "Auntie Celia's a total tech wizard. The moment I could flex my fingers she was teaching me everything she ever knew, and then some."

"That's nice," I say honestly. A nagging thought pushes its way to the surface. I'm almost afraid to ask – the image of Mrs. McIver's haunted eyes playing on a loop in my head – but I push on. "Where's...Where's your auntie now?"

"Oh, she's safe in London," Tabby says, as I try not

to make my sigh of relief too obvious. "As safe as she can be, keeping her head down. I kept trying to convince her to stay with Mrs. McIver and the others, but she's hell-bent on doing her own thing. Always has been a bit of a maverick."

"What exactly *is* she doing?" I say, fighting to keep the scorn out of my voice. "Does she do what you all do? Take people from their homes?"

"She patrols around London looking for survivors, if that's what you mean," Tabby says mildly. "Nobody took you from your home, Eva. You made that first step yourself, and I'm proud of you for doing it."

My scowl is definitely unladylike and mean, but I can't resist throwing it her way. To her credit, she doesn't seem fazed. I really don't know how she manages to be so nice all the time. I'd be impressed if I wasn't currently so wound up.

"Can I ask *you* a question?" Tabby continues. "You walked all the way to the end of your street, right? Because you were looking for us? That must've been really brave."

"What's your question?" I say with a sulk, once again regretting all of my bad decisions thus far.

Tabby smiles. "My question is, what encouraged you to keep going? Lila's hold is powerful. I could understand why you would've wanted to go right back inside the moment you opened the door. What encouraged you?"

The answer is so simple that it almost feels juvenile saying it. "I like the blossom trees," I murmur.

"The blossom trees," Tabby echoes. "They're beautiful. You're right. Springtime always promises something...better. Don't you think?"

I don't want to have this conversation, because it just reminds me of the fact everything around my home is destroyed beyond repair. I change tactics. Ever since my fireside talk with Mrs. McIver, there's been one pressing concern on my mind – besides my continuous worrying about Ali and Mum.

"When was there a war here?" I ask. "I mean, besides the First and the Second World Wars. I know all about those from Lila's history segment."

Tabby stops typing away at her computer, turning to me with a frown. "Who told you about the War?" she asks, before her eyes widen. "Are you...Are you remembering? What're you thinking?"

"Mrs. McIver mentioned it," I say quickly. "That there was war. Her husband died in it. It all sounded very sad."

"Ah." The excitement fizzles out of Tabby's eyes, replaced by concern. "That's...We wanted you to remember in your own time. At least, *I* did. Trying to see just how long Lila's influence lasts nowadays. It's like nobody around here at all understands the importance of scientific research, I swear to –"

"Tell me about the war," I interrupt. I have to. My attention span will only stretch so far.

Tabby chews at her lip, bringing one knee up to her chest as she swivels on her chair. I notice her socks have little rainbows stitched on. "Ummm," she draws the word out, clearly trying to decide where to begin. "It was sixteen years ago."

"Oh!" I can't help but laugh in relief. "Oh, that's not too bad then!"

There's a strained silence. Tabby refuses to look at me, slowly swivelling back to her computer screen. That probably wasn't the best thing to say. "I just mean, like, it was a long time ago," I try to rectify. "We can't dwell on the past, you know?"

"The past will always be our present if we don't do anything about it," she jabs at her keyboard as she speaks.

"But we're not in a war *now*," I say, only to pause. "I... *Are* we?"

"We're in a different kind of war," Tabby says. "We're in the aftermath." She suddenly freezes, her fingers hovering uselessly over the keyboard. "Oh, shit," she hisses. "Shit, shit, *shit!*"

"What is it?"

She only points. A red dot is beeping on the screen in front of her, ominous and persistent. It's moving, and it's moving fast. "Creatives!" she yells, tumbling out of her chair. "Divert, Darryl, *divert!*"

"Motherfu–" I hear Val begin to say, but she's cut off as Darryl wildly swerves the motor-home off of the road. I go careering forwards, my head narrowly missing the kitchen table.

"Hey!" I yelp, even though no one is paying attention to me. I grip at the edge of the table, hauling myself up.

"Oh God, oh God, oh God..." Tabby is mumbling to herself as she flicks a bunch of switches. One by one, the screens around her go black. The only one left is the one with the red dot, still moving, still gaining.

Val has sprung from her chair, and leaps at the skylight with almost unnatural ease, forcing it open with her elbow. She hoists herself up, again without so much as a groan, poking her head out to see the road.

"No sign," she shouts down. "But keep moving!"

Darryl doesn't hesitate as Bessie picks up speed. I didn't think she was capable of going this fast without combusting.

"There's a van!" Val suddenly yells down. "One of their vans!"

Hearing the urgency in her voice sends a cold wave of fear throughout my body. All the hairs on my arms stand to attention and I slump back to the floor.

We're happy, aren't we, Ali? I can hear myself say to my sister, not so long ago. Her and I sitting in the garden, before it all went horribly wrong. Push it down, lock it away, can't think about that. Can't breathe. It's as though the motor-home is collapsing in on me.

"Bloody shoot at them, then!" Darryl snaps. From where I am, I can see how fiercely he's gripping onto the steering wheel. His knuckles gleam white from the force.

I cower under the table. The idea of meeting the Creatives had been exciting before. These elusive, powerful men who help Lila bring the show to life. This is what I *wanted*. Why am I so frightened now?

Why do my hands shake as I press them against my head, hard enough to hurt, hard enough to stop me from *thinking* –

"Darryl!" Tabby's cry pierces my heart. "Whatever you do, don't stop!"

The tyres groan and creak underneath us. Through half-open eyes I see Val pull herself completely up. She's going on the roof – she can't go on the roof – she'll get herself *killed*.

"Stop it!" I hear myself scream, but I'm drowned out by the sound of gunfire, a constant *crack* of bullets.

"She'll be ok," Tabby is yelling, though it sounds like she's reassuring herself more than me. "It's Val!"

True enough, Val comes crashing back, landing heavily on her side. She groans a bunch of obscenities, panting harshly as she scrambles to her feet to close over the skylight. "Got their tyres!" she calls. "They're off the road, but keep moving! We're so close!"

Darryl swears to nobody in particular, wrenching the steering wheel to the right as we speed on. The rock music that's been consistently blaring finally dies out with a crackle. Silence hangs over all of us, ominous and foreboding.

"What happens if they get us?" I eventually croak.

"We're not gonna find out," Val says. Her eyes have that familiar hardness to them as she slumps to the ground, hands pressed to her left hip. Tabby sits by her side, the two of them a solid unit as I watch on. I'm still the outsider. I'm still someone they can't trust.

"I don't want them to get us," I find myself saying, needing them to believe it.

"We know, Eva," Tabby says, so gentle despite the panic around us. "Thank y –"

Her words are drowned out as Bessie goes faster and faster. There's a furious yell from Darryl – I instinctively reach for Tabby's hand – and then the world tilts and spins and crashes around us and

We're happy, aren't we, Ali?

Chapter 18

BEFORE, PART ONE: TABBY

A cacophony of clattering and shouting leaks from behind the closed kitchen door, getting louder and more intense as each minute passes.

Seven-year-old Tabitha sits on the grubby staircase. In her sweaty palms, she holds a rolling pin. Her mum had been planning on baking chocolate biscuits, and seeing as this kind of fun is a rare occurrence, Tabby was all too excited to help. Except, of course, Oscar has decided he's in a foul mood over something.

Usually, once her step-dad's arguing reaches its crescendo, he storms out to drown his sorrows in beer. A week is the longest he's ever stayed away. Tabby hopes that tonight is the night where her mother will finally kick him out for good.

The kitchen door is thrown open, and Oscar – a

six-foot glowering giant to Tabby – storms out, nursing his knuckles and swearing under his breath. Her mother staggers behind him, pleading with him not to go. Blood is trickling from the corner of her mouth.

Something inside Tabby's chest snaps and she leaps to her feet. "Leave her alone!" she hears herself shout, high-pitched and desperate, nowhere near as intimidating as she wants.

"Be *quiet*, Tabitha!" her mother snaps, barely throwing her a glance. "Go to your room."

Tabby's hands grip around the rolling pin to stop Oscar from noticing how much she's shaking. It's not even from fear anymore; it's from raw, red anger. "He's a bully," she spits, and then raises her voice as she looks right at her step-dad. "You're a big, ugly *bully!*"

Oscar's green eyes glint dangerously, and his mouth twists. She knows that look all too well, but she doesn't bound up the stairs in terror as he approaches. Instead, the rolling pin smashes against his cheekbone with all the strength she can muster.

For a moment, Tabby can't believe what she's done. She just knows it feels incredibly satisfying when Oscar roars in pain. He's bitten the inside of his cheek; now blood is dribbling from his mouth too.

Tabby's elation is short-lived when Oscar backhands her across the face. The force of his slap practically lifts her off of her feet, and her head crashes against the staircase banister as she falls back.

She lies on the stairs for a moment, stunned, the whole left side of her face throbbing.

"Control your brat!" Oscar shouts, slamming the door behind him. The force is so strong that a picture-frame of Tabby and her two cousins falls to the floor with a shatter.

Slowly, Tabby props herself up, waiting for her mum to appreciate the weight of what just happened. Instead, Tabby's mother grabs her shoulders, shaking her small body until her teeth rattle.

"What have you *done?*" she screams. Her dark eyes are wide with disbelief and rage.

Tabby tries to defend her actions, but when she opens her mouth no words come out. Her mum continues to shake her.

"You better hope Oscar comes back," she snaps. "And when he does, you better *grovel*, or you'll be answering to me for the rest of your life."

Tabby barely recognises her mother, and the moment she acknowledges this, she feels her heart break. No matter what happens, nothing will ever be the same between them again. Despite everything, her mum has chosen Oscar over her only child. "But, Mum –"

"Go to your room," is all her mum says. "Stay up there until I decide you can come down."

"I was trying to *help* you," Tabby says, eyes shining with angry tears. "He hit you, Mum. He's hit you before. We don't need him!"

Tabby's mother draws her hand back, and Tabby recoils. They both stare at each other, her mother's hand frozen in mid-air. Without another word, Tabby scrambles away and runs upstairs, breaths coming out in wheezy gasps.

Slamming her bedroom door behind her, Tabby lets herself cry for approximately one minute, and then curls her little hands into fists. Anger is a more useful emotion right now.

The sound of clinking glass from the kitchen confirms that her mum is drowning her own sorrows. If tradition is anything to go by, she'll have a bottle of wine and then pass out on the sofa. Tabby waits until she's certain her mum is at least two glasses in, and then carefully pushes open her bedroom door.

She sneaks across the landing, taking care to avoid the notoriously creaky floorboard near the top of the stairs, and then ducks into her mother and Oscar's bedroom. It's a complete state; empty glass bottles litter the frayed carpet, crumpled bedsheets trail across the floor, and there's a lingering smell of sweat and alcohol that clings to the wallpaper.

Tabby wrinkles her nose as she tip-toes towards her mother's dresser. Her cracked mobile phone is plugged into the charger, and Tabby tentatively picks it up. Having memorised the password from the time she saw her mum unlock it, Tabby's able to get into the contacts list in seconds.

She finds the number she wants, and presses the dial button. The ringtone is barely audible over the frantic pounding of her heart. Tabby resigns herself to the idea that nobody will answer, and nobody will help, but then suddenly –

"Hello? May? May, is that you?"

Tabby closes her eyes, breathing out shakily at the sound of her auntie's warm voice, which is simultaneously full of concern and disbelief.

"Auntie Celia?" Tabby whispers, glancing at the closed bedroom door. "Auntie Celia, it's Tabitha. I need...I need you. Can you come to the house, please?"

There's a moment's silence. When her aunt responds, she's in full control. "Hi, sweetheart," she says. "Give me half an hour. I'll be right with you. Stay in your room 'til I get there, ok?"

"Ok," Tabby says, wiping at her eyes. "Ok, Auntie Celia."

*

Never dressed in drab colours, luxurious hair always loose and natural, a Postgraduate degree in Engineering: Aunt Celia is everything Tabby wants to grow up to be.

Celia sorts everything out. Tabby's enrolled in a new school within the week, the study at Celia's home is converted into a bedroom, and no further contact with her mother or Oscar will be allowed.

At first, Tabby lets herself feel relief. No more going hungry at night, no more hiding away from Oscar and his foul moods, no more of her drunk mother screaming at her. Then the guilt comes. What will her mum do now? Will she be ok?

It's remarkable how quickly the guilt turns to

anger, and not much is needed to get Tabby's fists clenched. The nickname 'Tabby the Tyrant' is started by her older cousin, Michael, and it quickly spreads. He doesn't mean any harm, but Tabby's not exactly in a jokey mood these days. Thankfully, her aunt understands, and never yells at her about her bouts of fury.

"Sometimes, when you find yourself face to face with the beast, you know the best thing you can do for yourself?" Celia asks as she drives. She shoots Tabby a smile that could charm the meanest of strangers.

Tabby shrugs grumpily. She's in the back seat of the car, sent home from school in disgrace. Phoebe, a girl in her class, had made a comment about how Tabby's mum doesn't want her. It's true, which is why Tabby punched her in the mouth.

"Embrace the beast," Celia says. "Too much fighting only ever ends up leaving *you* in pain."

Tabby stares down at her scuffed fists with a frown. "I don't get it," she tells her aunt.

"You will," Celia says. "Because you've got us to help you."

*

The Brighton arcade on the pier is as noisy, crowded, and exciting as ever. A symphony of lights shine around the dark room, and families of all sizes are staking all their coppers on the various games dotted around.

There is an art to these coin machines. If you put

the two pence in *just* at the right time, you're guaranteed to push more coins forward, thus getting prizes. Now nine, and having never really had the luxury of toys before, Tabby has her eyes on particular fluffy caterpillar keyring.

She loves coming here, whenever it's a sunny weekend. It's just over an hour from London on the train, and it's so nice to get to the seaside and have all the sweets she can feasibly eat.

"Tabby," Aunt Celia is suddenly by her side. "How about having a go at the crane machine? Think you could win us a new blender?"

Tabby rolls her dark eyes, slotting another two pence piece into the machine. "It's a scam, Auntie Celia. Everyone knows that."

"That's part of the fun," Celia says. "The hope for some sheer, dumb luck. Your cousins have already lost at least a fiver."

Tabby's anger issues have stilled, thanks to Celia's loving approach and counselling sessions. Now whenever Tabby thinks about her mother and Oscar, it's with begrudging acceptance instead of rage. At her core, Tabby doesn't want to be an angry person. She wants to be kind yet firm, to see the good in people, just like her aunt. Besides, she's a *terrible* fighter.

Tabby slots her final coin into the machine, staring fiercely at the caterpillar keyring in the hopes this will *finally* be it, and then a strange, high-pitched alarm echoes throughout the arcade. It's not coming from one of the games, considering the way everybody has completely frozen.

Aunt Celia grabs her hand, just as the coins push the caterpillar forward. "Wait –" Tabby starts, but everybody is moving, running, pushing.

"Boys!" Celia yells. "Jasper! Michael!"

Tabby spots her older cousins in the crowd, and yells their names too. They're standing by the crane machine, startled and afraid. With a forceful shove from behind, Tabby gets swept up in the stampede, losing her grip on her aunt's hand. She falls face-first, *hard,* on the shabby carpet of the arcade. There's an awful cracking noise and she realises the right lens in her glasses has shattered.

"Auntie Celia!" Tabby bellows, desperately scrambling back to her feet. Her aunt is already pushing back against the crowd, sweeping Tabby up in her arms. She feels silly – nine-years-old is way too grown-up to be carried – but she clings onto her aunt with ferocity anyway. "What's happening?" she yells.

"Don't know," Celia pants. Jasper and Michael are here, they're all here, everything will be ok. "But if a lot of people start running, that's usually a sign to join them."

Tabby can't argue with that logic. Maybe it's some kind of terrorist attack, or a fire, or a robber? A robber could have stormed into this arcade, *definitely*, it's a perfect place to get lots of coins and prizes.

"It's World War Three!" A woman wails hysterically. "It's happened, it's really happened!"

Celia says a word that Tabby definitely can't repeat. "Moment we're outside, you have to run," she shouts at the three of them. "Run as fast as you can, you hear me? Oh, God, Tabs, your glasses."

"It's ok," Tabby says quickly, desperate to reassure her, because her aunt looks terrified and she is *never* terrified. This must be very bad. "I'll be ok!"

Sunlight bursts through as they approach the doors, and Celia flings Tabby to the ground. "Push through, get out, keep moving!"

Tabby's cousins grab her hands and they're all running. Celia will be right behind them, Tabby is sure, because Celia is strong and amazing and everything Tabby is going to be. Her vision is all blurry, but that's because her glasses are cracked, *not* because her eyes are filled with tears.

The sky, previously beautiful and blue, is now full of smoke. "Bombs," Jasper breathes, "these are the bombs."

Tabby has heard, of *course* she has, that trouble was looming and people were unhappy and things were going to go wrong. But all of that hadn't seemed *important,* because it wasn't happening to her in the moment, and the adults were supposed to sort it all out before it ever became an actual problem.

"No," she says out loud, but nobody is listening to her. She cranes her head, and to her immense relief Celia is behind them, ready to protect them all, her knight in shining armour. Tabby can't explain it, but seeing her aunt's expression in that exact moment, she knows that things will never be the same again.

*

Throughout the next few years of the War, Tabby is the reliable person to go to if you have a problem, and she honestly doesn't mind. It keeps her hands busy and her mind occupied; her and Celia are a solid unit, helping anyone who comes to them. If it's a gadget, Tabby can fix it. If it's companionship, she can offer it. Celia teaches her everything she knows, and Tabby is her best student.

An older girl, Valentina, lives across the street. She is beautiful, self-assured, and radiates power in everything she does. There is a deep sadness to her, but she never speaks of it, and Tabby never asks. Everybody has lost something in this, after all.

"I need you to fix my computer," she says one day. Tabby is utterly besotted.

"Anything you need," Tabby says. And then, because it's the adult thing to do, she adds: "It'll all soon be over, you know."

Valentina smirks, staring her down. Even though she's only younger by a few years, Tabby suddenly feels pathetically small. "The War? That'll always be here, Tabs."

The nickname comes from her being so good with computers; keeping *tabs* on people. Tabby isn't necessarily sure if she likes it, but anything is better than

Tabby the Tyrant. Thank God Valentina doesn't know about that one. "The fighting's dying down," is all she says. "The government's not going to keep it up forever. If people were unsatisfied, they had every right to be."

This seems a good, grown-up thing to say, but Valentina only responds with a condescending snort.

For a moment, the only sound is the Tabby tinkering with Valentina's sturdy computer. "What do you need it for?" Tabby asks, which in hindsight is a ridiculous question. It's hardly like Valentina can buy a new one at the moment.

"Pictures of my grandma," Valentina says immediately. "So I'd appreciate it if you just fucking fixed it."

Fair enough, is all Tabby can think, and does just that. Her and Valentina move from being acquaintances to good friends after that.

The people in charge, the people who started it all in the first place, enlist Michael for the War. He doesn't come back.

*

Seven long years of War, and Tabby doesn't know if life will ever be normal again, or if she even wants it to be. Celia no longer dances around the living room, and Tabby has long given up on her dream to be an Engineer. There's hardly any Universities left to go to – the last she heard, Birmingham has been completely wiped from the map.

One day, about a year after the War has finally ended, the televisions are delivered to every household. Tabby is grateful for them, especially because she can see how happy Lila is making everybody.

"She loves us," Celia whispers each night before bed, a hand on Tabby's shoulder. "She really loves us."

So every day, Tabby watches Lila with Celia and Jasper and knows they will all be ok, because how could they not be? There is nothing to fear anymore.

Chapter 19

I wake to the smell of putrid smoke and cold water dripping onto my face. When my eyes flutter open I see Tabby splashing her water bottle at me. This is getting to be a habit, waking up to her looking concerned.

"Eva!" she breathes my name in relief.

"I'm ok," I rasp, pushing myself up into a sitting position, scanning her face. There's a cut on her forehead, but it doesn't look too deep. My eyes stream from the smoke. The smoke. Where's the smoke coming from?

"You hit your head," Tabby is saying, "on the table. Had to drag you out. We're all...We're all ok, you know, but..." Her voice cracks on the last word, and I crane my head around to see what she's looking at.

Bessie lies on her side, up in a blaze of orange flames, oozing thick smoke that crawls its way up to tarnish the white clouds. Val is standing by Darryl; they both appear unscathed, but he's on his knees, staring in despair at the wreckage.

"Oh, Darryl," I say uselessly. He doesn't acknowledge me. He doesn't acknowledge any of us.

"He's been like that for the past ten minutes," Tabby admits, wiping at her forehead with a wince.

"I'm in *mourning*," he snaps, his eyes still fixated on his beloved motor-home. "You should be in bloody morning too, Tabs. All your tech, all our *stuff*, it's fucking *gone!*"

"Managed to grab a few things," Val says with a nod at her feet. There's a plastic bag and one rucksack, which I recognise as Mrs. McIver's bag of spare clothes.

"A few things!" Darryl laughs, but it sounds hysterical. "A few *things* are not the same as the amount of years and time we spent perfecting Bessie."

My eyes widen at the seriousness of this situation. "You can't track the Creatives anymore," I say, already knowing they've realised this way ahead of me. My eyes scan the area, like exposed prey trying to figure out where to hide. There's nowhere. Nothing but flat planes of grass and the burning sun. We've driven well off the road now, and any kind of civilisation seems impossible to reach.

"But they can certainly track *us*," Val says, "this smoke is like a giant arrow right to our location. We need to *move.*"

"I still have the phones," Tabby says, patting the front pocket of her dungarees. She's trying to be brave, but there's no hiding the fear in her eyes. "I can work with what I've got. I'm the genius, remember?"

"Darryl drove us off-course to the left," Val says as she points. "So we need to be moving in *that* direction to get to the boat. Be ready to run."

"Your hip –" Tabby begins, but is abruptly cut off with a glower.

Darryl staggers to his feet, swaying slightly in his misery. "You were my greatest achievement," he says to the burning vehicle, tears glistening in his eyes. "I will always –"

"Darryl!" Val snaps. "Cry about it later! *Vamos*!"

I'm wearing flip flops, courtesy of Mrs. McIver, which are useless to run in. I have no other kind of footwear. Not even socks. The possible risk of stepping on anything sharp doesn't outweigh the terror of getting caught by the people chasing us, so with a groan I kick them off, leaving them with the wreckage.

We run. Running like the desperate pack of prey that we are, as the sun sets around us and dusk provides us with some much needed shelter. Everything aches: my legs, my burning lungs, my poor feet. Multiple times I have to stop, so unused to this exercise, but then I'm dragged on.

I keep thinking of everything they've lost in the fire. All of Tabby's gadgets. She was so proud of them. I don't know why it hurts me, but it does, thinking of her loss. At least she still has my phone. What would I have done if...

"I can't," I wheeze, stopping for what must be the twentieth time. I clutch at my chest, legs shaking uselessly. "Two – two minutes!"

The others concede, clearly needing the respite too. "We're close," Tabby promises as she taps at her phone. She's breathing heavily too. Blood from her forehead has splattered onto her glasses. "So close."

Val clutches at her hip with a groan, her head bowed. Loose hair from her plait frames her face, damp with sweat. "Could do with a drink," she croaks. "Water."

"This is all we have left," Tabby says as she passes her the half-empty bottle from her pocket. Val takes a long gulp, showing great restraint. I would down it all in two seconds.

"Let's go," Val says, straightening up. Her eyes are glassy from what I can assume is pain. When Darryl attempts to take her arm, she shoves him away. "If you can't run, at least walk quickly."

I'm not sure if this is directed at me, but I grate-fully accept. My legs are minutes away from collaps-ing underneath me, and I still have the overwhelming need to comfort Tabby in some way. I tap her on the shoulder, and silently offer her my hand.

There's a moment where she looks as if she might cry, which is the exact opposite of what I wanted, but then she shoots me one of those bright smiles. Our fingers entwine, and with a firm squeeze, we set off together.

*

I can hear the water before I see it, the sound of

waves crashing over pebbles as we precariously stag-ger down the hill to the beach. The blisters on my feet have long burst, the blood congealed and dry around my toes. I barely acknowledge the pain anymore; the moment I see that seemingly endless stretch of water under the glow of the moon, I'm transfixed.

"Wow," I whisper as we all slow to a stop. I've the urge to take a running leap at it, to completely sub-merge my body, to cleanse myself of everything that's happened around us.

A shadowy outline by the water makes me gasp, and I automatically grab at Tabby's arm. My heart is still hammering away inside my chest, to the point where I feel it will never slow down to a normal rate.

"It's ok," Tabby says quickly. "We're expecting him. Carlos. He's taking us to Scotland."

I was hoping for backup with a bit more muscle. Carlos is a skinny man in a green checked shirt and white chinos, with a mop of unruly black hair. He holds himself like an awkward deer, ready to run away at the slightest inconvenience.

"Carlos," Val says, and then she's storming up to him, masterfully hiding her limp. "Did you snake us, you son of a bitch?" she snarls, grabbing the scrawny man by his collar.

"Valentina!" he sputters, face crimson. "What're – what're you *talking* about?"

"Don't bullshit me, Carlos." She shakes him with each word. "We just got run off the road by a bunch of Creatives."

"Well, don't look at *me*! Look at your motley crew!"

Val roughly lets go of his shirt. He stumbles back. "My crew can be trusted," she snarls. "You don't think I know how to cut the head off a snake?"

Val, trusting me? Sticking up for me? It takes me a second to appreciate the novelty of this. A warm feeling stirs in my stomach. It's the feeling of being wanted.

"Eva is definitely sketchy," Darryl chimes in, and a damp towel is thrown over the warm feeling, squelching it completely. "But there's no way she could've tipped anybody off."

Carlos straightens his rumpled shirt, throwing me a glare. "Well, it wasn't me. It wasn't anybody. You just got unlucky! Don't act like Creatives have never snuck up on you before!"

Val draws her fist back, but Tabby quickly grabs her arm. "He's right, Val, you *know* he is. It's nobody's fault, and we're all safe, and I'm sure we've lost them now."

She growls, yanking her arm away. We watch her pace for a moment. I've seen Val cocky, I've seen her irritated, I've seen her smug. I've seen her angry at *me*. I've never seen her with this sheer amount of rage.

"Let's just get on the bloody boat," Darryl says. If this is an attempt at calming her down, I don't like his survival instincts.

Val does stop stomping around, though, as if somebody has flipped a switch from 'self-destruct' to 'eerily calm'. "Alright," she says. "Everybody on the boat except Carlos."

Carlos' mouth drops. "I'm the only one who can steer the boat," he protests. "It's my boat!"

Val shrugs. "Consider it a promotion. You're now the watchdog."

"None of you can *sail!*"

"Can't be that hard, can it?"

He gapes for a good few seconds, eyes flitting between the four of us. I can see the sweat on his brow from where I'm standing, and look away. A pang of guilt stings my insides.

"All you need to do is tell us if you're responsible," Val continues. "I think I'm being perfectly reasonable, Carlos."

"If we leave him here, and the Creatives are still on our trail, it's a death sentence," Tabby says, her voice low. "You're not that cruel, Val."

"Yes!" Carlos points at her. "Exactly! Thank you!"

"It's not about being cruel," Val says, "it's about practicality."

"Jesus Christ!" Carlos has passed the borders of hysterics. He is well and truly flailing his arms around now. "I didn't do anything, Valentina! I swear on my entire extended family!" He fires words at her in Spanish, and she holds up her hand, stopping him in his tracks.

"Get on the boat, Carlos," she says. "Just wanted to make sure."

Stunned silence seems to resonate around us,

except for the gentle lapping of the waves. They seem to be toying with us, much like Val. Carlos has stopped flailing, staring at her in stupefied horror. "You bitch," he eventually says.

"Can't be too careful in this game," Val says with a shrug. "You've convinced me. Congratulations."

As much as I hate to admit it, Val clearly holds all the power here. Not just over me, but everyone around her. What I've witnessed is a masterful display of puppeteering, and I *would* be impressed if I wasn't so scared of her.

Tabby puts her hand lightly on Val's arm. "Thank you," she says sincerely.

"No need to thank *me*," Val says, "thank Carlos for not being a backstabbing weasel."

Carlos shakily adjusts his shirt, giving a short laugh as he does so. "You've completely lost it," he tells her. "Are you back on the booze?"

There's a silence that's only punctuated by Tabby glancing at Valentina and muttering, "Yeah, ok."

The next thing I know, Val has drawn her fist back and collided it with Carlos' nose. There's a sickening crunching noise and he howls, hands flying to his face as he tries to stop the flow of blood. I wince at the river of crimson spilling over his fingertips.

"You deserved that," is all Darryl says, as Carlos hops around in agony.

Val shakes out her hand, completely indifferent as she turns away from us and walks on. "D'you have a hat, by any chance?" she calls over her shoulder. "I think I'll make myself the Captain."

Carlos simply whimpers and whines before following.

Chapter 20

There was a solid period of my childhood when Mum would always read me and Ali *Peter Pan* before bed. Captivated by stories of swashbuckling pirates, enchanting mermaids, and a boy who refused to ever grow up. I remember being tucked up in my duvet, hoping to go escape to Neverland too. Who wants to grow up, anyway?

I'm thinking of Peter Pan as I walk around this wooden boat, its white sails tattered and ghostly in the moonlight. It's not exactly as glamorous as Captain Hook's, but it's an actual *boat*. I've never been on a boat in my entire life.

"Fuck me," I hear Val say with a laugh. "Carlos! You *do* have a hat!"

I follow her voice to the little doorway that leads to the cabins below. It's going to be cramped – there are only four bunk beds for the five of us, and I'm certainly not in the mood to squeeze up to anybody. When I peek down, Val is holding up a worn-out leather hat that *does* resemble a pirate's. The look on her face can only be described as gloating.

"I never wear it," Carlos sulks, arms folded defensively over his chest. The blood has dried around his nose, though he does keep sniffing in a self-pitying way. He walks up the stairs onto the deck – I've been paying attention to all the nautical terms – shoving past me as he does so. I pretend I don't mind, even though I do.

Tabby is sitting with her back pressed against the inside of the boat, staring up at the stars. Carlos had a few decent medical supplies, so a blue plaster covers the cut on her forehead. I've tentatively cleaned my feet with bottled water, but I don't have the stomach to properly fix them up.

The boat moves with a judder, and I stumble over to her. "We're sailing," I say obviously.

"Bon voyage," Tabby says with the ghost of a smile. "Let's hope Carlos doesn't steer us into a load of rocks."

She raises a very good point. What with the way he shoved past me and the way he was glaring at Valentina, he's certainly not happy with any of us.

"Does Val make a habit out of punching people?" I whisper to Tabby as I sit down next to her.

She shoots me a look that I can't quite pinpoint, giving a small shake of her head. I have the strong feeling that this question has annoyed her.

"I'm just *saying*," I throw my hands up in defence. "That Carlos guy was bleeding all over the place. Didn't you feel sorry for him? It was a horrible thing to do."

"Eva," she says with another one of those *looks*, "when we first met you, you threw a knife at us."

My mouth opens and shuts a few times while I try to think of an appropriate response. The best I can come up with is a huffy, "I don't think *that's* relevant."

Tabby stretches her legs out in front of her, rubbing at her neck. For a brief moment I imagine touching my fingers gently against her smooth skin to help her. "I used to agree with you about violence," Tabby says, "I want to still agree with you. Violence in general shouldn't be encouraged. And yet..." she gestures uselessly.

"Lila says it should only be used in important circumstances," I feel the need to clarify. "For people who *ruin* things. Carlos didn't ruin anything."

Tabby huffs. "That's ironic, considering she's ruined the whole *country* with her little crew."

My eyes roll so heavily I'm surprised I don't strain them. "Yeah, yeah," I dismiss, "whatever you say."

She surprises me by laughing. She's not condescending me. It's genuine; tinged with tiredness, but genuine. "Maybe we're both broken records," she says.

I like her. I shouldn't, but I do. She is everything Lila has warned me against, this beautiful stranger with her clever brain and unbearable calmness. At times I feel she is the lone lighthouse beaming that bright, bright light and I've no choice but to drift towards her.

"He did kind of deserve it," Tabby's voice brings me back to the moment. I realise I've probably been staring at her in silence for an uncomfortable amount of time, and quickly dart my eyes away.

"What?" I say uselessly.

"Carlos. He did – I know it looked bad, but – Val's an addict." The admission seems to bring her pain. For a while she just stares at her clasped hands, jiggling her knee. "Alcohol, mainly. But other things too. So when he asked her if she was drinking again..."

I've no idea what to say. My brain struggles to keep up for a moment, and all I can do is helplessly shrug. Tabby's clearly not done speaking, and I have no desire to interrupt her right now. I understand the weight of her words, even if she assumes I don't.

"She has been for as long as I've known her," Tabby says. "An addict, I mean. She's been clean for years now, even after everything she's been through. She's the strongest person I know. Val is the person to go to when you want to get shit done."

"I know," I say, because it's been so unbearably true since the day they came to my home.

"It's not my place to say anything," Tabby says, and there's such pain in her voice that I find myself reaching for her hand. My skin is probably clammy, but I give her fingers a reassuring squeeze anyway.

Tabby seems surprised by the gesture – maybe this whole time she thought I was some kind of heartless monster? – but then gratefully squeezes my fingers back. A little jolt of electricity seems to pass between our linked hands. Not literally, of course, but it feels...Good.

"Don't worry," I say. "I'm not going to say anything. My mum, she would always tell us…" And then I trail off, because I can't remember what Mum would always tell us.

Tabby doesn't press me for information. Instead, she just says, "So you can see why she did that? Right or wrong, the things she's been through, and for him to…You can see, can't you, Eva?"

"Yes," I tell her honestly, "I can see."

Her eyes bore into mine, as if she's trying to find out exactly what's going on in my jumbled mind. Eventually, she nods. "I know you do," she says. "And I see you, Eva."

"Rum!"

I'm jolted out of my thoughts by a very enthusiastic Darryl. When I glance up, Val is standing in front of us presenting a bottle of dark, rich liquid. Her hat's at a jaunty angle so her eyes are mostly covered, but I could spot that ever-present smirk from miles away now.

"You really could be a pirate," Tabby tells her affectionately.

Val only scoffs, uncorking the glass bottle with a satisfying pop. For a moment I think she's going to take a deep swig – she seems to be considering it too – but then she passes it over to Darryl. "Drink up, yo ho," she says. "We're on this damn boat for two days."

There's a small selection of food including dry crackers with thinly spread butter and tins of sugary sweet peaches. Adorable tiny glasses are passed around, courtesy of Carlos' cupboard. He continues to scowl by the wheel of the boat, avoiding us with a barely muttered *thank you* as I pass him a drink.

"Punch me in the nose and then steal my drink," he grumbles to no one in particular, snatching the glass from me. "Very classy indeed."

I leave him to sulk, pouring myself the teensiest mouthful. The smell is potent and sickly sweet as I lift the glass to my lips.

"Don't know if you really want that, Eva," Darryl is suddenly by my side, taking the glass from my hands. "It's 40% proof and it's going to be a waste if you throw it up."

"Who says I'll throw it up?" I retort, even though the smell *is* making me a gag. "I just want a sip. Is it like brandy? You said brandy was good for shock."

Darryl downs his drink without so much as a flinch. "It's all good for shock," he says morosely as he hands my glass back to me. "Sip it. *Slowly.*"

I do. It tastes disgusting, and burns all the way down my throat long after it's gone. "I'm really sorry about your motor-home," I manage, hoping he can't tell that my eyes are watering from whatever that drink was. "It was...cosy."

"It was a safe haven," Darryl says. He loosens his blue tie, his gaze fixed on nothing in particular as he stares ahead. "Took care of her for over five years. Never crashed once."

"You were just trying to get us here."

"More fool me," he retorts, only to immediately

shake his head. "Didn't mean that. I'm just...I'm so fucking *angry*."

I don't even mind him swearing, because technically it's alright when men do it. Anger is an emotion I'm becoming all too familiar with myself. Always there, always simmering.

"I got too confident. Maybe I let myself forget the seriousness of the situation." He shrugs, fingers tapping against his empty glass. "Been a long time since Creatives have tracked us down. Sneaky bastards."

I take another tentative sip of rum. It's not *so* bad once you get used to it. "Have *you* ever seen a Creative?" I ask, morbid curiosity getting the better of me. I'm imagining them with razor sharp teeth and blood-red eyes, perhaps with three heads. Monsters. They must be, to invoke such fear. But why would *Lila* surround herself with monsters?

It takes him a while to answer while my brain battles this conflict out. "Heard them first," he says. "They hacked into Bessie's system a couple of years ago. Spoke through our radio. Nearly had a heart attack."

I shudder. My sips of rum are now turning into gulps.

"I've seen one, once," Darryl continues. "Didn't want to get too close to him. But yeah, Eva. I've seen one."

"What was he like?" my voice has dropped to a whisper. The world seems to hold its breath as I await the answer.

Again, there's a tense silence, and then Darryl

shrugs. "Just a man," he says, very quietly. Beneath us, the ocean waves rhythmically crash against the boat, the spell broken. "Just a man, that's all."

Chapter 21

Rum, I've decided, is delectable nectar and it also makes me the most interesting person on this boat. I've had three of those adorable tiny glasses, and the burn I used to hate has now become an incredibly comforting sensation, tickling its way down to my toes.

This magic potion seems to be having the same effect on everybody else – even Val, the only one who's not drinking it. Maybe the good feelings are just infectious. They teach me sea shanties, the kind of music that can go from your blood pounding with excitement to your eyes filling with tears. We dance, rocky and off-balance, twirling round and round until I'm convinced I'll never not feel dizzy.

Val and Darryl share another cigarette as the night dwindles on. "We're both cutting down," Val finally explains, "and this is the easiest way to do it."

"Plus, we never know when we'll find a new packet," Darryl says glumly. "We have fifteen cigarettes left."

"Can I try one?" I'm emboldened by this sudden desire to just *do* things, try things, be borderline unladylike. Just for tonight. Just for a moment when nothing feels as scary.

Unfortunately, the two of them laugh with a shake of their heads. "Last thing we need is for you to choke over our valuable resources," Darryl says. "No offence."

"And maybe cut back on the rum," Val adds, "before you fall overboard."

I scoff. "You're not my mother," I say, and then the boat bumps over a particularly strong wave. I stumble backwards, landing right on my tailbone, but the wonderful drink has completely eased all sense of pain. "Ow," I say anyway, and start to laugh.

They laugh too, but not unkindly. Instead, they sit down by me, backs against the boat. I can't stop myself from giggling, but at the same time my eyes are suddenly stinging with tears. "It's going to be sad when Lila punishes you," I feel the need to tell them. "I'm sorry."

"Christ," Darryl says immediately. "Way to kill the mood, Eva."

"Lila won't get the chance," Val says with a deep drag of her cigarette. "None of them will. So don't worry your pretty head."

This doesn't offer me much comfort. The rules have always been so clear. Stay home, stay safe, watch Lila. Be a good upstanding citizen, a proper lady. I've broken all of these so, by that logic, I deserve to be punished too.

"Oh, Jesus Christ," Darryl suddenly exclaims, and

buries his head in his hands. "My CD collection! They'll all be charred to bloody ash. I've been collecting those for the past seven years!"

Val grimaces, patting his shoulder. "Ah. I *am* very sorry about that."

"No, you're bloody not," Darryl retorts.

"I am! I am," she says. "I liked some of them. C'mon, I liked the Green Day one, that was a great find."

"I'll need to start the collection from scratch," Darryl says miserably. "I bet I'll never find another Madness one. Those are like gold dust."

Tabby emerges from the cabin, with a newly topped up glass of rum. She's taken her glasses off, and looks strangely naked without them. "Should we discuss our plan of action?" she asks, her words slurring the slightest bit.

"Fuck no," Val says. "Not right this *second*. Let's rest and have fun while we can."

With that, she passes the cigarette to Darryl and digs into the pocket of her black cargo trousers, retrieving a packet of little white pills. I gasp before I can stop myself. "Don't take those!" I blurt. "*You* can't take those!"

The trio look at me as if I've suddenly grown an extra head.

"They're painkillers, Barbie," Val says slowly.

"Yes, sure, fine," I steamroll on. "But are *you* allowed to take painkillers?"

There's a long pause, and then Val throws a glare

at Tabby as the penny drops. "*Oh,*" she drawls, voice laced with distaste. "I see."

"I just wanted to explain!" Tabby jabbers, shaking her head rapidly. "Eva was like – 'cause you punched Carlos – she didn't get why what he said was so –"

"You don't need to fucking tiptoe behind my back," Val stands up with a wince that she quickly covers by scowling. "Sure, Eva, I punched Carlos 'cause I'm a sensitive addict, is that what you want to hear? Is that how you want to justify it? I punched him 'cause he's dickhead and 'cause I *wanted* to."

"I can *hear* you, Valentina," Carlos' voice shouts from the wheel. He's ignored.

"That's not – I don't *care* about you being an addict," I attempt. My speech seems so slow to me, and I struggle to form the words I actually want to say.

"And I don't care that you don't care," Val says. "It doesn't mean shit to me. Just don't act like you're doing *me* a favour by not caring. It's not a dirty little secret. I'm clean. I've been clean for the best part of six years." She throws Tabby a look that's a mixture of irritation and pure incredulity. "*You* know."

"I'm sorry, Val," Tabby says, raw and honest. "I didn't mean for it to be like I was..." She trails off, hanging her head in shame. Val approaches her and I tense, already bracing for some kind of conflict, but she just lightly shoves at Tabby's shoulder.

"Whatever," Val says, "just remember my number one rule. Don't patronise me."

"I'd never," Tabby says immediately. "You know that. Never."

There's a silence as Val's dark eyes flit between me and Tabby, and then she just shrugs in a tired acceptance. Darryl stands, and lightly touches Val's arm. She doesn't swat him away this time. "Stargaze?" is all he asks, the epitome of casual.

"Sure," Val says after a long moment.

The two of them walk away from us, to the other end of the boat. I let out a long breath that I didn't realise I'd been holding.

"That could've been a lot worse," Tabby admits, her voice shaky. "I probably *deserved* a lot worse."

I shake my head. "I don't think you did anything wrong."

"I hate the idea that I went behind her back," Tabby says. "That I hurt her in any way. She's...I'd die for her. I really would."

There's no way to doubt it. Her eyes hold such raw sincerity that I suddenly find myself blurting, "Are you in love with her?"

Tabby blinks owlishly. For a long time, she just stares at me in complete bewilderment.

"It's ok if you are," I hastily add. "Honestly! I mean, she's bad-tempered and really needs to work on her social skills, but I understand if you're in love. Being in love is a wonderful thing."

"Eva –"

"I'll tell you my secret," I say, because apparently my mouth won't stop moving. "I'm in love with Lila. I know you're going to laugh at me, but I'm serious. I'm in love with her, and when we finally meet her, it's all going to click into place. Don't laugh!"

"I'm definitely not laughing," Tabby mumbles after a long sip of rum.

I breathe out slowly, trying to get my over-excited heart back under control. "I know everyone loves her," I say, "but for me it's genuine. *Real* love. Like, the kind where I can see us kissing and holding hands and... I don't know, *baking* together, or something. Know what I mean?"

"Lila isn't capable of that kind of love," Tabby says, very quietly. Quietly enough that I can pretend she never said anything.

"I miss her. It's eased, but I miss her so much," I say, and then quickly shake my head to stop myself from thinking too hard. "I just wanted you to know that I understand, and that it's ok, if you –"

"I was," Tabby interrupts. "A long time ago, I was in love with Val. I'm not anymore."

I nod. This is an acceptable answer. "Because she's so irritable?"

Tabby laughs with a shake of her head. "No! She doesn't...She doesn't like girls the way that we do. I still love her, I love her to death, but not like that." She takes another sip of her drink, her smile soft. "She's my best friend."

"Oh." I suddenly feel like a fool, having just con- fessed my love for Lila like that. I slump back down to the floor, unable to properly meet her gaze. "I mean, that's good."

Tabby carefully sits down next to me, and offers the rest of her drink. I gratefully accept, taking a few shaky sips.

"She *is* annoying though," I feel the need to say. "Calling me Barbie all the time. Why does she do that?"

Tabby huffs a small laugh. "You never played with Barbie dolls? Barbie loves the colour pink, that's all. I mean, you have to admit, you *do* like pink. A *lot*."

I scoff, but ultimately end up giggling alongside her. "Yeah, yeah," I attempt, "I do, whatever."

"It's cute," Tabby says. "She's only teasing you. Don't let it annoy you."

"It doesn't, really," I admit. "I just wanted to complain."

There's a comfortable silence between us as we share the rest of the drink, licking residual sugar from our lips. "I had a pink tricycle," I eventually say. Something stirs in my stomach, dark and foreboding like an oncoming storm. The fog of alcohol is a safety net, and I resist the urge to push whatever I'm feeling away, if only for a moment. "When I was younger."

Tabby hums in acknowledgement.

"I outgrew it," I say. "I didn't want to, but suddenly I did. Everything seemed to...Everything went wrong from that moment, I swear."

"We all grow up, Eva," Tabby says gently, but I shake my head.

"I know. I know that. It was more, though. My mum made me give it away." I roll my eyes a little too hard, and make myself dizzy. "I made such a fuss about it. Because it was mine! Just because I was suddenly *older,* I had to give it away to *Jessica* down the street."

"Well..." Tabby is clearly struggling for the appropriate response. "I suppose it's better that it went to someone who'd enjoy it, right?"

"She never got to enjoy it." It's as if the words are coming from somebody else's mouth. I freeze, stuck on that cliff's edge again. *She never got to enjoy it.* I know why now. I know. The question is, do I jump, or do I hide?

Tabby is looking at me, very carefully. "Tell me," she says. "You can tell me."

"There was...It all exploded," I whisper. A tear falls from my eye, but I can't wipe it away. Every part of me is cold, so cold. The cliff has crumbled from underneath my feet. I am not jumping. I am helplessly falling down the abyss, and I will never be able to crawl out of it. Not this time.

The pink tricycle. Walking along the street as I pushed it by my side, the sun beaming down on my face. Worn-out sandals on my tiny feet. They slapped against the pavement rhythmically as I moved.

"The War," Tabby says. "The start of the War. 16 years ago."

"Stop," I manage through lips that feel frozen. I don't, I can't, I won't think.

"No, Eva," Tabby is gripping my hands, and there

are tears in her eyes too. "I'm so sorry, but we can't stop now. You have to keep going. Please. Please –"

Jessica waving at me as I approached her. So annoying, with her neat French plaited hair and perfect yellow sundress, all ready to take *my* toy. And then –

Smoke, putrid and thick. Screams. The horror is hitting me like a sledgehammer, slamming mercilessly against my chest. I can't breathe.

In a blink, Jessica's house was gone, and so was everything around it. I staggered back, tripping over my tricycle, running running running screaming – my Mum grabbing me, pulling me and Ali with her – we all ran –

I stagger to my feet, yanking myself away from Tabby, screams ringing in my ears.

"She better not throw up on my boat!" I dimly hear Carlos yell before I do, in fact, throw up.

Tabby hastily steers me to hang over the edge of the boat, holding my long hair back as I retch. I barely feel her. I barely feel anything. I only hear the screams.

Chapter 22

It takes me a long time to pull myself from the comforting numbness of sleep. When I wake in the cramped bunked bed, alone, I have no idea what time or day it is. I also don't care. Everything feels groggy and disgusting, my tongue far too big for my mouth. I've been warned about hangovers, but I still can't quite believe the rum I loved could be betraying me so brutally right now.

Each movement sends a pulse of pain throughout my head as I sit up, but that doesn't matter. I may have woken with a hangover, but that doesn't mean I've woken up foolish. I know what's happened. I will always know what's happened, and I can't go back.

There's a square mirror nailed to the wall, and I kneel down to look. I stare at my reflection until my eyes ache. Beneath me, the boat rocks gently over the waves, so that I have to hold my hand against the glass to keep myself steady. Hollowed brown eyes stare at another person entirely. A silly little girl playing dress-up to make herself forget the atrocities she's seen.

"Ali," I whisper out loud. My twin, my other half.

Out there somewhere with Mum. We were separated, I know that. I just need to remember *when*. "I'm coming for you both."

I am not a child anymore. As much as I tried to keep myself safe, I only ended up making myself hide. The pink butterfly clip in my hair no longer seems to shine, and I take it out. I reach for the scissors, and take hold of my long hair. Both of my hands shake and I take a few deep breaths to centre myself. I don't want to end up with a raggedy haircut on top of everything else.

Before I can even consider changing my mind, the scissors glide and cut with a sense of finality. Soft hair falls around me as I keep going, shorter and shorter, feeling lighter with each chop. By the time I've finished, the wooden floor around me looks like a very strange furry carpet.

My hair stops just at my chin, and I've attempted to cut shorter bits at the front. It's startling when I take a proper look at myself in the mirror, gently running my hands through it. I look older. Stronger.

"Sorry, Mum," I say, because oh boy, she is going to freak out once she sees me. "But I like it."

My knees protest as I stand up. I've knelt on them so long that for a moment the fuzzy sting of pins and needles is all I can think about. I stomp around to get my blood flow back, tugging my filthy pink dress over my head as I do so.

Mrs. McIver's bag of clothes lies on my bunk. I shake it out in front of me, sorting through each outfit until I find one that looks like it would suit me. There's a black jumpsuit that's loose and comfortable when I pull it on, with strappy sleeves and little embroidered silver stars across the bodice.

Last but not least, I pull the leather coat over my shoulders. It fits like a protective shield around my body. Although it's completely different to my pink dress, it's comforting in its own way. A new way.

The person in the mirror is like a stranger. Short chopped hair. Black clothes. Hardened eyes. My blistered, bare feet are the only reminder of how far I have come to get to this place.

I should probably get some boots.

Lila made me forget the War, probably to try and protect me, but she was wrong to do that. It's the first time I've ever considered Lila to be *wrong* about something. Even though I've not said it out loud, the admission burns in my throat, as if I'm betraying her.

I put the pink butterfly clip back on.

The others are on the deck by the time I emerge from the cabin. It seems to take them a moment to realise it's me and not a stowaway who's been lurking in the shadows, but then Tabby gasps softly.

"Eva!" she says, and she's beaming. "Wow! You look..."

I'm already self-conscious, my hands going to my short hair, an apology forming on my lips.

"You look *amazing*," Tabby continues, earnestly punctuating each word. My hands slowly drop to my sides. "Your hair! It suits you so much."

A smile tugs at the corners of my mouth. A real, genuine smile, and I notice with an almost painful thump of my heart that I'm happy. Despite everything, maybe I could be happy. "Thanks," I say, my cheeks flushed. "I just thought, you know, that it was...Maybe time."

"Looks good, Barbie," Val says, and then scoffs. "Can't really call you that anymore, I guess. Not with your new wardrobe."

I shrug, appreciating the sting of saltwater on my face as the boat surges onwards. "To be honest," I tell her, "I don't think I've liked pink for a long time."

Chapter 23

"Land," Carlos says as he points ahead.

I follow his gaze as the outline of buildings slowly come into view, poking their way through the watery morning fog. The fresh air is attempting to clear my head of the nightmare I had last night. Another dream filled with screams.

We've been on the boat for around two days, and I've been starting to feel jittery without solid ground beneath my feet. What once felt freeing suddenly felt never-ending, though that may just be my general state of mind at the moment. Nothing is satisfying me.

"What happens now?" I ask him. My voice sounds different. Older, maybe.

"What happens now is that I dock the boat, you go on your suicide mission, and I'll be hanging around to take any survivors back to your respective homes," he says, and then laughs, even though he's not said anything funny. "Let's hope Tabby's right about Lila's base being nearby, otherwise we're all better off digging some graves and jumping in them. Better use of all our energy."

"Tabby will be right," I say firmly. "If she's tracked this as the spot, then it'll be the spot."

"Listen to you," he scoffs. "Two days ago you didn't even know we'd had a war, now you're blindly following this little crew to your own death."

"I'm a fast learner," I mutter.

"And what'll you do if Lila's base *is* here?" Carlos asks, poking the wound with methodical venom. "Will you get her autograph before you blow her up?"

"Nobody's blowing anybody up," I say immediately, my heart skipping a beat at the very idea. "Lila did a lot of things for the greater good. Keeping us in our homes, that was to protect us. That's what she's all about. She does it because she loves us."

Carlos huffs. "Just as I thought. Still singing the same little fanatical tune."

"Finding the base means finding answers," I say selectively ignoring his jibes. "And that's what all of us want, isn't it? We all want answers."

Carlos turns his head to look at me. The area around his nose is mottled with purple bruises, though it's his glower that I find more disconcerting. "A haircut and a fancy coat don't make you any less of a loose cannon," he tells me. "Everybody knows it."

I shrug. "Maybe they like that about me," I say, and leave him standing by the wheel.

*

Tabby taps me on the shoulder just as the boat docks at the ruined town. Most of the fog has lifted, but that's not really doing us any favours. We're much more out in the open now. There's a worn-out sign-post where the name *Leith* is just barely visible. Once upon a time, I can imagine this place was beautiful, much like my home.

When I turn my head, Tabby is holding up a pair of boots. "Found these under my bunk," she says. "Maybe Carlos had a lady friend over. No clue if they're your size, but..."

"But my feet are a state," I finish for her with a smile. "Thank you. They'll be perfect."

I can feel her eyes on me as I pull the boots on my aching feet. Questions seem to hang in the air around her, but she doesn't ask any of them, and I don't speak up. Right now, I don't have the words. I know she understands this.

Val hops off the boat onto the gravel with minimal effort. Just once, I'd love to see her stumble, so I can be reminded she's not a superhero. "Give us two days, Carlos," Val says. "If we're not back by then, come find us. Sail around nearby in the meantime, but be careful. We don't know who's around."

Carlos huffs indignantly as he stares down at her from behind the wheel. "Me? Come find *you*?"

"If we're not back, it'll be because we're in some kind of trouble," Val says. "Which means whatever trouble has a hold of us will be coming your way. You want to fight that alone?"

"You could maybe annoy them to death," Darryl chimes in as he cautiously clambers off of the boat.

"Or I could just sail off back to England," Carlos says. "Which is sounding more appealing by the second."

Val and Darryl simultaneously fold their arms as they stare him down. A tense silence follows, which is eventually cracked by Carlos barking a nervous laugh. "Joke! I'm joking. As if I ever would."

"You're a part of the team," Tabby says, "God help us. And teams don't quit, do they?"

"Some do," Carlos gripes. "I think it's actually very noble and brave to know exactly when to pack it all in. It's a skill I've mastered over the years."

"Thank you for bringing us here," Tabby says, her tone softening into her familiar sweetness. "*That* was noble and brave of you. You're a good man, Carlos."

Carlos coughs, the faintest blush spreading across his cheeks as he avoids looking at her. "You're welcome," he eventually says. "Any time. Within reason. Two days, I'll be around, and I'll be ready for you all."

"Thank you so much," Tabby says, hopping off the boat before helping me down. These boots *are* too small, and it's taking me a while to get used to having them on my feet. She waves at Carlos, and I force myself to give him a smile too.

As the boat pulls away from the shore, the familiar feeling of despair punches me in the gut for a second, but I force it down. Carlos will be back for us. We will not be stranded. We will find Lila, she'll explain everything, and then I can show Mum and Ali around Edinburgh. They've never been either, and we'll all have a wonderful time.

"Carlos knows you're a lesbian, right?" Darryl says to Tabby, bringing me sharply back to reality. "Because if he doesn't, that was masterfully played."

Tabby shrugs. "I'm wearing fucking rainbow socks," she says. "If he hasn't clued in on that, that's his problem." She turns her head to Val. "Think we can trust him? He *was* a Vulture."

This means nothing to me, but I see Val's jaw twitch the slightest bit. Tabby must see the questioning look I throw at her, so she indulges me. "Remember Vultures? They were this group during the War. Went around doing all sorts, just because they could. As if people weren't miserable enough already, Vultures decided to loot and kill and –"

"Split up," Val interrupts before I can think too hard. Now that Tabby's mentioned it, Vultures *do* ring a bell. A flicker of a memory. I would hide with Mum and Ali as fires raged through the rubble.

"Tabby and Darryl, try to find supermarkets," Val continues. "Grab whatever you can."

"Coffee would be great," I add, which results in a lot of huffing from Darryl, even though it *would* be nice to have some coffee. I'm really missing my morning routine in this newfound world of chaos.

"Bottled water would be better, if only to rinse out these bloody clothes," Darryl says. "Is it only me who realises we all stink of smoke? If there are any Creatives about they'll smell us from a mile away."

"Decent point," Val says. "Guess I'm just used to the fact that you all usually smell."

Darryl opens his mouth with a frown, but then clearly decides to not press the issue.

"Eva and I will scout out the area," Val continues, much to my surprise. "We'll need to find some kind of shelter. How're the data signals, Tabs?"

Tabby has her phone out, holding it above her head as she squints at the screen. "Still strong," she says eventually. "We're close. Should be around an hour to walk to Edinburgh, maybe less."

Val checks her own phone for the time. I feel a certain pang, wondering how many messages I'll have missed from Ali. I hope she's not worried about me. As soon as we've met Lila, Tabby will finally have the chance to fix *my* phone. I'm sure of it.

"Ok," Val says. "It's nearly 8AM. We'll stay in Leith for a few hours before heading on. Meet back here at midday. Stay sharp, be careful, and don't get caught by Creatives."

"We'll endeavour to follow your instructions, in that exact order," Darryl says with a little salute. I salute as well, before I realise he's being sarcastic.

"Can't stress the last point enough," Val says, masterfully ignoring him. "If you get caught, we're all fucked, and we may not be able to help you even if you do send out an SOS. So just be smart."

Tabby tucks her phone back into her front dungaree pocket. "Good pep talk, Val," she says.

"Subtlety is an art." Val shrugs. "And I'm no painter."

Tabby and Darryl both seem to hesitate for a split second, until Val holds up her hand. "No goodbyes," she says. "Don't jinx it. See you later, that's all you have to say."

"See you, then," Darryl says quietly, before turning away. Tabby gives us one last lingering look, before following after him.

Strands of hair stick to my sweaty forehead, my throat dry as I stare at their departing backs. They move quickly, adapting their movements to keep close to the crumbled buildings, impeccably stealthy. Before I know it, they've soon turned a corner, out of sight.

"They'll be fine," Val tells me before I can say anything. "This isn't their first rodeo."

I don't think I know what a rodeo is, but now doesn't seem a good time to ask. I've not properly been alone with Val ever since the mini-argument back on the boat. The more I think about it, the more uncomfortably tight the pit of my stomach feels.

"Do not." She points a finger at me. "I don't need any apologies."

"How did –" I frown heavily. "Did I say something out loud?"

"No," Val says, "your expressions are just very obvious. It's *fine*, ok? There are far bigger things to worry about than hurt feelings, which I don't even have." She turns away, her eyes roaming the dilapidated town in front of us. "Besides," she says eventually, "you have enough going on in that brain."

A mutual silence of understanding follows. I don't need to say anything else, and neither does she. Instead, we just walk. Wispy clouds have covered up the already weak sun, so I'm grateful for my leather coat. The new boots pinch and rub, but they're certainly a better alternative than hot gravel, as I've so recently discovered.

"I don't remember all of it," I find myself saying. "It comes in flashes. A lot of it... still doesn't make sense yet."

"It'll come," Val says, her tone level with experience.

"I don't think I want it to," I say honestly. "I'm scared of what I know. But I'm also scared of not knowing. Does that make sense?"

"Perfectly," she says. "But living alone in the dark, in denial, that's not sustainable. For any of us." She tilts her head back to look at me, an eyebrow raised. "That was Lila's master plan, and look around you. Look at all the good it's done us."

I frown, still not sure how I feel about anybody bad-mouthing Lila, but hold my tongue. "You're just being facetious now," I say instead. "Lila's plan obviously wasn't to destroy Leith."

Val's eyebrow arches again. I don't know how she does that so effortlessly. If I tried, I'd look like a startled rabbit. "Keep a look out," she tells me. We've reached a squat, square building that looks marginally sturdier than the others. Its windows are boarded up with rotting wood, and I can't spot any door to let us in.

I fold my arms across my chest, watching as Val backs up. She jumps up and down for a moment. Then rolls her neck, one way, the other, full circle. Swings her legs back and forth. I watch this bizarre exercise routine for a moment, and then clear my throat.

"Wha —" Before I can even start my sentence, Val's taking a running leap at one of the boarded windows, her foot colliding against the wood with deadly accuracy. It splinters with a depressing groan, but it takes her a few attempts kicking at it until she finally breaks through.

While I give her a few moments to get her breath back, I peer through the hole in the window. Its dark and damp inside, but I can make out a few discarded desks and chairs. "It looks like a school," I say. I went to school, once upon a time. Ali and I sat together. I dimly remember summer dresses and sitting at my too-big desk, pencils sprawled over my books.

"It'll do," Val says, still panting slightly. "Somewhere to hide out. Maybe we'll learn something."

And that's when we both hear it — the comforting, familiar theme song of *The Lifetime Lila Show,* right here in this empty town.

We're keeping you safe,
so you don't wander and roam,
because after all — there's no place like —

We react in slow motion. Val's hand automatically moves to the revolver at her hip, but I'm running towards the sound, desperate, yearning, repenting. "Lila!" I hear my voice echo around the abandoned buildings, and then Val is by my side, yanking me back hard enough to dislocate my shoulder.

"Shut the *fuck* up!" she hisses, eyes frantically scanning the area until they land on the building in front of us.

It looks like it used to be some kind of shopping centre. Each of its three large display windows are filled with black-and-white TVs, all of them playing *The Lifetime Lila Show*. And then she's there, sitting at her desk, smiling her dazzling smile. I gasp.

"Good morning, you lovely viewers!" Lila trills over the show's cheery jingle. I'm rooted to the spot, mouth open, staring at her in wonder. She's ok! I suppose I had been worried that somehow she'd know I hadn't been watching her, but she's really ok and as beautiful and wonderful as ever. My mouth stretches in a wide smile to match hers.

"Lila," I whisper, wishing there was some way she could hear me.

"I hope you had a restful sleep, ready for a brand new day!" Lila says.

Val makes a disgusted noise in her throat, pulling me away from the screens. "Ignore it," she's saying. "Even that god-awful song is enough to make me sick. Eva! Snap out of it."

"But..." I whine, desperately trying to tug away, my

brain chanting *Lila – Lila – Lila* on a constant loop. "Just a minute. Let's just watch for a *minute.*"

"I'm not letting her steal another *second* of our lives," Val says, giving me a shake. "She drugged you up. Don't you get that? You can't remember the War, the aftermath, any of it, because of *her.* She kept us inside for years!"

"Shut up!" I snap, wrenching my arm away from her with a sudden burst of energy. "God, just shut *up!*"

My voice reverberates around the empty street, clashing against Lila's delightful chatter, and then Val's hand is forcibly pressing itself against my mouth. "*Ssh,*" she hisses, eyes wide and darting around. Her other hand grips onto her revolver, which is pointed over my left shoulder.

I remember we're supposed to be keeping ourselves quiet far too late. My eyes widen in apology, but I already know I've doomed us. I can see it in Val's eyes.

We are not alone.

A middle-aged man in filthy rags crawls his way out of the rubble behind Val, his face frozen in fixated horror. Tears sting my eyes as I helplessly stare back at him. "No," he growls out. "No no no no. No visitors!"

"No visitors here!" Another voice from directly behind me, gravelly and dissonant.

Val swallows, and I can feel the way her hand is tremoring against my mouth, until suddenly she rolls her shoulders back, her eyes narrowed. The flip has switched, and she is back in control. "Don't get scared now," she tells me, before aiming her revolver at the man behind me.

She fires.

Chapter 24

BEFORE, PART TWO: VAL

Valentina Lopez is fourteen and wonders if she will ever feel at home in Brixton. When her whole family moved from Mexico to drizzly England five years prior, with the promise of exciting opportunities, nobody had cared about how *she* felt. What was so special about Britain, anyway? She already knew, even as a child, that nowhere would be able to compare with the glorious food, the weather, the *people* of her home-town.

Her abuela sits in the front garden, otherwise known as a sad, square strip of grass. She reclines in this rocky deckchair every morning, no matter the weather, saying hello to each neighbour as they pass. Most say hello back. Some roll their eyes and mutter under their breaths, hurrying off to wherever they are supposed to go. Always in a rush, Londoners.

Valentina brings her abuela coffee. The good, strong stuff, with a tiny splash of milk. She would bring biscuits, but it seems like her selfish brothers have eaten them all. If Valentina had her own way, it would be just her and Abuela. Nobody else. She's the runt of the family, the only girl. A skinny little nuisance. When Abuela takes care of her, it's as though she's the most important person in the world.

"Going to rain," Abuela says glumly as she sips.

Valentina sits on the grass by her feet, craning her head. "It's a clear sky!" she admonishes. It's hardly scorching heat, but it's a beautiful day by London's standards.

"The sun has come out for you," Abuela says. "But trust me. It'll rain. It'll pour."

With a roll of her eyes, Valentina pulls her long hair up into a scruffy bun. "Cynic," she says, but with affection. "What would you like to do today?"

Abuela doesn't answer right away, just continues to sip at her coffee, gazing out into the busy street. Red buses honk at distracted cyclists. In the garden next door, a child laughs and squeals as she chases after ladybugs. Valentina angles her face to the sun, shielding her eyes as she basks in its warmth.

"Perhaps we should go to the fair, Maria," Abuela eventually says, a smile beginning to tug at her lips.

It takes Valentina a moment to register what exactly has been said. She has started to laugh, but the sound dies in her throat when she realises this is not a joke. "Abuela," she says, trying to keep her voice light. Waiting for her to smile, waiting for something. "I'm Valentina."

Abuela looks at her, really looks at her, and then her brown eyes widen. "*Si!*" she tuts, swatting at Valentina's head. "Of course you are! Do you think I don't know who you are, *mi amore?*"

Of course, there *have* been little things. Forgetting where she has placed her belongings, losing track of a conversation, mistaking recipes that she's been cooking for years. Others may not have noticed, but Valentina has.

She could say something. But to say it out loud makes it real, so Valentina laughs along with her abuela, bottles it back down, and prays this isn't the beginning of the end.

*

The War begins two years after her abuela's death, when Valentina's heart feels it has already been broken and will never be fully repaired. She envisions it beating in her chest, a long crack through its centre, desperately trying to do its job as her entire body wills it to be over.

London is ruined, but so is everywhere else, if the news is anything to be believed. They came with their rifles and their bombs and their big ideas for something new. Growing up, she was always told how society had been in a state of unrest for years, how it was only a matter of time before everyone grouped together and fought back. Abeula warned of oncoming storms, and they came in their thousands.

Nobody even knows what they're fighting for anymore – a world that has long been on fire? – but that doesn't seem to deter them. The government stepped in once riots got out of hand, which naturally only made things worse, and then they decided to go the whole way and just squash out anyone they disagreed with.

So now Valentina picks her way through streets of rubble, waiting for the sirens in case somebody, somewhere, decides to drop another bomb. Her family don't like her staying outside for too long, but *somebody* has to get food, and she's very gifted at petty thievery.

When she turns the corner and sees a group of men, all dressed in black, she knows she should probably be afraid. They're aptly known as Vultures; they swarm the streets at night, looting, rioting, pickpocketing any dead that they find. They're ruthless and cruel, but they're survivors, and Val has seen enough to not be fazed anymore.

So she walks up to them, squeezing down her fear, ignoring the names they fire at her. "I want to learn how to fight," she tells them, keeping her voice steady.

After the Vultures get over their initial surprise at her audacity, a teenage boy – probably only a year or two older than her – asks her what her name is.

He speaks in Spanish, and she later learns he's also Mexican. If he thinks they're going to bond over that, he's sorely mistaken, because she can spot a needy people-pleaser from a mile away, and Carlos is definitely that.

And when she shows them techniques that her brother has already taught her, they don't laugh at her. That's always a good start.

*

The grief is always there, but she's better at suffocating it. Vodka helps. So does wine, beer, whisky and cocaine, but vodka holds a special place in her heart. Alcohol typically isn't the easiest to come across, but that's the best part about being a Vulture. The group have taught her well; she's strong, cunning, calculated. On the top of her game. Sure, she spends every day numbing a good portion of her brain, but it could be a lot worse.

When the television is delivered to her house, around a year after the War is over, the initial reaction is to think it's some kind of trap – a *'Surprise! The War isn't really over, here's a bomb!'* kind of trap.

But nothing explodes. Instead, one early morning the television switches itself on and there's a woman. A beautiful, happy woman. The War may have been started by men, but a woman is now here to make everything better.

A weird thing happens to Val's face and it takes her a moment to realise that she's smiling.

*

"You need to leave this house," Val says loudly, hoping to drown out the noise of the television. A father and his two grown sons are seated on the floor, fixated at the black-and-white screen in front of them.

They do not react well to her breaking in. People rarely do. That's why she keeps her revolver strapped to her hip and a flip-up knife in her sock.

Ever since she'd forced herself to turn that damn television off, things have been insufferable. Val already lost seven years of her life to a War that nobody even really understood, and thanks to Lila's mind-numbing programme, she is now twenty-three.

Her parents and brothers refused to leave with her. They're probably in the exact same spots she left them in. She tells herself she doesn't care. Nobody ever paid much attention to her anyway, except her abuela, but now she's gone. Val is on her own.

Well. Not quite. Tabby is in the house next door, trying to convince an elderly woman to leave with them. Val figured an old lady wouldn't be much of a threat – Tabby's much better with machines than she is with her fists. Never in her wildest dreams did Val ever think she'd have teamed up with the geeky kid who used to live across her street, but Tabby is actually the biggest asset of them all. No matter all the atrocities, she still manages to smile.

The men are all screaming at her, practically frothing at the mouth. It's a pathetic sight. "You can't stay here," she shouts over them, "can't you see she's ruining you?"

Lila is playing that melancholy song from the sixties, *It's My Party.* It's still playing when all three of the men pin her down, grabbing at her long hair. She momentarily curses herself for not tying it up; she's made this easy for them.

"Shut up, shut up, shut up!" The father has a knife in his hand. A small one, but sharp all the less.

The sons hold down her arms at her sides. She bucks and kicks, twisting her head away. Everything she learned from the Vultures is already a distant memory thanks to Lila. It's still inside her, somewhere, but it's taking a long time to get it back. For now, all she can do is try to survive.

"Cut out her tongue," the man to her left says. "Shut her up, cut it out!"

Val's cheek is forcefully pressed against their filthy, rough carpet as the father uses one hand to hold her head down. Oh, she's fucked this one up. It's all going to get very messy. For a split second, all she can think about is how her lovely leather coat is going to be completely ruined.

Lips clamped, Val continues to struggle. Losing a tongue right now would *not* be convenient, seeing as there's too many people in the world she still wants to shout at. That, and she's guaranteed to bleed out and die right here in this disgusting home with these disgusting men, which isn't exactly how she envisioned going out. No, the only way she's leaving this world is after Lila and all her workers are dead.

The man to her left seems ecstatic that dear old dad likes his idea, and Val feels the pressure on her upper arm ease the tiniest bit. It's enough. She's just able to reach for her revolver as the tip of the knife is slicing against her lip.

Don't scream don't scream don't scream is all Val can think through the searing pain. Blood has splattered all over the man's face as he leans over her, desperate for another go. Vision blurred, sweaty hand clasped against her revolver, she fires upwards and straight into his chest.

Val's wound continues to weep blood. The sons have let go of her, scrambling towards their father in complete shock. There's no saving him, and she feels no guilt. Maybe she would if they weren't so prepared to carve her tongue from her mouth.

Hauling herself to her feet, she presses a hand against her mouth. It's slick with blood in seconds. "Fuck you," she attempts to say, but it's incomprehensible. They pay no attention to her anyway.

Don't worry, is what she really wants to say, *I'm sure Lila will make you feel all better in no time.*

*

Getting a good sleep is a luxury these days, so Val certainly doesn't appreciate being shaken awake by Tabby. Currently, they're staying in an abandoned shop in the backend of an alleyway, with Mrs McIver, the old lady Tabby successfully rescued months ago. The rescue mission that cost Val this goddamn scar.

"There's a man outside," she hears Tabby hiss at her. "I think he just escaped."

Or he's going to kill us, Val wants to say, but all she can do is force herself to get up and let Tabby lead her out into the alleyway.

A slim, tall man with scruffy blond hair approaches with both his hands up. He's wearing a blue suit. Who wears suits anymore?

"Ladies," he says desperately. East-end accent. "Ladies, do you know what the fuck is going on?"

Val rarely gives strangers the benefit of the doubt, especially a lone man. But he has alcohol, there's a flask in his hand. A cigarette is tucked behind his ear. No doubt she can handle this guy if things turn nasty. "Let Mrs. McIver know," Val says to Tabby. Her friend hurries back inside to do just that, and Val makes a big point of showing the man her revolver.

"Don't *shoot!*" he exclaims. "Jesus! I'm unarmed."

Val keeps her gun focused on his forehead.

"Hey," the man protests. "I'm *serious*. Don't shoot me."

Val gestures at the flask in his hand. "Whisky?" is all she says.

"Brandy," he responds, unscrewing the lid and

handing it over. She scrutinises him for a moment before putting her gun away, and then pours the brandy down her throat. It's like sweet syrup. "Nicked some from a supermarket, for the shock. What the bloody hell happened to your face?"

"Charming," she says, resisting the urge to touch the pink scar that runs its way down her top lip. "Don't worry. It was worse for him."

"I've been walking for days," the man says as she drains his entire flask in two more gulps. "All the way from Shadwell. You're the first people I've seen in all that time. Isn't that – I mean, what the fuck is happening? We were at War, and then we weren't, and then..."

Val takes the cigarette from behind the man's ear. "Got a light?" she asks.

He retrieves a lighter from his pocket without a fuss, clicking it a couple of times until a flame sparks. He's attentive. That's always nice.

"First people you've seen, huh?" she asks, taking a deep drag.

"Kind of. There are vans on the road, black vans. Hid from them. Think it's got something to do with..." his voice drops to a whisper. "Y'know, that bird on the TV. It wasn't just me, was it? It wasn't just me who was watching her. Did you...I mean, did you?"

Vans. Lila's cronies, no doubt, making sure people are staying inside. They'll have to try and gather some more information on that, and fast. "No shit," Val says. "We've all been brainwashed."

He gives a low whistle. "Fuck me," he says. She decides to not respond with something crude, considering she just drank all his alcohol. "So, you lot are fighting the good fight? Got a plan? Need a hand?"

"I doubt you've got anything to offer us."

"I can offer plenty." He reaches into his inside pocket again and brings out two CDs. "Found these in the shop too. *Chas and Dave Gold.* Bloody brilliant."

"Never heard of them," she says, taking another much-needed puff.

He stares at her incredulously. "No? Ok. We'll fix that. *Frankie Valli and the Four Seasons?*"

"Ah, *si*," she says as he brandishes the CDs in front of her, just in case she hadn't heard him. "I know them."

"Couldn't believe it. All I've been listening to is a bunch of old crooners for God knows how long. Finding these was like finding gold dust."

Val doesn't allow herself to find his enthusiasm cute, because she doesn't have time, and she doesn't care. He's freshly escaped, she's sure he's not lying about that. He's rambling too much and has a completely dazed expression. No doubt he'll remember atrocities soon enough, how they made him feel. He might as well have some company while he does. It's never pretty. When Mrs. McIver remembered the loss of her husband, she threw a vase at Tabby's head – thankfully missed, but still. As for Val, whenever the image of her abuela flashes in her mind, she drinks. It's very effective.

She outstretches her hand. "Valentina," she says.

The man is quick to tuck his precious CDs away, enthusiastically shaking her hand. "Darryl," he says. "Just Darryl. No wife, no girlfriend, nothing like that. As far as I'm aware."

"I don't care, Darryl."

He shoots her a disarming grin. "No, no, 'course not. By the way, don't know if this is at all helpful, but there's an abandoned motor-home about twenty minutes from here. Was tempted to break in and sleep in it, but aren't you glad I didn't?"

A motor-home. That *could* actually prove to be pretty useful. With any luck, Tabby will be able to hot-wire it. Val purses her lips, looking him up and down. "Can you drive?"

"Absolutely," Darryl says immediately, and then frowns. "Oh, Christ. *Can* I drive?"

Chapter 25

Val presses a flip-up knife into my hand, shouting something about my good aim, but I can barely concentrate with all the yelling and smell of gunfire and general panic that's ricocheting through the street.

There are four men, all with wide eyes and bared teeth, that close in on us. One has blood spurting from his leg after Val's bullet pierced through his shin. He's chalk-white, gasping out in pain, but still he moves towards us. She should have aimed for his heart.

It takes me three tries to press the button that flicks up the knife's blade, the handle damp with my sweat. Val has been keeping this hidden from me, but now she wants me to use it. To save ourselves from whoever these men are. Can they be the Creatives?

"Leave!" the one with the bleeding leg spits at us. "Don't need any more *bitches* around!"

Val cocks an eyebrow, biding her time. She waits until the man behind her has gotten close enough, and then she jams her elbow into his throat. He collapses, choking and wheezing, as she spins around with a bone-crunching kick to the ribs of the next attacker.

Seeing her in action like this makes me snap out of my paralysis. I can fight alongside her; she chose me to help her, and that's exactly what I'm going to do. Gripping the handle of the knife, I bare my teeth in a snarl towards the man with the bleeding leg. Swipe. Dodge. Spit. We do this demented dance back and forth, two animals trying to do whatever it takes to survive.

He reaches for me, and I slash at his hand. Spurts of blood nearly splatter me in the face. Neither of us scream. Behind me, Val's fists collide with another scrawny man's bearded face, who roars in rage as he reaches for her neck. She never lets anyone get close, always ducking, spinning, kicking. "Do you work for Lila?" she yells, blocking his flimsy punch.

The name provokes a howl from all the men around us; my attacker collapses to the ground, the gunshot wound clearly having bested him. I scramble away to stand by Val's side, knife still raised in my hand, the two of us finally a solid unit.

"They can't work for Lila," I hiss to her. "They're too disgusting. Anyone who works in television looks *smart.*"

Val mutters words under her breath in Spanish that I can't understand, but I feel she's probably insulting my intelligence.

"We left our houses," one of the men croaks.

"Escaped the poison, but it's still in us. Poison in our brains."

Val's head turns back to the shopping centre, where the televisions still play. It takes her a moment to consider his words. "Lila," she says, very quietly.

"You left your homes?" I ask, just to make sure I've got it right. "To stop listening to Lila?" A prickle of disgust prods my stomach, which I quickly have to get over, considering I did the exact same thing.

"So you're from here," Val says. When nobody answers, her eyes narrow and her voice cracks like a whip. "Answer me! Are you from this place?"

Each man hastily nods. Val looks at the man she shot, who remains sprawled on the ground, head bowed. "You," she says. "What's your name?"

He shudders and whines, repeatedly shaking his head hard enough for it to snap off his scrawny neck. I can't help but feel sorry for him, especially with the way he's bleeding all over the place. If he's lucky, he'll pass out soon enough.

"You don't even remember your name?" I say. "Would it be better if we gave you one?"

"He's not a stray cat, Eva," Val says with contempt. The remaining men are moving away, ready to scurry back into their hiding spots, clearly happy to leave their pal behind. Val fixes her steely gaze onto them. "Get away from the televisions," she says. "Stay hidden. It'll all be over soon enough."

"You're letting them go?" I ask, dumbfounded. These men attacked us, called us *bitches*. I would've thought Val would beat them bloody without batting an eye.

"They're no threat," Val says with a sniff. "But don't mistake my graciousness for stupidity. If these men *do* sneak up on us again and get in our way, I'll kill them. One by one. And I'll enjoy every second of it."

That's more like it. The men are quick to scarper, save for the injured one. He sits, utterly defeated, head still bowed. Val gestures to me. "Take off your coat," she says. "Bind his leg."

"What?" I feel my forehead crease into a heavy scowl. "No! I'm not ruining this coat for *him.*"

"Don't be a princess," Val says as she inspects the man's leg. "I only grazed him, but I need something to stop the blood."

"He was going to kill you," I say, just in case she's forgotten. "Why do you want to help him so much?"

Val looks at me as if I'm incredibly stupid, and then turns her gaze back to the man. He stares at her, a frightened rabbit in the face of a fox. "Congratulations," Val says, voice dripping in sarcasm. "You're our hostage. And you're going to tell us everything you know about this town."

Chapter 26

We find Tabby and Darryl in the same spot we left them, piles of disjointed shopping at their feet. I notice the way both their eyes light up only to immediately widen in surprise at the sight of us.

"We go out for supplies, and you come back with a grotty man," Darryl says. "That seems like a fair exchange of goods."

Val only huffs in response, practically throwing our unconscious hostage into Darryl's arms. He attempts to disguise his sudden yelp.

"Place is crawling with them," Val says. "Wouldn't have known until Eva decided to start yelling her head off about Lila."

I feel my chest tighten with anger. "I didn't –" I begin, only to cut myself off. She's right. I nearly got us both killed because I *still* can't seem to control myself. "I'm sorry," I say instead, my cheeks flushed with a sudden burst of shame. "You're right. It's my fault."

"It's a good thing," Tabby says immediately. "We could have been in trouble otherwise. Right? If we didn't know? Well, now we...Now we know."

I swear, my heart borderline bursts inside my chest for the act of kindness she's given me. The best I can do is shoot her a grateful smile, hoping my *thank you* is clear in my eyes.

Darryl attempts to sit the man down on the ground, but he collapses into the rubble. "Jesus Christ," he pants. "What did you *do* to him?"

"Shot him," Val says, the unspoken *'duh'* heavily implied. "Grazed. Nothing serious."

"I cut his hand," I say, not wanting my involvement to be left out.

"Yes," Val says. "And Eva cut his hand. *Ay Dios mío.* I need a cigarette."

Tabby kneels down to inspect the unconscious man. Even though half his face is covered by that scraggly beard, I can see the thin veil of sweat all over his pasty skin. Tabby grimaces. "Who is he?"

"He won't tell us his name," I say. "We should probably call him *something*, though."

Tabby sits back on her haunches, her nose crinkled. "Something generic," she suggests. "John? He looks like he could be a John."

"Sorry to ask," Darryl says. "I can see you've been very busy with *John* here – but any joy with finding somewhere to *hide?*"

In all the excitement, I'd forgotten about the little school. It takes us a good twenty minutes to make our way back, considering the shopping and the hostage we've acquired. Val leads us on, revolver never leaving her side, while Darryl unceremoniously drags the bearded man behind him. Every so often we stop, scanning the surroundings, before continuing on.

Tabby hands me a bottle of water which looks as though it's been gathering dust for decades – maybe it has – but I gratefully gulp it down. "You're ok?" she asks.

"I'm fine," I say. "You?"

Her lips quirk in a small smile. "Fantastic," she says. "We're alive, after all."

The feeling in my heart swells some more. I think, in all honesty, that she is too good for all of us.

*

We use my new coat – against my will – to tie Hostage John against one of the creaky school chairs. While he's still passed out, Tabby cleans and bandages his injuries with supplies she found from one of the shops. I feel it's a waste of our resources. I say nothing.

The school is damp and cold, and it certainly doesn't help that all the windows are covered. We've taped a bin-bag over our makeshift entrance, and the only source of light is the torch from Tabby's phone and a couple of lit candles. Occasionally, a breeze will blow at the bin bag and tiny beams of light will burst through. It'll be pitch-black when the sun sets, but I don't mind so much – I like the dark. It makes it easier to think.

Darryl has taken off his suit jacket and waistcoat,

and is dousing them in bottled water. He's rolled up the sleeves of his pale blue shirt, and it's interesting to see he *is* well-muscled.

Val is watching him, and something tells me she's acknowledging this too. She approaches him to stand by his side, pursing her lips at his efforts.

"They're still going to smell of smoke," she tells him.

"Don't ruin this for me," he says, before taking a swig of the water and sighing. "God, I wish this was vodka."

"Me too," she says, and then glances at me. "That was a joke, Miss. Priss."

I find myself flipping my middle finger at her, and am instantly horrified. Being around them is making me incredibly uncouth, not at all the lady I've worked so hard to be. "Sorry," I hiss, clenching my fist, nails digging into my palm, as if that'll undo my mistake. She only snorts with laughter, clearly enjoying herself.

"So, what exactly *is* the plan with our unconscious friend over there?" Darryl asks. "Shall we steal his lunch money?"

Val's eyes dart back to John, and she hesitates for a split second. "We question him," she says. "Get him to tell us everything he knows."

"And if he doesn't talk?"

"Then we beat it out of him," Val says.

Darryl tilts his head, giving a small shrug. "Makes sense."

"So," she pauses again. "It's a good plan?"

Darryl's forehead creases into a frown. "Who said that?"

This results in Val giving him a sharp hit in the chest, to which he only laughs. If she did that to me, I know I'd be wheezing for dear life.

"I can make you feel better. Reach into my pocket," Darryl tells Val. When she shoots him a glare, he raises both his eyebrows. "Don't know where *your* mind is, Val, but I found us a new packet of cigarettes."

Val's glare only darkens, though she does reach into Darryl's trouser pocket. "Share?"

At his nod, she opens up the packet, placing a cigarette in her mouth. She tilts her head towards him. Soundlessly, he gets his lighter from his back pocket. A few clicks, and he lights it for her.

They're playing a game with each other. Cat and mouse, except they keep switching the roles and the rules. It's almost mesmerising.

"Guys!" Tabby's voice brings me back to the room. "I think he's waking up!"

John is certainly not waking up very happy. He spits and swears at us, struggling against our makeshift restraints. We all watch him for a moment, wondering how long it'll be until he tires himself out. "Bitches!" he growls at us. "Stupid, interfering *bitches!*"

"Hey!" Tabby protests. "I just saved you from possible sepsis!"

Val takes a deep drag of her cigarette before kneeling down to meet John's eye level. "*Hola,*" she says sweetly. "We're new in town, as you might have

guessed. Just passing through, on our way to Edinburgh. Supposed to be some wonderful art and culture
in Edinburgh, right? They've definitely got a certain
show that seems to be *really* popular right now."

He spits at her. To Val's credit, she doesn't spit
back, just wipes her cheek with bland disinterest.
"Gross," she says. "That was gross, John."

John's brow furrows in a deep scowl. "Who the
fuck is John?"

Tabby is next to try to appease him. She kneels
next to Val, shooting our captive a smile. "My friend's
sorry about shooting you in the leg," she says. "But
we've made sure you're going to be ok. Maybe a teeny,
tiny scar, but that's by the by. If you promise to stay
calm, we could even untie you."

"This is all your fault!" John's voice cracks as it gets
louder, and he ignores Tabby's attempt to desperately
shush him. "All your snivelling, pathetic *fault!*"

Tabby frowns. "How do you work that out?"

John's wild eyes flicker between me, her, Val. His
chest heaves with shallow breaths, having forgone his
useless struggling. "They made that show because of
you. You...You *bitches* with your whining and your
crying and your – your grieving!"

The last word cracks against my stomach like a
whip. It is familiar, yet foreign, and I despise it. I
despise *him.* Before my brain can register my movements, my hand is flying towards his disgusting face.

"Eva," Val's voice, laden with ice, stops me in my

tracks. "Let's not get ahead of ourselves. We can hit him later."

I hope that's a promise. Through gritted teeth, my hand falls back at my side.

"All your fault," John repeats, practically frothing at the mouth. "Could've just carried on after the War, but no, no, no, you all had to make such a *fuss*. What you need is men."

"I think you've got the wrong end of the stick," Tabby says.

"Men to fight," John insists. "Men to keep you in line. Men to *fix* it."

Darryl seems to take this as his cue to step forward from the shadows, water bottle still in hand. John takes a few bewildered seconds, drinking the image of him in.

"You," John croaks. "You can help me."

Darryl remains silent, his mouth twisted in a combination of pity and disgust. John leans forward, desperate to meet his gaze. "That...That Lila was right about one thing, about how women should behave," John says. "She didn't need to drag *us* into it too. We didn't need her! You know what I'm talking about!"

"Lila's not right about a single thing," Darryl says. "It's not anyone's fault that she infiltrated all our lives." He tilts his head towards us. "It's certainly not *their* fault. We're all victims of the War here, mate."

John closes his eyes, his entire body trembling. "I am not...I am not your mate," he whispers. "You all should never have come to this town. They will get you. They will get us all and they will smear our blood on their – god damn – *televisions*, and she will laugh and laugh and laugh!"

Cold sweat tickles the back of my neck. This man is dangerous, this man is hanging on a cliff's edge by the skin of his fingertips. And we've stupidly locked him inside with us. Stupid, stupid, stupid.

"He's not going to tell us anything useful," Val says, standing with a huff. "Just preaching the same shit we've heard for years. Gag him."

"Valentina," Darryl says with a playful pout. "Let's not be hasty. I think John could end up being *extremely* useful to us."

John's eyes flicker open, and he stares up at Darryl with newfound hope. "*You'll* untie me," he says. "You'll let me go, won't you? You and me – we get each other."

"We absolutely don't, I'm afraid," says Darryl. "I think we're on completely different tracks here, to be honest with you. Just try and answer a few questions, preferably without spitting, and then we'll see what we can do about the whole untying situation."

"I'll talk to you," John says, before his eyes dart back to Valentina. "Not her. Not these women."

"Lila says we should be treated with *respect*," I feel the need to tell him, folding my arms across my chest. "Like the good old days."

"In the good old days, you knew your fucking place!" John's voice rises into a borderline scream, and that's when Darryl throws the rest of his water bottle in his face. He gags and splutters, momentarily stunned.

"Enough," Darryl says, eerily quiet, in a tone I've never heard him use before. It stops all of us in our tracks. Even Val raises an eyebrow in mild surprise. "Enough of this. Either you shut up and answer our questions, or we leave you here tied up for the rats to eat."

"Jesus, Darryl," Tabby hisses.

John seems to be thinking the same thing. His tongue darts out like a lizard, licking at his cracked lips. "I...Ok," he whispers, shoulders slumped in defeat. "I'll try. I'll try to – I don't know much, but I'll try to..."

Darryl tilts his head towards Val. "You'll answer *her* questions," he says. "Politely. With respect."

There's a strained silence, and then John slowly nods. Val is looking at Darryl in a way I can't quite describe, and then she slowly places the cigarette into his mouth. When she speaks, her voice is husky. "Thank you, Darryl," she says. "That was...enlightening."

"Happy to help," he says with the barest hint of a smirk, before nodding towards John. "Go on, then, darling. Knock 'em dead. Just not literally."

Val doesn't contradict him on the pet-name this time, I notice. Just pivots on her heel, approaching John again. "Let's try this again," she says. "*The Lifetime Lila Show.* We all know it. It's filmed in Edinburgh now, isn't it?"

"Yes," John says. "Yes. I – We think so. They came

through Leith, about a year ago. The people who work for her…"

"But you had already stopped watching the show by then, hadn't you?" Val says. "You and your little friends back there."

He nods, face suddenly screwed up in pain. "Wasn't easy," he says. "Nearly killed me, leaving my house. I just suddenly, one day, couldn't bear to listen to *her* anymore."

There's a disgruntled scoff and I realise it's come from me. I attempt to disguise it by clearing my throat, but John's already turned his gaze to me. "What?" I demand, and then throw my hands up in surrender. "I know, I know, I left my house too, but at least the reason was to find my family. That was for a noble cause. This guy left because he didn't appreciate good television."

"Thanks for your input, Eva," Val says, and then makes several gestures at me which I roughly translate into *sit the fuck down and shut the fuck up*. I mouth an apology as I do just that.

"Everyone was gone," John continues in a whisper. "Everyone…Everyone I'd known. My…I had a family, you know. I had a son. When I remembered, it just…"

"We've all been there," Tabby says, not unkindly. "The shock of it. The pain."

Tears trickle from his pale eyes, and I once again feel a pang of pity for him. "Those men came through town. The TV men in their smart suits. We hid until they'd all gone, but they – those they found, they took away with them."

"Killed?" Val asks.

"I don't know. No one knows. We should have been watching the show – that's what they said. And we should have been, we should have been, but..."

I can't listen to any more of this, and get to my feet. Walking away from this...this disaster of a man, I leave the classroom into the dark hallway. Rats scamper away from me as I lean my back against the dingy wall, breathing in through my nose, out through my mouth.

Moments later, Tabby has joined me. There's a silence as she stands beside me, leaning against the wall too.

"I hate that man," I say to her. I can still hear Val needling our captive with questions, but it brings me no pleasure.

"I know," Tabby agrees. "He almost makes me miss Carlos. Almost."

That warrants a tiny smile, which soon fades when I remember we're currently stranded. If John out there is anything to go by, we're doomed. "I can get that Lila's Creatives don't seem to be very good people," I say. "I meant it, you know. I don't want them to find us."

"Why're you still here with us, Eva?" Tabby asks me gently. "You trust us, don't you?"

"Yes," the answer leaves my lips before I can even appreciate the weight of it. "Yes. I do. I like you."

"But you like Lila more."

I struggle to find the words for a moment. "I need to meet her. To see her. She has the answers for us."

Tabby nods beside me as she unzips her rucksack. She hands me a cereal bar. "I hope she does."

I rip off the wrapping, suddenly appreciating how hungry I am. Mrs. McIver's soup seems like a lifetime ago. "I *do* like you, Tabby," I say. "I like all of you. I think you're going to help me more than...You're going to help me find Mum and Ali, aren't you? You're looking after me."

"I didn't want you to remember on your own," Tabby admits, after a pained moment. "Mrs. McIver wanted you to stay back at the hideout. It would've been safer, but I just...I couldn't do it. It felt so cruel."

"Thank you," is all I can say. "Thank you for helping me."

She bows her head, suddenly seeming so sad. I wonder what she's thinking in that brilliant brain of hers. Once I've finished eating, I gently nudge her shoulder. "Darryl's attitude back there was something else," I say, hoping to cheer her up. "What *was* that? It was almost sexy. Objectively, I mean, *I* don't find him sexy, but objectively it was —"

"I *know!*" Tabby turns to me, eyes wide with agreement. "Honestly, that was brand new!"

"Val was into it," I say. "Don't you think?"

"God, yes," Tabby says immediately. "She won't ever admit it. It's like she doesn't want to let herself like him."

I find myself thrilled with this exchange of gossip, because – forgive me – it's very fun. "I don't get that," I say. "If she likes him, she should just say she does. What's the point in *knowing* you like someone, and doing nothing about it?"

"I think she's probably a bit scared," Tabby says. "Not that she'd ever say that. Liking someone can be...Scary. I suppose."

There's a noticeable shift in the air. Everything suddenly seems slower, from our movements to our breathing. Our heads have tilted closer to each other, and I know full well what she means about it all being scary.

"Oh, Jesus Christ!" Tabby suddenly yelps, leaping away and stomping at the ground. "Not rats! Not rats! I can't fucking *stand* rats –"

I know we need to be quiet, and the only logical thing I can think to do is place my hands on her shoulders and kiss her.

The kiss reminds me of the remnants of my rum glass, sugary and sweet. For a moment, the images in my head I had of a life with Lila – dancing with her, baking with her, long walks in the park – are replaced with Tabby by my side instead. I think I prefer this version.

I'm jolted back to reality when Tabby inhales sharply through her nose, and I stop. "I'm sorry," I say quickly. "Sorry, I didn't mean to – cross a line."

"Oh, no, no," Tabby croaks. "It's – very nice. But are *you* sure that this is what you want to do?"

And I have to kiss her again, because how could I not?

-

Chapter 27

By the time we make our way back into the classroom, John has passed out again, his body slumped in the rickety chair. It's a relief, though it does pose quite an obvious problem.

"What're we supposed to do with him?" I ask, mainly meaning *When do I get my coat back?*

"I don't think Val thought that far ahead," Darryl says with a nod towards her. She's pacing back and forth, gnawing at her bottom lip as she concentrates. At Darryl's words, she glowers.

"We got what we needed to out of him," Val says. "Creatives stormed this place and they're filming in Edinburgh. We were right. *Tabby* was right."

Silence falls over us. Surely this is good news, but everybody looks a little too terrified for my liking. "I mean..." I begin. "That was always a very strong possibility, right? That's why you came."

"This is the closest we've ever been," Tabby says weakly. "Lila is literally...half an hour away from us."

I feel a little faint all of a sudden, but then to make sure Tabby doesn't feel threatened I grab her hand, giving it a squeeze. Lila is so close. The TV station is so close. Can she feel our presence? Does she know we're near?

"Jesus," Darryl whispers as he sits on top of one of the desks. "This may seem a ridiculous question, but what exactly *is* the plan here? I know we wanted to storm the place, which I always found *very* funny, because there's three of us – sorry, *four* of us now." He gives me a nod, and I swell with pride at being part of a team once again.

"Four of us against a sea of Creatives," Tabby says. "I know. I know. Shit."

Val raps her knuckles against the blackboard, and we all turn to look at her as if she's our saviour about to deliver a sermon. "Chill out," is all she says. "We know what we're doing. Don't lose your heads."

"With all due respect, Val," Darryl says, "we don't. Not really. Show of hands, did anyone at *all* actually think we'd get this far?"

The awkward silence is very telling. I can't exactly put my hand up, because that would be lying, and given our track record we should have all been toast a long time ago.

"By all means, be negative," Val says, her tone clipped. "If you're gonna be a snivelling baby, run back to Carlos. You can both whine together."

Darryl stands, his eyes narrowed. "Forgive me for being *slightly* apprehensive."

Val tilts her head as she considers him. "Maybe you *should* leave," she says after a deliberate pause. "After all, you're only good for driving, and we don't even have a motor-home anymore."

"Oh, God," Tabby mumbles to no one in particular. Her hand is clammy in mine.

"You are on bloody thin ice," Darryl growls. He and Val are practically nose to nose, glowering at each other with such intensity I'm surprised it doesn't physically hurt. "You want us to just blindly follow your lead, to not think for ourselves?"

Val's laugh is short and sharp. "*Please*, Darryl, if you have ideas, I would love to hear them."

"Guys," Tabby says. "Enough. Come on. We don't need to fall out with each other. We're all we have."

"It's bullshit," Val says, directing her glare onto Tabby. "From day one, you both wanted me in charge. Practically *begged* me. When you staggered out of your house, I was the first person you tracked down."

I look at Tabby. "*You* stopped Val from watching Lila?" I ask, in genuine disbelief. For some reason, it's never occurred to me to ask everyone how they met. In hindsight, this reminds me how self-absorbed I've been about everything, which leaves a deeply unpleasant feeling in my stomach.

"She'd stopped two months before me," Tabby says quietly. "We used to live on the same street. I found her so she could help me get my family to stop watching, too. Which she did. Of course she did, because she's amazing."

There is a loud thump as Val slams her hand against the blackboard again. She keeps her back to us for a moment, her breathing ragged. Darryl seems to be struggling with himself, on the brink of an apology despite his lingering anger.

"Val..." he begins, but then she whirls around to look at us all and he falls silent.

"Don't you think I'm tired?" Val demands, and to my horror her brown eyes are glistening with tears. "Don't you think I might have wanted to pack it all in *years* ago, to just stop? God, I would *love* to drown my sorrows and get a full night's sleep, but I don't have that kind of luxury. I do what I do because *nobody* else can, and nobody else is going to. There is nobody coming to save us. Do you understand that?"

Nobody ever comes for us, Ali's voice rings in my head. But that's not true. *These* people came for me. Val, with all her eye-rolling and coldness and brashness, saved me when I was sprawled out on the road. She kept me from strangling a small child back in the junkyard. She shot John in the leg to protect me.

"We're saving each other," I find myself saying. "Aren't we?"

"Do you even think we *need* saving?" Val fires at me. "Don't you just want Lila to sign your forehead?"

"No," I shake my head, needing her to understand. "It's not like that."

"Everyone is depending on me to get this done," Val says. "Everyone wants me to put a bullet in Lila's brain and magically fix everything. So that's what I'm going to do."

"Nobody is expecting you to fix the world, Val," Darryl says quietly.

"Aren't they?" she challenges, and then has to lean herself against the desk in front of her. When she speaks again, her voice is hollow. "I *have* to fix it. We have plans! You know we have plans. We're going to do this. We're so – we're so fucking close, but I need all of you with me."

Darryl carefully approaches Val, all the tension drained from him. He slowly gets to his knees and takes both her hands in his. She doesn't wrench them away. "I was being a bloody killjoy," he says sincerely. "And for what it's worth, now that I've had the time to think about it, this is all very exciting. Sometimes, when something is exciting, my initial reaction is to freak out."

"Oh, shut up, Darryl," Val groans.

"No, I'm serious. I was a dick, and I'm sorry, but you were also a dick."

Val takes a moment, but then nods. "I can admit that."

"That's my girl," Darryl says as he stands. "Then all is forgiven."

The atmosphere suddenly feels a lot lighter, and I can relax my tense shoulders. Tabby lets out her own sigh of relief.

"Can I make a suggestion?" she says tentatively. "We found some nice things. Let's take a breather to freshen up a bit, to eat something. Lila isn't going anywhere."

"People already know we're here," Val says. "We can't hang around pampering ourselves."

"Those men are hardly going to turn us in, are they?" Tabby replies. "You heard what John said. They're *terrified* of what the Creatives will do to them if they're discovered. They won't be frogmarching us to the TV station, it's a one-way ticket to being killed."

"Still a risk," Val says. "And they'd do it if the station offered some kind of reward or compromise."

"I don't think taking an hour to recuperate and strategise is going to hurt us," I say. "And I think you deserve to at *least* have some water and food, Val."

Darryl comes to stand by our side, the three of us staring Val down until she admits defeat. She opens her mouth to possibly argue some more, but then her eyes widen by the slightest fraction. Before I can do anything, there's a sharp crack and Darryl has fallen to the ground next to me with a strangled yell of pain.

I spin around in horror. Our hostage is loose, eyes wild and dangerous. He holds one of the chairs above his head, ready to bring it crashing down onto my skull too.

"Fuck," is the first thing I say, because nothing else can sum up this situation quite like that.

Chapter 28

My fist connects with John's greying face before the chair collides with mine. I barely register his howl of pain before I leap onto him like a wild dog, scratching him with my nails, pulling at his gritty hair.

John's got no choice but to drop his makeshift weapon, but the damage on Darryl has already been done, considering he's completely unconscious. Through my exertions, I see Val dragging him away, yelling at Tabby to watch him, before she's right at my side.

"Ok, *ok*, Eva! Get off him!"

I do as she says, scrambling away. John has deep scratch marks across his face from where my nails dug into his skin, which has only made him look more crazed and angry. I acted on pure adrenaline, but now fear is setting in, freezing my limbs. He wants to hurt us. He wants to kill us.

"Bitch," he breathes at me.

"Stop calling us that," I say, willing my voice not to shake. "We were going to help you. We were going

188 ~ EMILY RENNIE

to untie you and let you go. You didn't have to – you didn't have to hurt any of us."

John's face twists into a grin, even though he clearly doesn't find this funny. "You shot me first."

"That's – fair enough," I have to admit. I so desperately want to look over my shoulder to see how Darryl is, but I need to keep my gaze level with the danger in front of me. "But... our friend –"

"He'll be fine," Val tells me quietly, but even she sounds hesitant.

John takes a sudden swing at us, and I don't have time to react. Knuckles slam into my cheekbone. I bite the inside of my cheek as I fall. Tabby calls my name, but the ringing in my ears drowns her out. Metallic blood fills my mouth.

Through blurred vision, I force myself back to my feet. John's surprisingly strong for being so scrawny. Val sweeps her leg his shin; when he staggers, she delivers a crunching kick to his chest. He falls to the ground. Gets up. Charges at her again.

I let the blood dribble from my mouth. It's sticky against my chin. Val ducks from John's swinging fists, but takes a harsh hit to her collarbone. She's panting, clearly exhausted, but she never relents.

The discarded chair lies at my feet. I slowly bend down to pick it up, glancing back at Tabby as I do so. She's cleaning the blood away from Darryl's head, bandaging him up. Completely focused despite the chaos around her.

John swing another punch but this time his fist

is immediately blocked by Val. She grabs him by the wrist and wrenches with fierce precision. He screams like a baby as she forces him to his knees, her grip firm.

"Ssh," Val hisses. His scream trails off into a whimper. "You've been nothing but rude since we met you," she continues, voice laced with disappointment. "I thought we'd got past all this violence between each other, I really did."

"I will rip you apart," he spits at her, eyes watery with pain. "Lila will dangle your remains from her windows."

"Lovely image," Val says. "Shame you won't be around to see it."

There's a harrowing silence as her statement sinks in for him. I see him process the words, fighting back his panic. "You're not going to kill me," he attempts. "You wouldn't."

"You were going to kill *us,*" Val says. "Remember? A few minutes ago, when you were going to kill us?"

"I remember it," I say, voice thick with blood.

"No, no, no, no," John says, quick and desperate. "I wasn't really. I was – I just wanted to teach you all a lesson."

Val only nods, and then looks at me. "Lesson learned," she says, and I bring the chair crashing down onto his head. Val lets go of his wrist and he slumps forward, unconscious, and I drop the chair with a clatter.

"In hindsight," I pant, "bringing a brainwashed

person into a tiny dark room with us was always a stupid idea."

"And yet, we still have you hanging around," Val says, rubbing her collarbone with a wince. Before I can retort with something equally scathing, she holds up a hand. "Joke, Barbie. That was a joke. You make some very good points."

Tabby is already rushing over, eyes wide with horror. "You didn't really kill him, did you? Jesus Christ, did you kill him?"

"No," I say. John's breathing, and I know for a fact I didn't hit him hard enough. "Of course I didn't."

"We *should*, though," Val says. "Just out of courtesy. Is Darryl conscious yet?"

Tabby shakes her head, and then covers her mouth for a moment, eyes squeezed shut. Val swears under her breath, walking over to where Darryl is sat up against the wall.

"I'm sorry we scared you," I attempt, wiping at my bloody chin. "I wouldn't ever kill him, Tabby, honestly."

"It's ok, it's ok," Tabby says shakily. "I mean, I'm not naïve. I know what's got to be done, I've just never been so close to the action before. I'm more the stay inside, do the tech, fix the injuries kind of person. Are you two – are you alright? Let me see."

I inhale sharply as her soft hands touch my face. "Bit my cheek," I manage, "when he hit me. It's not that bad."

Tabby hisses in sympathy. "I'll see what supplies we have."

I'm given a bottle of water. I take a gulp, swilling it around my mouth, and spit. The taste of blood still clings to my tongue. I do it again, and swallow the painkiller Tabby hands me. "What're we going to do about..." I nod towards our unconscious hostage.

"Move him away from here," Val says. She's kneeling in front of Darryl, who is still very much passed out. "He'll wake up and count himself lucky. We'll be far away by then."

"We can't leave without Darryl," Tabby says incredulously.

"I know," Val says, as she draws her hand back and slaps Darryl across the face. The sound reverberates around the dingy classroom.

"Valentina!" Tabby snaps. "That's *not* how you treat someone who just got hit on the head!"

"Well, he needs to wake up," Val says, as if Tabby has just said something very stupid. "Darryl! *Vamos!*"

Miraculously, he groans, eyes fluttering the tiniest bit. "Wha..."

"Darryl!" I'm sure Val doesn't want anyone to know just how relieved she is, but it's obvious in her voice. "Darryl, c'mon. Wake up. We have to go."

His eyes flutter again. "Mhmm?"

Val runs a hand down her face, muttering to herself. "We don't have time for you to have concussion," she says loudly. "Understand? We have to *go.*"

"I don't think we can force him into rapid recovery,

Val," I have to say. "I mean, John also just got whacked on the head with a chair, and look at *him*."

"Then make yourself useful," Val says, "and move his body. Dump it somewhere away from here."

I open my mouth to challenge her, but the glare I'm thrown stops me in my tracks. Now is clearly not the time to argue. "I'll need help," I say. "I can't do it myself."

Val only gestures to Tabby. "Don't get caught," she says, as blunt as ever. It's almost as if her emotional outburst from before was a dream. "I'll stay with Darryl. I can wake him up."

"He's not going to wake up by being bullied," Tabby mutters as I retrieve my leather coat, shrugging it back on, immediately feeling better for it. "If anything, I think he'd rather stay unconscious."

I approach John, wrinkling my nose at the side of him. There's a thick gash on his forehead from where I cracked the chair against his skull. With any luck, he'll wake up in an hour or so with a splitting headache and will crawl back into the hole he came from, feeling sorry for himself. Unless, of course, he's dying right now. But there's not much I can do about *that*.

"I'll take the legs," Tabby says before I can, so I'm stuck with his horrible sweaty arms. Thankfully, he's not too heavy, but I'm still panting by the time we shove him out the window. He lands in a crumpled heap – I apologise even if he can't hear me – and we hoist ourselves out after him.

The weak sun is setting, and we welcome the

shadows. In the dark, we're safe. I know how to survive in the dark. "Bloody hell," Tabby whispers, breathing heavily. "I *hate* Val right now."

I huff in agreement. We haven't mentioned our kiss; perhaps there's no need. It felt like the most natural thing in the world to me, and maybe she feels the same. I hope so.

"There's no way we can leave our hiding spot now," Tabby continues. "Not until we're sure Darryl isn't majorly concussed. It's a death sentence for all of us."

The inside of my cheek continues to throb, and I tentatively touch the wound with my tongue. "Darryl should be fine, though, right?" I say. "I mean, nothing bad will happen to him?"

Tabby stumbles a little as she walks, and desperately rearranges her grip on John's legs. "I'm sure," she pants. "He's been through worse."

If Tabby thinks Darryl will be fine, then surely he will be. In the grand scheme of things, I'm very aware I've not known either of them for very long, but the thought of anything awful happening to them is making my throat feel tight and causing a static buzz in my stomach. It's not quite as strong as the way I feel when I think of Ali and Mum, but it's alarmingly close.

"Good," I say. I know it's dangerous to keep talking out in the open like this, but it's like neither of us can help ourselves. "Because we need to be a team, don't we, and it's not a team without –"

194 ~ EMILY RENNIE

"You don't regret our kiss?" Tabby suddenly blurts. "I mean, you don't feel weird with me, or anything?"

"Of course not," I say in surprise, doing my best to keep my voice at the level of a whisper. "No! I feel really...I feel really good about it."

She huffs an audible sigh of relief. "Oh! Oh, that's – me too. I feel good about it too." There's a pause, before she shyly adds, "I feel good about *you.*"

I can almost forget we're hauling an unconscious body in severely stressful conditions. At this point, Lila herself could swoop in and propose, and I don't think I'd even care. "Really?" I breathe.

"Very."

We leave John in an unceremonious heap, propped up against the doorway of an abandoned house. He's still breathing. Maybe his eyes are even fluttering. I take Tabby's hand and we kiss again, in a way that I am very, very sure about. I don't think I've felt this sure about anything for a long time.

"...Did you find any CDs in the store?" Val is saying when we crawl back through the window. It must have taken us around an hour overall, but Darryl is still the same as when we left him – unconscious – and Val hasn't moved from her kneeling position either.

Val glances up at us as we come back, giving a brief nod, and then turns her attention back to Darryl. I leave her talking to him, and take one of the shopping bags that's been left lying on the floor. There's deodor-ant, toothpaste, and a small aerosol that I discover is dry shampoo. Darryl and Tabby truly exceeded all expectations with their trip.

I douse my short hair in the spray, scrubbing at it ferociously until I feel human again, and hold it out to Tabby.

"Absolutely not," is all she says. "But you knock yourself out." She realises what she's said and winces, glancing back towards Val and Darryl apologetically.

"...And I shouldn't have called you useless," Val continues to him. "You're not useless. You're good for a lot of things."

"Like sex?" Darryl suddenly croaks, eyes fluttering open. Val stifles a yelp, and then hits him in the chest.

"Bastard," she manages. "Have you been conscious the whole time?"

"No." Darryl's eyes slowly close again, and he grimaces. "You kept droning on. I had no choice but to wake up."

Tabby and I are already hurrying over – she fumbles to grab some water, and I just want to check he really *is* alright. The pit of dread in my stomach is easing, and I poke at his cheek, just to make sure he's still responding.

"Ow," Darryl mumbles, as if by default. It's music to my ears. "Go 'way."

"*Si*," Val says, taking the water bottle that Tabby has handed her. "We need to stop crowding around him."

Darryl groans, forcing his eyes open properly, taking us all in. He gratefully accepts the bottle, sipping at it slowly. "What...What *happened* back there? Where's

—" His green eyes widen as he scans the room; he evidently moves his head too fast and moans, slumping against the wall again.

"It's fine," Val says firmly. "Don't panic. It's all taken care of."

"Y'killed him?"

"Not quite," Val says. "But it's still taken care of. He won't be back. If by some miracle he is, *then* I'll kill him."

Darryl groans again, tentatively touching his bandaged head. "Tabs?" he guesses, and Tabby nods. He swallows a few times, voice raspy. "Cheers. Gonna...be brand new."

"How's your vision?" Tabby asks. "Blurry, or ok?"

He shrugs feebly, closing his eyes again. "Just tired," he mumbles. "But...fine."

For now, that seems like the best response we can get out of him. He's certainly not going to be running laps within the next hour, but he's awake. He's awake and ok and everything is going to be fine. "I'm really glad you're alright," I tell him sincerely.

"Aw," Darryl says, giving me a feeble thumbs-up. "Cheers, love. Didn't know you cared so much."

"Me neither," I tell him, which makes him wheeze with laughter before he trails off in another pitying moan.

"We'll take our chances and stay here 'til morning," Val says as she gets to her feet, dusting herself down. "And then we're going to Edinburgh. You'll be fine by tomorrow, won't you?"

"'Course," he croaks. "I'm in my prime."

Val hesitates for a split second, and then kneels again to meet his eye level. "I'm glad you're ok," she says softly. "Really. I'm glad. Don't ever go unconscious on me again."

"I'll do my best," Darryl says. "Fancy giving me a healing kiss?"

Val huffs indignantly, but then presses her lips against his forehead in a sudden act of vulnerability. "Try to stay awake for a bit," she says. "Just sit still, get your strength back. Finish your water."

"You're so bossy," Darryl mutters, before he seems to remember something and points at her accusingly. "Oi! Earlier - did you *slap* me?"

"Don't be stupid," Val dismisses. "You were dreaming."

Chapter 29

I don't sleep much – even though I really could do with it – and it's not because the floor is cement and I'm using my balled-up coat as a pillow. My mind just won't stop buzzing, and I'm worried about what my dreams will bring.

Each of us has eaten and freshened up to the best of our abilities, but there's still a gnawing pang of hunger in my stomach. Now that the adrenaline from the fight has all worn off, I'm more aware of the pain.

Tabby snores softly next to me. Crows caw from outside. In the shadows, I can see the outline of Val as she sits by the window, keeping watch. I wonder if she ever lets herself rest.

Slowly, I push my aching bones up and approach her. She gives me a brief nod, so I deem it safe to sit beside her. In silence, she lights up a cigarette, leaning her head back as she inhales.

You smoke too much, I want to tell her. Instead, I choose the safer option and simply ask, "How are you doing?"

"Never better," she mutters.

"Did John hurt you?"

She scoffs. "Hardly."

"Yeah. We didn't really give him much of a chance, did we?" I say, and her mouth quirks into a tiny smile of appreciation.

"You did good, Barbie," she says, and then shakes her head. "Eva. Sorry."

I shrug. I'm not insulted by something as silly as that anymore, though my fingers still reach to touch the pink butterfly clasp in my hair. "Do you ever sleep?" I have to ask her.

"'Course I sleep," Val says, irritated. "You think I'm a vampire, or something?"

"Would make sense," I say, "with that attitude."

Val flicks cigarette ash. I hear, rather than see, her eyes roll. "I'm just keeping a lookout," she says. "Normally Darryl and I would swap, but he's got to rest. We need him for tomorrow."

"What if he's still sick?"

"He won't be."

"But what if he –"

Val holds up a finger, silencing me. "He has to be there tomorrow," she says firmly. "No arguments."

"If he's still feeling bad, I think he should try and find Carlos," I hiss. "Otherwise it's putting us all at risk. The whole point is for us to see Lila, and we won't be able to do that if we need to keep somebody from fainting the whole time."

"You're very chatty tonight," Val says, tone clipped.

"Weren't you the one I found passed out on the road not too long ago?"

I refuse to let her goad me on this. "You know I'm right," I tell her. "That's why you're grouchy."

Val sighs, rubbing at her forehead with her free hand. "I wouldn't exactly trust Carlos to come to Darryl's rescue," she says. "His instructions were clear. He won't come ashore and risk his life for no good reason, and Darryl *definitely* isn't a good reason. So he's coming with us, end of story."

She's clearly not going to budge on this. I can only hope that Darryl makes a miraculous recovery overnight. "What's going on between you two?" I feel empowered enough to ask. "You and Darryl."

"Me and Darryl?" she echoes, as if I've said something ridiculous. "There's nothing *between* us. We're friends who occasionally fuck, if that's what you mean."

"God!" I try to keep my voice low so I don't wake the others, but I hope she can feel the intensity of my glower. "Do you have to be so... *crude?*"

Val throws her cigarette to the ground, grinding it with the heel of her black boot. "Yeah," she says indifferently. "Do you have to be so virtuous? Does Lila tell you to save yourself until marriage, or something?"

"No," I mutter, folding my arms. "I just think it's unfair if someone clearly likes you and you just use them."

"Oh, give me a break," Val says. "Cut the act. You're doing the exact same thing to Tabby."

That stops me in my tracks, my mouth opening and closing uselessly. "Wha – I am *not,*" I insist through gritted teeth. "How dare you!"

"Five seconds ago you were salivating over Lila, and now you're making moon eyes at a girl who's too kind-hearted to know you're just playing a game," Val says. "At least be grown up enough to admit it."

"That's not it at all," I'm practically pleading with her to understand me. "Do you still think I'm some dangerous monster? I thought – I thought we were *friends*, or at least on our way to *being* friends, but – God, if that's what you think of me –"

"So, what should I think of you, Eva?" Val challenges. "Tell me."

"You should at least think of me as someone you can trust." To my horror, I feel my eyes sting with tears, but I blink them away. She is *not* going to see me cry again. "At the start, sure, I came with you because I wanted to meet Lila. That's not a secret. But I also came because I don't know where my mum and sister are. Have you forgotten that? I'm trying to find my fucking family, Val."

"We can't exactly help you with that right now."

"And I'm still here. Don't you get it? I'm *still here.* Whether you can help me with that or not, I've stayed, because I want to. Because I like Tabby, I like her a *lot.* I like all of you! Do you not believe me when I say that, or is it easier for you to still think of me as some kind of... brainwashed...?" I can't think of an appropriate word for myself, so I trail off uselessly.

"I can't have you messing with that girl's head," Val says. "She's too decent for that."

"I don't want to mess with *anybody's* head." My voice is raw, broken. Even after everything, Val doesn't trust me. Maybe none of them do, not really. "I never wanted to. I just wanted...I wanted things to make sense."

There's movement, and I tense as Val's fingers brush against my shoulder. "Just checking," she says, giving me a small pat, as if congratulating me for passing some kind of test. "No hard feelings. Got to be interrogated to show your true colours every once in a while, right?"

Tears that I haven't shed are blinked away in an ice-cold instant. I fell into her trap, the same way poor Carlos did back in Dover. "Jesus," I croak. "You're cruel."

"I'm practical," Val says. "Think of me like a mother-in-law. Got to make sure you've got good intentions when it comes to Tabs, don't I?"

"So, you don't think I'm a lying, manipulative freak?" I ask, just to double-check. "All of that was some kind of game?"

"First prize to you," she says. "I'd apologise, but we understand each other, don't we? We do what we have to do. You're one of us, Eva, there's no doubt about that."

I should be angry at her, but deep down, I know Val's right. Her methods are extremely unorthodox, but they work. A little *too* well. "Alright, then," I say. "So we all trust each other."

"For my sins, yes," Val says, and makes a little crossing motion. "All the way to the bitter end."

The bitter end. I wish she wouldn't say things like that. "What's your plan?" I whisper. "God, Val. Do you even have one?"

"Go to bed, Eva," is all Val says, turning her head away from me. "Tomorrow, we change the world."

*

"Eva. Eva. Evie! We have to go. We can't stay here!"

*

I'm the last one to wake up, disorientated and groggy. When I check the time on Tabby's phone, it's four in the morning, which explains why we're still shrouded in darkness. I must have only snatched a few hours of sleep. It'll have to do.

"Early bird catches the worm," I slur to nobody in particular, as I swallow down another painkiller.

"Got to move while it's dark," Val replies. She's plaited her hair again, wispy strands framing her face, and she moves with a familiar air of authority towards Darryl to shake him awake too.

Tabby scrapes her curly hair into her two buns, yawning. "It's a good tactic," she mumbles, "too tired to be nervous."

"Nothing to be nervous about," I say. "After today, we'll have our answers, and then...then it'll all be fine, won't it?"

Tabby rubs at her eyes, shoulders hunched. "Sure," she says. "I like the sound of that."

"You'll love Ali," I feel the need to tell her, reaching for her hand. "She'll love you too. My mum can make us all tteokbokki when we're back together."

"What's tteokbokki?"

"Oh, it's *so* good," I say enthusiastically. "Mum makes ours really spicy, I don't know if you like that. Her grandparents in Seoul taught her how to make it, years ago, when she was young. It's rice cake noodles, and gochujang, and fish cakes..." I trail off, because I'm only making myself hungry. "It's good. We can always make yours less spicy."

"I don't mind," Tabby says, but her voice sounds hollow.

I squeeze both her hands, pressing them to my lips. "It *will* be ok, Tabby," I say to her. "All of it. Lila won't hurt us. I can't explain, but I just...I just *know* she won't."

"Oh, Eva," Tabby says, her words catching in her throat. "I wish I could believe that."

She pulls her hands away from me, slowly getting to her feet as if she's aged fifty years. I look up at her, my forehead creased in concern, before standing too. Maybe she doesn't like the sound of tteokbokki, but I can't understand why.

Darryl is standing, though he's leaning half his

weight against the wall. The bandage on his head is stained a murky red, and even in the dim light of the candles, I can see he's paler than usual.

"Morning all," Val says, her cheery tone completely contrasting with the dismal atmosphere that drenches the room. "Feeling well rested?"

Nobody responds.

"*Ay Dios mío,*" Val mutters, "can you at least pretend?"

"I feel great," I say to help her out, forcing a smile onto my face, nice and wide.

Val points at me. "Excellent, Eva, that's the attitude. Maybe less of that terrifying smile, though. Looks like you want to rip somebody's heart out and eat it."

I stop smiling.

"Ok, here's the thing," Val says. "For the past six years, this is what we've been working towards. We need to appreciate everything we've done to get to this point. The people we've saved along the way, the alliances we've formed. We gave people hope, and that's not an easy thing to do these days."

Tabby tilts her head. "We're in the minority, though," she says. "Statistically, ninety percent of the country are still completely under Lila's control."

"I'm not arguing that," Val says, meeting her gaze. "The four of us, and the rebels with Mrs. McIver, we're all anomalies. There was something in us. Something that made us turn the TVs off. Part of us kept wanting to fight."

Goosebumps prickle my forearms. I know I want to

206 ～ EMILY RENNIE

fight, I'm just not exactly sure what I'm up against. I know I have this animalistic, desperate need for survival in me. I learned it from my family, I learned it from this trio, and I learned it from Lila.

"So," Val continues. "I'm not worried. Not with this team. We have a tech genius here who's gonna hack into the whole broadcasting system and shut it down."

"Uh," Tabby says. "I'm really glad you have so much faith in me, but –"

"We have a Lila fanatic who knows all the ins and outs of the show," Val talks over her. "The schedules, the segments, all of it."

"We do? Where?" I ask, eyes wide. When everybody stares at me, I throw my hands up. "I'm *joking*. That was a joke."

"I'm pleased you can make them," Darryl says from where he's slouched against the wall. "For a moment, I was worried."

Val turns her head to look at Darryl. "And you," she says, "I just can't do any of this without you."

There's a silence as he seems to take her words in, and he straightens up. "Oh?"

"Would make my life a *lot* easier if I could," Val says, with an irritated huff. "But I can't. You can fight, you're tall, and you have good arm muscles. So, I need you by my side, as insufferable as you are."

"Heartfelt," Darryl says. "I'm tearing up."

"Here's what we're going to do, then," Val says. "We make our way to Edinburgh. Leave everything behind but things you can fight with." She holds up the ruck-sack, giving it a shake. "Tape, spare bullets, painkillers. Eva, I trust you haven't lost my knife?"

"It's in my boot," I say. "I figured I'd hold onto it. I'm good with them."

"Aim for the centre," Ali's voice rings in my head. The two of us in the garden, practicing our throwing. Our aim. Sweat running down my forehead as I hold the kitchen knife in my hand. We can't let any Vultures or soldiers inside the house. *"Don't give them a chance to get back up."*

Val's voice jolts me back into the dark classroom. There's an icy chill prickling its way up the back of my neck. "Tabs. What've you got?"

"I'm an awful fighter," Tabby says, voice hoarse.

"All the more reason for you to have something on you. We'll do everything we can to get you to that control room, but you need to be able to defend yourself."

"Got my tie," Darryl says. "Someone sneaks up on you, get it round their neck and pull."

"Holy shit," Tabby hisses. "No! I'm not going to do that! You can't seriously expect me to kill someone in cold blood!"

"No one's saying that," Val says quietly. "Calm down."

I carefully approach Tabby, unclasping the pink butterfly clip from my hair. "Take this," I tell her as I unfurl her fingers. She stands rigid. "Just in case. Use enough force and you can at least distract them for a moment."

Tabby stares down at the clip in her hand for what seems like an age, and then slowly looks up to meet my eyes. Silently, she tucks it away into the pocket of her dungarees. "This is insane," she whispers.

"Welcome to the new world," Val says, slinging the rucksack over her shoulders. "We make our way to Edinburgh. We scope out the TV station. I'm sure they'll have Creatives guarding it, so it's a case of sneaking our way in, or fighting our way through them. Once we're inside, we get to the control room. Tabby works her magic, and we find Lila, and I –"

Val is interrupted as Darryl lurches from the wall. "One sec," he croaks as he staggers out into the hallway. There's a retching noise, and a few minutes later he returns, looking even paler than he did before. "All good. Out of system. Seeing the exact number of people that I'm supposed to be seeing."

"Oh, my God." Tabby mumbles. "We are completely fucked."

-

Chapter 30

A singular black van groans its way across the gravel up ahead, twenty minutes into our journey. It takes me a bewildered second to appreciate what I'm looking at, and then the breath leaves my body as Val gives me a forceful shove off the road.

"Hide, hide, hide!" she hisses at all of us.

No time to think. I'm crawling my way through the window of yet another abandoned building, the others close behind me. We flatten ourselves against the wall underneath the window. Blood roars in my ears.

Tyres scrape as the van continues to roll down the street. Beams of light hit the window. I forcefully clamp my hand over my mouth and nose, sure my shallow panting is going to give us away.

"No," I hear Tabby whisper, her voice merging into a whine of despair.

Val kicks her, which I don't appreciate, but I can't exactly snap at her about it. The headlights from the van seem to linger. Why won't they drive on? Do they know we're here?

"Can they track us from the phone?" Darryl

suddenly hisses, and icy dread trickles it way down my spine.

Tabby shakes her head rapidly. Of course they can't. She's too brilliant to let something like that slip from her mind. Her eyes are focused elsewhere. I follow her gaze, and have to dig my nails into my cheek to stop myself from making a sound.

I was wrong – this isn't an abandoned building. There's a woman sitting on the armchair in front of us. I can just see the back of her head, matted brown hair trailing over the flowery fabric. She's positioned right in front of her black-and-white television, which dons the phrase:

PLEASE STAND BY!

It's not time for the show yet. She's waiting for Lila.

The headlights outside flicker and move on as the van continues down the road. I slump against the wall, breathing in short, stuttering gasps. I don't have time to feel any relief. Tabby is already crawling over towards the woman before any of us can stop her.

"Stop, stop, she can still turn us in," Darryl says, panic edging its way into his voice. "We don't have time for any rescue missions."

"He's right," Val says. "That won't be the only van on the roads. We need to stick to the side-paths."

Tabby shakes her head, tentatively getting to her feet. The light from the television illuminates her face like some sort of angel as she presses two fingers against the woman's neck. "No need," her voice cracks. "She's already dead."

It is so cold in this house. I can barely feel my limbs.

Darryl gags, bending over. "Oh, Jesus," he moans. I'm tempted to join him, but I can't move. I can't think. All I can do is watch like some helpless child.

"Don't fucking throw up again," Val demands, before making her way over to Tabby's side, putting a hand on her shoulder. "There's nothing we could've done," she says, voice gentle. "She's been dead for days, Tabs."

There's a sombre silence, before Tabby turns her head away to look at the television. "We need to go," she says, voice hollow. "Before the show starts. How long do we have?"

I swallow a few times to find my voice again. "It's always playing by seven," I say. "That's when I would wake up. The music would already be on."

Tabby pulls her phone out from the front pocket of her dungarees. "It's close," she says. "The station. The signals are going crazy." She moves away from the woman in the armchair, clenching and unclenching her fist. "Let's get that crazy bitch."

"Level heads," Val says, "that's what we all need. Prepare for the fact there'll be more vans. If we need to split up, we know to head back to the dock for Carlos."

For some reason, my body feels as if it's being pulled towards the armchair. I don't want to look. I don't. And still, I approach.

The lady can't be any older than fifty. Her eyes are closed, and she seems peaceful. In fact, she could be sleeping. Something yanks at my heart, which is still selfishly beating in my chest while hers never will again. "I'm sorry," I say, to no one in particular. And then: "Why?"

"Could be anything," Val says. "Medical problem. Lack of food and drink. Things she would have had to leave the house for, but couldn't."

Tabby's hand finds mine, and she squeezes. I can barely reciprocate. "Don't think," she tells me, which is a strange thing for her to say. Normally that's *my* mantra. "Eva. Don't think about it."

I can't reply. There's that all-too familiar sick feeling that swells in my stomach. I will not cross that line, not now. I know Val wants to kick over the television, but she shows great restraint and simply unplugs it from the wall. "Let's go," is all I say. "Let's find Lila."

*

For years, I've spent most of my time wondering what the television station that hosted *The Lifetime Lila Show* would look like. A fairy-tale palace, fit for its princess, full of treats and delights. Maybe even painted pink, to match the prettiness from within. Now that I'm confronted with this brutalist building that has blended into the darkness, stabbing its way through the gloomy clouds, the disappointment leaves a sour aftertaste in my mouth.

"That can't be it," I whisper to Tabby. She continues to stare down at her phone, and then looks back up to the building that lies ahead. A few solitary lights blaze from three windows; two on the ground floor, and one on the top. I feel that *must* be Lila's dressing room on the top floor. She'll be doing her makeup, having her coffee. Getting ready for the day ahead.

"All the signals are coming from there," Tabby says. "That's definitely the station."

We've crawled our way through the thick, wild shrubbery that surrounds the pathway to the building – the only wildlife that seems to have survived this place. The sun won't rise for at least another hour, so I feel safe in the shadows and the leaves damp with dew. We keep ourselves crouched in the bushes, staring ahead at the station.

"It's awful," I say miserably. A sharp thorn has scratched its way along my finger, and I suck at the ruby droplet of blood. "It looks like a *prison*."

Val ignores me, pointing to what looks like an old block of flats further ahead. "A few seconds out in the open, but it's a solid spot," she hisses. "Aim for there."

It'll be more than a few seconds to get that far down the path. I glance at Darryl, who is breathing shallowly at the back of the line, pallid and bleary-eyed. I don't want to appear pessimistic in front of the others, but there's no way he's going to make it.

"All agreed?" Val doesn't wait for a response before she scrambles from the shrubbery, effortlessly moving in the darkness.

Behind me, Tabby swears under her breath before we follow after Val. My legs get tangled in the twigs and I crash to the ground, banging my knees. No time to think about it, I'm already up, already moving, already cursing myself in my head.

I collapse against the back wall of the block of flats, panting and sore, but in one piece. We've all made it without anyone spotting us, and I can appreciate that small victory.

"All ok?" Val asks, her own breathing laboured.

Tabby and I nod. A thumbs-up from Darryl as he bends over, retching again for a moment, before he straightens up. "Never better," he croaks.

Once again, we hear the scrape of tyres against the rocky path. All of us freeze, except Val. She simply presses a finger to her lips and gestures for us to keep our backs flat against the brick wall.

The sound of a van door opening. Boots on the gravel. The crackling of a radio. "Lila nearly ready?" a male voice says, so very close to us. Tabby's shaking hand fumbles for mine, and I grip it hard enough to break her knuckles.

More crackling; a muffled voice responding from the man's radio. I can't make out the words. Footsteps as the Creative walks forwards, finally coming into view, his back to us. He wears a smart suit, face covered by a visor helmet in matching black. Tall. A torch in one hand, his radio in the other. A rifle is strapped to his back. If he turns, he will see us, and there'll be a bullet in each of our brains before we can blink. A deadly certainty grips my throat.

He's inspecting the shrubbery, kicking at it with his boot. His radio crackles again. "Don't know," he responds to the question. "Sounds of disturbance. It'll be fucking rats, bet you anything."

The Creative's torch lingers on something that lies on the ground. Val slowly, carefully, pulls out her revolver as he kneels down to inspect it. Gloved hands pick up something small and shiny, and I don't need his torchlight to know what it is.

A pink butterfly clasp.

Tabby's legs buckle and I use all my strength to pull her back up, even though I feel like I'm getting repeatedly stabbed in my stomach. Val angles her head to look at us, and simply nods her head. Not angry. Just accepting what's about to happen.

"Found something," the Creative says into his radio. "Send more guys down to help with a look-out. Some kind of hair thing, could have always been here, but looks like it belongs to a girl."

His pal on the other end says something that has the man laughing crudely. He's still laughing when Val's bullet hits him square in the back, right between his shoulder-blades. The laugh abruptly trails off into shocked, sharp gasps. He falls to his knees as a rosette of blood spreads across his black suit jacket, and his helmet smacks against the torn-up road.

Maybe I should feel bad that he's dead, but I don't. All I feel is relief so strong that it's dizzying. This is the aftermath of the War, isn't it? Kill or be killed. None of us are strangers to that fact anymore.

"Good shot," Darryl says. "Nice and loud for all to hear."

"Shit," Tabby whispers. "Shit, shit, I'm so sorry, I'm so – It must've fallen from my pocket when we ran – Oh *God*, I can't believe it –"

"Stop," is all Val says. "It's ok. There wasn't any other choice, even if he hadn't found it."

Tabby buries her face in her hands, shuddering. I rub her back. "Please don't feel bad," I tell her desperately. Partly because I really don't want her to feel guilty, but also because there's not much time for her self-deprecation.

"Yeah, Tabs," Darryl says, giving her head a small pat. "Moment he saw us, he was going to kill us anyway. Val's right, there was no other choice."

Val is already dragging the Creative's body to our hiding spot, pocketing his radio. Without a word, she hands Tabby back the butterfly clasp.

"I nearly ruined *everything*," Tabby hisses. "How can you trust me not to mess up again?"

"Get a grip," Val says, before passing the man's torch to me. She rummages through his pockets, retrieving a set of keys. "Help me with this."

"I don't want to see his face," Tabby insists as I kneel down to remove the helmet.

"I do," I say, out of morbid curiosity more than anything else. Maybe he'll look like the monsters I've been imagining in my head.

The radio in Val's pocket crackles to life, just as I pull off the black helmet. "Harry?" a male voice says. "Harry, you ok? Sounded like a gunshot."

Val hastily passes the radio to Darryl, who clears his throat. "Yeah, yeah," he says gruffly, doing his best to disguise his East London accent. "All good. Thought I saw someone, so I fired my gun. False alarm. Was the bloody rats all along."

The Creative – *Harry* – is in his early thirties. Cropped dark hair. Sharp nose. Thin lips. I poke at his mouth hesitantly; no fangs. He's just a man. I don't know whether I'm relieved, or disappointed.

"We're sending more men down," the man on the radio says. "It's nearly show-time, and we can't have any fuck-ups."

"There's – There's no fuck-up," Darryl attempts. "Honestly, everything's fine. We can call off the search. Just focus on getting ready for the show, and I'll be back up in a second."

There's an eerie silence on the other end of the radio, and then: "What's my name?"

The question stops Val half-way through rummaging in Harry's right trouser pocket. "Motherfucker," she hisses.

Darryl has frozen, helplessly gesturing at Val. "Uh-hhh..." he drags out, hopping from foot to foot. "Ah, come on, mate. Don't be stupid! We've known each other for...for years?" his last sentence trails off into a question, and the radio abruptly goes dead.

"Astoundingly convincing," Val mutters as she holds

out her hand. Darryl sheepishly passes the radio back to her. "Eva. Put on the helmet and do up your coat. We can't wear anything else of his, it's all bloody and disgusting."

I look down at the helmet in my hands, and then glance back at her. "You want me to pretend to be a Creative?" I say. "Isn't that a better job for, you know...the *man* of the group?"

"It would be, if the man of the group wasn't dry-heaving every ten minutes," Val says, tone clipped. Darryl flips up his middle finger at her, before bending over with another feeble groan. "But you'll look the part – you're already in black. The coat covers you up well enough, and it means if anyone sees you, they shouldn't stop you if we get separated."

"But we won't get separated," Tabby says as she rubs fiercely at her face. "You should wear it, Val. Not Eva. It's too risky."

"It's riskier for the rest of us," Val says. "If we run into a Creative, Eva's just got to walk fast and with purpose, and they'll think she's one of them."

"And then I can use my knife on him before he gets a chance to say anything?" I guess her next sentence.

Tabby opens her mouth to protest again, but I shake my head. "It's ok," I tell her, "honestly. I don't mind. I'm kind of flattered you're trusting me with it."

"Just don't *actually* join the Creatives," Val says. "That would be really embarrassing for all of us."

Before I can properly roll my eyes, a piercing alarm stops me halfway, the noise reverberating throughout the town, pulsating in my brain. I clamp my hands over my ears with a groan. Over the din, we hear men shout as they run from the station, on the hunt. There's no way for us to sneak ourselves in now. A quiet entry is out of the question.

Without a word, Darryl digs into his suit pocket to retrieve his flask. The lid is unscrewed in seconds, and he takes a long swig of whatever alcoholic drink he's got inside.

"I've got us in a bit of a tricky situation," Val admits in a whisper as the alarm's incessant ringing ceases.

Darryl pockets his flask of Dutch courage, before craning his head from our hiding spot, gnawing at his lower lip. "No," he says when he looks back at the three of us. "Just need to go back to basics. What you need is a distraction."

"A distraction?" I echo. "Where can we order one of those?"

The first raindrop that has threatened to fall for the past hour hits the pavement. We all take a moment to look up at the grey clouds as they roll in the sky. When I look back, Val seems to have realised something before me and Tabby have.

"Darryl," she says. "Darryl. No."

"It's ok," he says. "Honestly."

Rain falls from the sky, thick and fast.

"They don't know how many of us there are," Darryl continues. His blond hair sticks to his forehead, soaked from the rain. He pushes it back. "You only need one person to grab their attention."

"No," Val repeats, brown eyes narrowed. "That's not how this is supposed to go."

"It's supposed to go whatever way it can," he says gently. "C'mon, darling. Can't you trust me?"

I can barely comprehend what's happening right now, only that Darryl is about to do something very reckless and stupid. I grab at his arm. "They have guns," I croak. "A lot of guns."

"I'm a fast runner," he says. "Back at school, I could do the one hundred metre sprint in like, twenty seconds."

"That's not very fast," Tabby hisses, tears in her eyes. "That's distinctly average."

Val keeps shaking her head. "It shouldn't be you," she says with a sudden sense of urgency. "I'll do it."

"No," Darryl says. "No. You're the leader. You have to lead. I'm your back-up, so I have to distract."

He cups her face, and kisses her. Just once. Then looks back at me and Tabby. "See you on the other side, ladies," he says with his trademark charming grin. "Can't wait to be back on that boat with you all, singing our sea shanties."

Before any of us can stop him, he's pulling away from Val, running from our hiding spot. Through the incessant hammering of the rain, there are gunshots. Men yell as they give chase, boots scraping against the gravel.

Val's eyes are screwed shut as we all press our backs against the wall, hard enough for the bricks to imprint on our skin through our clothes. When her eyes open, they hold that all-too familiar hardness. She peeks her head around from our hiding spot, and hisses, "He led them into the building on the left."

"He knows what he's doing," Tabby whispers back. "We can't worry about him."

"I'm not," Val says, and aims her revolver at the security camera that hangs above the doors to the TV station. "Send an alert to Carlos. Tell him to be waiting for us."

Tabby soundlessly taps at her phone, hands trembling.

"Top floor! We should get to the top floor," I say quickly. "Where the light is."

One shot, and the camera has fallen to the ground, cracked and smoking. "Top floor," Val confirms. "Go!"

We don't have time to think. I put the helmet on. My world is tinted black as it covers my whole head, and we run. We run to Lila.

Chapter 31

Scampering up flights of concrete stairs. Torch-light bouncing off the grey walls. The ground seems to sway under my feet as I take two steps at a time. I can't shake the sickening feeling that at any moment, a strong hand is going to grab my ankle and yank me back down into the shadows.

We pass the second floor. Can't stop. God, my knees and feet are throbbing. By the time we've careered up the final flight of stairs, Tabby is wheezing so hard I'm worried she'll faint.

Immediately, the atmosphere feels different from the bleakness of outside. The hallway is lined with plush red carpet, the kind a celebrity would walk up and down on, which makes perfect sense if Lila is up here. Dim, solitary light bulbs trail their way down the corridor, emitting a soft glow. On either side, there are doors. Thick doors, made of sturdy wood; not the best to kick down if it comes to it, but also not impossible.

"Ok," Val says after a moment of catching her breath. "Ok. We've made it this far, which can only be a good thing."

"We should split up," I find myself saying. My voice sounds muted to my own ears in this smothering helmet. Beads of sweat cling to my brow. The urge to wipe them away is itching at my insides. "Tabby and I can try to find the control room first while you look for Lila. We're too obvious together as a group."

Val purses her lips as she considers this, and then points up at a vent in the ceiling. Even from here, I can see the grill is loose and old. "Give me a boost," she says.

"You can't be serious," Tabby hisses. "What if you get *stuck?*"

"I won't get stuck," Val says. "Purely because I wouldn't be able to live with the humiliation. Now give me a fucking boost."

There's no time to argue about it. I knit my fingers together, trying not to grimace as Val's boot grinds against my skin. She places a hand on Tabby's shoulder and hoists herself up, ramming her other elbow against the wobbly grill. It doesn't shift. She hits it again.

I grit my teeth with the exertion of keeping her balanced. "Some – sometime *today*, please," I pant.

"It's not fun for me either," Val snaps back, with one final clang of her elbow against the metal. The grill moves, and she pushes it up and out of the way. She leaps up, arms trembling with the strain as she grips onto the inside of the ventilation shaft.

"How is it?" Tabby asks as Val disappears inside.

"Disgusting," comes the echoed response. "Lots of dead spiders."

I shake out my stiff hands with a groan. "If you find Lila, do *not* kill her," I say to Val. "We need our answers."

There's no response, but I know Val's heard me. I can't even contemplate the idea of her ignoring my advice, and I'm hardly going to hoist myself up into the ventilation shaft to chase after her; I need to stick with Tabby.

"And then there were two," Tabby mumbles.

I wish I could offer her some kind of comforting look, but as it is, all I can do is grab her hand and squeeze it. "I've got you," I tell her, hoping she believes it, because I've never been sincerer. "Whatever happens."

Tabby opens her mouth, struggling for words, and then shakes her head. "I want to say something heart-felt," she says, "but the you look really funny in that helmet, and it's putting me off."

"Totally fine," I tell her, pulling her onwards, "save it for later."

*

Time, being the traitor that it is, ticks away from us as we roam the corridors. We can't hear Val up in the ventilation shaft, but I can't afford to be concerned about that right now. Tabby is muttering frantically to herself as she scans her phone, moving from door to door.

"It's here," she insists. "The control room, it's on this floor, there's just so many bloody –"

We pause at the next corner; I peek my head around first to make sure nobody is coming, and we keep moving. "It's ok," I say, "we'll find it."

"Why would they make it so complicated for themselves?" Tabby hisses incredulously. "Like, how hard would it be to just have some signposts around here?"

Suddenly, I stop in my tracks; Tabby, engrossed on her phone screen, bumps into me with a stifled yelp. "Sorry!" I whisper immediately, pointing towards the door I've just spotted. CONTROL ROOM is emblazoned in golden letters across the oak wood. "It's just, that might be useful."

There's a pause. "Oh." Tabby adjusts her glasses, pursing her lips. "You know what, fair enough. Yeah, fair enough."

Naturally, the door is locked. I twist and yank at the handle anyway, just in case, to no avail. Trickles of salty sweat sting at my eyes.

"Let me try," Tabby says, gently moving me out of the way. She kneels down, rummaging for something in her pockets, and pulls out two hair pins. I watch in amazement as she starts to pick at the lock with ease.

"Where did you learn to do that?"

Tabby sticks her tongue out a tiny bit in concentration. For a moment, she reminds me of a bespectacled cat. "My cousin Jasper was a borderline kleptomaniac for a while," she says. "Never that serious, but he'd take things from the house. He taught me to pick the locks of the cupboards where Aunt Celia would hide the good stuff. I was young, so she'd never suspect me, but when she found out – *yikes.* Two of us grounded for a three months. Still, I never forgot how to do it."

There's a satisfying click, and Tabby breathes out in relief. "Try the handle now," she says, and when I do, the door creaks open.

"You're a marvel," I tell her, wishing I could give her a kiss. "Truly."

"Yeah, well," Tabby shrugs. "I still have no idea what I can do with the actual tech inside, and that's what –"

The sound of footsteps makes Tabby freeze, brown eyes staring up at me in horror. All I can do is help to her feet and hustle her inside, without so much as a good luck or goodbye. Tabby disappears into the control room just as a Creative turns the corner and spots me. I scan him quickly. Middle-aged, receding hairline, not in the best physical shape. He'll be easy to overpower.

"Come from the vans?" the Creative asks me, gesturing to my helmet. I nod. "Nice. I was just on my way to check on Lila."

Lila. I gesture with my arm to encourage him to keep walking, and I match his stride. He's short for a man, or maybe I'm tall for a woman, who knows. Either way our heights match perfectly, and he doesn't seem to find my presence strange.

"Kailan was doing her makeup," he continues, "but he got called away half-way through, so...Guess I'll need to *brush up* on my skills." He laughs, slapping me on the back. "Get it? Brush up? Because she uses...You know, how women use makeup brushes?"

I stay silent, partly to not give myself away, and partly because he's just not funny.

"Did you hear the alarm go off?" he says, trying to appear unfazed at my lack of laughter. "Heard some of the guys say we might have trespassers."

I can't *say* anything, so I simply tilt my head and give a non-committal '*hmm.*'

"Last thing we all bloody need," he says. "We can't delay the start of the show, Lila will be...Well, I mean, *you* know what she's like."

I like to think I do, but I'm about to find out for certain. A thrill trickles down my spine as we stop outside a wooden door. Lila is on the other side. I *feel* her. Is she adding the finishing touches to her outfit? Is she perfecting her hair? It's nearly show-time.

The Creative's voice jolts me back to the dark hallway. "What do you think? Could it be that same group from before?" his voice lowers as he leans in to me. "I thought we'd stamped them out already. They're like *roaches.*"

There's a clang from the ventilation shaft above us, and I inhale sharply through my teeth. The Creative frowns, his eyes darting upwards. "What was –"

I wait until he's close enough, and then drive my helmeted head forwards to smash him in the face with all my force. He crumples to the floor as my own brain rattles. I raise my eyes to the ventilation grill above me. "Did you hear all that?" I ask, knowing full well that she did.

True enough, the grill falls to the floor and Val drops to my feet in a matter of seconds, driving her boot into the Creative's head. "Masterfully done, Barbie," she pants. "I'm so proud."

"Tabby made it to the control room," I tell her, to which she breathes a small sigh of relief. "I think this must be Lila's room," I continue, before shaking my head. "No. It is. It definitely is. Can't you feel her?"

Val throws me a condescending roll of her eyes as she hunkers down to drag the Creative out of our way. He's been hit hard, so it's unlikely he'll spring up with perfect clarity anytime soon. Still, she binds his wrists and mouth with the thick masking tape from her rucksack.

She's trying hard to appear unfazed, but giving the way she's gnawing at her lower lip, I know she's nervous. "Tabby will do what she can on the signals," Val says. "I don't know how long she'll shut everything down for, but..."

"But it's better than nothing," I say, trying to fight the excitement out of my voice. "So...so let's go. Let's go, Val. Let's meet Lila, and get our answers."

"We don't need answers," Val tells me, her hand poised over the door handle. "We need change."

We both stare at the door. On the other side is the person I've been thinking about for the best part of my adult life. The woman who I once assumed was going to love me the way I loved her. The woman who I thought had been protecting us from the harshness of the world.

Suddenly, I'm seized with a sense of foreboding that's stronger than anything I've felt since I left my home – even recalling the War. This time it feels different. This time, it truly feels like the end of something.

"Eva?" Val asks me. "Are you ready?"

I lift my eyes to meet hers, and give a brief nod. Val's revolver is already in her hand. She must be low on bullets now. "What if..." I begin, but trail off. I don't even know what I want to ask. What if Lila hates us? What if they can find it in themselves to forgive her?

I think of Tabby. Brilliant, sweet, *real* Tabby, who is alone in that control room trying to disrupt the television signal. I think of Darryl, who has risked himself as a distraction just so we could make it inside. And Val, for all her grouchiness, who has protected us all to get to this very point. They've been working towards this for years. I can't be the one to slow them down.

My hand wraps itself around the door handle. I nod again at Val. "It's time," is all I say.

A creak as the door eases its way open. It's so *quiet* inside. As bleak as the rest of this building. Val shuts the door behind us with a gentle click, and I tug off my helmet. Fresh air hits at my grateful face, and I blink a few times to adjust to the half-lit bright lamps. The two of us are guided by their glow, pointed towards a very well-known desk.

"Oh, my God," Val croaks. She crosses herself, as if warding off a demon. I didn't think she was the religious kind.

My lungs burn as I realise my tense body has been holding my breath in. I make my way towards the desk, towards Lila, who is sitting in her chair.

"No," Val continues, anger pushing its way through. "No, no, *fuck!*"

I barely hear her as I continue to approach the desk. Lila's arms are tied to her chair. Thick, black tape covers her mouth, and she's wearing large headphones that frame her lovely face. The wire connects to a black-screened monitor behind Lila's chair – it keeps routinely flashing. Her eyes are closed, but somebody has swiped light shadow over her lids, and her lashes are thick and curled with mascara.

"Lila?" I whisper, even though I know she can't hear me. "What's happened to you?"

A thin trickle of blood begins to leak from Lila's nose. Behind me, Val hunches over, a hand pressed against her forehead. "We've been so stupid," she whispers to no one in particular.

I force myself to move away from Lila, looking up at the old-fashioned clock that adorns the wall. Half an hour until the show starts. Half an hour to get out of here before anyone notices.

"She's not the villain," Val's words drive their way into my heart, each one a perfectly sharpened knife.

"Jesus Christ, Eva, she was never the villain." Her voice cracks, and the two of us stand, helplessly staring at the poor, beaten woman in front of us. "She's the victim."

Chapter 32

Val doesn't seem to know what to do, which is alarming, because she always knows what to do. Now she just stands motionless, eyes wide with horror and disgust and fury. I look at her beseechingly, waiting for her to give me some kind of instruction, but it's as if she's frozen in time.

Up to me, then. My fingers hover hesitantly before I begin to tug at the tape that covers Lila's mouth. I don't want to hurt her; I'm not even sure if she can feel what's happening. As the tape peels back, her lips look strangely naked without any lipstick on. Even though Lila's always shown in black-and-white, her lips are always pristinely painted. Everyone knows that.

Val finally moves towards me, doing her best to get some semblance of control back on her face. We both watch as Lila's mouth moves silently to whatever is being blasted into her headphones.

"What the hell is going *on?*" I hiss. "What *is* all this?"

"I don't know," Val says uselessly, "I...Jesus, I don't know."

Tell me what to do, I want to say, like a helpless child. Maybe she feels the exact same way. "We don't have a lot of time," is what I opt for instead. "We need to do something."

"I just don't know if any of this is, like..." Val gestures to all the equipment that surrounds Lila, forehead creased in concern. "If we move her, will it hurt? Has she just been chained to this desk for the past few years?"

I rub my sweaty palms against my coat. "Let's take the headphones off," is all I say. "We can figure out what she's listening to."

There's a small nod from Val, and I hesitantly reach my hands out to lift the headphones away from Lila's ears. Audio continues to drone on, and I hold them up to sneak a quick listen.

Good morning, my lovely loyal listeners, a robotic voice buzzes. *On today's show, we're finally going to announce those competition winners! I hope everyone's as excited as I am –*

"It's the show," I whisper to Val. "She's listening to what'll be on the show today."

"She's getting a script drilled into her," Val says, and swears so vehemently that I can't help but flinch.

The plush headphones feel heavy in my hands, even though they can't weigh that much. I don't know what to do with them. Smash them to pieces? As tempting as it is, I don't have the time or the physical strength, so I decide to just yank the cable out of its socket. Silence. The only sound is the constant ticking of the clock, and mine and Val's shallow breaths. All we can do is watch.

Slowly, Lila's eyes blink open, like a beautiful doll come to life. I have to forcibly resist from leaning in to check what colour they are, just so I can finally know.

"Lila?" Val begins hesitantly. "Is – is Lila even your name? Did *they* give you that name?"

The woman's lips continue to move soundlessly for a moment, only for her gaze to suddenly snap on me and Val. Blue eyes, as blue as sapphires, just as I always imagined.

"Lila?" Val tries again.

The woman's mouth trembles. Eyes widen, scanning the room.

It may not be the best time, but I really want her to know. "By – by the way," my voice trembles with suppressed excitement and nerves, "I am *such* a huge fan."

"Oh my *God*, Eva," Val hisses at me with pure venom as she starts to loosen the restraints around Lila's arms, but I don't care. I've waited years to say it, and it might make Lila feel at ease for a moment if she knows her hard work has been appreciated.

Except Lila only screws her eyes shut and lets out a desperate, mournful wail, like a lost animal in pain. It's such a terrifying and awful sound that for a moment the ground sways beneath my feet.

"Shit," Val mutters, scrambling to finishing untying her. "Lila, please, I mean no disrespect, but you're going to have to shut up."

"We're here to help," I add, shooting her what I hope is a comforting smile, even though she's not looking at me. "It's all going to be ok, Lila, we're going to get all of this sorted –"

The machines behind Lila's desk begin to emit a high-pitched whine, red lights flashing on and off with rapid speed, before the entire system seems to give up. Even the lamps fizzle and die, plunging the room into darkness.

"Well," Val says after a moment, "let's assume, or pray, that was down to Tabby."

Lila has stopped making any noise now; she has reverted to complete and utter silence. In fact, I can barely tell if she's breathing. I just see her rigid out-line in her chair, even though all her restraints are gone now.

"Lila?" I try again. "Would you like to come with us?"

"No time for niceties," Val says, hoisting Lila up from behind the desk. To Lila's credit, she doesn't re-sist or make any kind of complaint, even though she'd well be within her right. I need to desperately talk to Val about her bedside manner one of these days.

The main lights in the hallway are also out by the time we shove ourselves through the door, but dim yellow emergency bulbs have clicked themselves on. Lila's limbs are wobbly as Val steers her forwards, like a startled fawn learning how to walk. Now that she's standing, I can see she's not that tall, even though she's wearing platform heels. She wears a green, floaty dress with slightly puffed sleeps, adorned with white polka-dots. It's a true 1950s, classic Lila look.

"Let's hope Darryl is still doing a good job distracting," Val pants. "Regular Creatives inside don't seem to have any guns, just the ones who drive the vans. Control room?"

"Back this way," I gesture as we hurry along down the corridor, Val more or less dragging the still silent Lila with her. For a dizzying moment I worry that we're lost, that I'll never find the room again in this maze of a building, that Creatives are going to snatch us any second and Tabby will be lost forever.

Then we turn the corner, and Tabby's torchlight bounces off my face. "Tabby!" I gasp as I take her in, and gather her into my arms with a fierce squeeze, just to make sure she's really there. "Tabby, you did it!"

"I – did *something*," she wheezes, "no clue of the long-term damage, but I more or less fried the whole broadcasting system, or just caused a massive power-cut, and smashed up a bunch of their equipment –"

I take her face in my hands and kiss her, pouring all my relief and hope and love into it, to the point where my knees feel shaky and I forget where we are.

Tabby seems to feel it too, because when she pulls back, her eyes are half-closed and she's in a daze. "Wow," she croaks, "thanks, Eva. I do what I can."

"If you're *finished*," Val's aggravated voice snaps me back to reality. "Can we please get back to *escaping*, lovebirds?"

It's at that moment when Tabby realises who Val is

holding up. Her mouth drops open, eyes wildly going between Lila and Val, and then she seems to piece it all together. "Bloody hell," she whispers in pure horror. "Ok. Ok, we're *so* out of here."

We don't know how much time we have left, or what's waiting for us outside of the station, but all we can do is run for the concrete stairwell. Val leads the way, slinging Lila's arm around her shoulder, half-carrying her down the stairs. The sound of my footsteps echo haphazardly as I run after them.

Behind me, Tabby screams. I stagger to a stop, nearly losing my footing on the stair. When I spin my head around, I can see one of her arms has been wrenched back by a Creative; a stunned young man who can't seem to believe what he's seeing.

"Who are you?" he demands angrily. "How did you get in? What have..." he trails off, his eyes widening as he seems to realise what exactly might be going on. "The broadcasting signal. What have you done? What have you stupid little bitches done?"

Tabby's free hand jabs itself upwards into his eye, and the man shrieks. It takes me a while to realise exactly what she's done to cause him such pain, and then I see my pink butterfly clasp gripped in her fist, glistening with blood.

Howling and swearing in rage, the Creative clutches at his ruptured eye. I reach up to give him a hard shove in his chest, and he falls backwards with a yelp. There's no time to praise Tabby for her quick thinking;

I can only grab at her arm and hurry down the rest of the stairs.

"Sorry," is all Tabby pants, holding up my clasp. "That – that was disgusting."

It was great, I try to say, but I need to save all the breath I have for running. Muscles aching, I tilt my body back to stop myself from tumbling down the last flight of stairs. Above us, we can still hear the young Creative yelling out in agony.

We burst through the station's exit after Val and Lila, blinking fiercely to adjust to natural light. So far, I can't see anybody waiting for us, but there's no time to relax. We have to keep going.

"Head back to Leith!" Val yells. "Darryl knows to meet us back there, head for the boat –"

I don't hear the rest, because behind us, there's a sudden explosion of smoke and raging red fire. The force lurches us all forward. Gravel scrapes at my face as I'm knocked to the floor with a scream.

Bewildered, stunned seconds tick by. I'm on my back, staring up at the sky. The grey clouds are blowing over; it looks like it could be a beautiful day after all. In the distance, a magpie caws as it soars through the plumes of black smoke.

I need to get up. Need to run. We all need to run. Body aching, I force myself to roll over onto my hands and knees with a pained moan. Fire roars through the entire building, its heat smothering. A putrid smell fills my nostrils. I feel as though I am right back home, about to give Jessica my lovely pink tricycle, only for the entire street to burn before my very eyes. I cannot go back there again.

Through watery eyes, I desperately scan the area for the others, and that's when I see Tabby's glasses. They lie at my feet, a thick crack running down the right lens. The sight of them abandoned on the road like this feels like a punch to the gut. I soundlessly pick them up, ignoring my protesting muscles. "Ta –" I begin, only to start violently coughing. "Tabby!"

I find her sprawled on the ground, face pressed against the road. A wedge of hard ice lodges itself in my throat, and my breath comes out in short, stuttered gasps at the sight of her. I run over to her immediately, forgetting all about the pain the moment I see her. "Tabby!"

Thankfully, I hear Tabby groan, and her limbs begin to stir. "Tabs," I say uselessly, practically choking on the relief as she attempts to lift her head up.

"Eva," Tabby croaks. "Wh..."

"It's ok, you're ok, it's all fine," I say through ragged breaths, helping her to sit up. "I have your glasses, but they're all cracked, are you going to be alright?"

Tabby isn't listening; she just stares in horror at the burning building ahead of us. "Darryl was in there," she whispers. "That's where...that's where he ran inside."

No. No, no. "Are...are you sure?" I ask stupidly, because of course she's sure.

Tabby points with a shaking hand. "Building on the left," she says, face slack with shock. "Building on the left. Darryl was in there."

I help Tabby to her feet, even though she barely acknowledges me. "He could've got out," I say, desperately needing to believe it myself. "He could've already escaped, made his way to the boat, he could've done that."

"Where's Val?" is all Tabby says. "We need to – we need to find Val, before the Creatives do."

It doesn't take me long to spot Val's tall figure ahead, outlined in smoke. She is already standing, gaze fixated on the burning building in front of her, and then she begins to run towards it.

"No!" Tabby calls out, only to start wheezing and spluttering. "Valentina, we have to go! We have to go!"

Val doesn't listen, and we have no choice but to run after her. A Creative staggers out of the TV station, shrouded in the billowing plumes of smoke from the building next door. Before he even has a chance to shout, Val has shot him point-blank without a moment's hesitation.

"Jesus!" Tabby yelps. "Valentina, please, we can't stay here!"

Val stoops amidst the burning rubble. When she stands, she is grasping something in both hands as if it's her last lifeline. A charred, dented flask.

Tabby's breath is a stuttered gasp as she grips onto my arm. There's nothing I can say. There's nothing I can do. I feel like there's two of me; one is standing on this desolated street. The other is watching from somewhere far away, in another place, another time.

"Oh, Darryl," Tabby whispers, eyes brimming with tears. "You idiot."

Val is looking past us, her own gaze hollow. She takes a few stumbling steps forward, mumbling something I can't make out.

Icy prickles make their way down the back of my neck, the unmistakable feeling of being watched. I turn. Lila is standing in the middle of the road, blood still trickling from her nose. Her green, floaty dress is ripped and stained with dirt. "Jamie," is the first word she utters, voice dry and croaky. Wild, blue eyes stare at me. "Where's Jamie?"

Chapter 33

Carlos' boat isn't waiting for us. Neither is Darryl.

My ragged breaths curls in wisps, even with the watery sun doing its best to shine. I barely feel the cold. Sweat from our desperate run clings to my arms, sticking uncomfortably against the leather of my coat. It's all I can focus on. As aggravating as it is, I'm grateful for the distraction.

I don't want to think right now.

Most of the helmeted Creatives were inside the building that exploded – *Darryl was too, Darryl was too* – so that's a glimmering comfort. They were the ones with the guns, and they were the drivers. So far, no van has chased after us, but that doesn't mean there won't be one. And the longer we stand here, desperately waiting for Carlos of all people, the more likely it is that any Creatives on foot will catch up with us.

When they find us, they won't be merciful. I'm sure of that. Considering what they just did to –

"I know it's silly," Tabby whispers to me, "but I just really...I kind of hoped he'd be here."

It's not silly. I'd been hoping the exact same thing.

Hot tears sting at my eyes as I shakily grasp her hand. Why isn't Darryl here? I know he's got a head injury. I know it was slowing him down. I know the building he was last in exploded in a fiery rage. Somehow, I still had a glimmer of hope that he'd already be here, waving down Carlos' boat for us, laughing at us for being so slow, ready to chat about our success with a cigarette already in his hand.

Val is pacing, eyes desperately scanning the grey seas. "I told you to send Carlos an alert before we even went into the station," she demands as she turns to look at Tabby.

"I did!" Tabby insists, voice cracking. "And – and he knows, he knows he has to come back for us, he *will* come back for – Honestly, Val, I did."

I can't bear to see Tabby so distraught, and reach out a hand to comfort her. Even though she recoils away from my touch, I don't take it personally. Something in me feels the exact same way. To give her distress some privacy, I avert my gaze.

When I turn my head and see Lila, I need to give myself a sneaky pinch. I can't *believe* she's here. Everybody who watches the show must be so annoyed right now, but Lila is here, with *us!* She's staying silent, which I can't blame her for, especially because we found her practically chained to her desk. I don't mind if she's silent. The fact that I'm standing right by her, soaking up her company, is more than enough for me.

I open my mouth to say something to her, but get

all tongue-tied again. Then all of a sudden, she breaks her silence once our eyes meet.

"How long?" she croaks.

How long has Lila been on the TV for? I swallow, doing my best to keep my face neutral. "It's...It's probably been a few years," I admit, voice shaking. "There was the War, and then..."

"Where's Jamie?" is all Lila asks again.

"I...I don't know," I have to say. It's awful to admit, but a tiny pulse of jealousy throbs in my throat at the way she says this stranger's name. "Who's Jamie?"

Lila looks around, taking in the world around her, as if for the very first time. Her breathing is ragged. "He's dead, then," is all she says, blue eyes glistening with tears that refuse to spill over.

"Dead?" I echo, flinching at the horrible word. "You don't know that. Why do you say that?"

"Because he would have come for me," Lila says. "No matter what, he would have come for me. But...but he's not here. There's only you. So...he has to be."

I'm sorry, feels like the correct thing to say. When I open my mouth, nothing comes out but a useless croak. "You don't know that," is all I can repeat. "Whoever Jamie is, he was probably just watching your show. Everyone's been watching your show. You're – Lila, you're a *celebrity.*"

This doesn't seem to excite her. If anything, she looks like she'd happily claw my eyes out if I carry on speaking. I tactfully dart my eyes back to the shoreline, ragged fingernails digging into my palms. The fear doesn't creep back in; it paralyses me completely. I screw my eyes shut. Carlos will be here soon. Carlos *has* to be here soon, otherwise...

"There!" Val suddenly shouts. "Carlos! *Vamos!*"

My watery eyes snap open, and I see a familiar wooden boat pulling itself into the shore. At first, I'm sure it's a hallucination, a desperate fever dream, until a familiar curly-haired man behind the wheel gradually comes into view. I could collapse with the relief, but Val is yelling at us all to run, so I blindly obey.

"Stay there!" Val is yelling to Carlos. "We'll come to you, be ready to move!"

When I throw myself against the grey waves, all the breath leaves my body for a good five seconds. I hear Tabby yelp at the impact as well, but I can't exactly offer any encouragement. Cold water seeps through my clothes, the chill setting itself into my muscles as I desperately wade towards the boat. No matter how hard I try, the tide keeps pushing against me. My limbs fight to just *rest,* if only for a moment. I swallow a mouthful of salty water, spluttering at the foul taste of it.

Hurried splashing from behind tells me that Lila has decided to follow us after all. This gives me the push I need to keep going. For a moment, I was sure she was going to stay rooted to that spot forever.

Of course, Val is the first to reach the boat. Teeth chattering, I make sure Tabby gets pulled up before me, and then I gratefully clasp at Val's hand. Lila soon follows. Once we've all clambered aboard, we stand in stunned silence, shivering. Unable to believe it.

"You took your fucking time," Val eventually snaps, shooting Carlos a fierce glare. "What, were you having a nice nap?"

Carlos flips up his middle finger. "Less of the attitude, Valentina," he says. "I was in such a good hiding spot and it took me a little longer to make my way here. Just be grateful."

"Grateful!" Val laughs, and not in a pleasant way. "You want me to be *grateful,* Carlos! Grateful that you finally bothered to show up?"

"Exactly," he says, far too smugly, and then he frowns as he takes us all in. "Wait. What happened to Darryl? Did you replace him with a hot lady?"

None of us can respond. Carlos' eyes dart between us all, scrutinising Lila, who keeps her head bowed. "Shit," he whispers in sudden recognition. "You – You actually kidnapped Lila? What was the point in that? Why isn't there a bullet in her brain?"

"She's not Lila," Tabby says. "I mean, yes, she's Lila. But not the Lila we all thought she was."

"What the hell does that mean?" Carlos asks incredulously, backing away as if we're all contagious. "She's either the host of *The Lifetime Lila Show,* or she isn't. I've not been chained to my television screen for a while, but that's definitely her!"

Lila lifts her blue eyes to observe Carlos calmly. "Boo," she croaks, and then cracks up laughing like a wild thing when he recoils, almost toppling over the side of his boat.

"You all thought she was controlling you," I say, the pieces slotting together as I say them out loud. "But it was the other way around. Those Creatives were controlling *her.* They made her do the show, she never asked or wanted to." I glance at Lila questioningly. "Right? Is...Is that what happened, Lila?"

Lila inclines her head the tiniest bit, no longer laughing. Her entire face has closed back down to a blank slate.

"I don't buy it," Carlos insists. "She could still pollute our brains!"

"You don't have much to pollute," Val says as she pushes past him. "Get this boat moving, *now.* We can explain when we're far away from here."

Carlos is still resembling a startled fish, mouth agape. "But, Darryl –"

"Darryl is obviously not coming," Val says, voice tight. "He thought he'd play at being a hero and got himself killed. Go figure."

Carlos swears under his breath, face pale, before moving up to the boat's steering wheel. Val keeps her eyes focused on the shore, revolver never leaving her hand. I see her lower lip tremble.

"Let's wait a minute longer," I say in sudden desperation, holding onto her arm. "He could still come back. He could still be ok."

Val only shakes her head. "No, Eva," she says quietly.

"He's gone. He's gone, and we can't stay. They'll all be coming for us now."

The boat judders and lurches forward. Before long, the coastline of Leith is fading in the distance. "No!" I protest, but clearly she's not listening. Desperate, I turn away from her, and run up to Carlos. "Stop it! Stop the boat, we have to wait!"

"Not a chance," Carlos says, his knuckles gripping the wheel hard enough to break it in two. "You'll be waiting an eternity."

I swear fiercely, though I'm not sure what I was expecting from him. Certainly not actual support. "Tabby!" I attempt. "Tabby, we can't just leave, we can't, it's not right!"

Tabby stays rooted by Val's side, head bowed, silent. Why has everybody around me suddenly become so *useless?*

"It's awful, Eva," Val says as I approach, panting heavily. "I know. But turning this boat around is the last thing Darryl would have wanted us to do. If we go back, he won't be there, but Creatives *will* be."

She's right. I know she's right. Still, the anger churns in my stomach, rising up to my throat. "They killed him, and we're running away," I say, fury spiking my words. "Why didn't we make them pay for it? They *killed* him!"

"I don't think they did," Val says, tapping her fingers against the rough wood of the boat. Salty seawater sprays our faces. "I don't think they killed him, I mean. I think Darryl saved us."

None of us respond right away, unsure what Val means. She shakes her head in frustration, clearly thinking we're slow.

"I'm sure of it," she continues. "He made it possible for us to escape, he did it on purpose."

The rage in my chest simmers down the slightest bit at her steady words. "On...On purpose?" I echo, the devastating explosion playing on a loop in my mind. "How could he have done that?"

"His lighter," Val says, her expression tinging on desperate. I don't know if she's trying to convince us, or herself. "The building he was in, it was apartments, right? They would have had plenty of things in there that could've..."

"Gone boom," Lila says unhelpfully, and then snorts with laughter. We all flinch. I feel personally let down by her crass behaviour, and haughtily turn away. She was the one who taught me the importance of being ladylike and respectful, so it feels especially cruel for her to be amused right now.

"For lack of a better expression," Val says through gritted teeth, "yes. Tabby, what do you think? It's possible, isn't it?"

Tabby rubs at her bare eyes and stays silent for a moment, before her head snaps up. "It smelled of gas," she says suddenly. "Could have been old cookers or boilers. A flame to those could have definitely caused an explosion. Jesus Christ, did he – *did* he do it on purpose?"

"He said he'd give us a distraction," Val says as she

slumps to the floor, back pressed against the side of the boat. Her brown eyes are wide and glassy as she stares ahead into nothing. "He certainly did that. Took out a lot of Creatives while he was at it."

Whatever anger I was feeling is dripping away; now, the pit of my stomach just feels hollow. Shaky breathing and the crashing waves are the only sounds, until I feel fingers tap at my shoulder. I turn to see Lila, and for a moment when I look into her blue eyes, everything seems calm. This is *Lila,* my hero, my source of guidance. Radiant, perfect Lila, who can make any frown turn upside down.

"Your friend," she says. "What was his name?"

"Darryl," I whisper. Salty tears sting the grazes on my cheeks.

Lila nods. "He had the right idea," is all she says. With that, she limps away, down into the cabins.

I stare after her, speechless, horrified. Who is this woman? Where is the Lila I know and love?

Chapter 34

Towards the back of the boat, there's an emergency box which contains a spare pair of glasses for Tabby, a half-full bottle of rum (which makes me a little sick just looking at it), various painkillers, and a flare gun. I'm not exactly sure what the point of the flare gun is, because if this boat capsizes I don't think anyone's guarding the shores, ready to save us. I decide not to bring this up.

Tabby rubs at the lenses of the glasses for a while, but they're still slightly streaky when she puts them on. "That's better," she says, pushing them up the bridge of her nose, attempting a smile. "I can see you now."

"Poor you," I say, hoping to lift her spirits a little. "I must look awful."

"Never," Tabby says. "It's kind of annoying, actually. No matter the imminent danger, you always look great."

She's definitely sweet-talking me, but I can't help blushing anyway.

Carlos approaches, which makes Tabby's expression

abruptly sour. "Boat's steady," he says. "Weather looks good. We should be back at the junkyard tomorrow night."

When I think back to staying in the junkyard, it seems like it happened to a different person, in a different lifetime. I hope Mrs. McIver has made some more soup for us. I can imagine how stunned she'll be to see Lila with us.

"It's a shame," Carlos is saying. "Darryl was a decent guy. Though it does make me the man of the group now, I suppose."

My eyes drift ahead to where Val is standing. She methodically lights up a cigarette without a word, even though she must hear everything Carlos is saying. Surprisingly, Tabby is the one who gets to her feet, fists clenched.

"You're not a replacement," she snaps. "Don't flatter yourself. You could *never* replace Darryl."

Carlos raises both eyebrows, clearly up for the challenge of a fight. "Easy there, pipsqueak," he says. "I'd *hate* to be a replacement Darryl. Imagine being Valentina's little lap-dog. I can see why he decided to cut his losses and bow out."

Tabby draws her fist back, but I grab at her arm just in time. "Don't," I tell her calmly.

Her technique is all wrong. To deliver a good punch, you should tuck your thumb over your four fingers, otherwise you're likely to break a bone. You have to keep your wrist as straight as you can, and make sure your stance is strong.

I make sure I've got all of that right, and then I punch Carlos square in the nose.

"Oh my *God!*" he shrieks, hands flying to his face. "What the *fuck*, Eva?"

Shaking out my hand, I shrug and tell him, "I thought your face looked like it was healing too nicely."

In the distance, I hear Val laughing. Carlos whirls around to face her, blood spilling over his fingertips. "Laugh it up," he says thickly. "Go ahead! Laugh 'til you choke!"

"*Gracias*," Val says. "I will."

Carlos wipes at his once-again busted nose, seething with anger. "Darryl died because you treated him like shit," he says. "He'd have done anything for you, but you knew that. That's why you had him on that leash for years. He *must* have been good in bed, huh? He certainly wasn't that good a driver, so why else would you insist he travelled with you everywhere?"

Val takes a deep drag of her cigarette. I wonder if she's going to stub it out on Carlos' face.

"Unless, of course, he sacrificed himself so he wouldn't have to lie horizontal with you anymore," Carlos says, face twisted in malicious glee. "Can't blame the guy for that, I suppose."

"Shut up," Tabby says, voice trembling with rage. "You don't know what you're talking about, Carlos. You don't know a single thing." Her head turns. "Don't let him bother you, Val," Tabby spits. "Once a Vulture, always a nasty little Vulture."

At that, Carlos fixes Val with a cold, hard stare. She matches his gaze, still without saying a word.

"If only you knew," Carlos says icily. "Your role model isn't exactly squeaky clean, either."

"None of us are," I say. "We're still good people trying our best."

Carlos barks a laugh. "Right," he says. "Well, consider me humbled." He gives his nose a final wipe, leaving a smear of sticky blood on his right cheek, and then staggers back up the steps to stand by the wheel.

"I can't believe you punched him like that," Tabby whispers to me in awe. "That was...*iconic*, Eva."

"Didn't see the point in you hurting your hand," I say, and give her a small kiss on the forehead. I glance towards Val, who continues to stand in silence. I can't figure out what's on her mind at all, yet my heart aches for her all the same.

Tabby seems to understand, too. "I'll check on Lila," she says. "Maybe she's ready to talk. You can keep Val company."

Now I'm nervous, unsure if I even *want* to keep Val company. There's no telling if she's about to fly into a rage, and she's still got that lit cigarette in her hand. "I don't know..." I begin, but Tabby has already scampered down to the stairs to the bunks. Still shivering from the cold, I tentatively go over to stand by Val's side.

"I don't bite, Eva," she says to me with the tiniest smirk. "Unless I *really* have to."

How are you? How are you feeling? Is Darryl really

gone forever? When I open my mouth, these questions jam themselves in the back of my throat. I stay silent.

"I'm just thinking about next steps," Val continues, flicking cigarette ash. "I don't know how long Tabby's damage to their tech will last. With their kind of intel, they could get it back up and running within the day. But if Tabby smashed up a bunch of their stuff, maybe not."

"Val –" I try, but I can't get a word in edgeways.

"I mean, not that there's much they can do without the nation's loveable host," Val says. "Unless they have back-up recordings, or the brainwashing works with *anyone's* voice." She seems to have stunned herself with this notion, and freezes for a split second before ploughing on. "Fuck. No, that can't be it, it's Lila, isn't it? Lila is their special ingredient, for whatever reason, otherwise they wouldn't have literally tied her to that desk. We need her to talk, and we need her to talk *now.*"

I hold out a hand to slow her down. "Tabby's trying to speak to her," I say, "and we should let her do it, not us. You and I aren't exactly...Subtle."

Val huffs irritably, before conceding. "Alright," she says, "Confused, terrified people will be staggering out of their homes before we know it, so we can expect riots in the streets, now *The Lifetime Lila Show* is up in flames. Creatives will be chasing after us, and we still know basically *nothing* about them. Currently, the only one with the answers we need is busy staring into space."

"We can't be angry at her," I whisper. "She's not...herself."

Val grinds her cigarette under her heel with a shake of her head. "Too much to think about," she says. "Like how stupid I feel."

"Don't." I'm aware I'm being no help whatsoever, but I want to at least try and comfort her. "Darryl won't think you're stupid –"

"I'm not talking about Darryl," Val interrupts immediately. "I'm talking about how I didn't even *consider* Lila wasn't the one to blame."

"I really think we should talk about Darryl, Val," I say.

She whips her head to me, fast enough to make me jump. "If you want to keep all your teeth in your mouth," she says icily, "then you'll stop bringing up Darryl. *Comprender*, Barbie?"

I shrink back under the intensity of her glower. "*Comprender*," I mumble, tongue anxiously flicking across my front teeth.

Without another word, Val closes her eyes and leans her head back. I suppose the conversation we were having is over. I still stay by her side, purely because I feel she needs *someone* with her, even if she'll never admit it.

We sail on in silence, until we're in the midst of the seas with no land in sight. Around an hour later, Tabby emerges from the cabin, shaking her head.

"Lila wouldn't say a word to me," she says. "Just

stared into space for ages. She's asleep now, completely out for the count."

Val scratches at her cheekbone with scowl, arm muscles flexing. "Who *will* she speak to, then?"

"There could be someone. A man called Jamie," I suggest. "Lila asked me if I knew where he was."

"That's not a lot to go on," Tabby says with a frown.

"It's *nothing* to go on," Val snaps. "We need to know what happened to her, *how* it happened, to make sure they don't get a new smiley blue-eyed woman taking over our brains. She's going to have to talk to us."

I shake my head. "She will. She just needs rest. It must be exhausting, speaking to the public all day. Let's just let her sleep."

Val looks like she's going to argue with me, but then she sighs, turning around to look out to sea. Tabby and I hesitate a moment before doing the exact same. The three of us stand, scanning the endless horizons.

"I can't believe Lila's really here," I say, heart thrumming in my chest. "She's not...she's not what I thought she'd be like."

Tabby exhales slowly, pressing a hand to her forehead. "She's not what any of us thought she'd be like," she says. "I can't...This is insane. All of it. Completely insane. I've not even had time to cry."

It takes me a few seconds to acknowledge what she means, and then the fact that Darryl isn't standing with us brings a hot, suffocating feeling to the centre of my chest. Tears prick at my tired eyes, and before long, they're spilling over. It's silent for a while, save for my muffled sobs that I do my best to swallow down.

"I was a Vulture," Val suddenly says. Her voice is so quiet, the confession is almost snatched away in the wind. Almost. Tabby stiffens the tiniest bit beside me as the heaviness of the words linger in the air.

"You...Were a Vulture?" she repeats.

"I had nothing else," Val says. "My abuela was gone, so I made the Vultures take me in. They taught me to fight and fend for myself. Certainly didn't help with my addiction, but for everything else, they were there."

"You were a Vulture." Tabby seems to be stuck on repeat. I'm not quite sure how to feel myself. At first, I thought Val was nothing but trouble; a kidnapper who had snatched me from my home to stop me from watching Lila. Now the fog has somewhat lifted from my eyes, Val has been nothing but a hero, a protector.

"That's what Carlos meant? About you not being squeaky clean?" is all I say. "Because you were...one of them?"

Flashes of memory keep knocking at the steel iron door that's been fixed in my brain. My family and I never personally ran into any Vultures, but we always hid from them, just in case. Practiced holding and throwing weapons, fighting with our teeth and nails and everything we could. Everybody knew how vicious they could be.

"I'm sorry for a lot of things," Val is saying. "But I can't apologise for trying to survive. I did what I had to do. I didn't have a family, not really. It was only my abuela, and then she...she..." Val let's out a shuddering breath, hunching over the side of the boat. For a moment, I worry she might be sick, but then she straightens back up, pressing the heel of her palm into her eyes.

"My abuela was ill," Val says steadily, as if she's rehearsed this for years. "I don't want you to think she was old and frail. She was never frail. But her memory...Out of nowhere, it was like she was slipping away. Forgetting how to do the most basic of things. Got worse, and no one could do anything to help."

"I'm sorry," I whisper. "That sounds...awful."

"She died before the War," Val says. "Part of me died too. Rest of my family would never give me the time of day. The Vultures treated me like I belonged."

I can understand wanting to belong. I can understand all too well.

"Did Darryl know?" Tabby asks her quietly.

"Yes."

Tabby nods in silent understanding. "And you couldn't tell me. We've known each other since we were kids, and you couldn't tell me."

"It's not like that."

"We weren't supposed to have secrets from each other."

Val sighs, fingers tapping against the side of the boat. "Everyone has secrets, Tabs," she says wearily. "Even you. Even Darryl."

"Well, we'll never know Darryl's secrets now, will we?" Tabby snaps.

She's so angry. I'm not used to her being angry, especially with us, but fury is crackling throughout her rigid body. What can I possibly say?

"I think..." I begin hesitantly. "I think we should all try and get some sleep."

"I don't *want* to sleep," Tabby says, practically bristling at the suggestion. "I don't want to pretend like none of this has happened. Maybe it's easy for *you*, Eva, but I can't do that."

I'm already shaking my head, swatting away her harsh words. "What're you – this isn't easy, Tabby. None of this is easy! Do you not think I care about Darryl? Because I've not known him as long as you? I still *care*."

Tabby's lips are clamped shut as a wave of shame sweeps over her face. "I didn't mean anything like that," she whispers. "I shouldn't have said it. I'm just..."

Her and Val exchange a look that does not go unnoticed. "It's ok," is all I say after a moment. "It's ok, Tabby. I know."

*

None of us have the energy to speak to one another. I stake my own quiet spot towards the back of the boat, and sit alone as the stars begin to peak through the cloudy skies.

I take off my coat, spreading it next to me so it

can dry, and stretch my limbs out to lie on the rough wood. I don't plan on falling asleep, but I must, because at some point later I'm aware of my eyes flickering open. My cheek is pressed hard against my coat; I'm going to have sleep marks imprinted on my skin for definite.

I'm not sure what's woken me up. I'm cold, but I'm used to that now. When I push myself up into a sitting position, groggily blinking, I see a figure ahead outlined in the shadows, standing by the side of the boat. Val. I keep quiet.

She's holding Darryl's flask. The odd glint of silver shines through the rest of its charred surface. She keeps turning it over and over in her hands, head bowed. My heartrate quickens, yet I remain rooted to the spot.

There's a flash of light as Tabby emerges from the cabins, making her way up the stairs. Any second now, she's going to see Val. I don't call out. I keep myself hidden in the shadows, where I feel most comfortable, and just watch.

Tabby seems stuck in time for a second, but then she hesitantly approaches her friend, who's back is still turned. "Please don't drink that," Tabby whispers.

Val doesn't jump in alarm, the way I definitely would've. She just soundlessly tips the contents of the flask into the churning seas below. "Wasn't planning on it," she says.

"Really?"

"No." Val huffs a quiet laugh as she turns to face

her, pocketing the flask. "It's all I could think about. Still, I couldn't do that to you."

"It's not about me," Tabby says. "It's about you. About treating yourself fairly."

"Do I *deserve* to be treated fairly?" Val challenges. "Or am I a nasty little Vulture too?"

A heavy silence lingers. Tabby is shaking her head. "I don't care that you were a Vulture," she says quietly. "I don't. I mean, I was *shocked,* yes. But I was more shocked that you never told me."

"I'm not proud of it, Tabby," she says. "Any of it. I've been...So ashamed."

"You were desperate," Tabby says. "We've all been desperate. It's not exactly the best time for moral compasses, is it?"

Val turns her head away. When she speaks, her voice is hoarse. "You don't have to be so forgiving."

"I *love* you, Val," Tabby insists fiercely. "You're one of the strongest, bravest, most trustworthy person I know. The things Carlos said to you – they were disgusting. And I shouldn't have blamed that on him being a Vulture, I should've blamed it on him be-ing...Carlos."

"I can't bring it in me to hate him," Val confesses. "Everyone grieves differently, and he's just...He's angry. Lost. For all of Carlos' *many* faults, I know he liked Darryl." At that, Val bows her head. "I really did love him, you know."

"Oh, Val," Tabby's voice cracks. "I *know* you did. He knew, too. That's why he was so annoying about it."

Val chokes a little with laughter, but then buries her head in her hands, shoulders shuddering. Tabby simply bundles her up in her arms, holding her tight. Even from here, I can see she's crying alongside her friend. "You're one of the best people I've ever met," Tabby tells her. "I love you, ok? We'll make sure Darryl hasn't died in vain –"

"Of course he has," comes Val's muffled voice. "It's all in vain. Every last bit of it."

Tears trickle from my eyes. I can't stand to watch alone in the dark anymore. When I rush towards them, neither of them seem particularly alarmed; they just open up their arms and welcome me as I throw myself into the hug.

For a long time, the three of us just grip onto each other, and we cry. We cry for ourselves, for poor Lila, and for our brave, sarcastic, selfless friend.

Chapter 35

"Mrs. McIver and the rest of them will be expecting you," Carlos tells us as we all clamber off of the boat. "Just keep walking straight, and you'll see the junkyard soon enough."

Apparently, Carlos has docked the boat as close as he can to our destination. Now that the sun is due to set, we're able to be less conspicuous while still having an hour or so of light to guide us. We've landed on another pebbly beach; green rolling hills stretch on in the distance, as far as the eye can see. It won't be an easy hike.

"You're not coming?" I ask. In the orange sunlight, the skin around his nose looks considerably purple, and I can't help but feel a little guilty.

"No," Carlos says. "I'm sticking to the seas for now. Keeping watch. If the Creatives are going to come from Leith, they might come by boat."

Tabby tilts her head, eyes narrowed. "That's...surprisingly noble of you," she concedes. Her voice is hoarse; I heard her crying all of last night. Whenever

I open my mouth to ask how she's feeling, the words die on my tongue.

"I know where I'm useful," Carlos says, "and I know what I'm good at. Just make sure that Lila doesn't slit your throats in your sleep."

Over the course of our two-day journey, Lila has still barely said a word. Val has tried bribing, coaxing, and yelling. I opted for pleading and grovelling. No matter the tactic, Lila continues to stay silent, blue eyes downcast. In this moment, she looks more like a lost puppy than a malicious murderer.

"I think we'll be fine," is all I say. "Won't we, Lila?"

Lila glances up at me, and scowls. Now she's more of a Rottweiler than a puppy. I've no choice but to look away, chastising myself in my head. Whatever I do, I can't seem to win her approval; I can only hope nobody notices how much it's devastating me.

Val hoists our faithful rucksack over her shoulder – suitably singed in the explosion, but still miraculously in one piece. "How long a walk are we looking at?" she asks Carlos.

"Three hours if you're fast," Carlos says, "five if you're lazy."

A shadow of a smile darts across Val's face. "Safe travels then, Vulture," she says, outstretching her hand. Carlos rolls his dark eyes before begrudgingly accepting the handshake.

"And to you," he responds. Now that Val's secret is finally out in the open, some of the animosity between them seems to have shifted. For now, they can understand each other. Both reformed Vultures. Both no longer hiding from their pasts.

The moment Carlos' boat begins to pull away from the shore, we start our trek. The journey on the boat has restored some strength. I've eaten and slept well, despite everything. As long as I don't think too hard, then everything will be ok.

"Everything *will* be ok, won't it?" I ask Lila. I've quickened my stride to walk next to her. "Nothing to feel, nothing to fear, and all that?"

Lila furrows her brow in frustration. "What are you *talking* about?" she demands, voice cracking at me like a whip.

My face flushes. When I open my mouth to explain, Lila is already storming ahead. Val hurries after her, but not before shooting me her infamous glower. I watch them for a moment, completely dejected, until Tabby links her arm through mine.

Tucking a strand of hair behind my ear, I keep my eyes downcast. "I keep messing up," I say.

She shrugs in solidarity as we walk together. "We're all messing up, Eva. Nobody knows what to say to her. Or what'll get her to talk."

I squeeze at Tabby's arm, grateful that she understands. My love for Lila isn't the same as it once was. I'm not some silly, infatuated girl. Still...

"Maybe it sounds stupid, or selfish, but..." I can't hide the tremble in my voice. "Why can't she be the person I *wanted* her to be?"

Tabby stays silent for a very long time. "I'm sure

her abusers thought the exact same thing," is all she eventually says.

I inhale sharply through my nose, momentarily stunned. "I didn't mean it like –" I begin, but her words keep ringing in my ears. The Lila I thought I knew was a cruel lie, so why am I so desperately trying to cling onto her?

"I'm not saying you're anything like those Creatives," Tabby says hurriedly. "It's just – *nobody* knows the real her, do we? Not a single one of us."

I squeeze at her arm again, nodding over and over. "You're right," I say. "You're completely right."

Tabby shoots me a comforting look, clearly understanding my inner monologue. "Listen," she says. "Let's catch up with them. We can all walk together, and just...Be cool. Yeah?"

"I can be cool," I say, desperately hoping it's true. I allow Tabby to lead my onwards, so that we're eventually side by side with Lila and Val. We carry on in silence for a while, as the sun sinks behind the wispy clouds.

"Not to bring it up again," Val eventually says. "But I feel we've still not properly introduced ourselves, Lila."

"I know all your names," comes the stoic reply. Lila keeps her gaze focused ahead, her breathing shallow. Beads of sweat dot her brow. Clearly, she's not been out for many walks as of late.

"And we know a little about you," Val says. "We know that, for six years, you've been on every TV throughout the country. And ever since your show started, people have been stuck."

Lila doesn't respond, though she does dart her eyes towards Val in acknowledgement.

"So, help us out here," Val says. "Turns out, you were the damsel in distress instead of the dragon. How did that happen? Who did this to you?"

"You've asked me this already," Lila grumbles.

"And you've not answered," Val is quick to reply. "So – What do you remember? What can you tell us?"

"The War," Tabby prompts, her own breathing laboured as we walk. "Do you remember the War?"

My grip on Tabby's arm tightens, waiting for Lila's response. Both Tabby and I were children when the War broke out, but Lila and Val must have been teenagers. Will Lila have blocked everything out, like me? Or will she be able to fill in some of my blanks?

"I remember the War," Lila says. "I remember all of it. I was fifteen when it started."

I try to keep my breathing steady and quiet.

"I remember having to evacuate my childhood home," Lila continues. "I remember me and my mum sleeping on dirty mattresses in a room full of strangers, while bombs kept demolishing cities. I remember how at the start it was all supposed to be for the *better*."

Val tilts her head. *"Si,"* she agrees. "To start fresh. That's what the government said."

"To start fresh," Lila repeats. "They tried to spin it back on us. We'd gotten too greedy. We'd forgotten how to coexist. Resources were running out; people were hoarding too much wealth. *We* were the problem. So when rebels began to stand up for themselves –"

"The government got angry," I finish quietly, heart stuttering in my chest. A lingering headache prods at my temples. Push it down. "And then where did they go, those people in charge?"

"That's easy," Lila says with a humourless smile. "They waited 'til all the rebels were killed off, and then they died themselves."

"And then you came along," Val says. "The host of *The Lifetime Lila Show,* the saviour of our nation, ready to steer us lost souls back on the right path."

Lila falls silent again. For her, it seems the conversation is over. I'm not sure if Val is satisfied, but it's certainly the most Lila has ever said to us, so I consider that a victory.

Once the sun has set completely, the chill is quick to set in. Lila is wearing one of Carlos' grey jumpers over her silky dress, but her teeth still intermittently chatter. She doesn't complain; if anything, she seems grateful for the freshness of the air.

Within the hour, I can see the outline of towering scraps of metal. We're close. I've no idea what's going to happen to us now, but we're close to some kind of sanctuary, and that's all I want.

"Oh, *shit,*" Tabby breathes, releasing her hold on my arm.

It takes me a few stunned seconds to under-stand what's wrong, and then my stomach flips. The

entrance to the junkyard, once so secure and protected, has been left wide open.

Tabby begins to run, and the rest of us chase after
her. The closer we approach, the more apparent the
disaster is. Everything is eerily quiet. There's no chatter, no smoke from a camp-side fire, no Mrs. McIver
to welcome us. The place is completely deserted.

For a moment, the four of us stand in silence. Val
slowly roams her eyes around the junkyard, taking the
abandoned sight in.

"I was promised a warm welcome," Lila says blandly.
She seems unfazed at this catastrophic turn of events.
"I thought I was a celebrity."

Nobody responds. *We're completely alone,* is all I
can think, a constant siren blazing in my head.

"Son of a bitch!" Tabby suddenly explodes with
rage. *"Carlos!"*

"Hold on," Val says quietly, but with enough authority to stop most people in their tracks.

Tabby, however, is not most people. She squares up
to Val, gesturing wildly at our surroundings. "They've
all gone!" she yells. "Everyone's gone! He *must've*
known. He's double-crossed us, Val. He's left us out
here with nothing!"

"Not necessarily true," Lila pipes up. In her hands
is a half-empty, dusty bottle of wine that she's managed to find within the rubble. "If anyone's a fan of
Sauvignon."

"In recovery," Val says, "but you go right ahead."

Lila unscrews the wine, gives it a tentative sniff,

and then takes a few long, deep gulps straight from the bottle. I watch in morbid fascination as she wipes her mouth with the back of her hand in a very un-ladylike manner.

"*Nowhere* around here has any signal," Tabby says in an undertone. "It's a safe space, which makes it a deliberate dead-zone. No chance of any Creatives tracking it down."

"So we can't even *try* to get hold of somebody?" I ask, already knowing the answer. A lump of dread is lodged in my chest. "What are we going to –"

"Alright, everybody," Val says loudly. "No panicking allowed. Look around, take whatever's useful. See if there's any kind of message for us. If they've had to move on, they'll have left us something."

Tabby has sat on a rusty metal table, head in her hands. I wrap my arms around myself, rocking back and forth on the balls of my feet. Every fibre of my body is begging me not to panic.

"Listen," Val says, "I'm open to suggestions here. If anyone has something to add, let's hear it."

"What if something bad happened to them?" I find myself whispering. "Do you think the Creatives found them before we –"

"*Not* helpful, Barbie," Val says through gritted teeth. "I believe I asked for helpful suggestions from now on. Anybody else?"

There's a billowing silence, and then Lila raises her hand. "I have an idea," she says. "We could all pack it in, lie down, and die."

Another silence, broken only by Val's irritated huff. "Again. I asked for serious ideas."

"That was completely serious," Lila says. "Do you see me laughing? Look around you. This is an apocalypse. Why are people in apocalypse scenarios always so keen to keep trying? In every movie and book, there's always scrappy survivors doing their best. Why do they *bother?*"

I can feel myself frowning, but don't really want to ask what she means. Lila storms back out of the junkyard, and the rest of us have no choice but to follow her.

"Your friend had the right idea," Lila says wildly. "Darren, Darryl, whatever his name was. He had the right fucking idea just cutting his losses."

Tabby's fists clench, and I hastily hold onto her arm in case she takes another wild swing. "Darryl died trying to save you," she says, her voice merging into a growl.

Lila laughs jarringly. "You came to *kill* me, not save me. Don't pretend. And now you're all stuck with me because it turns out I wasn't the master manipulator you thought. But that's not my problem!"

Tabby bows her head, unable to disagree. I also cast my eyes downwards, shame heating my face.

"Alright, then," Val says bitingly. "By all means, stay here and wait for those men to find and kill you. Jeopardise all of us who worked so hard. The only reason you're finally free from them is because of us. You're only proving to me that you're the selfish bitch we all thought you would be."

"Don't you think I know that?" Lila explodes. "I *loved* Jamie! I loved him with everything I had, and I left him. I left him to save myself, when he was better than all of us. And what can I show for it? What the fuck can I show for it?"

Lila collapses to her knees, hands in her hair as she weeps. Any stoic façade from before is long gone. She just cries and cries, gripping onto her head, chanting nonsensical phrases to herself.

"Lila?" I whisper, in an attempt to appease her.

She doesn't respond, though her lips keep moving soundlessly as she rocks back and forth. And then, the foreboding gleam of headlights in the distance, getting closer and closer. The sound of a van.

Tabby's hand finds mine. We grip onto each other as the headlights approach. Too late to run. The Creatives have found us.

Chapter 36

BEFORE, PART THREE: LILA

Tap precisely six times on a wooden surface top – and it has to be *real* wood, you can't jinx it – and you're guaranteed to have a safe day without you, or anybody you care about, suffering.

Luckily, Lila's bathroom has a sturdy wooden cabinet made from oak. When the thought pops into her head that today is definitely the day she will die, she raps her knuckles against the cabinet hard enough to burrow splinters into her skin. Once satisfied, she stares in the mirror and smears concealer over the dark bags that protrude under her blue eyes. She's been doing this ritual for the past ten years, so she doesn't see the point in stopping now, even though it always leaves a sour taste in her mouth and a useless buzz in her brain.

A cold glass of water, and she takes her medication. It's not working the way it used to. Maybe because there's a severe shortage of pharmaceuticals thanks to this pesky War that's going around. She could be taking placebos. In fact, the more she thinks about it, she's definitely taking placebos. Possibly poisonous placebos.

Lila chucks the last bottle of her little white pills down the toilet, and flushes.

By the time her makeup is finished and she clomps her way downstairs, her mother is seated at her usual spot on the sofa, listening to one of her old records that creaks as it spins. Mozart fills the squat household. Lila and her mother were relocated to this dead-end village halfway through the War when their actual flat back in Canterbury was blown up. Not only that, they were moved alongside a bunch of other displaced strangers. Never mind that they're now sharing a home with these random people; whatever her mother wants to listen to, that's what they're going to have to listen to.

"God, Mum," Lila says, barely containing her annoyance as she shrugs on her oversized fleece. "Can we not listen to someone who got their start after the twentieth century? For a change."

Her mother ignores her, as per usual. Lila doesn't take it personally, seeing as her own brain feels broken too; long before the War, but broken nonetheless. She makes her way to the kitchen, thinking she'll down a quick cup of coffee for courage. "I have to go to the market," she announces to the household. "We need food."

Lila is the only one who goes to the market, though calling it a market is bit of a stretch. It's a rickety row of tables at the end of the street, where scroungers have managed to find scraps that are decent enough to sell. It's shit, but there's nothing else, unless she walks for miles to find an abandoned supermarket somewhere.

Besides. There's a young man at the market who sells apples, and he's nice to look at it.

The record scratches and stops spinning. Silence is worse, in hindsight. "I'll be back soon," she says to the house, voice sounding ominously loud. Her mother blinks slowly, turning her head towards her.

"Lila," she says, as if she's only just recognised her. "Taken your medicine?"

"Yes," Lila lies. "Don't worry about me, Mum. I really do think I'm fine now."

Outside, the air is cold with the familiar chill of autumn. The spindly tree that stands alone right outside her front door sheds its last orange leaf. For some reason, this almost makes tears prick Lila's eyes.

There's two other people at the market, heads bowed as they rummage for whatever change they have. Lila takes her time walking past the tables. The young man who sells the apples is right at the end, red hair vibrantly clashing with his yellow scarf, a smattering of freckles dusting his nose. He sneaks glances at her. She pretends not to notice.

"You come here every other day," the man says as she nears his table, and the skin around his green eyes crinkles as he grins.

"I don't want to starve," Lila replies blandly, refusing to get sucked in.

"Ah, sure," he says with a nod. "That's absolutely fair enough. Well, please, take a good look at all this wonderful, home-grown produce."

"It's not home-grown," Lila says. "Come on. You find them by rooting through bins."

"Absolutely *not*. I grow them myself," he insists. "Swear to God. We have apple trees, orange trees, lemon trees –"

"Yeah, yeah," Lila says, dropping the meagre change she has on top of the table. "Whatever you say. Five red apples, then."

After taking her money, the man outstretches his hand for her to shake. "James Murray. My pa calls me Jamie, or he would, if he hadn't gone off to fight in a War."

Lila stares at his hand as various thoughts flash up in her head. He's been handling change from who knows how many customers. There's a cut on his hand, faint and healing, but a cut nonetheless. Could lead to contamination, which could lead to sepsis, which could lead to –

Suddenly, the world seems a little too bright, and she swallows. "Lila," is all she says. "I'm Lila."

Jamie's hand is still outstretched.

"I'm not going to shake your hand," she tells him.

And then: "Sorry. God, sorry. That must've sounded so rude. I just don't like shaking hands."

"It's a weird custom, you're right enough," he says, still with that lovely smile as his arm falls back to his side. "Hello, Lila. It's a pleasure to properly meet you."

Jamie gives her the brown paper bag of apples. She walks away without looking back. When she takes a look inside, she realises he's given her one extra.

*

"I'm a poet," Jamie tells her. It's wintertime, when the darkness rolls in by the late afternoon and the cold air bites and stings. The tip of Jamie's nose almost matches the brightness of his red hair.

Lila does her best not to laugh in his face. "No way," she says. "Really? I didn't think anyone wrote *poetry* anymore."

"It's a dying art," Jamie says. They both sit on his stall table, sipping hot chocolates that they bought from Lilly's stall; a nice old lady who, while definitely overcharging, *does* make good drinks. "Nobody has time for it. In fairness, sometimes thinking of rhymes can take all bloody night."

"Lots of poems from wartimes, though," Lila says. *"Dulce et decorum est."*

Jamie's eyes widen in surprise. *"Pro patria mori,"* he finishes. "I hope you don't expect me to be anywhere near as good as Wilfred Owen."

In a way, it doesn't surprise Lila that Jamie writes

poetry. He's an old soul; his favourite singer is Bobby Darin, who he plays on his record player every evening. He prefers a glass of whisky – tiny splash of water, certainly not with ice – instead of pints. He refuses to partake in any gossip, insisting it's better to be respectful to others.

Lila knows all of this because she can't seem to keep herself away from the market. She tells herself it's *not* because of Jamie. Home – if she can even call it that – has become even more stifling than usual. Her mother has become very close with the new man who's just been displaced from Liverpool, and the two of them spend every evening cosied up on the sofa.

So now, every time she goes to the market, Jamie writes Lila a small poem. They *could* be romantic, if read a certain way. At first, she thought it was weird, possibly a reason to be alarmed, because who does that? But they're sweet, and *he's* sweet, and in this strange, scary world, Lila craves sweetness. She doesn't allow him to get too close, because once he is, she knows he will never write for her again. So she continues to play it cool, and every time she collects her apples there's a new handwritten poem in her bag.

*

Four months later, when Jamie asks her on a date, she laughs, because she assumes he's joking.

"There's nowhere to *go*," she tells him, once she realises he's actually serious.

"There's plenty," he says. "You just need to know where to look."

In the good old days – around five years ago – there were restaurants. Bars. Public parks. Now there's rubble. "Jamie," Lila says, "you're a nice guy. But we can't go on a date."

"Why not?" he asks, sounding genuinely surprised. "You think I'm nice, I think you're nice. Downright lovely, in fact. Prettiest blue eyes I've ever seen."

"You barely know me," she says, even though that's technically not true. She likes to think she knows him well, at least. "You probably write mushy poems for every girl that comes here, hoping to catch at least one of them."

Jamie's eyes widen and he stares at her, looking so horrified that she almost feels guilty. Almost. "*Lila*," he admonishes. "Do you really believe that?"

"Maybe," she says, and then can't help but blurt, "I just don't understand why you'd want to."

"Because I like you," he says immediately, like it's the easiest thing for him. "You're funny. You're quick. Smart. I like the way you roll your eyes when it's impossible for you to hide your annoyance – like right now. You always buy my apples even though I'm pretty sure you don't even like them."

"I don't *mind* them," she says, "but I do prefer peaches."

"I work with what I have," he says morosely. "I agree entirely! Peaches are the superior fruit, but we've only got the apple and orange and lemon –"

"I'll go on a date with you," Lila interrupts, because if she doesn't, she's going to kiss him.

Jamie's green eyes widen, and when he shoots her *that* smile, she doesn't know how to tell him about who she is, because then he might go. Lila doesn't think she could let him go from her life now.

"But it's just – I have a thing," she suddenly blurts, while her brain screams *shut up shut up shut* up on a constant loop. "There's something I've not told you, something about me."

Jamie takes a bite out of one of his red apples as if he doesn't have a care in the world. "Uh-huh," he says.

"I..." The words catch in her throat. "I'm not great at the moment. I don't have any medicine for it left, and I've just had it so long, I don't see any way out of it. It's – It's me, but it's *not* me, it's..."

Jamie, to his credit, is not backing away in alarm. He only looks at her, nodding, his smile gentle.

"I have OCD," Lila says, and it's like the rock that's been pressing on her chest lightens a tiny bit. She finds herself smiling. "Obsessive Compulsive Disorder. That's what...Yeah, that's what I have."

There's a pause, and then Jamie says, "Yeah. Don't take this the wrong way, love, but I kind of guessed that months ago."

For a moment, Lila is floored. Years of her life have been spent masking her intrusive thoughts, hiding her compulsions and rituals. Just how closely has Jamie been paying attention? "Oh," is all she says. "Well, it's not the cutesy, commercialised version where I like things colour-coordinated. That's not what OCD is. I mean, maybe some people who have it do that, and that's fine, but I'm talking more – You don't mind?"

"Mind?" he echoes incredulously. "Why the hell would I mind? Just let me know whenever you need anything, or what I can do to make things easier. So. I'll come round to your house tomorrow afternoon? How does four sound?"

Lila blinks, trying to process what exactly is happening, but then squares her shoulders. "If you're late I'll think that you've died," she says, waiting for him to finally be scared away.

Jamie only shrugs. "I won't be late. I won't be early. I'll be right on time for you."

"Ok, then," Lila says, her voice cracking the slightest bit. "In that case, I can't wait."

*

"It's like poison in my brain," Lila tells him one night in his bed, when she feels she finally has the courage. "I don't know if I'll ever find the right antidote."

"Maybe you don't need to think of it that way," Jamie says. "Maybe it's not a question of a miracle cure. Maybe it's a question of learning and adjusting alongside it. Asking for help, and not hiding."

There's a silence, where she has to look away from him for a moment. "Nobody's ever said that to me before," she admits softly.

*

"I really do love you, you know," Lila tells him two years later. It's become easier over time to let herself say it. At first, the thought terrified her. Loving someone meant to inevitably lose them. All her life, Lila feels as though she's been fearing the worst. When the worst happened, and the world fell around her, it was almost a relief. Almost vindication. But now the War, for all the good it did, is over. Through it all, they have survived, and they are here. Together.

Jamie shields his eyes from the sun, shooting her that warm smile she loves so much. "I should hope so," he says.

Seated underneath a pink blossom tree, in the field where Jamie took her on their first date, Lila lets out a long breath. She was never really one to stop and smell the flowers, but being with Jamie makes her notice the little, beautiful things. She doesn't want to take the fact they're being dusted with little pink petals for granted, when not so long ago this would have been considered a miracle. It seems that even in the darkest of atrocities, flowers find their way to bloom. Maybe she can too.

"Feels nice," she says, "to not worry about anyone else being carted off to war, or when the next bomb will drop. Let's continue to be grateful, alright?"

Jamie scoots closer to her, retreating underneath

the shade of the tree. "Absolutely," he agrees. "Shall we shake on it?"

It's not gone unnoticed that Lila's obsessions and compulsions also seem to have stilled, at least for the moment. They ebb and flow, of course, never the linear pathway that she would like. Still, Lila hasn't worried about germs or illness for a solid six months, and certainly not from Jamie, so she laughs as they shake hands like little kids making a pact.

Jamie's gaze turns a little more serious. He doesn't let go of her hand. "Lila," he says. She loves the way he says her name, lyrical on his tongue. "I wrote you another poem."

"I can't wait to hear it," she says, only slightly teasing. A light breeze blows at her dark hair as she leans in closer to him.

"It's more something I'd like you to read," Jamie says. "It's short, and in very small writing, but I'd still like you to try and read it."

"Ok," she says, already distracted as she kisses at his irresistible, freckled cheek. "Then let me read it."

Jamie takes her by the shoulders and moves her back so they can look at each other again. He's usually so confident, so sure of himself, but right now he looks nervous. "Close your eyes," he tells her. "And hold out your hands."

Lila frowns, but does as he says. She feels something small and box-shaped in her open palms, and her eyelids spring open in surprise. A grey, suede, unmistakably ring-sized box. "Jamie," she says uselessly.

"Lila."

"This isn't a poem."

Jamie gently puts his hands over hers, and they open the box together. Inside is a simple silver band, gleaming in the sunlight. With trembling fingers, Lila holds it up, and sees the flowing words of Jamie's poem engraved onto the ring itself. "Fucking hell," she croaks.

Jamie is watching her anxiously. "It's too much," he says. "Isn't it? Like, absolutely overkill. People say there's no time for romance in this world anymore, but I just *can't* agree, because without love, or hope, then – then what do we do? So I thought, what's the best way to propose to the person I love the absolute most, and I went to Georgie – you know, the lady who deals in all the silverware and what have you –"

"This is a proposal," Lila states obviously, just to make sure. "You're proposing to me."

Jamie's face is getting redder by the second, and he can't even blame the sun, considering he's sitting in the shade. "I'm trying to, yes."

"Why would you do that?"

"Why would I...Did you not just hear what I said, about you being the person I love the absolute most?"

Lila's gaze flicks from the ring to Jamie, her heart thumping painfully in her chest. Inscribed along the band are the words *Yours completely, as long as you'll have me. All my love, forever. Jamie.*

"But... how do we start?" Lila whispers. "How do we repair everything, fix everything?"

Jamie cups her face, hands warm and soft against her skin. "How about we start with just us?"

After he's slipped the ring on her finger, they press their foreheads together, as if to imprint this memory into the universe forever. Pink blossoms twirl gently around them in the spring breeze, and in this moment, it really could just be Lila and Jamie left in the world, and she wouldn't mind at all.

*

Progress is not linear, Lila tries to remind herself, whenever she wakes from a nightmare convinced she is going to harm Jamie, or when she finds herself scrubbing her hands twenty times in one afternoon.

Jamie has noticed, because he always does. Living together makes it impossible to hide. At first, he tries to help her alone, but eventually he asks the question she doesn't want to hear. "We can try and find you medication again," he says. "It's out there. People deal in medicine."

"I'm not taking antidepressants from some back-alley bin," Lila tells him. "It's fine. I'm fine. No miracle cure, remember? I can sort it myself."

Except Jamie doesn't listen to her, and one night he comes home with a busted nose and bruised cheek-bone, a torn package in his hands.

"What have you *done*?" she asks him in horror, whilst knowing full well.

"They wanted a load of money that I didn't have,"

Jamie says, with a hint of a smile. "So I snatched them. Got a little roughed up, but there's plenty in there, a good six months' worth."

She doesn't respond, because she can't find the words. Rage simmers in her chest, which he is quick to pick up on.

"I'm here for you, Lila," Jamie says quietly. "If you're lost, I'll find you and bring you home. Just let me find you."

"I'm not a child."

"I never said you were. But you're not *well*, love. It's not your fault, it's not any kind of failure. You don't have to struggle alone. I'm your husband, through sickness and in health, right?"

"You're infuriating," the words come out of her mouth before she can stop them. "Always tiptoeing around me, making out I'm completely crazy. I never asked you to go out and get me these random pills, that was your choice."

"They're not random pills. They're the exact ones you used to take for your OCD," Jamie says firmly. "I triple-checked, Lila. I wouldn't give you anything dangerous."

It's all well and good him saying that, but she can't trust him. Even though this is *Jamie*, the person she loves most in this wretched world, she cannot trust him. As soon as this thought crosses her mind, it's as though a knife has been twisted in her stomach.

"I don't want them," is all she says. "And you shouldn't have gone behind my back."

Right on cue, the Bobby Darrin record that Jamie has been spinning stops playing. Silence fills the bedroom as they look at each other; Jamie sitting on the bed, Lila standing in the doorway.

Jamie is left alone to sort out his bloody nose, and without so much as a goodbye, Lila leaves their small house. The winter air immediately sets itself into her bones – she didn't bother grabbing a jacket – as she sets off walking, not even caring where she's going. All she wants is a moment's peace.

Hot tears stream down her cheeks. She scrubs them away with the same ferocity that she wishes she could do to her own brain, weaving through alleyways, her boots on the cobbled streets the only sound.

Lila doesn't think she can do this anymore. Any of this. She's simply too tired.

As soon as the thought enters her head, she spots a tall silhouette at the end of the alleyway, shrouded in darkness. Lila freezes in her tracks. Maybe she should be afraid, but for a moment, all she can feel is relief.

"Are you Death?" she croaks, already feeling silly for even suggesting it.

The figure walks towards her, coming into view. A tall, older man with a neatly trimmed black beard, speckled with grey. "No," he tells her. His voice is rich and deep and for a moment, it's like being wrapped up in a protective blanket. "Not at all."

Lila's mouth trembles. "Who are you, then?" she asks. It's difficult to explain, but it's as though this man has somehow been waiting for her.

The man steps closer. Vultures used to roam alleyways in the height of the War, but this man doesn't look like a Vulture.

He's dressed in a smart black suit, with a deep maroon waistcoat. Completely out of place nowadays; it's as though he's stepped out of a classic novel.

"A better question is, who are *you?*" he says, a twinkle in his eye. "Out here in the cold, alone. Have you lost your way?"

"Everybody's lost their way," Lila says with a hint of a smile. She doesn't feel threatened. For a moment, her panicked brain has stilled in the presence of this stranger.

The man nods his head sombrely in complete understanding. "Everybody *has* lost their way," he agrees. "So much suffering in the world. So much pain. The War was supposed to help all of that, but it just made it worse."

"Exactly," Lila breathes. "Yes. That's exactly it."

"What we really need is for somebody to guide us," the man says. "For somebody to encourage. To lift the people up again. To protect them from all of this pain."

His words strike at her heart. For a moment, she feels faint. "Is...Is that even possible?" she asks, voice catching. "For it all to go away?"

He puts a hand to his heart as he looks at her, seemingly straight into her soul. "You're in such pain," he says sympathetically. "I can see it. I can feel it. We can do something about that together, my sweet girl."

290 ~ EMILY RENNIE

Once again, tears trickle from Lila's blue eyes. "I'm so scared," she whispers. Why she's saying all this to a complete stranger, she has no idea, but she can't stop herself. "God, I'm so scared. I'm so tired."

"I know," he says, kindly outstretching a hand to her. "I can make that go away for you. I can save you from all those worries in your head. What's your name?"

"Lila."

"Lila," he echoes. He says her name in complete admiration, that she can't help but feel proud. "Beautiful. *Beautiful*, Lila. You're perfect, just what we've been looking for. Let's go for a walk, shall we? Soon there'll be nothing to fear at all, I promise you."

*

"If you're lost, I'll bring you home," Jamie had once said to her. "Just let me find you."

Find me, Lila tries to say, but her world has gone dark, and the only words that can come out of her mouth are the carefully scripted ones that these men drill into her.

Jamie. Find me.

Chapter 37

A black jeep screeches into view, braking haphazardly in front of us. I turn away, grimacing, raising a hand to shield my eyes from the harsh headlights. In my sock, the flip-up knife seems to singe my skin; out of the corner of my eye, I know Val's revolver is already cocked. Whatever happens, these Creatives will not take us without a fight.

The driver's door swings open. I clench and unclench my spare hand, my palm damp with sweat. Undoubtedly, their priority will be snatching Lila, so I step in front of her so she's shielded from view. If they want Lila, they'll have to get through me first.

A woman dressed in a red jumpsuit and combat boots steps out of the jeep; dark skin, curly hair that frames her head like a halo, a gun also in hand. Her eyes scan us, one by one, until her gaze falls on Tabby and she smiles.

"Auntie Celia?" Tabby breathes, dumbfounded.

The woman raises her brown eyes to the heavens with a grateful sigh. "Tabby. Thank *God*."

Tabby runs to her, leaping into her arms with an overjoyed squeal. "Auntie Celia!"

My knees buckle. Two seconds ago, I was sure we were dying. Could it be that someone has actually come to save us? Not just anybody, but Tabby's beloved aunt? "Hello," I find myself croaking, feeling the need to introduce myself before I collapse from relief. "I'm Eva."

Celia continues to hold Tabby to close to her as she shoots me a warm smile. I immediately feel safe in her presence. "Yes, Eva," she says. "Of course. I've been well briefed on you."

Well briefed by Tabby? This sends a little thrill down my spine. Tabby mentioning me to her aunt must mean she really *does* like me.

"How did you –" Tabby begins as she pulls away, but then her voice cracks. "How did you find us? Did you know we were coming? Where's everybody else?"

Unfortunately, Celia has noticed Lila, who is still rooted to the spot on the ground. There's a sharp inhale of breath, and then a *click* as Celia cocks her revolver. Her gun focuses on Lila's forehead. "Would somebody like to explain to me what the hell is going on?" she says calmly.

Through blood-shot eyes, Lila stares down the barrel of the gun, unflinching and unafraid.

"Don't shoot!" I beg. "You can't shoot her. She's done nothing wrong."

The gun doesn't waver. "Nothing wrong? A television showed up at my house one day with nothing but *her* talking to me, and I forgot everything I knew. Nothing *wrong?"*

Tabby spreads out her palms. "Aunt Celia," she says firmly. "Trust me. Trust Eva. We can explain everything, but please, put your gun away."

Celia shoots me and Lila a look so scrutinising, it's like I'm under an interrogation lamp. For a moment, I'm worried she'll go ahead and pull the trigger, but then she slowly lowers her revolver. "Where's the Cockney boy?" she asks.

There's a tense silence, which is abruptly broken by Val of all people bursting into hysterical tears. It's such a bizarre sight that we all gawp at her in shock. I know I've seen her cry, but never like *this*.

"Um..." Tabby begins uncertainly. She clears her throat as her eyes flicker from Val. "Darryl didn't...Darryl didn't make it back, Auntie."

Celia breathes out slowly in understanding, and reaches a hand out to Val, who recoils from the touch.

"I'm fine," Val says, while clearly being anything but fine. She scrubs at her face, as if her tears have somehow humiliated her. "I'm – sorry. Sorry, Celia. I'm just – very relieved to see you."

"Oh, sweetheart, it's ok," Celia whispers, holding out her arms. "I'm so sorry. He really was a good man."

Val hesitates a moment, but then allows herself to be hugged, even though her face twists in discomfort.

"Cry all you like," Celia tells her. "Nobody expects you to be made of stone."

"It's much easier to be made of stone," Val says

through her hiccups, pulling away. "God, Celia – how *did* you find us? There's not supposed to be any signal out here."

"There isn't," Celia says. "But you're talking to a pro. Now, get in the jeep, I'll explain everything on the way." She throws Lila a distrustful glare. "You. You stay in the sight of my rear-view mirror, but if you so much as try *anything* –"

Lila still doesn't move from her spot. "If you're so worried," she says in an undertone, "then leave me here."

Celia is clearly tempted, but after receiving a firm stare from Tabby, she sighs. "That won't be necessary," she says. "If my niece says you can be trusted, then I suppose you can be trusted. We'll just need to give everybody a warning about our special passenger on the way."

"Where are we going?" Tabby asks. The way she looks at Celia is nothing short of adoration, and I don't blame her. Without a doubt, her aunt is a force to be reckoned with, and I'm so grateful for her arrival that I could weep.

Celia cups Tabby's cheek, giving it a gentle squeeze. "Home," she says.

*

Even though the car journey is long, it still somehow passes me by in a blur. Tabby sits in the front seat, while I squeeze in the back with the others. Val is in the middle, between me and Lila, which is probably for the best.

We fill Celia in on everything that's happened. I do most of the talking. When it gets towards the end, and I think of the explosion, my words trail off and Tabby has to continue on my behalf.

According to Celia, the television signal is still completely disrupted. She passes Tabby her mobile (after going into a load of tech talk about establishing a signal through to Mrs. McIver), telling her to send a message through so that everyone is suitably warned of our arrival.

"Whatever you did, it worked," Celia tells us. "The only thing on the television is a bunch of squiggly colours. We've turned all the radios off, just in case Creatives try to reach people through there."

"It's not going to last forever," Tabby admits. "I did what I could, with what I had. But those men don't have Lila anymore. That's got to count for *something*."

Lila has resumed her silence; she just stares out of the window, even though it's pitch black outside. At Tabby's words, she tilts her head the slightest bit. It's impossible to tell what she's thinking.

"It's a victory," Celia says. "A bloody massive one. Bask in your success for a moment, all of you."

Val mimes toasting a glass. "*Salud*," she says, before glancing at me. "Coca Cola only, of course."

I hit her arm, even though it *is* nice to have her teasing me. It's almost like her breakdown never happened, which I'm sure is just the way she wants it.

"How did you find us, Celia?" I say. "Carlos left us in a total dead-zone! For no reason!"

"That's Carlos for you," Celia concedes. "Can't expect a leopard to change its spots. Or a Vulture to change its feathers, I suppose."

"Good one," Val says. I strain to hear a hint of sarcasm, but she sounds sincere.

"Thank you," Celia wrenches the wheel, taking a sharp left. I narrowly avoid whacking my head against the window. "I managed to track your movements on the boat, through Tabby's phone."

Tabby folds her arms with a huff. "My phone's supposed to be impenetrable."

"Sure," Celia says in a smug tone. "Except like I said, you're talking to the pro. I taught you everything you know, babe."

Tabby scoffs, but then nods her head in acknowledgement. "Fair," she says. "Fair enough. As long as you show me how you did it later."

"Done," Celia says. "Anyway, I'd always planned to meet you on the other end of your journey. When I saw which way Carlos was heading, I thought something was up. What did he tell you?"

"That he was taking us back to the junkyard," Val says. "And that everyone was waiting for us. You can imagine we were a little alarmed when we found the place empty."

"Bastard," I say, with real scorn. "I hope he hits a bunch of rocks."

Celia laughs. "Carlos is a slippery one," she says.

"Can never pin him down. He'll show up when you least want him, and then disappear when you actually do. He'll be around, I'm sure, ready to grovel his way back in."

He'll have a hard job, if I have any say in the matter. I glance at Val to see if she's sporting a similar scowl, but she's tilted her head back, eyes closed. I suppose this is the exact behaviour she expected from Carlos.

"You said we were going home," Tabby says. "What does that mean? To Brixton?"

"Not quite," Celia says. "But home is where family is, right? And everybody is there. Mrs. McIver, Jasper –"

"*Jasper*?" Tabby squeals again, practically leaping out of her seat. "Jasper's here?"

Celia laughs, eyes flicking up to look at me in the rear-view mirror. "Tabby's cousin," she says, even though there's no need. "He's been searching for trapped survivors across the North. He finally made it home."

"And where are you calling home?" Val asks. "Another junkyard?"

The jeep barrels over a bump in the road, and I cling to the seat in front of me with a muffled yelp. Celia makes Darryl's driving look like a professional taxi service.

"I think we can do a little better than a junkyard, after all your hard work," Celia says with a smile. "Don't you?"

Chapter 38

We arrive at an actual house. Not a cramped bunk on a boat, or an abandoned bus, or a draughty old classroom. A sturdy, two-floored house, with a fire-place already crackling golden flames in the living room. I walk around, my fingers brushing against the red sofas, the heavy velvet curtains pulled across the windows, the frayed mismatched cushions, just in case I'm hallucinating all this comfort.

"How did you find this place, Aunt Celia?" Tabby breathes as her eyes roam the cosy room. "It's like the War never happened to it."

"Darryl actually clued us in on this area, months ago," Celia says with a tiny smile. "He'd been driving around and saw it could be a safe spot to hunker down in. It didn't look like this when we found it, believe me. But all of us wanted you to have somewhere nice to come back to."

Knowing this makes me feel even closer to Darryl. He looked out for us the entire way through. When we eventually see him, we can thank him properly.

Before I can collapse onto the sofa, Mrs. McIver

enters through a door that looks like it leads to a kitchen. I'm swept up in a hug within seconds and I find myself clinging to her as if she's a long lost relative, tears pricking my eyes. She hugs each of us in turn; when she reaches Val, she clasps both her hands in silent sorrow.

"You did us all proud," Mrs. McIver tells her. "You all did. Not that I had any doubt."

"Darryl's the reason we're here, really," Val says with a ghost of a smile. "I want you to know that. We couldn't have done it without him."

Mrs. McIver gives Val's hands a squeeze, her pale eyes glistening. "Everyone will know it," she assures her. "For years and years to come, people will know it."

Lila lingers in the doorframe, lost and uncertain. When she meets Mrs. McIver's eyes, the older woman flinches, abruptly turning her head away. Without a word, Lila leaves. We hear her footsteps go up the creaky stairs.

Mrs. McIver shudders. "I don't trust that woman in this house," she mutters. "No matter what you say."

"She's harmless, Mrs. McIver," Tabby says. "I'm ninety-nine percent sure. We've been travelling with her for days now, and she's not some criminal mastermind. She's a victim of the War, just like all of us."

My eyes dart to the ceiling, wondering what Lila is doing up there. Her anguished wailing back at the junkyard plays on a loop in my mind. "Tabby's right," I say. "She's not who any of us thought she was."

Behind me, Celia enters the living room, arms

folded. "Lila's gone straight to bed," she says, forehead creased. "Do we bring her down and interrogate her?"

Val rubs her forehead with an aggrieved sigh. "I've tried," she says. "We've all tried. Tonight was the most she's ever said to us, but still nothing about how all of this actually *happened.*"

"Maybe she needs some time to remember it all," I say, with a twinge of discomfort. "You know. Like I did."

Mrs. McIver turns away with a sigh, and picks up a folded pile of tartan pyjamas from the floral-patterned sofa. "I made these for you all," she says, and then falters. "You might think it's silly, but I had to keep my hands busy. So – there's a pair for..."

Unable to finish her sentence, Mrs. McIver hands the pyjamas to Val, who huffs a small laugh. "No problem," she says. "I'll wear Darryl's, and Lila can have mine."

"They'll be too big for you," Mrs. McIver frets. "I can take them in, but it'll take me a few days, and I wanted you to –"

Val cuts her off with a simple look. "They're great," she says sincerely. "Thank you."

There's so many things I want to do. Now that we're finally in a safe spot, the extent of my injuries are clamouring for attention, all the way from my throbbing cheek to my battered feet.

The house has two functioning bathrooms, so I don't feel guilty about hogging one of the showers. I stand under the scalding water, lathering my hair in lavender-scented shampoo and scrubbing my whole body until there's not a trace of grime left. I brush my teeth until my entire mouth is tingling and stinging, being as mindful as I can of my healing cheek. I take two of the painkillers that have been left for me by the sink, and the soft pyjamas from Mrs. McIver feel like a hug when I put them on.

Once I've made my way back to the living room, I find Val sitting in the armchair, adorned in her own oversized tartan pyjamas. Her long, dark hair is also freshly washed, and is still damp as it pools over her shoulders. She looks softer, younger.

There's an old-fashioned record player in the corner of the room that I instantly gravitate towards, flicking through the albums. To my delight, there's a Bobby Darrin one. I put it on, despite Val's irritated groan, hoping that Lila is able to hear it from upstairs.

"I know we can't stay here forever," I say, collapsing on the sofa, as Bobby croons quietly in the background. "I know Creatives will be looking for us. But this is just *really* lovely."

Val hums in agreement, before shifting in the armchair with a wince. I notice an icepack resting against her upper-thigh. "Hip," she says at my questioning glance. "Keeps clicking."

I hiss through my teeth in sympathy. "I'm sorry."

"Don't be," Val says. "I'm the one who's fucked it."

Suddenly, the kitchen door swings open; Tabby comes bounding through, also adorned in the home-made pyjamas. She yanks a young man into the room with her. "Eva! Meet my cousin, Jasper!" She beams, pushing the aforementioned man forward.

Jasper gives us a sheepish wave. He's so much taller than Tabby; side by side, they look like a comedy act. His black hair is shaved at the sides, but delightfully curly on top, and his dark skin has smatterings of white pigmentation across his forehead and nose. "Hi," he says. "Anyone want a hot chocolate?"

"Yes," is my immediate reply, and then I remember my manners. "Yes please, Jasper. I'm...I'm Eva, by the way."

"Figured as much." He holds his palm out for a high-five. I tentatively slap it. "Be good to Tabs, yeah? Or I'll have to mess you up."

Tabby rolls her eyes, hissing at her cousin to shut up. The idea of this skinny man beating me in a fight is quite funny, but I nod fiercely anyway. "You have my word," I say.

"Excellent." Jasper's smile holds the same genuineness as the rest of his family. I immediately like him. "Not directing this question at you, Val – no offence – but would anyone like some Baileys in their hot chocolate?"

Val scoffs with a sarcastic thumbs-up. Jasper's expression suddenly turns serious.

"I really am so bloody sorry about Darryl," he says. "I know I only met him a few times, but – I liked him. A lot. All of this, it's so shit. It's *so* shit."

"Yeah," Val says quietly. "I know. Thanks, Jasper."

"If there's anything at all that I can do –"

"You're doing it already," Val says, "by making that hot chocolate."

Jasper nods hastily, and dives back into the kitchen. A moment later, his head pops around the door. "So – was that a yes to Baileys? Anyone? I really want to open this bottle of Baileys."

I say yes without even knowing what Baileys is, and pray it won't betray me the way rum did. Tabby says she'll have some too, and Jasper looks thrilled as he closes the kitchen door behind him.

"Good luck," Val says, a little smugly.

"Baileys is *nice,*" Tabby insists at my look of sudden alarm. "You'll barely taste it in the drink, anyway. Promise."

"This is Jasper we're talking about," Val says. "She'll taste it."

Before I can make a run for the kitchen to stop Jasper from completely ruining my hot chocolate, there's a sudden creak. I turn my head to find Lila in the doorway, in her tartan pyjamas like the rest of us. There's silence as she takes us in, and then glances down at her clothes.

"Hi, Lila," I say, willing my voice not to squeak. It is *so* weird seeing her like this, bare-faced and in casual-wear. She suddenly looks so young. "How...How are you?"

"God," Lila eventually says, with another look at us. "We look like a really shit girl band."

I'm so taken aback, that I laugh. Tabby does too. Even Val cracks a small smile. Lila hesitates for a moment, before stepping into the living room. Her own mouth quirks the tiniest bit, and then I see her eyes widen a fraction as she takes in the spinning record player.

"I put it on for you," I say, shooting her a timid smile.

Lila walks over to the record player, and soundlessly lifts the needle. Bobby Darrin abruptly stops singing *Dream Lover.* "I'd rather not listen to that, thanks," she says, voice quiet.

I falter. "Oh, ok. Well, there might also be an Elvis one, if you'd prefer –"

"I can't fucking stand Elvis," Lila says matter-of-factly, as she turns around. She takes a moment to compose herself, and then squares her shoulders. "I just wanted to say thank you," she says. "Thank you for getting me out of that...that place. You didn't have to do that."

"Yes, we did," Val says simply. She gestures towards the sofa. "You can sit down, you know."

Lila shakes her head, and remains poised like a startled bird ready to fly away at a moment's notice. "I know you're expecting answers from me," she says. "There's a lot I want to know, too."

"I'm sure there is," Tabby says gently. "And whatever you need, we want you to know that you can come to us. We're not your captors, ok? We're...I mean, we can be your friends, if you want us to be."

Intertwining Tabby's fingers in mine, I nod in agreement. "She means it, Lila," I tell her. "When I was lost, Tabby and Val proved themselves to be amazing friends. Darryl, too. I really...Without them, I don't know what I would've done."

At that, Tabby gives my hand a squeeze, shooting me a warm smile that makes my stomach flip. I can't resist lifting her hand to press it against my lips.

Lila watches us in silence, and then bows her head. "I'm sorry for everything I said about your friend," she says quietly.

With that, she leaves the room.

*

When I crawl into bed after two mugs of (thankfully delicious) hot chocolate I'm so grateful I could weep. I wrap myself in the blue blanket – slightly scratchy, yet still the softest thing I've felt in a while – and bury my face in the pillow.

I'm sharing a room with Tabby, which is exciting. The fact I'll be able to be so close to her, just the two of us, is something I don't want to take for granted.

"This is amazing," I slur to her. "You have to lie down with me."

Tabby stays standing, and then tentatively brushes her hand across my forehead. I'm momentarily transported back to being a child, when Mum would tuck me and Ali up in our beds, stroking our hair.

My eyelids flicker shut and I sigh in contentment. "C'mon," I say. "Let's sleep."

"I need to talk to my aunt," Tabby says quietly. "I won't be long."

With great effort, I force my eyes open. "You don't need to go right *now*." I reach out my hand. "Stay with me. Please?"

"I can't, Eva," Tabby says. "I'm sorry, but I really need to...I really need to talk to Celia."

She sounds so sincere that I know it's useless arguing. In fairness, it's been a long time since Tabby has seen her family. I can appreciate that. When I find Mum and Ali, I know I'll want to spend a lot of time with them, too.

"Ok," I concede. "Well, I'll try and stay awake, but..." I trail off in a yawn.

Tabby chuckles a little, keeping her warm hand pressed against my head. "Don't wait up for me, Eva," she says. "You need the rest."

By the time Tabby has gently closed the door behind her, I'm already drifting off into a deep, deep sleep.

Chapter 39

When I wake up, I'm alone, the bed next to me completely undisturbed. Tabby must still be with her family. The glow of the full moon shines through the gap in the curtains; on the wall, the clock tells me I've only been asleep for an hour. I could snuggle back under the blanket, but I'm craving another hot chocolate. Truth be told, I'm also missing the company of my friends. It's too quiet in this room.

I sneak down the stairs, not wanting to wake anybody up on my way. The house is silent and dark, save for a gleam of light poking through the gap in the living room door. Snatches of whispers are heard as I approach.

"It's not going to be easy," I hear Celia say. "There's loads of people out there that need to be found."

"But it's not impossible," comes Tabby's reply. "Is it?"

My hand lingers over the doorknob as I strain to hear.

"Not impossible, no," Celia says. "But we'll need a

308 ~ EMILY RENNIE

lot more information to go on, sweetheart, and according to you, Eva's still not remembered it."

My heart hammers in my chest. They're talking about me. Why are they talking about me?

There's a silence, and then somebody sighs. Biting my lip, I incline my head the slightest bit to peek through the gap in the door. With a jolt, I see Val. I have to quickly move away before she feels my eyes on her.

"I think she remembers everything," Val says in an undertone. "We *all* think she remembers everything. She's just in complete denial."

Celia hums in stoic agreement. "Tabby. What *has* Eva said to you?"

"This isn't fair," Tabby says instantly, voice tight. "I'm not going to talk about this when she's sleeping upstairs."

Thank you, I almost say. As usual, Tabby is the only one talking any sense. My hand is still poised over the doorknob, trembling with indignation. Anger stirs in my chest.

"It's not fair on her to keep this up, either," Val says. "Especially now that Darryl – Come on, Tabs, you saw her. She still expects him to walk through that door. Denial is her natural default."

"Well –" Tabby cuts herself off. "Well, what's wrong with that? Just for a bit longer? Isn't it easier?"

Celia tuts. "Now you just sound like *The Lifetime Lila Show,*" she says. "That's the whole reason that bloody thing was invented. To hide your grief. To numb you."

"I can't be the one," Tabby whispers. There's such raw pain in her voice that I close my eyes, as if that'll block all of this out. "It'll hurt her too much."

"No," Celia says gently, "you're the best person to tell her. The two of you have a close bond."

I can't bear any more of these riddles, and move away from the door as if I've been struck. No longer caring about being quiet, I run up the stairs, back into the safety of my room.

I can't keep still. I pace around, head throbbing, flashes of conversation barreling their way through the barriers so carefully placed in my brain.

"There's no telling what she'll do. No telling at all."

"Oh, Eva, I wish I could believe that."

"You talk to your sister a lot?"

"Maybe it's easy for you, but I can't –"

The bedroom door creaks open and I stop in my tracks. I don't need to turn around to know it's Tabby. I let her stand there, and busy myself with picking up my discarded blanket, folding it neatly.

"I can't wait for you to meet Ali," I tell Tabby, keeping my back to her. My hands shake, and I have to refold the blanket again. "You really will love her."

"Eva?" Tabby whispers. Her voice is thick with tears. "You heard us downstairs, didn't you?"

I only shake my head, doing my best to ignore her. "We're going to have a lot to catch up on," I say. "So I'll probably stay with her and Mum for a bit, if you don't mind. Not forever, I'm not leaving you, or anything like that." I attempt to brighten my voice, but it keeps cracking. "Can't get rid of me that easily!"

"I didn't want to do it like this," Tabby says. I hear her close the bedroom door behind her.

"Ali's going to be really interested in all your tech stuff," I say. "She'll understand it better than I did. She's really smart."

"Eva," Tabby says again.

Inhaling shakily, I put the blanket down, before I finally turn my head to look at her. "Please don't," I whisper. "Not yet."

Some time ago, I stopped asking about my phone. I see it now in Tabby's hand, as she slowly holds it out towards me. "Please," Tabby says quietly, "please take it."

"*No*," I insist. Tears spill from my eyes, and I furiously wipe them away. Tabby is crying soundlessly too as we stare at each other, in a complete standoff.

"Eva, it's time," she says. "I wish it wasn't, and I'm so, so sorry —"

I snatch my phone out of her hand. "You were supposed to *fix* it, not go through my things!"

Tabby shakes her head, loose curls bouncing. "Please," she says, "I just want to be here for you. I want you to know that I'm not going anywhere, that I'm —"

"You can't promise me that!" I explode. "*Darryl's* gone! Darryl's gone, and he promised he'd come back, but where is he? Where is he, Tabby?"

I'm shoving her before I even realise what I'm doing. It's too late for her to react, and her back slams against bedroom door with a painful thump. She wheezes in surprise, and when I look into her wide and desperate eyes, I'm horrified at myself.

"I'm so sorry," I blurt. "I'm so sorry, I didn't mean to do that, I didn't mean to, I'm so sorry."

The idea of hurting Tabby is too much to bear, and feel my legs buckle from underneath me as I weep. I clutch my phone to my chest, rocking back and forth, tears streaming down my face.

Soft hands touch my knees; Tabby has crawled over to me. She remains silent, allowing me to cry. "It's ok," she whispers. "It's ok, Eva."

She presses her forehead to mine, and I mimic her deep breaths until my tears stop. I can't hide anymore. Not from Tabby, and not from myself.

With shaky hands, I unlock my phone. It takes me a few attempts to click onto my messages, already knowing what I'll find.

Morning, Ali! Hope you and Mum are doing ok.
Not delivered.

Any ideas for this competition? I think I'd like a new coffee pot.
Not delivered.

Hi Eva, it's Ali. All fine! It's the first day of spring today. Are there flowers in your garden?

Not delivered.

There was no data or Wi-Fi at my house. There never was.

I was never talking to Ali, and she was never talking to me. In my Lila-infused confusion, I've been responding to myself, and blissfully forgetting about it after my afternoon nap. All the messages I've tried to send are lies.

I'm sobbing, smashing my fists against the floor, in complete agony. *"Ali!"* I scream, over and over, until it's completely nonsensical and my knuckles are bloody. "No no no no, Ali!"

Tabby wraps me up in her arms, rocking me. Eventually I give up and collapse against her, my useless phone left discarded on the floor. My body heaves and I cling to her, all of my grief out for everyone to see. The dark cloud over my head has finally burst open, and I let the rain come.

Chapter 40

BEFORE, PART FOUR: EVA

"We're happy, aren't we, Ali?" I ask my twin sister.

The two of us are sitting in the garden, tired from playing, as the hot summer sun beats down. Any minute now, I expect Mum will shout out the window for us to put some sun-cream on.

"Duh," is Ali's immediate reply. She's out of breath from riding my tricycle; I generously let her borrow it, even though we're definitely getting a little too big for it. "Don't be weird, Evie."

"I'm *not* being weird," I say with a scowl. I would shove her, but the heat is making me lazy. "I'm only asking because Mum's been moody."

Ali lies down, stretching her arms over her head, not even caring about getting grass stains on her dress.

"Mum *is* moody," she agrees. "But we're still happy, me and you, so she'll be happy again soon too."

I can't really argue with that logic, so I lie down next to her. "In just two years, we'll be ten," I say. "Josh says when he's ten, he's having a huge party, because it's double-digits. Our party'll be even bigger, because there's two of us, so that's *double* double-digits."

"I'm five minutes older than you," Ali says. "I should really have a party all to myself."

My head immediately snaps to look at her, eyes wide in disbelief, but then Ali cracks up laughing. "I'm *joking*, Evie!" she says. "As if."

I try not to make my sigh of relief too obvious, even though the thought of not sharing my party with Ali has made my stomach drop. She seems to be having fun teasing me today.

As if reading my mind, Ali then makes a bunch of kissy noises. "I bet you fancy Josh," she says, and I kick her leg. There's no strength in it, so she only laughs as if I've tickled her.

"I *don't!*" I insist. Josh is a quiet boy in our class who always stammers whenever the teacher asks him a question. I like him as a friend, but that's it, and I say as much until Ali finally drops the subject.

"Do you think Mum will let us have a really big party, then?" she asks, a hint of excitement in her voice.

I shrug, idly tugging at blades of grass. "We've got loads of time to plan it, if we tell her we want one now," I say.

With that, the two of us immediately sit up, on the same wave-length. "Let's ask her right now," Ali says eagerly. "We'll ask, then if she says no, we'll give her some iced tea and we'll tidy up the kitchen, and then she'll *have* to say yes to us."

We grip onto each other's hands in excitement, a mutual look of determination in our eyes. Who can resist double the charm? Certainly not our mum. Our bare feet slap against the tiled flooring as we barrel through the house, only for us to stop suddenly at the living room door. We can hear the low sound of the TV. Lately, Mum has been glued to the screen, except it's always boring news. It's weird; Mum *never* lets me or Ali watch so much television.

I linger over the door-handle, and then turn to Ali. "You're braver than me," I say, suddenly nervous. "You go and ask first."

Ali rolls her brown eyes, muttering under her breath about me being a huge baby as she pushes the door open. "Mum!" she beams, tossing her long, black hair over her shoulder, charm exemplified. "Eva and I want to ask –"

Mum hastily scrambles for the TV remote, but it's too late. Ali and I collectively gasp at the news footage of a blazing explosion. It looks like it's happened in a crowd of important people; I recognise one man who's in the newspapers a lot.

"Cool!" Ali blurts. "It's like an action movie!"

The screen goes black. Mum holds the remote in her hand, shooting Ali a silencing glower. "Go back outside and play," she demands. "Do you have any sun-cream on? Put your sun-cream on, *now*. Do you want to look like lobsters?"

"What *was* that?" I say, trying not to sound too scared. If Ali finds it cool, then I don't want her to think I'm a wuss. "Was that real?"

Mum's eyes narrow, and she jabs her finger at the doorway. *"Out!"*

Mum's voice only raises like that when she's really serious, so Ali and I quickly scarper back to the garden. Ali re-stakes her sunbathing spot, sulking a little.

"We'll try again at dinner," she huffs. "Mum is *so* moody."

I stay quiet. For the rest of the day, right up until I'm tucked up in bed, all I can think about is that explosion. When I close my eyes, I see the fiery glow, burning everything in its wake.

*

In the middle of the night, a baby is shrieking, over and over again. I feel like doing the same whenever I picture Jessica's house disappearing in a blaze of flames.

After it happened, we all ran and ran, leaving our home behind. Everybody else on the street did the same, except for Jessica's family. It was too late for them.

Once we were far away from our street, breathless and terrified, Mum knocked on every door she could.

We were turned away countless times, until a stranger finally let us in.

"It's just me and Rosa," the lady said, rocking her baby in her arms. *"There's not much room. But stay as long as you need to."*

That was a week ago, and we're still sleeping on the floor of her living room. The radio is never off; the adults circle around it from day to night, waiting for *something*. Anything. I don't understand any of the news.

I shift in my sleeping bag, trying to switch my brain off. The baby upstairs keeps wailing, the noise pounding in my temples.

"Somebody attacked our street," Ali says suddenly. She lies next to me, eyes fixated on the cracked ceiling. "Someone evil. A supervillain, like in the movies."

"Supervillains don't exist," I mumble. "Not the ones with silly names and capes and powers."

Ali mulls this over for a moment. "Maybe they look normal, then," she says. "Like everybody else."

Suddenly, I'm overwhelmed with dread, and jolt upright in my sleeping bag. "What if all this is my fault?" I whisper, breath stuttering in my throat. "I really, *really* didn't want to give my tricycle away, and I was so mean about it, and now Jessica –"

"Don't be stupid." Ali sits up with me, tucking a strand of hair behind my ear. "*'Course* it's not your fault, Evie!"

I hunch over with a moan. Even my twin can't

comfort this despair in the centre of my chest. "I'll never be horrible again," I vow. "Never, never, never —"

Mum stirs from her sleeping position, slowly propping herself up. I hold my breath, worried she'll be angry that I've woken her, but she only rubs at her eyes.

"Eva," she slurs. "What's all this about being horrible?"

I burst into desperate tears, flinging myself at her. Mum holds me close, shushing me gently. I feel like the baby upstairs as she soothes me. "It's ok, love," she says. "Cry it out."

"Eva thinks the explosion's her fault," Ali pipes up. "But I told her that was stupid."

I shoot her a glower through my watery eyes, gripping onto Mum's arms hard enough to leave marks.

"It wasn't your fault, darling," is all Mum says. She sounds so tired. "Of course it wasn't. If anything, it was mine."

Ali and I simultaneously gasp. I pull away from Mum, staring up at her in horror. "*You* made the explosion?" I whisper, unable to believe it. Our gentle, lovely mother could *never* do this. Ali's words about supervillains looking just like everybody else ring in my head, and icy dread trickles down my spine.

"No, no!" Mum says hurriedly. "No, that's not what I meant. Sorry, I was — I was being hyperbolic."

"That's a big word," Ali says.

"Yes, it is." Mum pats my head as I move to sit next to Ali. She sighs, shoulders hunched. "I mean, it's my fault that I didn't tell you about what was happening, and...I'm so sorry."

We both stare at our mother as we wait for her to elaborate. Ali keeps crossing and uncrossing her arms, forehead pinched with worry.

"I was trying to protect you," Mum continues. "That's all I wanted to do. But I kept you in the dark, and that wasn't fair. You've seen things that you *never* should've, but if you'd been aware of what was going on, then maybe – I don't know. I didn't know what to do for the best."

"Did you know an explosion was going to happen?" Ali asks hesitantly.

"They've been happening all over, for a while now," Mum says, inhaling shakily. "I didn't know it was going to happen to us. Clearly, that was naïve, and I was burying my head in the sand. I was a coward. I should've told you everything, and the truth is – the truth is, this is a war now."

I stay silent as I let this sink in. A war, like the kinds Ali and I have been learning about in school. I think back to that explosion on the TV, the man running away. A politician. Mum takes another shuddered breath in, before carrying on.

"People are fighting, and we're stuck in the middle," she says. "I don't know how long it'll last. It's been brewing for a long time, so maybe it'll fizzle out sooner than we think. The truth is, nobody really knows what's happening. All we can do is...Is stick together."

Ali sniffles forlornly. "So – there's a *war*, and we're homeless now."

"There'll be others like us," Mum says. "Lots of people. There'll be places for us to go, I'm sure of it." She strokes our hair, feigning a smile. "The three of us could make a new place nice and pretty, couldn't we? The main thing is, we're all together. That's all we need."

All of us together in our house would be better, I want to say, but bite down on my lip. I know Mum is trying her best to be brave, so I need to do the same.

Both Ali and I wrap our arms around Mum, burrowing ourselves into her embrace as if it'll shelter us from the world itself. "Will it happen again?" I whisper. "Will anything like that happen again, near us?"

Mum's grip tightens around us. "I don't know," she says quietly, and that's what scares me most of all. Mums are always supposed to know. "I wish I could tell you that you'll never see anything like that again, darlings. But... I just don't know."

Eventually, our mum is able to soothe us back into our sleeping bags, stroking our foreheads as we try to relax.

"My perfect pair," she says wistfully. "Never change."

Hearing her say that makes my heart ache. I sneak a glance at Ali, but she's already snoring gently. I burrow myself in my sleeping bag and do my best to copy my twin.

*

For our thirteenth birthday, Mum gifts us with second-hand mobile phones. Ali generously opts for the one with the cracked screen, no matter how many times I insist I don't mind. I'm just grateful to have some connection with the world around us, to have a better idea of what's going to happen next. It's also nice to play some music.

Mum does her best to keep up our schooling as society lies in ruins around us. In the scraps of time when we're not searching for the next place to stay, or foraging around for necessities, she recites stories. She painstakingly writes out maths equations on dusty surfaces. She stresses the importance of the world around us, regaling us with childhood tales of her growing up in Seoul.

Then there are the other lessons. The lessons for survival. If it's not soldiers we're running from, it's a new group called Vultures. We've heard the horror stories, but have been lucky enough not to encounter any in person. Still, that doesn't stop Mum from arming us with any weapons we can get our hands on.

We're used to moving around by now. We've slept in bus shelters, abandoned shops, moved in with total strangers in cramped flats. Currently, we're staying put in a small room that used to be some kind of café, if the faulty coffee machine and array of dirty cups are anything to go by. Even though an emergency housing agency was set up two years into the

War, we've had no luck getting a permanent place, no matter how many times Mum has tried.

"High demand right now, I guess," Ali jokes, every time Mum returns from queuing into the early hours of the morning. I can't resist smirking with her, even though nothing about it is funny. Still, sometimes it's just better to laugh.

Until one day, when Mum returns, she's beaming in a way I've not seen her do in a very long time. "We've done it," she tells us breathlessly. "We've bloody done it! We've got a house!"

For a moment, Ali and I can't speak. We just stare at her in stunned silence, and then Ali gives a loud squeal, leaping onto our mother. I'm quick to follow, and Mum squeezes us fiercely. "Now, it's not going to be perfect –" she begins, but is immediately cut off.

"Who cares!" Ali says. "You're amazing! It's going to be perfect, because you're *amazing!*"

"Charmer," Mum huffs a laugh. "It's in Birmingham, so it'll be a bit of a journey. We'll head off first thing tomorrow morning –"

"Birmingham!" I say in fascination. "We've never been to Birmingham before."

"A real adventure," Mum says, brushing my hair back from my face. "So, we'd all best get some sleep, right? Dream of home décor, loves."

*

There's not much in Birmingham, and the house is

small and crumbly, but when the three of us finally step inside our new home, I couldn't be happier. Finally, a proper place to call ours. We've not had this since Ali and I were nine. There's nothing that can't be fixed up with a bit of team effort and hard work, so we painstakingly roll up our sleeves and make the house our home.

Our new neighbours, Steve and Jonathan, gift us a half-empty pot of duck-egg blue paint. Ali's favourite colour. We spend a whole afternoon painting our front door blue, splashing each other with flecks of paint, laughing in the sunshine.

By the time Ali and I are fifteen, we've settled into a semblance of normality. The War isn't over, but it does seem to be dwindling, and in our new little corner of the world we can almost forget about it. Mum tutors the children in the neighbourhood, and Ali already has her eye on a handsome teenage boy at the end of the road, which I can't entertain.

"Don't be jealous, Evie," Ali teases me. "We can share him, if you like."

I don't know how to tell her, because *surely* she must know by now. Is she waiting for me to say it? Do I even have to? It shouldn't be a big deal. Steve and Jonathan are married, and everyone here loves them. They're helpful, compassionate, welcoming to all. There's nothing they wouldn't do for their neighbours, and everybody extends them the same courtesy.

So, if I were to just *say* that I only like girls out loud, would it matter to Ali? I'm positive it wouldn't, but I still swallow my words back down and mutter some-thing about how she can have the boy all to herself.

One day, there's a knock on our door, and Mum opens it to find Steve in a panic. My first thought is that soldiers have set up base in our village, but once Mum invites him inside it's clear that's not the issue.

Mum offers him a cup of tea, which he refuses. This is rare. He doesn't even sit down, just paces around our living room. "I'm sorry, Eun," he keeps saying to our mother, "I just didn't know who else to...I didn't know who else to come to."

"You're welcome here any time," Mum says, trying to keep him at ease. "You know that. What's wrong?"

"It's Jonathan," Steve pants. "His leg – I don't know what else to do."

Jonathon was enlisted to fight in the War, a few years ago, on the government's side. He didn't want to, but I suppose they didn't give him much of a choice. When his leg was severely damaged, he was sent home without so much as a thank you. Now he can't walk much; when he does, it's with two canes.

"What's happened?" Mum says calmly.

"He tripped the other day," Steve says, running a hand down his face. "He was trying to grab a book for me, and he fell. Sliced his bad leg on the side of the glass table. Jesus, the blood, it was like it would never stop."

Ali and I wince at the image. Poor Jonathan.

"So, I did all the typical first aid stuff," Steve con-tinues, his words practically tripping over each other.

"And for a while it seemed like it would be ok. But this morning – the wound looks awful, and he's got a fever, and none of our medicine is helping. I don't know what to do."

Mum considers this for a moment. "Possible infection," she finally says. "And if that's the case, painkillers won't cut it. Let me see him."

When Mum returns an hour later, her forehead is creased with worry. I make her a cup of tea as she collapses into our thrifted armchair, rubbing her temples. "It's an infection, alright," Mum says as I pass her the steaming mug. "A bad one. He'll need a doctor."

"Good luck with that," Ali mumbles. I give her a fierce poke in her side. She's right, but even so, she shouldn't say it out loud.

Mum doesn't respond for a while, cradling the mug in her hands. "Steve asked if I could look after Jonathan, while he went to search for medical help," she says quietly.

"We can do that," I say, eager to be useful. "We can all stay with Jonathan, can't we? Make him meals, look after him, until Steve comes back."

Ali hesitates. When I turn to shoot her a questioning look, she shrugs uneasily. "I'm sorry, it's just – Look, I don't want to sound awful, but...how likely is it that Steve could even make it to the next *town?*"

At that, I falter, aware of Ali's point. Steve isn't exactly the pinnacle of health himself, with his bad asthma. He can barely walk the length of our street without wheezing. Both him and Jonathon are in their mid-sixties, and the War has made them frail and tired.

"Yes," Mum murmurs in agreement, "that's what I told him."

Eyes wide, I look between Ali and Mum. "But we can't just *not* help," I say, horrified. "We have to do something!"

"We are going to do something," Mum says, taking a sip of her tea. "*I'm* going to do something."

I rub my arms, which are now prickled with goose-bumps, because I know exactly what our pragmatic mother is about to do. Ali knows it too, and her expression has abruptly soured. "*No*, Mum," is all she says.

"You didn't see how ill Jonathan is," Mum says calmly. "He needs to be with his husband."

"Did Steve ask you to do this?" Ali demands, voice shaking with barely supressed anger. "He can't ask you to do this, Mum. It's not fair. You can't go out there searching for some – some random doctor!"

Mum puts her mug down on the small side table, movements slow and deliberate. "Of course he didn't ask me," she says. "I offered, because it's the right thing to do."

"The right thing to do, is to stay with your *children*," Ali spits. "Not leave us alone in the middle of a War."

"I'm not leaving you alone," is the instant reply. "You're going to stay with Steve and Jonathan until I get back."

This does nothing to appease Ali, who only scoffs

in disgust. I rub at my forearms again, trying to push down my fear. "Where are you going to go?" I whisper.

"No further than Manchester," Mum says. Clearly, she's got this all figured out. "And...And if there's no luck there, then..."

"Then what?" Ali snaps. "You'll keep looking for this miracle doctor? You'll leave your kids in the dust, just to fuel some kind of stupid...stupid *hero* complex?"

Years ago, Ali would never dare speak to our mother in this way. I know times have changed, but I still recoil in horror as the words fly out of her mouth. Stupidly, I half-expect Mum to scold her, to send her to her room, to ground her.

Mum stands, "I'm sorry," she says, tired and sincere. "But if there's even a slight chance of saving a man's life, I'm going to take it. Think of how much they've both looked after us, ever since we moved here. They'd do the same for us, and you both know it. We have to protect each other, otherwise –" Mum's voice cracks. "Otherwise, what's the point?"

Ali's lower lip quivers, but I see her blink back her tears with ferocity.

Silently, Mum outstretches her hands to both of us. I hesitate for a split second, before going to interlink my fingers with hers, squeezing hard. Turning my head, I look to Ali, waiting for her to do the same. She stands rigid.

"Ali," I attempt. "Please."

"I'm not staying with Steve and Jonathan," is all Ali says. "If we're old enough for you to leave, then we're old enough to look after ourselves in our own home. Aren't we, Eva?"

My mouth drops open at her sheer defiance. I know for a fact that *I* want to stay with Steve and Jonathan. This is the first time we've ever majorly disagreed over something, and my grip on Mum's hand tightens.

"You're staying with them," Mum says, in an all-too familiar voice. It's the quiet, low tone which shows she means business. "You can stay here during the day, you can do whatever you like. But you're not staying in this house alone at night. Not with Vultures out there."

At that, Ali's demeanour shifts. She suddenly looks afraid. "Vultures don't come here," she says, but she sounds uncertain. "Not in a village like this."

"Vultures will go anywhere when it's dark," Mum says. "You know that."

I clutch at her hand. "Why don't we come with you?" I plead. "We can help you look for a doctor, can't we?"

Mum only shakes her head. "No. No. You can sulk and you can be furious with me, I don't blame you for that. Just know that I love you with everything I have, the two of you, and that's why you're not coming with me. That's why you're staying in a cosy bed, safe and well-fed. I won't have any more arguments."

And so, we say nothing else. We gather some clothes in silence, and stand outside our front door, as we watch our mother hurry away down the street. When she reaches the end of the road, she turns around and gives us a wave. We wiggle our fingers back. I blow her kisses until she's completely out of sight.

I breath out slowly, turning my head to look at Ali. "Think she'll find a doctor?"

"Sure," Ali says. I know the anger is still there, but she's doing her best to quell it in my presence. "When Mum's determined, anything can happen. Look at our house."

My lips quirk in a smile, and we walk over to our neighbours' where Steve welcomes us with open arms. When I dream, I see Mum standing at the end of the street, waving and waving.

*

On the fourth day with no Mum, my faith in her ability to find a doctor is dwindling. I don't say this to Ali, but I wonder if she's thinking the same thing. It's difficult being next door, so we spend most of the days in our own home and garden, while the sun is out. We've barely seen Steve; he's glued to Jonathan's side in their bedroom, and stress and worry fills their home like poison.

To distract ourselves, we sit down in our living room and play a game of cards. Ali keeps winning, which is entertaining at first, but soon gets really annoying.

"You're cheating," I insist, snatching the cards from her. "Let *me* shuffle this time."

"I'm not cheating!" she says indignantly. "It's not my fault that I'm better at –"

We're interrupted as a high-pitch, blazing alarm pierces the entire neighbourhood. The cards fall from my hands, as we stare at each other horror. We know that sound. That's the sound to evacuate as soon as you can. Bombs are coming.

Slowly, as if moving through treacle, we get to our feet. *Ali,* I try to say, but nothing comes out of my mouth. The world around me distorts and blurs.

"Eva? Eva!" Ali is shaking my shoulders, sharp nails digging into my skin. "Listen to me!"

I blink slowly, trying to concentrate on her face in front of me. She keeps swimming in and out of focus as the sirens wail and howl.

"Mum's not back," I croak.

"I know. I know." Ali exhales shakily. "But we can't stay here."

I remain rooted to the spot as Ali runs around the house, bundling what little items we have into our worn-out duffel bag. She seems to be moving in fast-forward, while I'm stuck on complete pause. *Useless.* Utterly useless.

"Eva!" Ali's voice jolts me back to life, tinged with desperation. "Eva, please. I can't do this alone. We have to *go!*"

Hearing my twin plead like that snaps me into a semblance of clarity. I force myself to bend down and help her pack what she's gathered into the bag. "Next door," my voice sounds distant, like somebody else is speaking from far away. "Steve and Jonathan."

Ali has ripped out a piece of paper from one of

Mum's notebooks, and is frantically scribbling a message for her, on the rare chance that this house will still be standing by the time our mother gets back. "I know," she pants. "Come on, they're the adults, they must have some sort of plan. We'll message Mum the moment we're out of here."

"There might not be any signal," I say in an undertone. "She might not be able to –"

"Fucking hell, Eva!" Ali suddenly yells. "I know! I know all that! Do you want to stay? Do you *want* to sit in this house and wait for the bombs to fall on us?"

I'm so startled by Ali raising her voice at me that tears spring to my eyes.

"Or, let's say we miraculously *do* survive it," Ali continues wildly. "Vultures will be coming to pick through the rubble. They'll probably already be on their way, if they can hear the warning alarms. How many do you think the two of us could take on, and still come out with all our body parts?"

I open and close my mouth uselessly. I'm still kneeling on the frayed carpet, staring up at her, my hand uselessly poised over the zip of the duffel bag. I do my best to hold my tears back, but they soon fall. All the while, the sirens blare.

The strength seems to leave Ali immediately. She slowly kneels down next to me, head bowed. "I'm sorry," she whispers, reaching for my hand. "I wish...I wish I knew what to do. I wish Mum was here."

Even after everything that we've gone through, it's rare to see Ali admit defeat.

"We need to go," I tell her, giving her hand a strong squeeze. "You're right. We don't have a choice."

Tears fall from Ali's eyes. She hastily scrubs at them with her free hand. "I'm ten minutes older, after all," she attempts to joke. "You have to do what I say."

"I know." My voice catches in my throat. "You shouldn't be the only one who's brave. I'll be brave for the both of us, ok?"

"Ok," she croaks. "Ok, Evie."

Outside, it's chaos. Those who have cars are careering down the village road, others are frantically running and screaming. Before I can let fear freeze me again, Ali is hauling me along to next door. Steve and Jonathan gave us a spare key, but in my panic I can't remember where I've put it. Ali is hammering her fists against their window and front door while I desperately rummage in the duffel bag.

"Come on, come *on!*" Ali yells at nobody in particular. Her voice is drowned out in the wailing sirens. "Steve! Steve, Jonathan, we have to get out of here!

Finally, I find the silver key inside the pocket of my packed jeans. "Here!" I thrust it towards Ali with shaking fingers. She wastes no time in unlocking the front door, and yanks me inside.

"Steve!" I shout, voice cracking. They *must* have a plan. Jonathan fought in the War. They're the adults; they know what to do when the alarms come. I stumble through the dark living room, heading for the staircase. "Steve, Jonathan! It's Eva and Ali!"

Ali is right behind me when I burst through into

their bedroom – the time for polite knocking is over – and find them both lying on the bed, as if none of this is happening. I allow a flicker of rage to spark in my chest. Mum trusted Steve to look out for us, but he's doing *nothing,* he's doing –

"Oh," Ali whispers. "Oh, Steve."

Steve is holding an unnaturally still Jonathan close to him, head bowed. His shoulders shake, and his breathing stutters as he silently cries. It's awful of me, but the first thing I can think of is how Mum has gone to find a doctor for nothing. Then, the horror of it hits me and I stagger back, bumping against the wall. Jonathan is dead. There's nothing anyone can do for him now.

Eventually, Steve lifts his head, as if in slow-motion. He stares right through us both with glassy eyes. It's like we're nothing but shadows.

"Steve?" I croak. "The sirens. We…We can't stay."

"Sirens," he repeats blearily, glancing around the bedroom. He doesn't let go of Jonathan once. "Yes."

Ali takes a step towards the bed, and then falters, looking anywhere but at Jonathan. "What do we do?" she says shakily. "What do we do now?"

Again, he takes a long time to respond. "You'll need money," Steve finally murmurs. "Money, and food. Downstairs. Take whatever you want."

It takes me a moment to appreciate what's happening, but then I realise. Steve is not coming with us. He's staying with his husband until the very end. I see my twin's legs buckle, and I rush to help her. She only stares, wide-eyed at Steve, shaking her head.

"Go now," he tells us. "Don't stop for anyone, just keep moving. You have to just – to just keep moving until you find somewhere safe."

"We were supposed to be safe *here*," I whisper. Nobody is listening to me. Ali is still rooted to the spot, dumbfounded.

There's nothing we can do for Steve and Jonathan. We're on our own now.

*

We walk for days, leaving the home we worked so hard on. We walk until I'm forced to refer to the house as a distant memory, and the pang of longing no longer feels like a knife twisted in my flesh.

Four months with no Mum. I was right about there being no signal; we can only hope that one day we'll get to a place where there is some, and can finally contact her. I understand Ali's rage from before, now. Why did Mum have to take it upon herself to try and fix everybody else's woes? What good did it do *any* of us?

"Positive attitudes only," Ali tells me. Frustratingly, now that *I'm* feeling anger, she seems to be more optimistic. "*When* we find Mum, not *if*. We'll find her. We're the dream team, you and I, Evie."

We find refuge in a small village. An elderly woman tells us there's a spare room for us that we can share, which we gratefully accept, even if the two of us have to sleep cramped in one bed. We won't be here for long, so we make do.

Sleep is my only solace at the moment. Being awake feels like so much effort, and I can't summon the energy to do anything. Ali's ways of coping seem to be the exact opposite to mine.

On the third morning in this new place, I'm rudely awoken by my twin. "Come on, Eva." Ali shakes my shoulder as I try to bury my face in the rock-hard pillow. "We should get some fresh air. Walk around the village, see what's up."

"*Nothing's* up," I grumble. "There won't be a village fair or a market, Ali. There's a War going on."

"You never know," she says. "It's worth exploring, while it's a sunny day."

The spring sun mocks me with its cheeriness as I'm yanked out of the front door – Ali is surprisingly strong despite our lack of good food. I stand, sulking, as she wraps a pink scarf around my neck. "It's sunny, but still chilly," she says. "Got to bundle up."

"You are so *annoying*," I attempt, as she keeps wrapping the scarf around, covering up my mouth with the scratchy material. Eventually, I concede and start laughing, because the whole thing is so ridiculous. Ali seems delighted.

We walk around for a little while. We're mostly in silence, but the understanding, comforting kind. Every so often we'll glance at each other and smile.

I hate to admit it, but Ali was right to get me out of bed. It's good to be outside.

"Wow!" a little voice pipes up.

Ali and I spin around in surprise to find a young boy – probably around seven or eight – standing in middle of the street. His face is in good need of a wash, and his blond hair practically brushes his eyelids as it flops over his forehead.

He points at us. "You look exactly the same!"

"Yeah," Ali and I say simultaneously. When she folds her arms, I fold mine. She tilts her head to the left, and I copy. The boy, as predicted, gasps in fascination. Despite everything, this simple trick of ours makes me crack a smile. It's just like old times, when we'd annoy our mother.

"We're twins," I tell him.

Ali shakes her head, purposefully widening her eyes. "Don't listen to her," she whispers. "She's my evil clone, escaped from the lab!"

The boy swivels his head between the two of us, mouth still agape. "*So* cool," he says. "Where did you come from? Are you with all those men who have the guns?"

In a flash, my body has tensed up, banter from seconds ago long gone. "What are you talking about?" I demand.

"They came the other day!" the boy says, eyes wild with excitement. "Men with really big guns."

Ali and I glance at each other, both immediately on edge. "Do you know which ones they were?" Ali asks.

"It's either men fighting on the government's side, or the rebels. Which group has been here?"

"Well..." the boy furrows his brow. "Who're the good guys?"

Ali raises an eyebrow, mouth twisted in scorn. "Does it matter?"

"What she means is, neither of them are good anymore," I say. "They're both dangerous, and you should keep away."

The boy chews at his chapped lips, clearly mulling this over. "But then what are we?" he asks. "Good, or bad?"

"We're the ones left stuck in the middle," Ali says. "Just trying to survive."

The boy sagely nods his head, and then cocks his fingers into a gun shape. "Come on, then! I'll be on the side of the rebels!" he crows. "You be the governors. Bang! *Bang!*"

"Stop that!" Ali snaps, swatting at his hand. "This isn't a stupid game."

"I'd rather he was playing than crying," I say to her in an undertone. "Let's just get out of here."

Before we can even turn around, the boy is zooming to block our path. "I'm Liam!" he says, fingers still poised at our heads.

I resist the urge to push him out of the way; God knows how annoying Ali and I were at his age. At least there's only one of him. "Bye, Liam," I say.

Liam ignores me, and centres his fake gun at Ali's heart. *"Bang!"*

"Oh, no," Ali says in a voice dripping with sarcasm, throwing her hands up. "You got me!"

The boy sulks at our lack of enthusiasm, and storms off in a huff. We watch him go, and I can't help but snort with laughter.

"Well," I say. "This place was nice while it lasted, I suppose."

"Yeah," Ali sighs. "Better pack up and get moving. The further away we are from any of those soldiers, the better. Can't trust any of them."

"Roger that," I say, linking arms with her. I want to thank her for getting me out of bed, for lifting my spirits, for all the effort she's putting in, but I can't find the right words. She knows, though. Ali always knows.

*

The next morning, we're up at six, just as the sun is rising. I wait outside with our bag while Ali thanks our host. She's better than me in the mornings; I'm not at all sociable and still feel half-asleep.

I'm rubbing the grit from my eyes when a small boy dashes past us. I recognise him from yesterday.

"Morning, Liam," I call after him.

He doesn't stop, just shoots me a wave. "They're back!" he yells in excitement. "I'm going to go see them!"

Too disorientated to understand what he's talking about, I simply yawn. "Who's back?"

Liam's too far away to hear me. I watch his little legs sprint off down the street, and he ducks under a maze of red tape that definitely wasn't there yesterday. Squinting, I step forward, trying to get a better look.

"All good to go?" Ali's voice suddenly says from behind me. I pull my eyes away from where Liam ran to.

"Mmhm," I mumble with another yawn. "Heading south?"

Ali doesn't respond right away, forehead pinched with barely-disguised worry.

"They said there's a better chance of signal in the south, didn't they?" I prompt.

My twin keeps gnawing at her bottom lip. When she eventually meets my gaze, my heart starts to thrum in my chest.

"Ali?" I ask hesitantly. "What is it? Is it...bad news?"

What a stupid thing to say. Life is perpetually bad news at the moment. Even so, I can't stop the tremor in my voice.

"Ali, just tell me. It's ok. We can deal with it together."

Finally, she speaks. "It was just on the radio," she murmurs. "An attack on Manchester. More bombs."

Now my heart feels as though it's stopped entirely. It sinks down in my chest, a dead weight. "Where Mum was going?" I whisper.

"We don't know if she was actually there," Ali says,

but her words buzz and drone in my ears. "We just need to keep trying to get in touch –"

"No," I interrupt. "No. We need to stop kidding ourselves. She left us behind, and now she's dead."

Ali flinches. "*Eva.*"

"You're thinking it too!" I say wildly, thrusting my finger into her chest. "You've *always* thought it, from the moment she walked away. I know you, Ali!"

She opens and closes her mouth helplessly. "Sure," she eventually says. "I've thought it, but that...that doesn't make it *true* –"

I'm turning on my heel and storming away before she can finish her sentence. I'm so angry, and I can't bear to listen to Ali's efforts to calm me. I want to be angry; I *need* to be angry. If I'm not angry, then I need to face the fact that our mother has gone forever.

"I hate her!" I scream. "I hate her, I hate her, *fuck* her for doing this to us!"

"Eva!" Ali is chasing after me. "For God's sake, *stop!*"

I spot the group of men too late. They stand behind the maze of red tape, rifles raised. Immediately, I fling my arms up to show we're unarmed, staggering to a halt.

"Stay where you are!" a soldier barks at us. "Get back!"

I'm panting, already berating myself for leading us both here. As my eyes roam the area, I spot little Liam. He's crouched on the ground, sobbing in fear, as a soldier aims his gun at his little head.

"*Hey,*" I try to say, but nothing comes out of my mouth. I can only stare.

Ali is right behind me, and takes a step forward. "What's going on?" she demands. She's trying to be brave, but her voice is shaking. "That boy lives here. This is his street."

"This is army territory now." The soldier standing above Liam has a raspy voice that reminds me of nails on a chalkboard. "Not a space for civilians to trespass."

The thought of a tiny child trespassing is enough to make me want to laugh like a wild thing. Once again, I'm frozen. There is so much noise, and I don't know what to do. I should never have brought us this way. I should have stopped Liam from running.

"*For fuck's sake,*" Ali is screaming over Liam's desperate wails. "*He's just a boy!*"

She ducks under the red tape before I can grab her arm and pull her back.

"Stay where you are!"

"He's a boy! What's he going to do to you? What's he going to –"

It happens very quickly, and then everything is slow. The bullet hits Ali square in the chest and she is flung in the air, back arched like a graceful dancer, arms spread out in surrender. Rosettes of blood bloom across her dress.

The world is quiet when she falls to the ground.

"Ali?" I eventually whisper. My lower lip trembles. "Ali?"

I take a step backwards. The soldiers aim their guns at me, and a high-pitched noise in my ears drowns out their words.

"Get away from the tape. Go. Leave now."

I can't leave my twin. In all the commotion, Liam has ducked under the tape and is already running away. I can't be mad at him. He's just a kid.

I take another step back. And another. All of the soldiers' faces merge into one indistinguishable blur. *That's my sister,* I try to say. No words come out of my mouth. I brought her here, she was only following me. We were supposed to stay together.

Ali?

*

I am alone. Completely alone.

I head south, because I have no other plan. I don't cry. I barely sleep or eat. I just walk.

For months, there's nothing but decimated streets, until I find a sole bungalow. It stands alone against the rubble, like it's been waiting for me. When I get inside, I find a bed, a sofa, and a kitchen with functioning plug sockets.

"Thanks, Ali," I say out loud, the first words I've spoken since it happened. I can't explain it, but it's really like my twin has looked out for me.

Unfortunately, there's still no signal. I tap at my phone, holding it high above my head, but nothing to

Mum sends. In a fit of rage, I throw it to the ground, and then immediately decide I don't care.

I don't care about anything now.

Time is moving so painfully slow. I could've been here for months, maybe even a year. My low appetite ends up being a bit of a blessing, as it means I can save whatever food I have in the duffel bag.

I'm woken up in the middle of the night by the sound of a car outside. If it's soldiers, they're welcome to shoot me. I should never have run away. I should've stayed with Ali, but I was weak. I was a coward.

My movements are slow when I go to open the front door. An old-fashioned television lies on the door step, and I see taillights through the fog as a car speeds away.

"Leave me alone!" I scream. I'm running from the bungalow to chase after them, bare feet scraping against the tarmac. "Just leave me *alone!*"

Finally, I'm sobbing. I didn't think I'd ever break through this numbness, but I'm sobbing and yelling and cursing all of them until my voice is raspy and unrecognisable. When I stagger back to the bungalow, the TV on the doorstep is playing a cheerful little tune without me even turning it on.

I stop in my tracks. Part of me wants to kick it over and shut it up, but I hesitate. There's something about the music that's calming me, and it's quite nice to have something other than my own thoughts to occupy my time.

I pick up the television, and close the bungalow door behind me.

Chapter 41

"Hi, Eva."

I inhale sharply through my nose at the sound of Lila's voice, but resolve to keep myself still under the covers. Silence lingers, heavy and smothering.

That overwhelming, all-encompassing feeling that rocked through my body, back when Val turned off my television for the first time. I can appreciate what that was now. It was grief. Raw and real and devastating.

It's been two weeks since the...the incident. I've stayed in my bed for most of it, no matter how many times people have tried to console me. Even though it's not her fault, rage simmers through my veins whenever Tabby has attempted to sit in the bedroom to talk. This is a surprising new tactic, trying to get *Lila* of all people to speak to me.

"It's a nice day, you know," Lila continues. For a second, I'm transported back to sitting in front of my television, listening to Lila enthusiastically tell us all about the first day of spring. An ache pangs in my chest for the naïve, oblivious girl I used to be.

"You can ignore me if you like," Lila says at my resumed silence. "Most people here do."

At that, I sit up in bed with a frown to look at her. She's wearing an oversized black hoodie that emphasises the brightness of her eyes, and her tartan pyjama trousers. Her dark hair is tied back, which is almost like an act of bravery, having her face completely open and exposed. In her hands, there's a small black notebook.

"*Still?*" I have to say. "What, even Mrs. McIver? They can't still think any of this was your fault."

"It was my face and my voice," Lila says. "Why *should* they trust me?"

I can't think of an appropriate answer, so I just allow myself to sit on the edge of the bed. When I pat the spot next to me, I don't really expect her to sit. Except she does. Lila perches next to me, blue eyes downcast. The black notebook rests on her lap, and she traces her fingers over it.

"It's funny," she says. "My disorder made me worry I was an evil monster for years. I would do anything humanely possible to stop that from being my fate, and I somehow ended up being the villain, anyway."

When I hesitate, she shoots me an apologetic look. "Obsessive Compulsive," she tells me. "It doesn't matter. I mean, it matters, but – the point is, I understand why people treat me like I'm...bad."

"You're not bad. You helped *me*," I feel the need to tell her. "You weren't a monster, you were kind. Supportive. Even if it was all a lie, you made me feel safe."

Lila huffs quietly under her breath. "That's the problem," she says. "That's how they trapped me. I wanted to feel safe, too."

I hold my breath. I'm scared that if I so much as move, Lila will take flight, and I want her to keep talking. My eyes drift to her notebook.

"It's easier for me to write my experience down," Lila says, catching my gaze. "So, that's what I've been doing. Anything I can remember, anything that's vaguely useful, it's gone in here."

I nod slowly. "That's good," I say. "That's a good idea. We don't need to talk about anything right now."

"It's alright." Lila exhales quietly. There's a small silence before she continues. "Before it happened – I wasn't dead, but I felt it." The more she speaks, it's as if she's visibly getting lighter before my eyes. "I felt dead. A zombie. Even though I had...I had someone with me, nothing felt like it could be ok."

"The man you were looking for?" I ask tentatively. "Jamie?"

Lila doesn't respond for a while, absent-mindedly picking at the loose threads of the bedsheets. "Jamie was my husband," she eventually says. "And my best friend."

"I lost my best friend, too," I say before I can appreciate the weight of my words. Now that they're out in the open, a sour taste tingles in my mouth. I have to close my eyes for a moment and wait for the wave of nausea to pass. "Ali. My twin."

"I'm sorry."

I swallow, but the lump in my throat refuses to shift. "Yeah," is all I can whisper. "Me too."

We sit in silence for a moment. I think of the others downstairs, wondering what they're doing. Wondering how much time we have left before we need to run away again.

"Tabby misses you, you know," Lila suddenly says. "She's always talking about you."

It hurts to hear, because I miss her so badly too. All I can do is shrug. "Well. She shouldn't have strung me along. If she'd just said *something*..."

"What *should* she have said?" Lila challenges. "What would you have done in that situation?"

I glower at nothing in particular, unable to answer. Deep down, I suppose I always knew something was wrong. Tabby *had* tried. Several times. I can't deny that. I can still be angry, though.

"I don't think it was deliberate," Lila continues. "I just don't think any of them knew what to do for the best."

Tears prick at my eyes. I let them fall, completely numb. "When I watched you on TV, I could forget all about it," I admit. "I wanted to...I wanted to keep that feeling for as long as I could. Because otherwise, she really *is* gone, isn't she?"

Lila doesn't respond for a moment, and then shrugs feebly. "I don't know if it works like that," is all she says.

I press the heels of my palms into my eyes, taking in a few deep, shuddering breaths. Sometimes, the pain lurks in the sides of my brain, not as intense. Other times, it's like I'm choking on it, and I can't breathe.

"I left Jamie alone, you know," Lila says, very quietly. "I let him down so badly. If I hadn't been so stuck in my head, then maybe none of this would ever have happened."

Slowly, I lift my head, taking her words in. "I don't think it works like that, either," I tell her. We look at each other. The television star and the number one fan, except we're neither of those things. We're two young women in the same boat, navigating this sea of grief and turmoil together.

"How's it been?" I finally summon the courage to ask. "In the outside world?"

"Now that I'm no longer on the air, you mean?" Lila says. "Reports of riots, just like Valentina predicted. People going mad on the streets, all over the country, looking for me."

"Fuck," is the first thing I can think of to say. "But – still nothing from the Creatives?"

Lila shakes her head, staring down at her lap.

"Right," I breathe. "Ok. So, shit's hitting the fan, and they're still quiet."

The question is, whether the Creatives are being deliberately quiet or not. I decide not to voice this out loud, and instead pat Lila's shoulder.

"It's going to be alright," I say. "After all, when life gets tough, you just need to put on a big smile, nice and wide."

Lila grimaces. "Urgh," she says. "Who told you *that*?"

"You...You did."

"Oh, Jesus." Lila raises her eyes heaven-ward. "Well. You *can* do that if you want, or you could go down-stairs and let yourself be with your girlfriend."

I haven't ever referred to Tabby as my girlfriend. Despite my feelings towards her right now, I can't help but like the sound of it. Breathing out slowly, I stare down at my knees, wondering what I should do. I really do need to get out of this room – at the very least, I could take a shower.

"I still don't really want to talk about Ali with any of them," I say. "Not even Tabby. I want to...I want to keep her all to myself for a bit. You know? Keep her with me a little longer."

"Talking about her won't make her disappear," Lila says quietly. "If anything, it'll do the exact opposite. But it's alright. I get what you're saying."

I look away for a moment, thinking of my brave, selfless, stubborn twin. My other half. I can't mope in this bedroom while there's trouble going on. It's like I can feel Ali's hands on my shoulders, giving me a jostle.

Come on, Evie.

When I turn back to Lila, it's with a small smile. "Alright, then," I tell her. "What's our next move?"

Chapter 42

Lila is waiting for me at the bottom of the staircase once I've showered and dressed back into my (now washed) jumpsuit and leather coat. She doesn't notice me right away; her eyes are fixated on the wooden banister. I see her clench and unclench her fist for a moment, and then with seemingly great effort, she moves away.

"Tabby and Val are in the living room," she says once she's spotted me. "If you want to see them."

I don't know if I do. Part of me wants to run and hide back up the stairs, but I still follow Lila into the living room to find Tabby and Val on the floor, tinkering with an old radio. When I step inside, both their heads snap up to look at me.

"I'll leave you to it," Lila says. Before I can open my mouth, she's left me, closing the door behind her. I falter, and then look at the two women that have simultaneously saved my life, and betrayed me.

It's weird seeing them, knowing what I do now. I swallow the sudden lump in my throat, and turn my head away.

"*Hola*, Eva," Val says, a tinge of hesitation in her voice. "How are you?"

I look back at them. Tabby is staring at me, her expression flickering between hopeful and nervous. Once again, the anger inside me splutters. I don't answer Val's question, and instead gesture to the radio.

"What're you doing?" I ask monotonously.

Tabby holds up a screwdriver, shooting me a nervous little smile. "Just giving it a bit of reboot," she says. "So we can be aware of any reports. There's been a few –"

"Riots, I know," I interrupt.

Neither of them meet my eyes for a moment. Val clears her throat. "We need to get a message out to the public, before the Creatives do. Something concrete for the people to listen to, so they know what's been going on all these years."

"Radio broadcast is our safest bet," Tabby continues, keeping her gaze steadfast on her work. "Jasper and Celia have helped us source all the equipment we need. Then, once we get a message out there, we should be able to disrupt the signal before Creatives can trace it back to us."

None of this means much to me. The radio crackles to life with a final twist of Tabby's screwdriver, and she breathes out slowly in satisfaction. "There we go," she murmurs, beginning to fiddle with the dials. "Let's see if we can reach any survivors..."

I'm not sure how they expect me to react. Maybe to sit down with them and help, like nothing is wrong.

I could do that. I could squash everything all the way down again, put on a smile, act like I'm interested.

Instead, I turn for the door. "I want to go outside."

Neither of them seem defensive at the bite in my voice. "Good idea," is all Val says. "Get some fresh air and keep an eye out. We've been going in pairs to patrol around."

"If you like, I could..." Tabby hesitates. "I could patrol with you. We could talk."

My jaw tightens automatically, and I have to remind myself to inhale. "I'd really rather be alone," I say through teeth that are slightly gritted.

Tabby and Val give each other a pointed look. "I get it," Tabby says. "Completely. But it's just safer if two of us go outside, you know? Nobody goes out alone, just in case. We don't need to talk. I can walk behind you, or in front of you, or –"

"Fine," I interrupt. "Whatever. Fine."

Relief floods Tabby's face, but I'm already turning away from her before she can say another word.

Outside, the air is cool and calm. The street is lined with trees that used to flourish with pink blossoms. Now they lie bare, spindly branches drooping as if they're mourning with me. Remnants of petals trail down the road. I stoop down to pick one up.

"They never last as long as we'd like them to, do they?" Tabby says quietly from behind me. "But they're so beautiful when they're here."

I don't respond. I drop the petal from my hand as if it's burned me, and I start to walk.

"I know you're angry with me," Tabby says.

I march ahead, stoically ignoring her.

"It probably doesn't help," Tabby continues, "but I'm so angry with me, too. I keep thinking about how much better I could've handled everything. Every single day, I've gone over and over it in my head."

I keep quiet as she hurries to match my quickened stride.

"I don't want you to think that I was...dragging out your suffering. That's the last thing I ever wanted, Eva."

"Stop it!" the words fly out of my mouth. I spin around, eyes blazing, as Tabby abruptly stops in her tracks. "Oh my God, just *stop* it. You do such a good job of acting so sweet, as if you actually liked me."

Tabby's mouth drops open uselessly. "What are you – I *do* really like you, Eva!"

"You're a liar."

"No!" she protests. "No, I never lied to you. Not – Not really. The battery inside your phone *was* dead, and it did take me a while to get it –"

All she's doing is stoking the fiery rage that burns in my chest. My voice raises. "You could've just left me alone! But no, you had to get me on your side. Were you that lonely, with no girls like me around who might look your way?"

Tabby's expression shifts from stunned to incredulous. "I don't know exactly what you're insinuating," she retorts, "but if we hadn't helped you, you'd have been left passed out on the road, Eva!"

I turn away from her again, and resume storming ahead. The fallen pink blossoms that litter the streets are tarnished with mud and grit.

"Eva," Tabby attempts from behind me, "please."

The desperation in her voice makes my useless heart twinge, and I slow down my pace. It takes me a few moments to get control of my breathing, because I *refuse* to cry. "It feels like..." I begin as I stop walking, angling my head slightly. "It feels like you were all laughing at me."

Immediately, Tabby opens her mouth to protest, but I hold up my hand.

"No. Let me finish. I don't know how else I'm supposed to feel about it. You knew the moment you took my phone that my twin was dead, didn't you?"

There's a moment where Tabby looks anywhere but at me. When her eyes finally meet mine, they're glittering with tears. "I didn't know for sure," she says quietly. "I knew it was...I knew it was very likely, yes."

I turn my head away from her again. My eyes fixate on the tree in front of me, and I brush my fingers over the barren branches. "She was shot by a soldier," I eventually say. "She didn't do anything wrong, but he still killed her. Like she was nothing."

I let the words linger in the air, before turning my head to look back at Tabby. My smile is humourless and tired. "I don't even know what side the soldier was supposed to be on."

Tears fall from Tabby's brown eyes, her gaze never leaving mine. "I can never appreciate your loss," she whispers. "I know that. But, I...I lost my cousin in the War. Michael. He was only eighteen."

I allow the words to sink in as I slowly turn around. "Oh," I breathe. "Oh, Tabby. I'm sorry, I really didn't...I didn't know that."

"Why should you have?" she says, her voice wavering. "I never told you. It wasn't like it was a secret, but – I could never say it out loud to you. The show made us all forget him, for a long time."

My eyes dart away from her. I'm unsure where to focus my gaze. I hear her shakily exhale, before she continues. When she speaks, her voice is low.

"You called me sweet," Tabby says. "But I wasn't always. I fought hard to actually be nice, you know." She takes a deep breath, before continuing. "Before the War, when I was a kid, my mum signed over full custody to Celia, because I was getting in the way of her new boyfriend. The boyfriend who would beat both of us up."

I snap my head up again. Finally seeing her. All of her. "Tabby," I whisper. The idea that anyone could hurt her is unthinkable.

"I'm not telling you all of this for pity," she insists. "That's not it. I'm telling you, because I don't want to keep anything from you, Eva."

What do I say? Do I thank her? Do I stay mad at her?

"And...we've both lost Darryl," she continues quietly. "I know it's not the same. I know that. But I can understand what it's like to lose someone, and to wish it was different."

Heat spreads throughout my body, and I swallow a few times, trying to keep control of my catapulting emotions. "I'm not mad at you," I finally say. "I'm mad at literally everything else."

We both can't resist laughing. It's fleeting and breathless, but we're laughing together anyway. Slowly, I outstretch my hand towards her, waiting for her to take it. I've missed her warmth, her soft skin.

Except she hesitates. And then: "I've been looking for your mum," she suddenly blurts.

The shocking words stab their way into my skin, and I flinch. My hand lowers. "My mum's gone too," I say quietly. "She's been gone for years."

At that, Tabby falters. "You... saw her? I mean, did you..."

"I didn't see her die, if that's what you mean," I snap, voice scraping in my throat. I don't even feel that guilty when Tabby flushes in shame. "My mum left us. It was to help another family, but she still left us. She'd been gone for four days when the sirens came."

"You were mad at her?" Tabby asks hesitantly.

"Ali was. I wasn't at first, not really, but then...then we heard that even more bombs had fallen." I scrunch my eyes closed for a few seconds, trying to fight back another gut-punching spasm of pain. "My mum is dead too, Tabby. I've known it for years. Whatever you've been doing, you shouldn't waste your –"

Tabby is already shaking her head. "On Bessie, I had a lot of databases." She speaks rapidly, as if afraid

I'll cut her off at any moment. "I kept track of where all the televisions were delivered to, in every postcode across the country. When we crashed, I lost the physical computers, but I kept everything backed up. I still have those databases."

"What're you talking about?" I gripe. The last thing I want to do right now is listen to a load of technical jargon.

"I searched for Jeongs in the UK," she says. "Your name came up, obviously. When Ali's didn't, that's...that's when I knew for definite, but I didn't know how to bring it up. I knew you'd eventually remember, the same way all of us did once we'd broken free from the show, and I wanted you to feel safe with us. When the memories of the War came back to you, I thought – but then you kept talking about Ali, and I didn't know what to –" Tabby's words trip over each other, and she trails off in a weak groan.

Her words flip and tumble in my brain, as I try to grasp onto them. "Why are you telling me this?"

"Because I've been going through the rest of the Jeongs," Tabby says, seemingly relieved that I'm responding. "A lot of them didn't match up. But then I found a woman. A television was delivered to Eun Jeong, in Newcastle."

Icy cold fingers creep their way across my shoulders and spine. "My mother's name was Eun," I croak.

Tabby grips onto my hands, squeezing them in suppressed excitement. "The ages matched up," she breathes. "I've no idea if she's still in Newcastle. But I'm sure we could find out."

Oxygen won't properly fill my lungs. The air sputters out of my mouth, and I try to gulp it back in. "Oh my God," is all I can wheeze.

"I'm not saying this to get your hopes up," Tabby says. "We don't know if this Eun is alive, and we don't know if it's your mum. Not yet. I'm telling you because you deserve to know, and I don't want you to ever feel like I'm hiding things from you."

"You're...You're really looking for her?" I whisper. "For me?"

"If you don't trust me anymore, I get it," Tabby tells me. Her voice shakes the slightest bit, but she perseveres. "If you want nothing else to do with me, I get that too. But I really *do* care about you, Eva. So much. I'm sorry for everything you've gone through, that you had to do it alone."

I look back at the bare tree. The all-too familiar ache in my chest fades the slightest bit. It's still there, of course. For now, it's just not as consuming. "I'm not alone," I tell her. "None of us are. We have each other."

My hands move of their own accord. I cup Tabby's face, and kiss her. I've kissed her before, I know, but this feels new. This feels important. Neither of us have anything to hide now; we can be figure this out together. Shaky, patch-worked, but honestly together.

The way she kisses me back, raw and true and sweet, tells me she feels the exact same. We don't say anything else for a while, and link arms as we begin to walk back.

"Has Lila told you much?" I eventually ask.

"Bits and pieces," Tabby says. "She's told us a bit more about Jamie. He was her husband. It sounds like...It sounds like he was a wonderful person."

I nod, thinking of the love Lila holds in her eyes whenever she mentions Jamie. Anyone can see how much he meant to her. "How's Val been?" I dare to ask. "Is she...You know, with Darryl being...dead. Is she doing ok?"

Tabby considers this for a moment. "She's actually being a lot more open about it," she says. "Which is strange for her. Maybe it's because we're able to actually sit and be with our feelings for a while."

I understand that, all too well. "I'm glad she's talking about him," is all I say. "I miss him. I don't want us to just...not mention him."

"Me neither," Tabby says sincerely. "I want to talk about his crappy music and his loud laugh and how fancy he looked in his blue suit, forever."

The corners of my lips tug into a small, genuine smile. "Let's talk about all of them," I say. "Michael. Ali. Darryl. They deserve to be celebrated." I tilt my head up, to look at the cloudy skies. "They deserve to be remembered."

Chapter 43

When we get back to the house, it's eerily quiet. Tabby and I stand in the hallway, taking in the sight of flung-open doors and upturned furniture. Not a person is in sight.

"Shit," is all Tabby says. "This can't be good."

Well, I think, *it was nice while it lasted*. Before I can reply out-loud, Val flies down the staircase. Her hair is tied back in its long plait, and she's dressed in her black cargo trousers and vest.

"What's going on?" I demand. "Have the Creatives found us?"

"I don't know about that," Val pants, "but Lila's gone."

My stomach flips, and my legs suddenly feel very unsteady.

"Gone?" Tabby echoes, eyes wide. "What do you mean, *gone?*"

"I mean, she's done a runner," Val says.

I have to catch my breath; for a moment, I'd assumed the very worst. I allow myself to feel a flash of relief that Lila is actually alive and breathing, but then panic floods back in. "Are you sure?" I press.

Val rubs at her forehead, jaw clenched. "We've searched everywhere in the house," she says. "Lila's not here. I don't know how, but she must've sneaked out. Celia and Mrs. McIver are searching the area now, in the jeep. You didn't see anybody on your patrol?"

"No." Tabby chews her lip. "Not a soul."

In fairness, we'd been talking too much to pay attention to anything urgent, but it's best not to let Val know that. Instead, I scowl. "How do you lose the host of *The Lifetime Lila Show?*" I hiss. "She's on everybody's Most Wanted list!"

"Believe me," Val's voice merges into a growl, "I'm not thrilled about this either."

There's a crash and a yelp, and suddenly Jasper comes bursting into the hallway. His clothes are covered in flour. "The radio!" he pants. "There's a message on the radio!"

Immediately, we're running after him to the kitchen. I see a mixing bowl broken on the floor; Jasper must've dropped it mid-baking, in his panic. On the counter, the newly fixed radio is turned all the way up, just in time for us to hear:

"And now, a pre-recorded message from *The Lifetime Lila Show.*"

There's a slight pause, and then a man's voice fills the kitchen, velvety and warm. "To our lovely viewers," he says. "Please do not despair."

I gasp. Val immediately shushes me, her eyes narrowed as she listens.

"You all know, deep down, that Lila would never leave you for good," the voice continues. "You also know, deep down, that you *need* her. Lila doesn't want you to suffer, or argue with each other. None of us do. Lila wants us all to be content. Didn't you feel content watching the show?"

"Shit," Tabby breathes. "Do you think the Creatives have fixed up their –"

Val's shushing intensifies. "Jasper," she hisses, "did Lila have access to the radio?"

"I don't know," he says in a whisper, wiping a smear of flour from his cheek. "She was upstairs for a while, and when I went into the living room, the radio *was* in a different spot. Maybe she..." He trails off, wincing. "Uh-oh."

Dread trickles down my spine. The man's voice on the radio suddenly softens, like he's coaxing a stray child.

"And now, I speak directly to Lila. All of us here are sure you've had enough of your little break from the studio. The audiences are waiting for your return, as are we. Didn't we fulfil our promise, and make your pain stop? Didn't we look out for you?"

His voice suddenly hardens. "Enough is enough. As the host of the show, you have a duty for your country and your citizens. Look at their suffering. Look at their pain. For years, you have healed them. Don't turn your back on the people who depend on you."

"Turn it off," Val tells Jasper. "Cut the signal. We can't risk radio broadcast right now."

I hold onto her arm. "Wait," I say. "If Lila heard this too, we need to listen right to the end."

"So, we shall be waiting for your swift return, just like the people of our nation are," the man says. "This country has always built back better, through all the wars before. This time is no different."

Tabby scoffs in disgust. I echo her sentiment, my skin crawling.

There's a small pause in the broadcast, and then: "A final note, Lila."

The man's voice no longer sounds soft and comforting. His quiet tone holds such sinister power that it feels as though he is standing right behind me, whispering in my ear. Goosebumps prickle my arms.

"Yours completely, as long as you'll have me. All my love, forever. Jamie."

With that cryptic message, the recorded broadcast ends. We're left with a dull crackle, until Val twists the dial with an aggravated huff.

"Perfect!" she snaps. "Not only has Lila heard a threatening guilt-trip of a message. They've also got key information on her dead husband. No *wonder* she's ran away. What were you thinking, leaving her alone?"

Jasper gawps in surprise at her outburst. "I was just trying to *bake!*" he protests. "Since when was *I* Lila's minder?"

I wrap my arms around myself, forehead creased in

concern for Lila. "She won't have gone looking for the Creatives, will she?" I say anxiously.

Val gnaws at her lip, pacing around the kitchen. "If she has, we're fucked," she says, ever so helpfully. "We've no clue where she could be, or *when* she managed to sneak out, seeing as Jasper was busy whisking eggs."

"Keep it up," Jasper grumbles, folding his arms. "I know who *won't* be getting any of my pavlova."

Without a sound, Tabby picks up the radio, holding it to her chest as if it's a cuddly toy. "We just need to think," she says quietly. "Do we try and get a broadcast out there now? Do we risk it? Lila might not even hear it."

I gasp suddenly as a thought catapults into my head. "Her notebook!" I say. "Lila had this notebook, and she was writing everything that she could remember. There might be something in there that'll help us."

Val's eyes widen a fraction in acknowledgment. "*Si*," she agrees. "She's been scribbling in that thing for days. Check all the rooms!"

Lila wouldn't be the kind to leave her precious notebook out in the open for any of us to read. She'll have hidden it, and she'll have hidden it well. With that, we frantically begin the search. I start with the living room, chucking cushions over my shoulder, rooting through the cracks in the sofa.

I can't stop thinking of her out there, alone, purposefully walking into danger. Every minute that she's gone adds another lodge of dread in my stomach.

"Here!" Tabby yells from upstairs. Moments later, she's bursting into the living room, panting, holding up the black notebook triumphantly. "Inside the lining of her mattress!"

Now that we actually have it in front of us, I'm hesitant. "Maybe we shouldn't," I say. "Whatever's in there, it's private and important. She wasn't ready to share this with us."

"We don't have time to worry about anyone's hurt feelings," Val says. "We need to know where she could've gone, we need to know what happened to her, full-stop. Open it, Tabby."

Sharing my trepidation, Tabby falters for a second before squaring her shoulders. She flips the notebook open. *"Somehow, I've fucked up an entire country,"* she reads aloud, *"and I really have no one to blame but myself. And the bastards who did this to me, I guess, but a lot of the responsibility falls on my shoulders."*

I slowly sink down into the disrupted sofa as I listen. My tongue tingles in my mouth. No matter how hard I swallow, I can't satiate the sudden dryness as Tabby reads Lila's innermost thoughts out loud.

"I convinced myself the only way to survive was to be alone, even though Jamie was the best thing that ever happened to me. It's not like I was waiting for a man to save me from having OCD, that's stupid. It had nothing to do with saving. It had everything to do with being understood."

Tabby lifts her head from the book, biting her lip. "This feels really wrong," she admits, flipping over the

page. "We're rooting through her only coping mech-
anism."

"Skip all the personal shit, then," Val insists. "We
don't have time. Has she said anything about *how*
they took her away?"

Eyes skimming the new page, Tabby clears her
throat before continuing. "Ok. Here: *I can't remember
much about the man in the alleyway. Just his voice. He
told me he could make the poison in my brain stop, and
I was desperate. I went with him willingly.*

*"We got into his car. I don't know how he did it,
but this man had me spilling everything about my life.
About my past. About my home with Jamie in Canterbury. It was like the more I told him, the more relieved
I felt. He gave me something to help me sleep. When I
woke up, I didn't know where I was."*

"*We're* near Canterbury," Val says in sudden alarm.
"About an hour's walk away. She never mentioned she
was so near her old house."

"She never mentioned much to us at all," I point
out, rubbing at my arms. I'm shivering, no matter how
much I try to hide it.

*"They'd play Bobby Darrin, after I told them how
much Jamie loved his music. I didn't understand what
the hell was going on. A lot of the time, nobody would
even speak to me. It was like I was a puppet. They'd do
my makeup and fix my hair, while scripted lines were
drilled into my head. They kept playing the same music,
over and over, until something snapped.*

"When the music started, it's like I was a shell of

*myself. I could feel myself smiling, hear myself talking,
but I couldn't do anything to stop it. Every day these
men would tell me I was making a huge difference
to people's lives. How for years, everybody's grief and
misery had been weighing the country down. What they
needed was a warm, traditional woman to save them. I
should've been proud of my hard work, for everything I
was doing."*

My body shudders, as if physically trying to repel
what I'm hearing. I'm just as guilty as any of those
Creatives, for loving the show, for wanting Lila to be
this picture-perfect, pin-up host.

*"There were so many men there. I tried to remember
what they'd wear, because they'd alternate between
different colours,"* Tabby reads aloud. *"It was my only
way of knowing what day of the week it was. Mondays,
Wednesdays and Fridays, they wore black. Tuesdays
and Thursdays burgundy. And at the weekends, they..."*

Tabby stops. From where I'm sitting, I see the notebook in her hands begin to tremble, even though the
rest of her body is stiff and frozen. Her eyes scan over
the rest of the page, and as they do, her face gets more
and more ashen.

"Tabby?" Val says slowly. "What is it?"

"I..." Tabby swallows. "I don't know. It's just..."

I tentatively approach her, feeling my own heart
rate pick up. "Tabby?" I gently take the book from her
without any fuss. She remains rooted to the spot.

"What's going on?" Val demands, ever the caring
nurse. "Are you sick? Are you gonna faint? 'Cause if

you're sick, go to the bathroom, and if you're gonna faint, sit down."

Tabby blinks fiercely a few times, before shaking her head. "No," she says. "I'm not going to faint. I just don't know what I'm thinking right now."

My eyes scan back over what Tabby has read, up to the part where she abruptly stopped. I linger over the last sentence. I read it again. And again.

And at the weekends, they wear blue, three-pieced suits.

Chapter 44

Lila stands outside the front door of the home she walked away from all those years ago. Somebody is already inside, music blasting behind the closed windows.

Rabbit, rabbit, rabbit. Chas and Dave. Lila never cared for Chas and Dave. She certainly doesn't care to hear them now. Whatever sick game these men are playing, she's not going to be their prize for a second longer.

*

When Val comes back into the room, her face is pale and her brown eyes are glassy. "My gun is missing," is the first thing she says. "She's taken my fucking revolver."

*

Valentina's revolver feels very comfortable in Lila's hand. She's checked; there's two bullets left. One for the first man she sees inside, one for her. She's never fired a gun before, but how hard can it be? Today, the fates have smiled on everybody.

Lila nudges the unlocked door open with her foot, the gun held high. The obscene music bleeds into her ears. She takes a deep breath, and steps inside.

*

"There's a car over the road." Tabby already has a screwdriver in hand. "Jasper and I can maybe hot-wire it."

This morning, I put the flip-up knife back in my sock. I reach for it now, passing it to Val. I feel like I should be shaking, but I'm not. My body is eerily still.

"Do you think – the whole time?" Val whispers. Her fingers tighten around the knife.

The sheer nausea in my stomach is so overpowering that I can't answer right away. "I don't know," I say hollowly. "It might be a coincidence."

"I don't believe in coincidences," Val says as she pockets the knife with a sense of finality. "Not any-more."

*

This used to be Lila's home, somewhere for her and Jamie to start completely anew. Everything looks different now. No more pictures on the walls, no more

Charles Rennie Mackintosh vases filled with flowers. It's all bare and empty, a shell of what it used to be.

Lila cocks the gun, keeping herself flush against the peeling walls. In a way, the setting is very apt.

*

"This isn't going to work," Val says over the sputtering of the car engine. We've been careering over pot-holed roads for five minutes, but it looks like our luck is running out.

Underneath my skin, I feel like my veins are thrumming. The world is a little too bright. "She can't have got that far," I hear myself murmur. My words don't mean a single thing. Lila could have made it all the way to her old house, for all we know. We don't know anything at all.

"Either way," Val says, "we'll have to find her on foot."

"We don't have time, we don't have *time!*" Tabby frets. The car engine sputters as we lurch forwards. With a final groan, the car rolls to a juddering stop.

From the backseat, I watch Tabby take a deep breath in. Then, she exhales out a furious scream, slamming her hands against the wheel, over and over. "Fuck, fuck, *fuck* him!"

"Tabs!" Val's voice cracks through the air. "Save the despair for later. We've got to."

Tabby gives a final punch to the wheel, fist hitting against the car horn. The noise reverberates throughout my body. "If he wasn't already dead," she grinds out, "I'd kill him myself."

*

Slow steps up the stairs, music getting louder by the second. Of course this man is in her old bedroom. They'll *never* stop violating her. She'll never be fully free from their grip.

Lila exhales slowly. Years ago, she had stormed out through this door in front of her, leaving Jamie alone on the bed. She's relived that moment so many times. Standing here, she half expects to see the ghost of her former self push past her.

Rabbit, rabbit, rabbit.

Revolver in hand, Lila slowly turns the door handle, and pushes it open to confront the beast inside. A tall man in a blue, three-pieced suit stands by Jamie's old record player. "Lila," he greets her with a disarming grin, as if they're old friends.

He is not alone. The gun in Lila's hand wavers. Tears fill her eyes.

"We don't need to do anything rash," the man says casually, over the constant music. He speaks with an East London accent, much like his clearly beloved singers. "I'm actually really pleased to see you. We just need you to come home, Lila. Come back with me, and everyone will be alright again."

A single tear trickles down Lila's face. She wants

to whisper his name, just to make sure, but her lips won't move.

In the man's arms, he is holding up a hostage with flame-red hair, a knife pressed to their neck. A male hostage, his mouth gagged with tape, his wrists bound together with rope. When their eyes meet, his green to her blue, it's like they're the only two people in the world again. Here he is. Her Jamie.

*

The crack of a gunshot alerts us to the house at the end of the street. We've been sprinting down every road, every alleyway, every corner of the city, so exhausted we could collapse. Now, the three of us stand frozen on the cracked pathway, breathing raggedly. Overgrown ivy trails across the house's brown bricks. Everything is boarded up, except the front door, which is swinging wide open. It creaks miserably in the breeze, a constant groan that jars my eardrums.

"If that was Lila –" Val begins. "If that was Lila, then she's got one bullet left."

Tabby's grip tightens on her screwdriver. Val flips up her knife. I'm the only one without a solid weapon, but that's alright. Right now, I don't think anything could stop me. "Whoever's in there," I say, "let's finish what we started."

Chapter 45

Lila's back is to us when we burst through the bedroom door. She whips her head round. Her hair has fallen loose, wild eyes burning through the stray strands that frame her face. Instantly, I spot the revolver in her hands, but there's no time to feel any relief.

"This fucker's got Jamie!" Lila screams. "He's won't let him go!"

Jamie? I don't get a chance to even open my mouth before Val cuts in. She stretches out her hand, quick and efficient. "Give me my gun," she tells Lila steadfastly. "You've already wasted a bullet. Eva, Tabby, get her out of here. Let me –"

Val's words blur and trail away. All of our eyes are now fixated on the Creative at the back of the room. He stares at us, with all-too familiar eyes, a gagged hostage in his arms. Bile rises in my throat, as Lila screams again.

"What have you *done* to him, what have you done to Jamie, you bastard!"

The Creative glances back at her, before deliberately

pressing the knife in his hand against the hostage's –
Jamie's – neck. This is wrong, this is so devastatingly
wrong.

"Darryl?" is the first thing Val croaks, before Lila
fires her gun wildly again.

The ceiling is already smoking from the previous
misfired bullet, and this shot splinters the dusty mirror above the Creative's head. He ducks with a yelp,
and Jamie slips from his grip. "That's seven years of
bad –" the Creative begins, before Jamie takes the opportunity to stomp on his captor's foot with as much
strength as he can muster.

Unfortunately, it's not a whole lot of strength, and
he ends up landing with a thud onto the wooden floor.
Lila surges over to him, chanting his name, desperately tugging at the tape on his mouth. I don't know
what to do, where to look.

Val grabs Darryl – it can't be him, and yet it really
is – by his collar. "Nice suit," she tells him, before driving her fist into his jaw. The knife in his hand clatters
to the ground and I instantly swoop down to snatch
it, pointing it at his chest.

"I'm not going to fight you, Val," Darryl croaks. "I'm
happy to see you. I'm happy to see all of you, really –"

Val's grip on his collar tightens, and she slams him
against the wall. "You son of a bitch," she hisses. He
gasps out in pain as she drives his back into the splin-
tered mirror. "You're a Creative. You've always been a
Creative, haven't you?"

He doesn't gawp in offence, doesn't start a myriad

of protestations. He stays deathly quiet, as blood trickles from his beaten nose. "We all have our reasons, darling," he says. "We all have to survive."

Val's hold on him loosens for a split second in sheer disbelief, but then she quickly catches hold of herself. Behind us, there's a sob. Tabby has knelt at Lila's side, helping her with Jamie. There's several layers of tape over his mouth that look painstakingly tough to get off, and his green eyes are glassy and unresponsive. For all I know, he's mentally somewhere else entirely. Somewhere safe, a fake bubble-wrapped world like the one I used to know so well.

With great effort, Tabby forces herself to look up at Darryl, eyes blazing with horror and disgust and fresh tears. "Reasons to survive," she repeats icily, wiping at her face. "That's funny. You know, considering you happily let us believe you were *dead."*

My hand trembles, and I force myself to square my shoulders, to lift my chin in defiance. I will not let Darryl see a single moment of weakness from me.

He meets my gaze, and when he does, my traitorous lower lip quivers. The left side of his face is already a smarting red. Darryl at least has a shred of decency to look away at Tabby's words, eyes flickering to the side. "Well." He spits blood. "You left me for dead, in fairness."

"Were we supposed to let Creatives kill us?" Val demands, and then barks a laugh. "Maybe that was your plan all along, huh? Lead us to our deaths, except we all got away? Must've been a really rough day at work for you!"

There's a soft groan. Lila has finally removed the final piece of thick tape from Jamie's mouth. "Jamie?" she whispers as she cups his face. "Jamie, it's me. It's Lila." She's desperately yearning for any sign of recognition. She doesn't get one. Jamie stares right through her as if mindlessly gazing at a television screen.

Lila's despair is so potent that we all can't help but watch her. She rakes her fingers through Jamie's red hair, shuddering as she holds him close to her. Suddenly, I'm transported back to Steve and Jonathan's bedroom, watching the inevitable, and have to forcibly remind myself that it's not the same.

Jamie's not dead. Yet.

Slowly, Lila lifts her head. There's no trace of tears; just pure rage that burns with ferocious vigour as she directs her eyes to us all. "I can see this is some kind of very fucked up reunion for you all," she hisses. "But I only want to know three things. How he found my husband. What he's *done* to my husband. And why we haven't *killed* him yet!"

"It's Darryl," I whisper. All the while I am staring at a ghost, I am staring at a total stranger. "Our friend."

"Except he was *never* our friend, clearly," Tabby adds as she stands. The screwdriver trembles in her hand. "I don't get it. I don't get the *point* of it, Darryl. You helped us. You were with us every step of the way. You – we *loved* you! We loved you so fucking much."

"Tabs –" he begins, but she slashes the screwdriver against his face. He's abruptly silenced.

"No!" she screams. "No, no, you do not get to call me a cute nickname and act like you care about me! You don't get to do that!"

A thin line of blood blooms across Darryl's cheekbone. He opens his mouth, but then closes it. Val lets go of his collar, as if the fabric has been singeing her palms this entire time.

"You want to talk to us? Then answer Lila's questions first," Val says, eerily calm. "You owe her that much. If she finds your responses helpful, *then* we can have a nice discussion. Does all that sound fair?"

I shift my eyes to glance at Tabby. There's something in Val's tone of voice that is all-too familiar to me. The last time I heard her speak like this, Carlos had a broken nose within ten seconds. Tabby inclines her head the slightest bit, and I know she feels it too.

"Sounds fair," Darryl says after a pause. "Yes. I want to – I want to talk to you. I never thought I'd have the chance again, honestly, so that would be –"

Val clicks her fingers, cutting him off. "On your knees, then," she says. "Hands behind your back, against the wall. No funny business from you. Move so much as a *centimetre* and I'll slit your throat."

It's like their old game of cat-and-mouse, except with much more serious consequences. I see Darryl swallow, and he breaths out slowly as he descends onto his knees.

"As attentive as ever," Val tells him. "Go on, then. How did you find Jamie?"

Darryl's nose is bleeding. He seems to wrestle with wanting to wipe it, and wanting to follow Val's orders. I make sure to keep the knife pointed at his neck. "A television was delivered to him in North London. According to our records, that's where he's been for the past seven years," Darryl says. "Before that, I've no clue where he was."

Lila mouths something silently, gaze flitting back to Jamie. "So, what did you do? Drug him? Bundle him in a van and drive him down to our old home, just to try and get me back for your sick little show?"

"I don't know the specifics," is the only thing Darryl says, "but I do know what's been happening all over the country." His voice is methodical, as if he's practiced this speech hundreds of times before. "You heard the radio broadcast. People are losing their fucking minds without you, Lila!"

"That's not my problem," Lila grinds out. "I never asked to be your saviour, and Jamie never asked to be a pawn in your game."

Darryl shakes his head. "They can't cope without you. They're desperate."

"I was desperate too!" Lila's voice rises. "We were *all* desperate!"

I feel a muscle in my jaw twitch. It's taking all my effort to not break down and scream right now. I don't need to look at Val or Tabby to know they're experiencing the exact same emotions, if not ten times stronger.

Val angles her head. "Will that do for now, Lila? Or do you want to hear more of his snivelling?"

Val doesn't wait for an answer. Before I can blink, she's driving her knee into Darryl's face with alarming speed. There's a crack as the back of his head slams into the wall, and his eyes roll back. He's unconscious before he hits the floor.

Tabby hunches over slightly. I worry she's about to be sick, but it turns out she just wants to have her own kick, right into Darryl's chest. With those thick boots of hers, it's bound to leave a mark.

I don't have any energy to have a go myself, so I let Val root through our rucksack to find the appropriate equipment to tie Darryl up. My attention is back on Lila and Jamie; I make my way over to them slowly, outstretching my hand. Lila stares at me as if I'm a venomous snake, but then slowly accepts my help. Together, we get Jamie to his feet. Once up, he stands unaided, swaying ever so slightly.

"We need to call Celia," I say. "And Mrs. McIver. They'll know what to do about – Jamie needs medical help."

Tabby's phone is already in her hand, fingers trembling. She doesn't look at me. Before long, she's urgently telling Celia the address, but my attention is elsewhere; Jamie has slowly begun to walk around the room. He still doesn't approach us, doesn't speak, doesn't acknowledge anything that's happened. He just shakily walks around, like a new-born fawn out on his very first stroll.

"Jamie?" Lila whispers again, watching him helplessly.

The young man finally turns around, green eyes meeting her blue. His lips quirk up in the tiniest of smiles, and I hold my breath.

"I saw you on the TV," is the first thing he says out loud, voice dry and hoarse. "You're really good."

There's an awful silence as the weight of his words sink in. Lila takes a shuddering inhale, tears trickling from her eyes. "It's me," she tries. "It's just me. It's Lila."

Jamie nods, but it's not in the kind of recognition Lila has been hoping for. It's the recognition of a fan. I know it all too well.

"You should...you should get back to the studio," he insists, biting at his dry lips. They crack and bleed, but still he continues, each word a knife to the heart. "You really are...so wonderful on the show."

Chapter 46

The moment we're back home, we're tying an unconscious Darryl to one of the kitchen chairs that we've brought into the living room. Tabby and I can still barely look at him, but Val is nothing but practical as she winds the ropes around his arms and chest. Once satisfied that Darryl won't be waking up and escaping any time soon, she immediately leaves for the kitchen, and we've no choice but to follow her.

Upstairs, Jamie is sleeping in Lila's bed, and she's superglued to his side. Mrs. McIver is doing her best to nurse him physically, but it's the mental that's proving to be the most disconcerting. Was I as bad as him, when I first left my house?

I've bitten the skin around my nails so much that it's all cracked. I can't stop thinking of the blurry car ride back to here; the way Lila touched the sleeping Jamie's red hair, his face, his hands, as if imprinting him onto her skin. "He's alive," she had croaked, tears glistening in her eyes. "He really is alive, isn't he? I'm not dreaming it."

"You're not dreaming it," I'd told her quietly. I don't

know why I feel a pulsating jealousy. Maybe because Jamie is back in her life, but Ali will never be back in mine. It's useless thinking like this; useless and cruel. I'm happy for Lila, I'm happy for them both. Still, feeling a normal reaction like jealousy is a welcome escape from whatever I'm feeling about Darryl.

"So," Tabby's voice brings me swiftly back to reality. "What the fuck are we going to do with him?"

Val doesn't respond right away. She sits down in one of the kitchen chairs, rubbing her temples.

"We should kill him," Tabby suddenly blurts. I gasp involuntarily, hissing her name in distaste. I don't even know if I disagree with her; it's just such a blunt, awful statement from her sweet mouth.

Still, Val stays silent. She just reaches for a cigarette, flicking her lighter a few times. I notice the way her fingers tremble.

I reach to clasp Tabby's shoulder. Her lower lip quivers, and she keeps her eyes steadfastly anywhere but at us. "I *grieved* him," she says. "I grieved my friend. I don't know who that man is sitting in there, but he's not my friend."

After a deep drag of her cigarette, Val finally speaks. "We need to question him before we kill him, Tabs," she says mildly.

"What is there to question?" Tabby demands. "He's a Creative, their man on the inside. The moment we let him loose from those ropes, he's going to finish what he started and kill us all."

Although I know she's right, I still find myself

shaking my head hesitantly. "If he wanted us dead so badly, there was always *ample* opportunity," I say.

"*Si*," Val agrees, taking another drag. "Exactly."

There's a colossal crash from the living room; Val instantly stubs out her cigarette and we burst through the kitchen door. Darryl's chair has overturned. Groggy and disorientated, he moans, muffled from where his face is pressed into the carpet.

"Going somewhere?" Val quips dryly.

There's another moan. I don't feel any pity. Next to me, Tabby is breathing harshly through her nose, fists clenched at her sides.

Val squats down next to Darryl, grabbing onto his hair and lifting his head. "Let's get one thing straight," she says, as she brushes the blunt edge of her knife along Darryl's cheekbone with her other hand. "We didn't bring you back here so we could have a friendly catch-up. You're here for one reason only, and that's to explain everything you know about the Creatives. The more you keep stalling, the more you try to joke with us, the more my patience wanes. And it's already *very* thin."

Darryl swallows, attempting to angle his head away. "Valentina," he says. "I'd concentrate a lot better without you waving that knife in my face. C'mon. It's me. I'm not going to – I'm not going to hurt you."

"The fact you can say that without a hint of irony," Val says monotonously, "is remarkable." She abruptly lets go of Darryl's head, and his face smashes back into the carpet. He lets out a strangled yelp.

386 ~ EMILY RENNIE

"I can't – bloody say anything – if I'm all horizon-tal," he wheezes. "Val. Val, darling, let me –"

Immediately, Val hoists the chair up before he can even finish his sentence. "Do not call me darling," she says in a low, dangerous voice. The kind of voice that hints she's moments away from swiping her knife across his Adam's apple.

There's a tense pause, and then Darryl nods. Blood slowly leaks from his nose. "Sorry," he concedes. For a moment he looks so pathetic, that my eyes sting and I have to avert my gaze.

"First of all," Val says. "Do the Creatives know where we are? Did you tip them off about this location?"

Slowly, Darryl shakes his head. "They shouldn't," he says. "Finding this street felt like my own personal back-up. A safe haven, in case..."

"In case what?" I snap. "In case we were actually successful in rescuing Lila? All you did was create an even bigger web to trap her in. It's no coincidence we've ended up so near her old house."

"It wasn't a coincidence," Darryl agrees, "but it was just a very weak gamble. I figured, if you all *did* come back here and Lila *was* with you, there was a chance she'd recognise the area and make her own way home. I didn't expect you to figure it out, but I guess that was stupid of me. If anyone was going to figure it out, it'd be you three, wouldn't it?"

He shoots us a small smile that none of us return.

"Or," he continues, "a more likely alternative: if everything went south for me, I'd have a safe space of my own to escape to. And clearly, things did go south for me."

"Enough rambling," Tabby's voice merges into a growl. "Start actually *talking*. The whole time – Were you one of them?"

He bows his head, seemingly unable to meet any of our eyes. "It's complicated," is all he says.

"Complicated?" Tabby echoes incredulously. "*No*, Darryl. It's really not. Just say it with your chest. You're a fucking *Creative!*" She storms over to him, jabbing her finger into his blood-splattered tie.

Darryl doesn't flinch as he holds Tabby's furious gaze steady in his own. "If you want to call me that made-up title," Darryl says, "then I can't exactly disagree, can I?"

Val waves her knife dangerously close to his throat again. "Patience," she repeats, "is waning thin."

Shifting in his chair, Darryl gives a small nod in defeat. "Then, the answer is yes. Ever since you met me, I was in on the show, yes," he murmurs.

His confession lingers in the cold living room, and then Tabby covers her mouth with her hands, as if she's about to be sick. "Oh, *God*," she moans. "The whole time. The whole time, you were...Were you sent by them? To spy on us? To be their man on the inside?"

Darryl's silence is enough confirmation. The knife in Val's hand lowers the slightest bit; it must be taking all her strength to not thrust it into his chest, but she remains still.

"When I was a boy..." Darryl begins, only to be immediately cut off as Tabby groans.

"Let me guess," she says dryly, "you weren't given enough hugs? I don't care about whatever sob story you're conjuring up."

"It's not a sob story," Darryl says. "It's just what happened. If you want me to explain myself, you're going to have to actually give me a chance."

Tabby skews her mouth, glowering. She's clearly torn between keeping her mouth shut or continuing to tear strips off Darryl. Personally, I don't care about insulting him; I just want *some* kind of clarification.

There's a pause, and Darryl shakes his head. "Sorry, Tabby. I didn't mean to snap at you like that, I just –"

"Oh, spare me," Tabby mutters, arms folded tightly across her chest. Silence swells, and then she sighs in aggravation. "Go on, then. Speak."

Darryl pauses again, before shifting uncomfortably in his seat. "Obviously, the War wasn't good for any of us, but it hit my parents hard," he says. "Dad died when I was a teenager, fighting for a cause he didn't even understand. It's not like he was a great guy or anything. Kept Mum under his thumb their entire marriage. It sounds bad, but I think part of me was relieved that she could finally be *free*, but..."

We wait for him to continue; the words seem to sour in his mouth.

"But his death, it rotted her. I watched the grief physically eat my mum up from the inside. She couldn't do a single thing for herself – wouldn't eat, wouldn't sleep, wouldn't even bloody wash herself. I did whatever I could to help her, but it was never enough, and then she..." he trails off, eyes darting towards Val. "Well. You know what she did."

Val tilts her head in acknowledgment. "I remember what you told me," she says, voice low. "But you could have been lying to me, couldn't you?"

Immediately, Darryl throws her a fierce glare. "Don't you dare," he snaps, "don't you dare make out that I'm the kind of person who'd lie about my own mother *killing* herself. Bloody hell, Valentina, I'm not that –"

"In fairness, Darryl," Val says smoothly, "I'm not the one who spied on my friends for over five years, and I certainly didn't help kidnap a woman and numb the country."

Darryl flinches at her words, already shaking his head. "Neither did I!" he insists. "Jesus, it wasn't like that. I was promised – I was promised a way to fix everything. To fix the nation. Isn't that what everybody wanted, after the War? A chance to just – to just feel *better?*"

Nothing to feel, nothing to fear, and vice versa. I swallow down the sudden lump in my throat, goosebumps prickling all the way up my arms. Darryl keeps going, words burrowing their way into my skin.

"That man you heard on the radio – he was the one who encouraged me. He found me on the streets and looked after me, when I was just a scrawny kid who had absolutely nothing left." At that, Darryl's voice softens, as if in adoration. "He promised me peace.

Said there was an end to everyone's suffering, and I was welcome to join the team and help pave a new future that was reminiscent of the glorious past. Gave me some purple pills and suddenly everything just – washed away. For the first time in years, I could sleep at night."

Lavender Slumber, I open my mouth to say, and then slowly close it. Darryl had *laughed* at the concept of those pills. Had he been taking them in secret the whole time?

"I wanted to cling onto that feeling," Darryl continues. "And I wanted everyone else to be able to feel that way too. So, I joined this group. All men. At first I was just driving around, scouting out remaining towns and cities. I didn't know what for. The whole process, setting up the show, it took months."

Darryl stops, swallowing a few times. I wonder if he's about to ask for water, and then I wonder if I even want to give him any. Eventually, he continues.

"With Lila – I really didn't know how far it went, ok?" Darryl raises his eyes to the ceiling, face twisted in pain. His breathing is beginning to get laboured. "When I started the show, I was a snivelling boy who was only good for driving the vans. I didn't *meet* Lila. All I was told was – we were making her happy, and she was making *us* happy. It was an escape from her miserable life as much as it was for all of ours."

Tabby huffs a small, humourless laugh. "Oh, come on now, Darryl."

"It's true," is all he says. "You don't have to believe me, and it probably doesn't change anything, but –"

"You're right," I interrupt coldly. "Even if we did believe you, it doesn't change a single thing. Either way, you've played an active part in brainwashing a woman against her will and plastering her all over the TV."

When Darryl's green eyes meet mine, I can't bring myself to look away. "Alright, Eva," he says quietly. "You look at me and tell me watching that show didn't make you feel safe. Didn't make you happy."

My breath stutters, throat unbearably dry. "But it was a *lie*, Darryl," I whisper. "All of it was a lie. My sister – my sister is *dead*. I'd rather know that, and remember her, honour her, than live in a fantasy."

Tabby's hand reaches for my shoulder, and she gives me a comforting squeeze. I brush my fingers over her knuckles, keeping myself grounded. Darryl is the first to break away from my gaze, head bowed.

"Then you're braver than me," he says gruffly.

His admission only deepens this overwhelming sadness. It clings to my bones. It dries my throat even further than I thought was possible.

"So, you drove the vans," Val says coldly. "When did you get promoted to a spy?"

Darryl slowly angles his head to look at her. "The show had been running for over a year," he says. "Word was spreading about rebels breaking into houses and getting people out. So, a few of us were told – we had to find out who was behind it all, who was doing disrupting our newfound peace. I was picked, and sent off to cover London ground."

"Your job was to turn us in," Val says simply. "Wasn't it? To find us, and deliver us to the TV station."

Darryl inclines his head in a tiny nod. "The others were hell-bent on killing you the moment they heard about two women dragging people from their homes. I was sent in with no real clue, but then – then I met you."

If he's expecting Tabby and Val to soften, he's going to be waiting a long time. The two of them stand rigid, venom practically burning in their eyes.

"At first, I just wanted to get to know what you were all about. How long you'd been doing this, when you'd stopped watching the show. I didn't mean to – I didn't mean to stick around, you know? It was supposed to be *simple*. You weren't supposed to be so strong-willed and resilient and fun to be around. You weren't supposed to *care* about me."

"We weren't supposed to be *people*, you mean," Tabby says through gritted teeth. "We were supposed to be blemishes on your perfect world. Easily disposable. *Traitors*."

Darryl shifts again in his chair helplessly. "When you said you wanted to go all the way to the top, to find Lila, I knew...I knew I wouldn't be able to stop you. I knew you'd do whatever it took. So I stalled us. As much as I could."

"All those times, when we'd been so close to finding

the station..." Val says slowly. "Did you tip your little friends off?"

"Sometimes," Darryl says, "but other times, no. They found you – *us* – all by themselves." His eyes meet mine again. "I'd never really seen somebody who'd only just stopped watching the show, until *you*, Eva. When I saw the state you were in, something felt...wrong. *I* felt wrong."

"Must've been hard for you," Val says tightly. "To come face to face with a Lila fanatic and have to pretend you were repulsed. Did you tune into the show while the rest of us were asleep, just to get your fix?"

Darryl ignores the jibe, staring at us beseechingly. "I'm not going to say these feelings happened overnight," he says. "But then...in Edinburgh, when we saw that woman, dead in her armchair..." he falters, his words trailing away.

"A sudden change of heart?" Tabby asks sarcastically. "Don't try it. You led us directly to that TV station and tried to kill us with that explosion. Too cowardly to actually stab us in the back yourself?"

Immediately, Darryl shakes his head, green eyes wide and earnest. "No, no, that's where you're completely wrong," he says. "I did set off the explosion, that's true, but I did it to give you a fighting chance."

I feel myself frown, taking in the weight of his words. The explosion *did* mean we could escape with Lila, I can't deny that.

"I didn't want..." Darryl's voice is low, and he hesitates before continuing. "After everything, I didn't want – it was easier for you to think I was dead, than to realise what I was."

The door behind us slams into the wall as its kicked open. Before I can acknowledge what's happening, Lila is storming towards Darryl, a sharp kitchen knife in her hand, teeth bared like a wild animal.

"No –" I blurt uselessly, holding out a hand as if that's going to stop her perfectly justified rampage.

Lila's reached Darryl in seconds, arm pulled back to plunge the knife into his chest. Darryl doesn't shout or protest; he simply screws his eyes shut, twisting his head away without a word. Accepting his fate.

"What did you do to my husband?" Lila hisses. "What did you *do* to him?"

In the split second of hesitation that follows, Val knocks the knife out of Lila's hand. As it clatters to the floor, Val grips onto the smaller woman's wrist, holding her back. "You don't want to do that," Val says calmly.

"I absolutely fucking do," Lila pants. Her eyes are glassy with rage and her entire body trembles. "Just because *you're* too much of a coward."

Val arches an eyebrow. "It's not a question of cowardice," she says. "Trust me. Eva, pick up the knife."

I stoop down, grasping the knife's handle. It's heavy in my hand, as I centre it at Darryl's chest. For a fleeting moment, I envision jabbing forwards over and over, breaking his heart into pieces, the same way he's done to mine.

"Valentina could kill me in a heartbeat," Darryl

agrees. "But there's no *fun* in that, is there, Val? If I know you, you'll want to drag my torture out as much as possible."

There's a pause as he and Val look at each other. "He's right," Val says. "We're not finished with him yet."

"Well, when *will* you be finished with him?" Lila's voice rises. "Because from where I'm standing, there's too much talking and not enough *punching.*"

My arm is beginning to ache from how tightly I'm gripping onto the knife. I allow myself to lower it for a second or two, but make sure it's clearly in Darryl's line of sight so he doesn't get too comfortable.

"Is everyone getting packed?" Valentina asks calmly. "We'll need to be out of here soon."

"There's no need to rush off on my account," Darryl says. "I told you, it's extremely unlikely anyone else knows you're here –"

Lila's hand strikes him across the face, and he's abruptly silenced. For a moment, the only sound is Lila's harsh breathing as she stares him down. "They're packing," Lila grinds out, eyes locked on Darryl's. "We're ready when you are."

"Then go back upstairs," Val says. "All of you. We need a group discussion on next steps."

"And are you staying down here to slit his throat?" Lila says. "Otherwise, I'd rather be here for the show."

Val inclines her head slightly, and simply gestures for us all to leave the room. "Give me a few minutes," she says. "I want to make sure I've got everything we need out of him."

Without another word, Lila storms from the room. I watch after her, holding out the kitchen knife to Val, but she only shakes her head. "Keep that," she tells me. "And make sure Lila doesn't get her hands on any more."

My eyes dart back to Darryl. I don't want her to be alone with him; I don't want him to try and twist his way back into our lives.

"Leave us," is all she says. And then, softer: "Please."

*

Upstairs, the entire household is crammed inside Val's bedroom. Tabby and Jasper sit on the bed somberly; Jasper keeps jiggling his knee as if he wants to jump out his own skin, no matter how many times his cousin hisses at him in annoyance.

"I don't believe it," Tabby keeps repeating. "About him trying to save us with that explosion. I don't believe a word that comes out his mouth. He's just trying to save himself, the way he's been trying to save himself this whole time."

I don't know what I believe. My heart aches; I want to comfort her, I want to weep, I want to go back downstairs. Lila is ignoring all of us, completely fixated on knocking against every wooden bedpost in a clear attempt to calm down from the fury that burns inside her. Celia has attempted to console her, but it's as if she's talking to the air.

"Jamie's memory will come back," I speak up, doing my best to reassure her. "It will, Lila. He's just...he must be in deep, that's all."

Lila doesn't glance up from her task, continuing to count under her breath. Watching helplessly, I don't know if I should stop her, or leave her be until she's satisfied. Whatever the case, I can't seem to keep my mouth shut.

"It *will*, Lila. All his memories – they're still in there, locked inside of him. It'll all come flooding back to him once he's had the chance to rest."

"What if it doesn't?" Lila eventually croaks. "What if I've ruined him forever?"

I shake my head, desperate for her to understand. "No. You didn't ruin *anybody*. It's not your fault."

That seems to register, judging by the dangerous glint in her eye when she finally looks at me. "You're right," she concedes. "Your tied-up friend in the living room, it's *his* fault."

"He's not my friend," I say quietly. "He was never my friend."

Right on cue, Val soundlessly enters the room, walking over to the window ledge as if we're all invisible. She perches on it, head angled to stare outside at the barren trees. "I've locked him in the kitchen," she says before any of us can ask. "He's not going to get out of those ropes anytime soon, trust me."

"That's great," Lila says monotonously. "So, when do we kill him?"

"Killing him means there's one less Creative in the world," Jasper agrees. "He's dangerous. He can't be trusted, no matter what he says."

"We don't kill in cold blood, Jasper," Celia murmurs.

"We don't, maybe." Jasper points towards Val. "But *she* does. She knows just how to do it, don't you, Val? You agree with me, right?"

Val doesn't respond for a while, still seated on the window ledge, staring through the glass. Her shoulders are hunched the slightest bit, the only giveaway that Jasper's words have hit home. "'Course I agree," she says hollowly. "Nobody's arguing with you, Jasper."

The floorboards creak as Mrs. McIver slowly makes her way into the bedroom, shoulders stooped. "Everything's packed," she says in a weary, gravelly voice that I've never heard before. It strikes me just how much she's trying to keep herself together as our matriarchal figure.

Celia offers her arm to the older woman, but she's batted away. "We'll find somewhere new," Celia says softly. "Somewhere just as special."

"I don't care about the house," Mrs. McIver scoffs. "I mean, of course I'll miss a comfy bed and actual kitchen, but I can survive without them. I'm just not sure..." she breaks off in a watery chuckle. "Christ, I'm getting too old for this life."

Lila is staring at her in silent expectation, as if

she's afraid to ask her question out loud. Mrs. McIver shoots her a small glance.

"He's awake," Mrs. McIver tells her. "He seems happy enough. Still confused, still no clue where he is, but happy."

Breathing out slowly, Lila nods. "Ok," she murmurs. "Ok. That's...that's good, right?"

"Better than him being hysterical or overcome by grief, sure," Val says as she stands from the window ledge. "That'd *really* slow us down. Think we can get him into one of the cars without a fuss?"

Mrs. McIver seems to consider this, before nodding. "He's not going to lash out in protest," she says. "He doesn't have the strength, and it doesn't seem his character."

"Can I see him?" Lila asks. "Now that he's awake? I can help."

I hesitantly gnaw at my lip, unsure if that's a good idea, for numerous reasons. Mrs. McIver seems to be on my wavelength, because she shakes her head. "Best not, hen," she says, her voice gentle. I didn't think I'd ever hear her speak to Lila so kindly. "Don't want to upset yourself."

"I'm already upset," Lila counters. For a moment, I worry she's going to put up a fight, but then she collapses next to Tabby on the bed. "Fine. Fine. I just want to get away from here, I just want to..."

Val observes us all, like a queen surveying her desolate kingdom. "Get your things," she says firmly. Everybody looks at her, desperate for clear orders.

400 ~ EMILY RENNIE

"Pack up the cars. I know what you want me to do, and I'll do it. You just be ready to go."

I stare at her, dumbfounded. Even when everybody else clears out the room, Tabby and I remain, rooted to our spots.

"Val..." Tabby begins, and then falls silent.

"They're happy for me to do it," is all Val says, "but are you?"

Tabby looks at her, giving a helpless shrug. "I don't – he's not our friend, Val. He's dangerous, he's clearly unhinged. He's...he deserves everything he gets."

"So, we'll let the cold-hearted Vulture kill, because that's all she's good for," Val says mildly.

"*No*," I say simultaneously with Tabby, shaking my head. "No, Val, that's not it. It's not like that."

"It's ok," Val says with a small, humourless laugh. "I *am* good at it. I know what's got to be done. I'm the only one here who can."

She angles her head back to stare out of the window again. Tabby and I soundlessly watch her, before we have no choice but to leave.

Chapter 47

Outside, in the cold fresh dusk, the world is holding its breath. We're packing whatever we can into the black jeep. Mrs. McIver is already asleep in the front seat, deep worry lines etched onto her forehead. She's devastated by it all, in a way I've never seen before, and I worry the impact it's going to have on her health.

"It feels wrong to be leaving Val alone in there," I say, glancing back at the house. All the curtains in the living room are still drawn shut.

"Val's the best person to be alone with him," Tabby says bleakly. "I don't have the guts for what she's about to do."

Hearing the raw anger in her voice doesn't make me flinch. It just makes my heart stutter with pain. "Do you *really* want him dead, Tabby?" I ask her quietly.

Tabby doesn't answer me as she keeps methodically packing bags into the boot. "It's going to be a tight squeeze," she mutters, observing the jeep.

Across the street, Jasper is attempting to hot-wire another car. Occasionally, we hear him vehemently swear, so I'm pretty sure it's not going well.

"You can always sit in my lap," I tell Tabby, hoping it'll make her smile.

"Ha," she says without humour, hoisting a duffel bag into the car. She rests for a second, breathing heavily through her nose. "Ok. I think that's every –"

"Fuck," I say suddenly. "My leather coat. I've left it upstairs."

Tabby whips her head around to look at me. "Leave it," she says. "We can find you another one." Her steely resolve weakens a tiny bit at my pleading look. "*Please*, Eva. Don't go back in that house."

"I'll literally be two minutes," I tell her. "I know exactly where it is."

"I *know* you're lying about this stupid coat," Tabby accuses. "This is a ruse to get involved with whatever's going on inside."

"I'm not lying," is all I say. I *did* leave my coat inside. Whether it was on purpose or not is my business.

"*Please*, Eva," Tabby's voice cracks, "just let her do it. Let her finish it. It's what he deserves."

I squeeze her arm. "No matter what he's done, that's not how you operate," I tell her gently. "That's not you, Tabby."

When I kiss her, I taste salty tears. She doesn't say a word. I pull away, but keep my forehead pressed against hers, wishing I could go inside that brilliant mind to know exactly what she's thinking.

We're interrupted as Celia approaches, and I carefully pull away. "Go help your cousin," Celia tells her. "He's taking far too long."

"He's the klepto," Tabby grumbles. "He should be able to break into and hot-wire a car all by himself."

"*Was* a klepto," Celia corrects, giving Tabby a small push. "And if memory serves, you were his little apprentice, so there's no use getting on a high horse, my girl. Go."

With a huff, Tabby obediently heads over to Jasper. She looks at me over her shoulder, silently begging for me not to go back inside, but I've made up my mind. When I turn away, I feel the fury from her eyes burn into my back. She'll have to forgive me.

I don't want Val to be alone for this.

Everything is so quiet when I sneak back into the house. Part of me feels I should just storm in, metaphorical guns blazing. I don't owe Darryl the courtesy of a heart-to-heart. Still, something makes me hesitate, and I linger outside the living room door. It's open just a crack, and I can't resist peeking in.

Darryl has been brought out of the kitchen; he's still tied to the chair, but he's entirely focused on Val, who stands in front of him. Although the knife is still in her hand, she's no longer aiming it anywhere.

"I will never understand you," Val is saying. "I will never understand why you've done this, how you could *ever* think this was the right path to take."

I see Darryl's jaw clench, his gaze shifting to the carpeted floor. He doesn't respond.

"You brainwashed the whole country," Val whispers.

Darryl's head snaps up. "But what's wrong with that?" he immediately challenges.

Val stares at him in stupefied silence. "I can think of a few things," she finally says.

"I just meant – is it really so terrible?" He lolls his head back, with a half-hearted laugh. "You saw first-hand what the War did to people, we *all* did. My mum – Christ, when I had the chance to get that image of her broken body out of my head, yes, I took it. I'm not going to apologise for that."

Val paces back and forth, and I shrink away from the door in case she can somehow sense my presence. I wouldn't put it past her.

"If you're going to kill me," Darryl says, "I'd much rather be untied for it."

Val doesn't respond for a moment, though she does stop in her tracks. "What difference would it make?" she asks monotonously. "The outcome's gonna be the same whether you're tied up or not."

"True," he agrees with a small, albeit hysterical, laugh. "I'd just really like one last cigarette. I don't suppose you have any to spare?"

Soundlessly, Val walks behind the chair, and begins to saw away at the ropes with her knife. Darryl breathes out slowly in relief as the pressure around his chest and arms loosens. "Cheers," he says. "Nice to have a bit of dignity back."

"Don't get too comfortable," Val says, "I just think even liars deserve to die standing."

Slowly, Darryl gets to his feet. Throughout this entire exchange I've been holding my breath, waiting for either of them to pounce. So far, that doesn't seem to be happening. "I never lied to you, Val," Darryl says, and then hesitates. "Ok, yes, I did. Of course I did, I won't insult you. I lied about who I was and my background, but everything else –"

"Everything else!" Val's voice raises and she lifts her knife. "Darryl, everything else is redundant!"

"No, it's not," Darryl says. "It doesn't have to be. We're – we're here together, you and me, against all the odds. I died for you, technically. I was never lying about how I felt towards you, towards Tabby, towards all the others. You're *good* people. I thought you'd all be...all be...You were supposed to be wrong, and we were supposed to be right."

He outstretches his hand to her, and then seems to reconsider. His arm flops uselessly at his side. "I wanted to protect you from them," he says. "In the end, with the explosion, that's what I decided to do. Too little, too late, maybe. But that's –"

"You're *one* of them." Val spits at his feet. "You should've protected us from yourself, and left us alone the moment you fooled yourself into thinking you cared. I never needed saving, you little rat."

"I thought the world needed Lila," Darryl insists. "Maybe it doesn't need *her*, exactly, but it needs something. Look around you. It *needs* it."

"No," Val says with a shake of her head. "No. The world needs to heal. Not hide." At that, her voice cracks, and she lowers her head. "God, Darryl," she breathes. "What do you expect me to do here?"

Darryl takes a tentative step closer to her. "Do

you love me?" he asks. "Maybe not now. But did you, ever?"

"You're a Creative," she whispers.

"You're a Vulture."

She reacts as if he's struck her. "Are you really going to use that against me?"

"No. Not at all, darling, that's my point. We're two sides of the same coin. We're two people who have done what we had to."

"You can't seriously be comparing us." Val laughs, wild and desperate. "I told you everything, *everything* about myself. You helped me when I was in fucking withdrawal. I opened myself up to you, I trusted you more than *Tabby*. More than Tabby! Was I insane?"

Darryl slowly gets to his knees, hands up in surrender. Val stares down at him, shuddering with barely suppressed anger and despair.

"I grieved you," Val says. "I thought – I thought it was all my fault. I as good as killed you, because I couldn't stand to not have you by my side. Because I wanted you with me, I always wanted you with me, because – Yes, I loved you."

I close my eyes, willing myself not to make a sound.

"Of course I loved you, idiot," she continues. "You know I did. You were my best friend, my partner. That doesn't change what's happened here."

He nods, considering her words. "You're all out of bullets," Darryl says. "So you can't blow my brains out. It'll have to be the knife."

My own grip tightens around the screwdriver, but Val is as still as stone.

"What we shared with each other," he continues. "The secrets, the stargazing, the fun, all of that was real to me. All of it. I don't care about the big picture anymore. I thought I could, but I really don't."

"Or you just want the easy way out," Val says. "Like any Creative coward."

Darryl moves his hand to his suit jacket. I prepare myself to burst through the door, ready to knock a gun out of his hands. Surely, Val has checked him for weapons. She's not an idiot.

"I can give you something," Darryl says. "Something to prove to you I mean what I say."

There's a slight hesitation, but then Val nods. He pulls a small memory stick from his pocket. "About two years ago, I nicked this from Tabby," he says. "Before you ask, no, it didn't have any important data on it. But it does now."

"Pictures of you and your Creative friends?" Val asks dryly. "Did you do poker nights?"

Darryl shoots her a smile that she doesn't return. "Funny, Val. Very good. Do you want to hear what's on here, or should we do some more of this friendly banter before you slit my throat?"

Val grumbles something under her breath that I can't hear, before gesturing with her knife. "What is it, then?"

"All the details on the rest of the Creatives," Darryl says. "I've been collecting it, as insurance. Don't get me wrong, you all played a blinder with disrupting the signals, but they've got back-up footage."

"Back-up footage?" Val echoes, as if the idea had never occurred to her. I see her jaw clench. "Of Lila?"

"Pre-recorded," he confirms. "Currently it's useless, what with all the signals going up in smoke. Still, they're out there. Trying to recuperate, to set up somewhere new. I have all the info, right here, to stamp them out for good."

Val stares, dumbfounded, at the memory stick in his hand. "Is this an ultimatum?" she demands. "You give me what I need, so I spare your life?"

"Who said anything about sparing my life?" Darryl challenges. "All I want is one last cigarette."

Val snatches the memory stick from his hand. Without another word, she digs into her pocket and hands him over the cigarette pack. "I'm obviously going to cross-reference all this data," she tells him. "Tabby's going to have to run this on her computer."

"Obviously. Got a lighter?"

They appear to be nearing the end of their conversation. I need to get out of here, before they both realise I've been spying. I can't imagine Val will be too pleased with me if she knows I've heard all of this intimate conversation. I just need to go upstairs, grab my coat, and leave before anyone notices.

The traitorous staircase creaks on my way down. I'm two seconds away from the front door if I sprint, but it's too late. In an instant, Val is opening up the living room door, shooting me a very unimpressed look. "Eva," she says, voice dripping with irritation. She throws me the memory stick. "Give this to Tabby."

I clutch it to my chest, face flushed. "Val, listen, I –"

"Get out of here," she interrupts. "Get in the car. We're leaving in five minutes."

I've no choice but to obey. Just as I close the door behind me, I hear Val lower her voice as she addresses Darryl.

"Goodbye, *querido*," she whispers.

Whatever happens next, I'm not around to see it.

EPILOGUE

It's summer. Not so long ago, the trees outside were barren. Now, fresh green leaves have sprouted on every branch. They gently wave in the warm breeze, occasionally tapping against the bedroom window, as if they're saying hello.

Tabby and I sit on the floor of our current sanctuary – a cottage in an abandoned village that we discovered last month. Outside, the overgrown plants seem to cocoon us from the rest of the world. If ever there was a time for privacy, it's now.

"This should be it." Tabby hesitantly passes me the microphone. She fiddles with the dials of the radio, brow furrowed. "Now, if it doesn't work – if it doesn't work, I'll have to play around with it some more, but –"

I silence her by taking her hand in mine. "The fact you've tried is enough," I tell her sincerely. "Whatever happens. Thank you."

Staring down at the radio, I allow myself a few seconds to summon up courage. We've used this tech a *lot* in the past month. Tabby has painstakingly been searching for every radio signal in proximity to speak to the general public. We've told the people about Lila, about the Creatives, about what we're going to do. It's been risky, but we're gathering crowds. We're gathering momentum. With the public on our side, all of us can revolt against the institution that tried so hard to silence us.

And now, there's something else I have to do. Is she out there? Has she heard our message?

Tabby shoots me a gentle smile and then gives me a thumbs-up with her free hand. "Ok. You ready? It's ready."

With that, I take a deep breath. I lift the microphone to my lips. Swallow a few times. And speak. "Eun Jeong? Are you there?"

For a while, there's only static.

"Eun Jeong," I say again. "Hello? Are you there!"

My hand is still clasped in Tabby's. She gives my fingers a gentle squeeze the longer the silence goes on.

I begin to lower the microphone. Thankfully, I never really got my hopes up in the first place. It was always a very, very slim chance that she would actually be –

"Eva?" a familiar voice suddenly responds through the crackling radio. She sounds older. She sounds tired. But I know, immediately, that it's her.

I nearly drop the microphone, but hastily scramble to catch it before it clatters to the floor.

"Eva?" the voice again.

Tears stream down my face. I don't even need to

look at Tabby to know she's crying too. I lift the microphone to my lips.

"I'm here, Mum," I manage. "I'm here."

*

One week later, I walk past the overgrown weeds and thorns, to meet Val on the road outside the cottage. She leans against Celia's black jeep, cigarette in hand. According to her, this really is her last ever one. I'll believe it when I see it.

"*Hola*, Barbie," Val says. "I hear from Tabby that you're both heading north."

I nod. My leather coat is in my arms; the sun is beating down too fiercely for me to be wearing it right now. "My mum's waiting," I say, a smile tugging the corners of my mouth. "She's going to hate my haircut."

Val laughs. She flicks ash, before taking another deep drag.

"And your plan?" I say. "Tracking down all the remaining Creatives?"

"*Si*." Val angles her face to the sun. "Guess Darryl really was good for something after all. It should be fun."

I hesitate. There's a lot I want to say to her, but I only hold out the leather coat. "You can have it back, if you like," I say.

Val gives a simple shake of her head. "It's yours," she says. "Suits you better, anyway."

I'm sure that's a lie, but I shoot her a grateful smile. I really do love this coat. "You don't have to..." I pause. "You don't have to track them down alone, you know. My mum understands. There's a lot of places between here and Newcastle."

She grinds her finished cigarette under her heel in silence. When she eventually looks up, her eyes are warm. "You need to get home to your mum," she tells me.

With that, she slings an arm around me as we begin to walk back up the garden path. I turn my head to her. "Did you do it?" I dare to ask. "Did you kill him?"

Val doesn't respond. I don't think she ever will.

The front door opens before we can reach it, and Lila comes outside. Immediately, she sits down on the doorstep, face angled to bask in the sun.

"You're in the way," Val tells her, but she's smiling.

Lila doesn't bother turning her head, eyes closed in bliss. "Hi," she says. "Sit down with me."

I oblige, stretching my legs out. Val rolls her eyes before doing the same. There's a comfortable silence, as we just enjoy the warmth of the sunshine.

Lila shields her eyes from the sun, shooting me a glance. "When're you heading off?" she asks.

"This evening," I say. "Better to travel in the dark."

"Taking the shitty car?"

"Yeah," I say with a grimace. "So, we'll see how far we get before we have to inevitably walk."

Lila laughs. It's nice to hear her sound genuinely happy. "Well, we'll miss you," she says sincerely. "You know you've left your poor girlfriend to do all the packing?"

"She enjoys it," I say with a smile.

Inside, I can picture the scene perfectly. Celia and Jasper helping Tabby cram items into a suitcase. In the kitchen, I already know Mrs. McIver is making us soup. For some reason, tears prick at my eyes. I'm going to find my mum, but I know I'll always have a makeshift family now, no matter what.

"How's Jamie?" I ask, the same way I do every day. The young man tends to keep to himself around the cottage, scurrying from room to room like we're contagious. For the past month, he's not spoken a word to any of us, except Lila.

"He's not bad today," Lila says. "When he talks about...who I was before, who *we* were, he seems ok. His memory is still really jumbled, but it looks like some of the pieces are slotting back into place. I don't know. Sometimes he looks at me and it's like he hates me."

"He doesn't," Val tells her. "It might take some time, but he will come back, and you'll both be supported when he does."

Lila's lips tug in a small smile of appreciation. "Thanks," she says. "For everything."

"Well." Val shrugs as she stands up, stretching. "I don't know what'll happen next."

"None of us do," I say. "But maybe that's alright. At least now we have an actual say in our lives."

Val shoots me a tiny smile before heading inside.

I'm content to stay with Lila for a while longer and we resume our comfortable silence. The birds chirp their pretty songs; yellow flowers bloom through the weeds. In this moment, everything is good.

It's not long before I remember what's happening later, and I tingle with nerves. "God," I mutter. "What am I supposed to do until the sun sets?"

At that, Lila turns her head to me, a sardonic smile tugging at her mouth. I smile back.

"I've an idea," she says. "We could always watch some TV."

THE END

ACKNOWLEDGEMENTS

I know every author tends to start an acknowledgements section with 'there are so many people to thank' – but there really are! I first have to thank Editor extraordinaire and dear friend, Ashanti Bloomfield, who has had such unwavering faith and enthusiasm for this book since day one. Her support was game-changing – if you are looking for any editing or proofreading services, Ashanti is your girl. Check her out on Instagram @ashanti_tanita

Another pivotal person in making this book is Natcha Chirapiwat, who designed the beautiful cover and blurb. An incredible artist and photographer - check out her work at https://nchrpwt.wixsite.com/portfolio

I need to thank my boyfriend, Lawrence, for always encouraging me to keep writing. Lawrence, you make me feel like a bestseller every day. You also happen to be quite good at maths, which is useful when you're self-publishing. Love you, Lawrence!

To my family, for their constant support in my creative endeavours, and for gifting me with impeccable Glaswegian humour and resilience. This will be your first time ever reading this book – which is nerve-wracking. I always admire your honesty, but if you didn't like this one, keep it to yourselves. Deep breath now – Mum, Dad, Beth, Gran, Al, Papa, Gordon, Pel, James, Will, Jen, Alistair, Ewan. Love you all endlessly.

To Sam – my first editor from when we were wee

11-year-olds. You've been reading my stories for 15 years now – some of them were really bad. Some of your editing was also really inappropriate. I do mean it when I say I couldn't have done secondary school without you, and I'm endlessly proud and full of love for all of the Mitchells.

To my therapist, Amy. Thank you for your incredible help and insight. OCD is a weird one, but you never made me feel weird (even though I certainly felt doo-lally at the time). You helped me understand and look after myself, and I've never felt more stable (she says...)!

To my friends – all of you. Thanks for always listening to my ramblings, for supporting my work, for spurring me on...and for encouraging me to laugh at myself when it's very necessary (Jake). A special shoutout to my partner in crime, Phoebe, who has been behaving like an agent in getting this book out there, alongside any of my other writing. You always go above and beyond, and I love you.

And to you, the reader, who took a chance on this book. Thank you.

Emily Rennie is a London-based writer, producer, and performer. She has a Masters in Creative Producing from Mountview Academy of Theatre Arts and a BA in English & American Literature and Drama from the University of Kent. From the honest one-woman play about chronic illness, *'Can I Call You Back?'* at Theatre Peckham, to being long-listed for the Funny Women Comedy Writing Award for the TV pilot *'I'm Not That Weird'*, Emily enjoys writing across a wide array of media.

When not writing, Emily is making new theatre with her Co-Producer Phoebe White over at *Rennie and White Productions,* giving a platform for up-and-coming writers, directors, actors and other creatives. She also makes silly comedies with *Big Licks Theatre Company*, where her play, *That's A Bit of Sheer-luck! A Sherlock Holmes Parody'* had a sell-out Edinburgh Fringe run.

Emily can be found on Twitter (she refuses to call it X) @EmilyRennie3 and on Instagram @emilyrennie1

Big Licks Theatre Company Instagram: @biglickstheatreco

Rennie and White Productions Instagram: @rennieandwhiteprods

Milton Keynes UK
Ingram Content Group UK Ltd.
UKHW020952311023
431661UK00016B/791